D0954070

**Also available from
Susan Mallery
and Harlequin HQN**

**Watch for the next Fool's Gold romance,
coming soon!**

SUSAN MALLERY

DREAM WEDDING

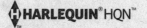
HARLEQUIN® HQN™

ISBN-13: 978-0-373-77841-6

DREAM WEDDING

Copyright © 2013 by Harlequin Books S.A.

Recycling programs for this product may not exist in your area.

The publisher acknowledges the copyright holder of the individual works as follows:

DREAM BRIDE
Copyright © 1999 by Susan W. Macias

DREAM GROOM
Copyright © 1999 by Susan W. Macias

HARLEQUIN®
www.Harlequin.com

Printed in U.S.A.

CONTENTS

Dear Reader,

I'm a big fan of sisters—probably because I never had a sister and desperately wanted one growing up. I wanted someone to talk to and hang out with. When my parents were making me crazy, I wanted someone there who would understand.

This 2-in-1 is a reissue of two of my older books *Dream Bride* and *Dream Groom.* They were reader favorites when they were published over a decade ago and these stories celebrate the love sisters share. There is the family connection and, of course, the wonder of each of the sisters falling in love. But these stories have a little extra twist. Because my sisters come with some unexpected magic.

It seems there's a family legend about a gypsy girl who was saved from certain death and how, as a reward, she passed on a very special nightgown. Rumor has it if a woman wears that nightgown on the night of her twenty-fifth birthday, she'll dream of the man she's going to marry. While that's kind of exciting, it can also be inconvenient. What if you don't believe in legends...or you're already engaged to be married?

I hope you'll enjoy these two books and the legend of the Bradley sisters. And if you happen to have a sister—biological or of the heart—please give her a hug from me.

Happy reading,

Susan

DREAM BRIDE

CHAPTER ONE

"I WISH I was going to dream about the man I was going to marry," Cassie said and grinned. "I know how excited you are about it."

Chloe Bradley Wright looked at her sister. "Oh, yeah. Too excited for words." She fingered the soft lace of the nightgown she held. "Do I have to do this?"

"You don't *have* to do anything."

If only that were true, Chloe thought with regret. But she did have to wear the stupid nightgown. It was her twenty-fifth birthday and time for her to participate in the family legend. Not that she believed in magic or happily-ever-after. As far as she was concerned, falling in love or caring about someone was a one-way ticket to heartache.

She opened her mouth to express her opinion, then pressed her lips tightly together. *She* might not be a believer, but her sister, Cassie, had more than enough faith for the both of them.

Chloe stared into the face that was nearly as familiar as her own. Cassie was adopted, but younger by only six months. The two girls had been together since Cassie was four weeks old and they were best friends. Chloe had shared her admittedly cynical opinion on more than one occasion, but Cassie's belief in the legend had never wavered. Who was she to try and change her sister's mind now? It was just for one night. What could it hurt?

"I'll wear it," she said, trying to sound gracious.

Cassie leaned forward and hugged her. "I knew you would," she said and bounced off the bed. Her short, thick brown hair swung around her face. "I'll go tell Aunt Charity. Won't she be surprised?"

"Probably not," Chloe muttered when she was alone. Aunt Charity had a sixth sense about these things. No doubt the older woman figured she already knew whom Chloe was going to dream about.

"I'm not going to dream about anyone," she said aloud as she pulled her T-shirt over her head, then slipped out of her jeans. "It's just a nightgown. It has no mystic powers. It's now the twenty-first century, for heaven's sake! No one believes that kind of thing."

She unfastened her bra and tossed the garment onto the floor, then picked up the nightgown. The cotton was cool to her touch and she shivered involuntarily.

"It's nothing," she insisted. But she hesitated before pulling the soft fabric over her head. What if the legend was true? What if she was really going to dream about the man she was destined to love? What if—"What if people have been abducted by aliens lurking in cornfields?" she asked aloud.

"Oh, I don't think those stories are true," her aunt said as she entered the bedroom. Charity raised dark eyebrows. "So how much did Cassie have to twist your arm to get you to wear it tonight?"

Chloe shrugged as she smoothed the nightgown in place. "Not too much. I figure it's an inevitable rite of passage for Bradley women, as inescapable as birthdays and taxes. I'm just sorry she's going to be disappointed in the morning."

"Yes," Charity said as she moved to the bed and pulled back the covers. "It will be sad. Cassie is one of those rare types who is a true believer. There aren't many left."

Chloe had turned twenty-five that very day, but suddenly she felt like a ten-year-old with a favorite relative staring at a less than perfect report card, all the while telling her the low grades were fine, as long as she'd tried her best.

"You can't tell me you believe in the legend," Chloe said as she plopped down on the edge of her bed.

Charity settled next to her. The older woman was of average height with the Wright family's dark eyes and hair. She had to be in her mid-fifties, but she could have easily passed for someone a dozen years younger.

"I've traveled all around the world," Charity reminded her. "I've seen many amazing things. As for magic and legends?" She shrugged. "Who's to say what's real and what isn't?"

Chloe snorted indelicately. "Give me a break. So you're saying that this nightgown is several hundred years old and is magical?"

"You never know."

Chloe fingered the soft cotton. "It's in pretty good shape for an antique."

"So am I, dear." Charity patted her hand.

"You're hardly an antique." She drew in a deep breath. "It would be nice if it were all true, but I just can't take that step of faith."

"That's the reporter in you."

"Agreed. But someone in this family has to be practical. Between you and Cassie, you've always got your heads in the clouds."

"I'm back," Cassie announced as she bounded back in the room. She held something in her hand and before Chloe could figure out what it was, she tossed it in the air. Dozens of red, pink and cream rose petals drifted over Chloe, Aunt Charity and the bed.

"My contribution," her sister said with a smile as she settled in the small wingback chair by the closet door.

Chloe pulled rose petals from her hair. Her irritation faded in the presence of such loving support. Who was she to fight against tradition?

"You win," she said as she stood up.

Charity rose as well. "It's best, dear. You'll see." She waited until Chloe climbed into bed, then tucked in the covers. "Sleep well."

When she'd left, Cassie moved close and crouched down. "Dream of someone wonderful," she instructed. "Rich and handsome and very loving." Her wide dark eyes softened at the thought. "Someone who will want to be with you forever."

"What a romantic," Chloe teased. "I'll do my best."

Cassie straightened. "In the morning, I want details. Lots of them."

"I promise. Oh, and thanks for the party. It was great."

Her sister smiled. "My pleasure." She walked out of the room and closed the door behind her.

Chloe leaned up on one elbow and clicked off the lamp, then settled onto the bed that had been hers since she'd turned thirteen. The room had been decorated several times, but except for three years in high school, she'd slept here her whole life. Everything about the room, the house and even the town was familiar to her. Yet tonight, it all felt different.

"Atmosphere," she told herself softly. It was all the talk of magic and legends. Even a confirmed cynic like her was bound to be affected.

She pulled the covers up to her chin and closed her eyes. Memories from her twenty-fifth-birthday party drifted through her mind and made her smile. She'd wanted something small, friends and family only. Cassie and Aunt Charity had prepared dinner. The presents had been mostly gag gifts, which she preferred. Nothing sentimental for her.

She had a busy week planned at the magazine. She mentally listed all she had to do in the next few days.

As her mind relaxed and she started to get sleepy, thoughts of the legend intruded. According to family lore, several centuries ago a young woman had saved an old gypsy from certain death. In return the gypsy had given her a magic nightgown. If the women in her family—the Bradley family—wore this nightgown the night of their twenty-fifth birthday, they would dream of the man they were destined to marry. The union would be long and happy.

"Yeah, right," Chloe muttered as she turned on her side. "He'll probably come riding up on a white horse and sweep me away."

She knew exactly what she was going to dream about—what she always dreamed about. Nothing. Her nights were as quiet and uneventful as an empty drawer and that was just how she liked them. The nightgown wasn't magic. The legend wasn't real. And she was suddenly very, very sleepy.

HE APPEARED OUT of the darkness, not on a white horse, but in a Jeep that roared up the side of the mountain.

"This isn't happening," Chloe told herself even as anticipation filled her. She clung to the side of the rocks as the wind whipped at her hair and made the hem of her nightgown snap like a sail.

"Nightgown?" She stared down at herself. Dear Lord, she was naked except for a thin layer of lacy cotton. What on earth?

"You're dreaming," she told herself. "That's all. Just dreaming. Go with it and you'll be fine."

But the reassurance didn't keep her heart from pounding as the Jeep drew closer. The man inside stopped it a scant two feet from her, then climbed out.

He was tall—substantially taller than her five feet nine inches—and lean. "At least he's really good-looking," Chloe said to herself. "I mean if I have to dream about some strange guy, I don't want him to look like the king of the nerds or something."

The man didn't speak. Instead he walked over to her, ripped off his shirt, then pulled her hard against his gleaming chest.

"I like this," she said, feeling the masculine length of his body pressing into hers.

"Hush, love. I am your destiny."

"Uh-huh. And I'm a direct descendant of Queen Victoria."

She stared into the greenest eyes she'd ever seen. The dream was amazingly real. She could feel the wind, the heat of the man's body, his breath on her cheek. She swallowed. She even felt him pressing up against her. Wow! She had to get out more. Her subconscious was obviously way too bored with her life.

"I want you," the man said.

"Then take me, big boy. I'm yours."

He kissed her. Chloe stifled a shriek of both shock and pleasure. Talk about going for it. His mouth claimed hers in the most perfect, masterful way. She felt small and delicate and incredibly free. This was a dream, after all. She could say or do anything she wanted and no one would ever have to know.

She clutched his face and pulled back. "I have one request," she said.

"Make it. I'll do anything for you."

"Great. Just don't disappear on me until we're finished, okay? I hate those sex dreams where I wake up about thirty seconds from the good part. It does *not* make for a restful night."

Instead of answering, he swept her up in his arms and carried her into the cave. There a fire burned low. Their bed was soft, fresh, sweet-smelling straw. How nice of her brain to supply the details.

The stranger made love to her with a tender thoroughness that left her breathless and trembling. He touched and kissed every part of her. Much to her relief, she didn't wake up before the good part. In fact the good part happened at least twice. He even made her scream once and she'd never been a screamer.

"Who *are* you?" she asked when they at last stretched out together. They were both slick with sweat and breathing hard. She traced his perfect body, her fingers lingering on a scar on his left forearm.

"Your destiny."

"So you said, but do you actually have a name, or should I just call you Mr. D.?"

He raised his head and stared at her. His gaze was so intense, she felt as if she could see down to the bottom of his soul. Whatever lurked there called to her. She wanted to respond, but didn't know how. This was still a dream, right? It wasn't real. But for that second, she desperately wanted it to be.

"You'll know me," he told her as the world around them faded to black.

She tried to grab on to him, but his hand slipped through hers. Before she could even cry out, he was gone and she was alone.

"How was it? Start at the beginning and talk very slowly."

Chloe blinked at the bright light and realized it was

morning. She glanced around in confusion, then saw she was back in her own room, in her familiar bed. Cassie bounced on the mattress next to her and grinned.

"So, who is he? Who did you dream about?"

"What?"

Chloe sat up slowly. Her head was spinning and she couldn't quite wake up. Maybe because she didn't feel rested. It was almost as if she'd spent the night running around. *Or making love with a handsome, mysterious stranger.*

She pushed the last thought away. Nothing had happened. She'd had a couple of weird dreams. They were probably the result of too much chocolate cake and ice cream. They didn't mean anything.

Cassie was still in the oversized T-shirt she regularly wore to bed. Her thick hair was mussed, her face flushed from sleep. "Do you mean to tell me you didn't dream about anyone? Not even one guy?"

Chloe sat up and hugged her arms to her chest. Her body ached pleasantly and there was a definite dampness between her legs. Too weird, she told herself silently. But she did *not* believe in family legends. The dream had been a fluke, not a prophecy. She wasn't going to encourage Cassie's flights of fancy.

"I didn't dream of anyone," she said slowly, instantly picturing the handsome man who had swept her into that cave. It was all too embarrassing. What was she supposed to say? That the sex had been great, thank you very much? She couldn't admit anything to anyone.

Cassie's smile faded. "But I thought it was real." She sounded as if someone had stolen her last hope.

Chloe grimaced. She had done exactly that. But she couldn't tell the truth. She just couldn't!

"I'm sorry," she said and touched her sister's arm. "It's just a nightgown, kid. Like any other."

"Okay. Aunt Charity warned me the legend might just be a story, but I didn't want to believe her. I guess I'm going to have to." Cassie looked as if she was going to say more, then untangled herself from the covers and stood up. "I'll go start the coffee."

When Chloe was alone, she collapsed back on the pillow. She felt strange inside. Off center somehow. Was it the dream?

"There is no legend," she said aloud. "The dream was just my subconscious's way of telling me it's time to start dating. I'll take the hint. Today in the office, I'll look around for a likely candidate."

But as she walked to the bathroom, instead of trying to figure out which eligible men would interest her, she found herself picturing *him*. She shivered…not in fear or irritation, but at the memory of what his touch had done to her.

A hot shower went a long way to restoring her spirits. As she toweled off, she checked her arms and the tops of her breasts. Nothing. Just her regular skin. She'd half expected to see the lingering marks from his lovemaking.

"I must remember to ask Aunt Charity if insanity runs in the family," she said as she chose her clothes for the day.

Fifteen minutes later, her hair was dry and she was dressed. She headed for the kitchen and that healing first cup of coffee. As she reached for the coffeepot, Cassie flipped on the small television. They usually watched one of the morning shows while they ate breakfast.

Chloe had the pot in one hand and a mug in the other. Then a familiar voice filled the room and she froze.

"The gem exhibit is an exciting find," *he* said. "But I

can't take full credit for bringing it to the university. It takes a very large committee to pull this kind of thing together."

Goose bumps puckered up and down her arms. She set the coffeepot back on its burner so she wouldn't drop it, and put the mug on the counter. Then, very slowly, she turned to face the television.

The camera focused on the perky hostess of the local morning show. Then the picture on the screen panned right. A man came into view. A handsome man. A man who, until sometime last night, she'd never seen before. But she knew him. She knew every inch of his body. She'd touched and tasted him, she knew his scent so well, she could have found him in the dark.

"Why do you think you're always the one to make the great discoveries?" the woman asked.

The man smiled. Chloe felt her heart shudder in her chest, and she began to tingle all over. She might not want to remember, but her body wouldn't let her forget.

The man smiled. "Just lucky, I guess."

The hostess practically sighed. "Unfortunately we're out of time. Just to remind our viewers, Arizona Smith will be lecturing at the university on his fabulous gem find. There are still tickets available, but they're going fast. The gems themselves will be on display throughout the month. Mr. Smith, it's been my pleasure having you here this morning."

Chloe's mouth twisted. The woman was practically cooing. So much for professionalism, she thought, refusing to acknowledge the white heat inside of her that some might call jealousy.

So her mystery man had a name. Arizona Smith. Which meant he was real. She thought about the night-gown, the Bradley family legend, the dream. Oh, Lord, it couldn't be true. He was *not* her destiny. He couldn't be. She didn't want a destiny like that. She avoided relationships.

It doesn't matter, she told herself fiercely. *The man is in town for maybe a week. It's not as if I'll ever run into him.*

"I've got to get to work early," she told Cassie.

"Don't you want your coffee?"

Chloe was already heading out the door. "I'll grab some on the way," she called over her shoulder, and made her escape to freedom.

ARIZONA SMITH WAS everywhere, Chloe thought with dismay as she sipped her coffee at the small diner across the street from her office. His picture had been plastered on three buses and on four different billboards she'd spotted on her way to work. Even now he was staring at her from the bench directly in front of her building—or at least his *picture* was. She couldn't escape the man.

"Deep breaths," she told herself. The trick was to keep breathing. And moving. If he couldn't catch her, she would be safe.

It was too weird. All of it. Maybe she'd seen his picture over the past couple of days and not really noticed. Somehow it had gotten lodged in her brain and only surfaced last night. A perfectly plausible explanation.

If only the sex hadn't been so good.

"I don't believe in destiny," she reminded herself again as she left the diner and made her way to the foyer of her building. The magazine office was on the second floor. She stopped by reception long enough to pick up her messages.

"Jerry wants to see you," Paula, the receptionist-gofer called. "Something about a special assignment."

"Great." That was what she needed. Something challenging to take her mind off her temporary insanity.

She dropped her things at her desk, then headed for her editor's office.

Bradley Today was a small but prestigious magazine that came out twice a month. Chloe had gotten a job there when she'd graduated from U.C. Berkeley with a degree in journalism. Eventually she planned to make her way to New York, where the big magazines were published, but for now she was gathering experience and building her clippings.

"You wanted to see me, boss?" she asked as she stepped through the open glass door.

"Yeah, sit." Jerry waved to the seat opposite his desk.

It was only eight-thirty in the morning, but his long-sleeved shirt was already rumpled and his tie hung crooked. If the clothes hadn't been different from the ones he'd worn the previous day, Chloe would have sworn he'd slept in them.

"It's like this," he said, then stuck one hand into the pile of folders on his desk. He pulled one out, looked at the label, shoved it back and grabbed another. "Nancy's pregnant."

Chloe nodded. Nancy was one of their most experienced writers. "She's been that way for about seven months."

"Tell me about it. Babies. Who needs 'em? Anyway, she says she's too far along to be running around for me. She wants to write stuff that lets her stay in the office. Can you believe it?"

His outrage made Chloe smile. "Wow. How insensitive of her."

"Exactly. Does she give me any warning? No-o-o. She calls me at home last night and drops the bomb. So now I pass it along to you. Good luck, kid." With that, he tossed her the folder.

When she touched the stiff paper, Chloe felt the same shivery chill she'd experienced the previous night when she'd slipped on the nightgown. The tiny hairs on the back of her neck rose. She knew exactly what she was going to find inside that folder, and there was nothing she could do to change it. It was, she admitted, inevitable.

"He's in town for about three weeks," Jerry said. "Follow him around. Shouldn't be hard. He wants this piece as much as we do. Decent publicity and all that garbage. Get to know the real man. Write me something brilliant and it just might be your ticket out." Jerry looked at her. "A bigger publisher or maybe even a book deal. Do it right, kid. Breaks like this don't come along very often. Now get out of here. I'm busy."

With that Jerry picked up his ringing phone and probably forgot she'd ever been in the room.

Chloe gingerly took the folder and returned to her cubicle. She didn't want to open it. Maybe if she waited long enough, it would go away. Wishful thinking, she thought, and drew in a deep breath. She flipped back the top cover and saw him. He was standing on the edge of a mountain, leaning against an outcropping of rock. She recognized the clothes, the place and the man. She knew that just around the corner was a cave and in the cave was a fire and a bed of straw.

"I don't like this," Chloe whispered. "It's too strange."

"I brought it," Paula said as she walked into the tiny space and dumped a stack of folders onto the spare chair pressed up by Chloe's desk.

"What is it?"

"Research. All the stuff Nancy had gathered on that Smith guy. She said to call her at home if you want any tips." Paula's gaze drifted to the photograph. "Wow, he's good-looking. Just like that guy in the movies. You know—Indiana Jones. Although he doesn't really look like Harrison Ford. He's taller. Still, I wouldn't shoo him away if he turned up in my bed." She waved her fingers and left.

"Apparently I wouldn't either," Chloe said glumly. So much for escaping her destiny. In the space of twelve hours a strange man had invaded her subconscious and now her work. What was she supposed to do?

But Chloe already knew the answer to that. An assignment like the one Jerry had just handed her was one any junior writer would kill for. Talk about a stroke of luck.

Or destiny, a little voice whispered.

"I don't believe in little voices either," Chloe muttered, "So I'm going to get to work now."

She spent the rest of the day reading through Nancy's notes, clippings from other articles and some information she'd pulled from the Internet. By four-thirty her eyes hurt and she had a major headache. She still didn't have a strategy for dealing with everything that had happened, but she needed to get one and fast. Her first meeting with Mr. Smith was in the morning at the university. Nancy had already set it up. He was taking her on a private tour of the gem exhibit.

She gathered up all the papers and stuffed them into her briefcase. Maybe she could work better at home.

Forty minutes later she pulled into the driveway of the Victorian mansion that had been in her family for generations. Safe at last, she thought as she climbed out. She walked up the steps and into the foyer.

"It's me," she called. Cassie's car hadn't been in the garage, but Aunt Charity's had.

"We're in the kitchen."

Chloe made a face. Aunt Charity had spent much of her life traveling the world. She seemed to know someone from every possible corner of the globe, and at one time or another they all liked to visit. Who was it this time? A tribal elder from Africa or some obscure prince from the Middle East? She felt that familiar wave of resentment toward her aunt Charity for not being around when she'd needed her the most. But she filed those unpleasant thoughts away. She just wasn't up to dwelling on that tonight. And she wasn't in the mood to play hostess, either.

Still, she straightened her shoulders and forced herself to smile as she crossed the hallway and entered the kitchen. She already had her arm extended so she could shake hands with Charity's mystery guest.

She came to a complete stop just inside the oversize room. Her jaw dropped. She told herself to close her mouth, but her body wasn't paying attention.

He was as tall as she remembered. Lean, powerful and too good-looking by far. Not a tribal elder, or even a prince. No, he was much more dangerous. He was Arizona Smith—the man from her dream.

CHAPTER TWO

"Arizona, this is one of my nieces. Chloe. She's the journalist. Chloe, this is Arizona Smith. I think you were watching him on the morning news show earlier today, weren't you?"

Charity's question hung in the air, but Chloe didn't answer. Arizona shifted uncomfortably in his seat at the round table. He was used to fans being tongue-tied in his presence, but Chloe Bradley Wright didn't look like the rabid fan type. Plus, she was staring at him as if he'd grown a horn in the center of his forehead. He brushed back his hair, casually letting his fingers touch the skin there, just to be sure.

"Hi, Chloe," he said, and held out his hand. In the past he'd found that polite, social niceties often put people at ease.

Her gaze dropped from his face to his hand. She still looked panicked, but she responded automatically. "Mr. Smith. What a pleasure." Her attention shifted to her aunt. "You didn't mention company for dinner. I think there's a roast, but it's not defrosted. I could put it in the microwave and—"

"All taken care of," Charity said, and patted the empty chair next to hers. "Get yourself something to drink and join us. Arizona and I were just catching up on old times. He has some wonderful stories. I'm sure you'll be interested in them."

Chloe didn't respond right away. Her gaze settled back on his. Arizona read concern in her eyes and something that looked like apprehension. He held in a sigh. No doubt Charity had been telling tales out of school again. The older woman loved to brag about his exploits. Okay, he was willing to admit that there had been a time when everything they said about him was true, but that was long ago. These days his life was practically boring. At least when it came to his conquests with women.

Chloe moved to the refrigerator. "Would either of you like anything?"

"I'm fine, dear," Charity said.

"Me, too." Arizona motioned to the bottle of beer in front of him.

Chloe gave him a tight smile, then collected a diet soda for herself. She walked back to the table.

Arizona told himself it wasn't polite to stare, but Ms. Chloe Bradley Wright was very easy on the eyes. Tall, at least five-eight or -nine, slender with big brown eyes and a cascade of reddish-brown curls that tumbled to the middle of her back. She might not have a lot of curves, but she was woman enough to get his blood pumping.

If he had a type, she would be it. Fortunately he didn't have one, nor was he looking for anyone to keep him company during his brief visit to Bradley.

"I'm trying to convince Arizona to stay with us while he's here," Charity said, picking up the conversation where they'd left it when Chloe had arrived home. "I've explained there's plenty of room and he won't be any trouble at all. What do you think?"

Chloe was staring at him again. Whatever the reason for her attention, he found he liked it. She blinked twice, then looked at her aunt. "What? Oh, sorry. I was—" She took a sip of her soda. "It's just I've been staring at your picture all day. I can't believe you're sitting here in my kitchen."

Her words hung in the room like dust motes floating on a sunny afternoon. The silence lengthened. Chloe sucked in a breath and flushed, as if she'd just realized what she'd said.

"That came out wrong," she said quickly.

"Not to me it didn't." Arizona winked. "The fan club can always use a new member. Did I mention I often take care of initiation myself?"

He was teasing…for the most part. Chloe's flush deepened. Maybe the little town of Bradley would be more interesting than he'd first thought.

He glanced over and saw Charity's speculative gaze. Ah, so his friend was thinking about a little matchmaking. He drank his beer, unconcerned by her efforts. He'd dealt with much tougher than her in the past. As they said in Australia—no worries.

Chloe cleared her throat. "Now you've seen me at my worst, or close to it. I don't usually make a habit of putting my foot in my mouth. What I meant was I'm a reporter with *Bradley Today* magazine. The writer who was going to follow you around for the next couple of weeks and write the article won't be able to do it. Our editor assigned me this morning. I've been busy doing research."

A reporter. Assigned to him. He liked that. "Should be fun."

"Yes, well, I left a message at your hotel explaining the situation."

"I've been with Charity most of the day," he said. "I'll be sure to listen most attentively when I get back to my room."

"You do that. There'll be a quiz in the morning."

She smiled then. A real smile without thought or purpose. Her face lit up, her eyes sparkled and he found himself leaning toward her, already planning what he could do to make her smile again.

Chloe reached for her briefcase and unzipped the leather, unconstructed bag. "I believe we have an appointment at the gem exhibit at nine-thirty in the morning. Does that still work for you?"

In more ways than you know, he thought, but only said, "Yes."

"Good." She made a notation in her date book. "It will take me a couple of days to get up to speed. I have Nancy's research, of course, but I want to do some of my own. I'll try not to be a pain with all my questions."

"My life is an open book," he said.

Charity coughed. "*Really,* Arizona? Oh, good. I was afraid there were some stories you wouldn't want me telling, but with your life being so accessible and all…" She turned to her niece. "Later I'll tell you about the time a tribal elder's daughter paid him to teach her how to please her husband. It seems that there was a problem with—"

Arizona groaned. "Charity, have you no shame? That is private."

"I thought you were accessible. I thought you wanted to share yourself with the people."

"Not that much of myself. There are some things Chloe should learn on her own."

Chloe raised her eyebrows. "How kind of you to say that, but don't worry. I'm not interested in any lessons on pleasing the men in my life."

"They're all satisfied?"

"Completely."

In her tailored slacks and linen jacket, she looked professional and confident. He wondered if Charity saw the slight tremor in her niece's hand as she picked up her can of soda. Chloe was lying through her teeth. Which either meant she wasn't pleasing her man, or there wasn't a man to please. He found himself wanting it to be the latter.

Charity chuckled. "I'm sorry, Chloe. I'm giving you completely the wrong idea about Arizona. It's true that he can be a charmer when he wants to be, but for the most part he's a decent and kind man."

Arizona winced. "I thought you were my friend."

"I am."

"You're talking about me as if I were the family dog."

Chloe leaned forward and rested her elbows on the table. "So you don't want to be thought of as decent and kind? Secretly you long to be—" She pressed her lips together.

Indecent. His brain filled in the word and he shifted in his chair. What was going on between himself and Chloe? This didn't make sense. The banter was fine—he enjoyed people who were fun and funny. But the sexual innuendo wasn't his style. Too obvious. Was it the lack of female companionship in his life, or was it something else? Something about Chloe specifically?

Before he could analyze the situation, the front door opened and a female voice called out a greeting.

"That's Cassie," Charity said, rising to her feet. "My other niece. She's the baby of the family."

"That's hardly fair," Chloe protested. "She's younger by all of six months. You make her sound like she's still a teenager."

"Or that you're an old woman," Charity teased.

"Thanks."

A young woman entered the kitchen. Her gaze settled on Arizona. "I saw you on television this morning," she said and grinned. Her short dark hair accentuated her large eyes. Where Chloe was tall and slender, Cassie was a good five or six inches shorter, with plenty of curves.

A nice enough young woman, Arizona thought as they were introduced, but not intriguing. Not like her sister.

"So you're a famous explorer," Cassie said as she reached for a pitcher of iced tea and poured herself a glass. Heart-shaped earrings glinted at her earlobes.

"That would be me. Larger than life."

Cassie settled next to him and sighed. "Do women gush when they meet you?"

"Only if they're incredibly discerning." He glanced up and caught Chloe's smile.

"Are you married?" Cassie asked.

"Cassie!" Chloe frowned at her sister. "Don't be personal."

"Why not? Well, are you?"

"You proposing?"

Cassie sipped her tea, apparently unruffled by the conversation. "No. I'm involved with someone. But Chloe is single."

Arizona shot her a glance. So there *wasn't* a man in her life. Funny how that piece of information was suddenly fascinating.

"Thanks for sharing that particular detail," Chloe said and rose to her feet. Her aunt stood by an electric frying pan sitting on the counter. "Can I help?" she asked.

"I'm doing fine. I'm cooking Arizona's favorite for dinner," she said.

Chloe glanced in the pan, then over at him. "Pot roast?"

"Yup. You'd be amazed how hard that is to find in some places."

"I'll bet."

"There's chocolate cake and ice cream for dessert,"

Charity added. "Both you girls will be staying for dinner."

It wasn't a question. The sisters exchanged knowing looks, and Arizona was pleased that he wasn't the only one Charity bossed around.

"You don't have to if you have other plans. Although I would very much like the company." The latter comment he addressed to Chloe.

"Oh, we aren't busy," Cassie said. "I'm only seeing Joel and I can call him and cancel."

"Joel would be your young man?" he asked.

"Uh-huh. We're engaged to be engaged." She held out her left hand. A thin gold band encircled her ring finger. The diamond set there was so small it looked like a grain of sand.

"It's lovely," he told her.

She beamed.

Cassie started asking him more questions. He answered automatically, most of his attention focused on her sister. Chloe didn't rejoin them at the table. Instead she moved around the kitchen, doing odds and ends that to his mind looked like busywork. Almost as if she was staying as far away from him as possible. Did he make her nervous?

There was something between them, he thought. Some kind of a connection. He knew there were people who would dismiss a feeling that they'd met someone before. He didn't. He'd traveled too much and seen too many things he couldn't explain to overlook the obvious.

When he looked at Chloe there was heat and desire, but there was also something else. An intangible he couldn't explain but that he wouldn't ignore, either. He wanted to get to know her better. At least circumstances were conspiring to assist him in his quest. If she was going to be writing about him, she could hardly spend the three weeks he was in town avoiding him.

She turned and opened a drawer. As she choose forks and knives, one fell to the floor. She knelt down to pick it up. The movement prickled at the back of his mind. As if he'd seen her kneel before. But when he probed his mind, the image that appeared to him was of Chloe completely naked, kneeling on a bed of straw.

Not that he was complaining, but where on earth had that thought come from? He swore silently and forced himself to pay attention to Cassie and her list of questions. Thank God he was sitting down and no one could see the obvious and rapid physical response to his vision. Clearly he'd been without a woman for too long. He'd outgrown the appeal of a bed partner in every port, but he was still a man who had needs. At some point in time he was going to have to do something about them.

Cassie stopped her bombardment long enough to get up and fix a salad. Chloe walked over to the table and began setting it.

"Pot roast, vegetables, mashed potatoes and salad," she said. "Not very exotic fair. Are you sure you wouldn't like me to run to the gourmet store and grab a bottle of chocolate-covered ants or something. Just so you'll feel at home?"

Her voice was low and teasing. She stood close enough that he could inhale the scent of her. "I think I can handle this."

He wasn't talking about the food, but did she know that?

"If you're sure," she said and picked up his empty bottle of beer. "I'll get you another one."

Cassie sliced tomatoes into the bowl of lettuce and cut-up vegetables. She grinned at him. "So when was the last time you had three women waiting on you?"

He thought for a second. "It's been a couple of months. I was staying—"

Small bits of radish hit him in the face.

"Hey!" He looked up and saw Chloe prepared to launch another assault.

"That was an incorrect answer," she told him. "You should try again."

He eyed the piece of radish. "Charity, you're not protecting me from these bloodthirsty nieces of yours."

"You were just bragging how you can handle things. So you're on your own."

"I'm seriously outnumbered."

Chloe tossed him another piece of radish. This one he caught and popped in his mouth.

"No one here is impressed," she informed him, her eyes bright with laughter.

The teasing continued throughout the preparation of the meal. Arizona enjoyed watching the three women work together. They moved with an easy grace that told him they did this often. Their banter reminded him that on occasion his chosen life could be very solitary. Sure he loved what he did, but his lifestyle didn't allow for a home of his own, or many intimate connections. He had lots of acquaintances, but few friends.

He tried to distance himself from the situation, to observe instead of participate, but the trick didn't work this time. He kept finding himself pulled into the conversation. The sense of family was strong and he was the odd person out. As the three women joined him and began dishing up food, he realized he was the only man at the table. He liked that in a group.

When everything was ready, Cassie plopped herself next to him and smiled. "I have a ton more questions."

Chloe took the seat opposite his, while Charity was next to her. He rubbed his chin thoughtfully. "I don't know if I can answer anything without first getting an agreement that everything we discuss here is off the record."

There was a stunned moment of surprise followed by a burst of laughter. Both women looked at Chloe, who raised her hands in the air. "Fine. I won't take notes, record the conversation or make any attempt to retain it in my brain. I'm sure that important secrets will be shared here tonight, but the public will just have to stay uninformed."

"So how long are you in town?" Cassie asked.

"Three weeks."

"Where were you before you got here?"

"South America. I was making arrangements to ship the gems. Before that I was in India."

Chloe passed him the bowl of mashed potatoes. As he took it from her, she shrugged. "You'll have to forgive her. Cassie works with preschool children. She doesn't get out much."

Cassie gave her sister a mock glare. "Oh, and you've traveled the world yourself. I know you have a lot of questions, too. You're just pretending to be sophisticated."

Arizona leaned toward Chloe. "It's working," he said in a low voice.

Her dark eyes flickered with an emotion he couldn't quite register, then she smiled and looked away.

"What do you usually look for?" Cassie asked as he finished serving himself and passed on the mashed potatoes. "Bones and stuff?"

"I'm not that disciplined," he admitted. "I know it's

important to study the details of life in lost civilizations, but I don't have the interest. I want to learn about the unusual. The mystical and unbelievable."

Cassie frowned. "What do you mean?"

"Magic. Objects that cast spells or connect the wearer to whatever gods that society worshiped."

Chloe put some salad on her plate and gave him an innocent smile. "Remember the last Indiana Jones movie, Cassie? It's the one where they were looking for the Holy Grail—the cup Christ is said to have used at the Last Supper. Arizona looks for stuff like that."

Arizona wasn't fooled. Chloe might have just been assigned the story, but she would have spent the day doing research. She had to know that he loathed being compared to that fictional movie character Indiana Jones. There was no way he could compete with that kind of hero and come out anything but second best. Tweaking the tiger's tail, he thought. She obviously wasn't a pushover. He liked that in a woman.

Cassie stared at him wide-eyed. "Really? So you're interested in legends?"

"All kinds. Old stories, myths about the past."

"Family legends?"

There was something about the way she asked the question. Chloe focused on her sister. "Mr. Smith doesn't want to hear about that," she said, her expression tight. "It wouldn't be interesting."

A mystery, he thought as he glanced from sister to sister.

"Just because it didn't work for you doesn't mean it's not real," Cassie said. "We have a family legend. The Bradleys do anyway. That's the family on our mother's side."

"Cassie, I don't think—" Chloe began, but her sister waved her off.

"Ignore her," Cassie said. "She's a cynic when it comes to stuff like this."

"I'm intrigued," Arizona admitted. As much with the idea of a family legend as with the mystery as to why Chloe didn't want him to hear it.

"The story is that several hundred years ago an old gypsy woman was being chased by some drunken men. They were throwing stones and yelling at her and she feared for her life." Cassie waved her hands as she talked, providing animation for the tale.

He spared a glance for Chloe. She stared at her plate as if it had suddenly started forming signs and symbols in the mashed potatoes.

"A young woman heard the commotion," Cassie continued. "She lived in a small cottage on the outskirts of town. I think she was being shunned or something but no one knows for sure. Anyway, she invited the old woman in and protected her from the men. In return the woman gave her a magic nightgown."

"Really?"

Cassie's humor faded. "I'm not making this up."

"I don't doubt you. It's just clothing isn't commonly used to carry magic. It doesn't age well, is easily torn or destroyed. But it's not unheard of. What's the magic?"

"This is the good part. Every woman in the family is supposed to wear the nightgown on the night of her twenty-fifth birthday. If she does, she'll dream about the man she's going to marry. He's her destiny and as long as she marries him, they'll live a long and happy life together."

"I see." Interesting story. He'd heard several like it before in different forms. It was a common theme. Related stories were the idea of sleeping with a piece of wedding cake under the pillow, or the stories about St. Agnes Eve.

"Any punishment for not sleeping in the nightgown?" he asked.

She shook her head. "I don't think so. Aunt Charity? You're the one who knows the most about it."

Charity shrugged. "There have been rumors of unhappy marriages when the woman didn't pay attention to her dream and married the wrong man, but I don't think there's a penalty for not wearing the nightgown."

"I'd like to see the nightgown," he said.

"Is that really necessary?" Chloe asked. "It's just a nightgown. I mean you've probably seen a dozen just like it."

"Ignore her," Cassie said, rising to her feet. "She's crabby because the legend let her down."

More intrigued because Chloe was obviously hiding something, Arizona leaned toward her. "What don't you want me to know?"

"Nothing." But her dark gaze avoided his. "It's just a story. It doesn't mean anything."

"It means something to your sister."

"Cassie has always been the dreamer in the family."

"Oh, and you're the practical one?"

This time she looked directly at him. "Absolutely. I only believe in things I can prove."

"Not magic?"

"Magic is skillful sleight of hand at best, smoke and mirrors at worst."

Before he could answer, Cassie returned to the kitchen. She handed him a soft cotton-and-lace nightgown. The fabric was old, but it didn't have the look or feel of something from a couple hundred years ago. He fingered the lace. Sometimes objects spoke to him. Not in words, but in images or sensations. A prickling along the back of his neck or a—*She stretched out on the straw and reached up for him. Her eyes were bright with passion, her lips wet from his kisses. Slowly, so neither of them could doubt his intent, he knelt beside her and placed one hand on the inside of her knee. Inch by inch he drew his hand up toward the most secret part of her. The nightgown offered only token resistance, tightening slightly before sliding out of the way.*

As quickly as it had appeared, the image faded, leaving Arizona feeling aroused and slightly disconcerted. He hadn't really seen much of the woman's face. Just her mouth. But he'd formed an impression of her, one strong enough to identify her.

Chloe.

"What do you think?" Charity asked, her gaze far too knowing.

He hoped his expression didn't give anything away. He cleared his throat before speaking. "It's antique enough to pass muster in a vintage clothing shop, but this isn't more than fifty or sixty years old."

Cassie's mouth drooped with disappointment.

"Hey, that doesn't mean the magic won't work," he told her. "Who wears it next?"

"I do," Cassie said, then raised her eyebrows. "Of course my birthday isn't for about six months. However, if you want to talk about a recent experience, ask Chloe. She wore it last night."

"Really?"

Chloe flushed slightly. "It was my birthday yesterday. Big deal. I wore it. Nothing happened."

He studied her, the smooth skin, the high cheekbones and firm set of her chin. She was lying, but about what?

"No dreams at all?" he asked.

"None worth mentioning."

"Maybe you should let us be the judge of that. After all, if you're so interested in my story, maybe you should share yours with me. Just to be fair." As he said the words, the image of her in the nightgown popped back into his head. No way, he told himself. It hadn't been him. He wasn't anyone's idea of destiny. The fates were smart enough to know that.

A timer dinged on the stove. Chloe rose to her feet. "Saved by the bell, and I mean that literally. The cobbler is ready. Why don't the three of you go on into the living room. I'll serve the dessert and bring it to you."

"Ah, Chloe, you're no fun at all," Cassie complained.

"I know. It's my lot in life."

"Don't worry," Charity said as she linked arms with him. "We can use the time to convince Arizona to stay here instead of at some boring hotel. What do you think?"

Cassie clapped her hands together. "That would be great! Say yes, Arizona. I swear I won't bug you every minute with questions."

"Just every *other* minute," Chloe muttered.

Cassie grinned. "Actually, she's telling the truth, but would that be too awful?"

"Not at all," Arizona said.

He *was* tempted. He would have accepted the gracious invitation except for one thing. Chloe. Something about her called to him. He could still picture her in the nightgown and he was hard with wanting. If anything happened between them, he didn't want to worry about upsetting Charity by taking advantage of her hospitality and therefore be unable to make love with Chloe.

Talk about an ulterior motive, he told himself. If Charity knew what he was thinking, she would want him neutered for sure.

Cassie took the nightgown from him and folded it. "We're supposed to wash it by hand using water from the first rain after the first full moon following the wearer's birthday. I've marked the full moon on my calendar. I don't want to forget. Chloe might not believe, but I'm determined to make sure the legend happens to me."

Arizona stood up and caught Chloe staring after her sister with an incredible look of sadness on her face. He wanted to ask her what was wrong, but this wasn't the time, and even if it was, he didn't have the right. He was just a guest in the house. Of course there was the detail of the article Chloe wanted to write. She was going to spend the next three weeks chasing after him, and if she played her cards right, he just might let her catch him.

CHAPTER THREE

"THERE IS a perfectly logical explanation," Chloe told herself as she exited the freeway and headed for the university. "Things like this happen all the time. It's nothing to worry about. I'm not going insane."

She braked at the stop sign and shifted her car into neutral. Her mouth curved up into a smile. "The fact that I'm talking to myself is not an indication of mental imbalance. I've *always* talked to myself. The trick is to not answer. At least not out loud."

The intersection cleared. She shifted into first and accelerated. Okay, so she was still feeling very strange about the dream she'd had two nights ago. Being exhausted didn't help. She hadn't been able to sleep at all the previous night, what with trying to make sense of everything. Obviously she'd seen Arizona's picture somewhere in the past, and his image had been lodged in her subconscious. It happened all the time. Cassie had been talking about the nightgown legend for weeks before Chloe's twenty-fifth birthday. The combination of life pressures, family-legend expectations and Lord knew what else had created a very real dream. But it was only a dream.

The fact that Arizona had invaded her life the next day was merely coincidence. The world was full of them.

"I'm going to be fine," she said aloud. "This article is a great opportunity for me. I'm going to turn in a dynamite project, impress the socks off my editor and write my way into a job with a big New York publisher."

She drew in a deep breath. The spring air was warm, the sun bright, the sky clear. At the next stop sign Chloe glanced around at the budding trees and green lawns that marked the outskirts of the university campus. For the first time in months she had the top down on her little sports car. The wind ruffled her hair and made her want to laugh. She would get through all this. She'd always been a survivor. If nothing else, she would keep reminding herself that Arizona Smith was just a man. Okay, he was very good-looking and the sight of him made her heart race. And maybe when they'd shaken hands yesterday she *had* felt a slight electrical charge, not to mention the fact that she didn't even have to close her eyes to picture him naked, next to her, on top of her, touching her everywhere as he—

"Stop it!" she commanded herself. "Don't go there. It's way too dangerous territory. Keep it light, keep it professional."

With that she turned into the parking lot by the exhibition hall. She found a parking spot by the main walkway and put up the top on her convertible. She'd barely finished collecting her leather briefcase when a black four-wheel-drive Ford Explorer pulled into the spot next to her. As she stepped out of her convertible, she had the feeling her car looked like a gnat buzzing beside an elephant. Then the tiny hairs on the back of her neck all stood up and a shiver raced down her spine. She couldn't think about cars or even breathing because she knew. *He* was there.

Sure enough, a tall, handsome guy climbed down from the driver's seat and circled around the front of the Explorer. Arizona wore khakis and a long-sleeved dark green shirt. His hair needed a trim, his boots were scuffed, and none of that mattered because there was a glint in his green eyes that made her wonder if the devil was half so appealing as this man standing in front of her.

"Morning," he said. "I thought I saw you zipping by me on the freeway. You were talking to yourself."

Chloe tightened her grip on her briefcase, then faked a casual chuckle. "Dictating, actually. I'm a journalist. It's an occupational hazard."

"I see." His gaze traveled leisurely over her body. The attention was as tangible as a blast of hot air. She found herself wanting to move close and rub up against him, just to make the moment complete. Before she could make a total fool of herself, he turned his attention to her car.

"Nice," he said, pointing at the silver BMW Z3 convertible. "You ever pretend you're James Bond?"

Chloe rolled her eyes. She'd heard the question before. Yes, the car had been featured in Pierce Brosnan's first film as James Bond, but that wasn't why she'd bought it. Some of her trust money had become available a couple of years before, she'd needed a new car and she'd always wanted a convertible. She'd bought the car on a whim and had never regretted it even once.

But she wasn't about to explain that to Arizona. She was in a lot of danger with this man. He was the subject of a story she intended to write, so she had to get the upper hand. His respect for her professional abilities was required. But she had a feeling he wouldn't care about her years of study or how many articles she'd written. He exuded power the way flowers exuded scent. He would respect someone who gave as good as they got. She was having enough trouble trying to forget about the dream and ignoring her unexplained attraction to him. She refused to let him best her in a game of wits.

She made a great show of glancing around the parking lot. "I don't know if you've noticed, Dr. Smith, but Bradley is firmly located in an area referred to as the Sacramento delta. This part of California is completely flat. So unless you plan on scaling a building or two, this four-wheel-drive monstrosity you've rented seems a great deal like overkill to me." She kicked the closest monster tire and smiled. "Of course, you're the expert in archaeology. Perhaps there's something I should know to explain this."

Their gazes locked. Chloe didn't dare back down. Better to have gone too far than not far enough, she told herself.

A slow smile pulled at his mouth. His eyes brightened with humor. "Yeah, yeah. You called me on that one. I couldn't help it. I hate little cars." He took her arm and led her toward the exhibit hall. "Let's get one thing straight. I prefer Arizona to Dr. Smith, okay? Let's keep things informal."

The victory was sweet, although not enough for her to ignore the tingling in her arm or the way her heart fluttered in her chest. "Works for me. I want you to feel comfortable."

He looked at her. "I do. I feel very comfortable."

If they ever made love, they would be in danger of experiencing spontaneous combustion.

She didn't know where the thought had come from, but she knew it was true. Dear Lord, the man turned her on. But she couldn't let him know.

"Good. Then you won't mind answering all my questions."

They'd reached the building. Arizona held the door

open for her. "Not at all. We can talk about anything you'd like."

The hallway was dim and it took a minute for her eyes to adjust. They stood facing each other. "I have a whole list of things I want to ask you."

"I think I'd rather talk about you."

It took a minute for his words to sink in. Chloe's body screamed a gratified "Yes!" when she finally absorbed the meaning of his statement. Her brain resisted. Was this teasing or testing? She didn't allow herself to think it might be an invitation. He couldn't possibly know about the dream. Did the attraction go both ways? The thought both excited and terrified her.

"That's not very subtle," she told him, pleased that her voice was calm. Shrieking would have been so unattractive.

"I can be if that's what you would prefer."

"What would you prefer?"

She hadn't meant to ask that question, but it was too late to call it back. Once the words were out, she really wanted to hear the answer.

The devastating smile returned. "I'd like to take you to an island in the South Pacific. Somewhere isolated and romantic."

"I'm sure you have just the one in mind."

"Of course. You'd like it. The indigenous population has a society based on a female deity. The social structure is matriarchal. In their eyes, men pretty much have one use."

Chloe was grateful for the dimness of the foyer. She could feel herself flushing. Based on what she'd read about him, he was probably telling the truth about the island. Despite herself, she laughed.

"I should be insulted," she told him.

"But you're not."

"No, I'm not." How could she be, when every cell of her being responded to him. Not just because he was good-looking. In fact, that was the least of his appeal. Much of what drew her was his energy. She felt like a cat seeking out the warmth of the sun. She wanted to bask in his glow.

"Don't you have some gems you want to show me?" she asked in an effort to change the subject.

"Absolutely." He led the way down the hall toward the exhibit hall.

She fell into step with him. "You're not what I expected," she admitted.

"So you've been doing your homework. Did you think I'd be more scholarly?"

"No, although I'm sure you're the expert everyone claims. I guess I didn't think you'd be just a regular guy. I try not to form too much of an impression of someone before I meet him. I don't want to be writing the article in my head too early. But in your case, that was more difficult than usual. There's a mythical element to your press clippings."

"Tell me about it." He stopped suddenly and turned to face her. "Despite the press trying to make it seem otherwise, I'm not Harrison Ford or Indiana Jones." His mouth twisted. "I can't tell you how many times those comparisons have been made."

"How often do you come out ahead?"

"Good question." His features relaxed a little. "We're running about fifty-fifty. You wouldn't believe the people who have trouble understanding that he's an actor portraying a fictional character. What happens in the movies has very little to do with real life. But people have expectations."

"You don't want to disappoint them," she said guessing.

"Of course not. But I'm not a larger-than-life character. Who can compete with a movie legend? This is real life. I don't get a second take to make sure the line is said just right."

"I would guess that the fans who most want you to be like Indiana Jones are the ladies," she said.

He groaned. "They bring me hats like his. And whips."

Chloe wasn't sure what to say to that. "I see."

He winked. "Of course some of them have been quite satisfied with reality."

I certainly was.

She jumped. Had she said that or just thought it? Her gaze flew to his face. He was watching her expectantly. Her heart, which had stumbled a couple of beats, resumed its steady thudding. She must have just thought it. Thank goodness. Arizona could never know about that night— or her dreams.

"Chloe, I'm sorry. I was just teasing. If it bothers you, I'll stop."

His statement didn't make sense for a second. Then she realized she'd been quiet and he probably thought she'd been insulted by his comment. "It's fine," she told him.

He shrugged. "Seriously, there was a time when I enjoyed all the press and comparisons. I worked hard to live up to the hype."

"A girl in every port?"

"Something like that."

"What happened?"

"I grew up. It got old. I've learned that quality is the most important part of a relationship."

That surprised her. "So you're a romantic at heart?"

He shoved his hands into the front pockets of his

slacks. "Yes. But not the way you mean it. If you're asking if I believe in love, the answer is no."

That didn't make sense. "You said you believe in magic."

"Of course. One doesn't have anything to do with the other. Magic exists. Love is the myth."

"No way. I've never seen magic at work, but you only have to look around to know love is everywhere. Parents and their children, couples who have been together fifty years, kids with their pets. How can you deny all that evidence?"

He stepped toward the wide double doors that led to the exhibit. "It's surprisingly easy," he said, pulled a key from his pocket, turned the lock and pushed open the right door.

As she moved to step inside, she was instantly assaulted by cool air. The light was even more dim inside, with only an illuminated path to guide them. A shiver rippled up her spine, but this one was from nerves, not attraction. Chloe instinctively fingered the heart-shaped locket she wore around her neck.

"This way," Arizona said with the confidence of someone who could see in the dark.

They'd taken about two steps when a voice stopped them. "You can't come in here," a man said. "The exhibit isn't open yet." Seconds later a bright light shone in her eyes, blinding her.

"It's okay, Martin," Arizona said. "This is Chloe Wright. She's a journalist. I brought her by to show her the exhibit."

The light clicked off and a security guard stepped out of the shadows. "Oh, sorry, Dr. Smith. I didn't know it was you." The fiftysomething man smiled. "Let me know if you need anything."

"I will, Martin, thanks."

When they were alone again, Arizona motioned to the dark draperies on either side of the lit path. "The entrance is going to have blown-up photographs showing some of the ruins, that sort of thing. Robert Burton, a friend of mine, is composing appropriate music. Whatever the hell that means."

Chloe chuckled with him. "Probably something with a South American flavor."

"Probably."

They continued down the walkway toward bright lights. Dark drapes gave way to glass cases exhibiting tools, bowls and animal hides fashioned into primitive clothing. Arizona briefly explained the significance of the items.

"I constantly offend my colleagues," he admitted, not looking the least bit concerned by the fact. "I know I should be interested in this kind of thing." He motioned to a row of cutting knives. "They are the basis for understanding how a people lived day by day. But I'm a true romantic. I find the living more interesting than the dead, even the long-dead, and I prefer magic to reality. I don't care what they used to skin their kill. I want to know how they prepared for the hunt. I want to learn the rituals and hear the songs." He shrugged. "As I'm frequently reminded, religion and magic have their place, but a good knife in the hands of a skilled hunter can keep a family alive for the winter."

Chloe studied the honed cutting edges. "But religion feeds them as well—their souls rather than their bodies. That has to count for something."

"Exactly."

Arizona beamed at her as if she were a rather dull student who had finally come up with the right answer. She barely noticed, being too busy wondering where on earth that thought had come from. She was way too pragmatic to be concerned about the state of anyone's soul.

"I'm glad you see my point," he told her. "However, there are a few people I can't seem to convince. They're much more into the physical than the spiritual. We need to go through here."

He led the way into a brightly lit alcove. There was a closed door at the far end. He knocked once. Another security guard stepped out. "Yes, Dr. Smith?"

"Jimmy, I made arrangements to show Ms. Wright the gem collection. You ready to unlock the cases for me?"

The guard, a young man of Chloe's age, nodded seriously. "Yes, sir. Let me get the keys and disable the alarm."

When he disappeared back into the room, Arizona winked at her. "Jimmy is in charge of the gems. He's very proud of that. He'll be accompanying us. With him around, we can unlock the cases and you can actually touch the stones."

"I'd like that." She stared at him. "How long have you been in town?"

"A couple of days. Why?"

"You seem to know everyone's name. Or is that just a habit with security guards?"

"I told you. I'm interested in the living."

Jimmy joined them, cutting off any further chance for conversation. He led the way to the last room. The walls were plain black. Tall glass cases formed a staggered line down the center. Spotlights illuminated their precious cargo.

Arizona nodded at the first case. "We'll start at this end and work our way down." As Jimmy unlocked the case, Arizona sighed heavily. "I found them, but do they trust me with them now?"

"Sorry, sir," Jimmy said without cracking a smile. "I'm following the rules."

Chloe moved close to the display. The door opened and Arizona reached inside to pick up a huge pink stone. It was the size of an orange, with an irregular shape. He held it with a reverence that made her nervous about taking it from him when he offered it to her.

"This will heal you," he said. "Arthritis, stomach trouble, anything internal. I don't think it would work on a broken bone, although I could be wrong. Some of the incantations were written down. We've found pieces on tablets and animal hides. The tribe is obscure. The language is tough. Not related to other Indian tribes in the area. I don't have any of the incantations with me, so just think good thoughts while you hold it and hope for the best."

She took the stone from him. It was heavier than it looked. The top was bumpy, but the bottom was smooth and fit perfectly into the palm of her hand. She studied the way the light glinted off the facets.

"They didn't find the stone this way, did they?" she asked.

"No. It's been cut. There are definite markings. That's one of the mysteries. The tools we found aren't strong enough or sharp enough to have done this, so how did it happen?"

She handed him back the stone. "Do you have a theory?"

"Of course. But you're going to have to come to my lecture series to hear what it is."

He put the stone back in the case, waited until Jimmy locked it, then moved to the next exhibit.

There were stunning gems used in religious ceremonies, more healing stones, some of undetermined purpose. Arizona talked about them all, as if they were well-loved friends. When they were at the last case, he removed a huge diamond nestled in a flower-shaped bed of gold. The object was so heavy, she had to use both hands to hold it.

"Close your eyes," Arizona instructed. "Focus on the stone."

Chloe did as he requested. Instantly, the diamond began to glow. She frowned. That was impossible. For one thing, she had her eyes closed. How could she know if something was glowing or not? For another, she didn't believe in the mystical. But she could feel the heat and would have sworn she saw the light.

"This is a loving stone," he said. "It would have been used in ancient weddings to bind a couple together."

Instantly she could see the cave, the two of them entwined on their bed of straw. Which was crazy, right?

As the image filled her brain, the stone definitely brightened. Chloe stiffened and opened her eyes. She stared at the diamond. Nothing about it had changed. It wasn't glowing at all, and now that she was paying attention, there really wasn't any heat.

Arizona took the stone from her and returned it to Jimmy. After thanking the guard, he led her out of the exhibit hall. There was a small garden behind the building. Stone benches surrounded an inverted fountain.

Still confused by what had happened, she settled on one of the benches. He took a seat next to her.

"What did you think?" he asked.

"It's very impressive. I can see why you enjoy your work and why you have such a following. You've brought a great find to national attention."

He dismissed the compliment with a wave. "I haven't

done anything that special. I followed a few clues, refused to give up when other people did, but I'm no hero. There are a lot of great scholars out there. I'm just some guy interested in pretty rocks and religious icons."

"You're selling yourself a little short, aren't you?"

"Not really. When I met Joseph Campbell I was so impressed, I couldn't talk. He was my idol. I don't say that lightly. I've met many impressive people, but he was the best."

Interesting. She made a mental note. That information could add some depth and human interest to her story. "Are there any important people you haven't met yet who intrigue you?"

His smile was slow and lazy. It should have warned her. He relaxed back in the bench. "Yesterday I would have said yes, because until yesterday I hadn't met you."

It was a line, she reminded herself. But it was a good one. "Not bad."

His smile didn't fade, but something dark and dangerous crept into his expression. "I wasn't kidding, Chloe. I know you felt it, too. The energy when you were holding the diamond. Did the stone glow when you closed your eyes? That's supposed to be significant."

She tried swallowing, but her throat was too tight. When coughing didn't clear it, she decided to ignore both the sensation and the question. She opened her briefcase and pulled out a small handheld tape recorder.

"I'd like to ask you a few questions," she said.

He eyed the machine. "Obviously we're on the record."

"We have been all morning."

His gaze sharpened. "Really? That surprises me." He crossed his ankle over his opposite knee. "Ask away."

The sun was warm, but the heat filling her body came from the inside. There was something about him, about his relaxed posture. She angled away from him, but even so, the bench was suddenly too small. She felt confined and much too close. She could inhale the masculine scent of his body. Her mind didn't want to focus on questions or interview techniques. She wanted to move closer still; she wanted to run away.

Neither possibility was wise, she reminded herself, so she dug out a list of questions she'd prepared the previous night when she couldn't sleep.

"You traveled with your grandfather for most of your formative years," she said.

"That's right. He showed up one day when I was about three or so, and took me with him. One of my first memories is riding a yak somewhere in Tibet." He stretched out his arms along the back of the bench. His strong tanned fingers lay within inches of her shoulder and she tried not to notice.

"Grandfather traveled in style," he continued. "At heart, he was an adventurer. Fortunately the family had money, so he was able to go where and when he wanted. He'd run guns into Africa before the Second World War. He knew heads of state, from Nixon to obscure tribal elders in kingdoms the size of a grocery store. He would decide to spend a summer somewhere or maybe a winter, but we never stayed longer than a few months. Grandfather loved to be moving on."

Chloe knew this from her research. "He arranged for tutors?"

Arizona nodded. "Sometimes several at once. I studied for hours every day. When I was fourteen, he put me in university, Oxford, then I moved to Egypt for a year or so. India, South Africa. I have an assortment of degrees." He grinned. "None of them practical."

"Are you an adventurer, too?"

"In a manner of speaking. I've tried to be more methodical, to use what I know to discover the past. Grandfather wanted to travel for the sake of being gone. I want to accomplish something."

She looked at him. From where she was sitting, he looked like a fairly normal guy. Perhaps he was a little too good-looking, but otherwise, he seemed to be much like the rest of the world.

"You're staring," he said. "Is there a reason?"

She shook her head. "You're so different from anyone I've ever known. My family is one of the founding families of this town. My mother's maiden name is Bradley. The Victorian house has been ours for generations. I've traveled some, but not like you. Bradleys have been in this valley for more than a hundred years."

He shrugged. "Roots aren't a bad thing."

"I know. I'm not unhappy with my life. I'm just wondering what it would be like to have lived yours." She tried to imagine always moving around, never knowing where one was going next. The thought wasn't pleasant.

She remembered the running tape and the fact that this was supposed to be an interview. "Okay, next question. I know your mother died shortly after you were born. When did your father pass away?"

If she hadn't been studying him so closely, she wouldn't have noticed the subtle stiffening of his body. "My father is alive and well. At least he was the last time he called me."

"But you grew up with your grandfather. He took you away when you were three."

"I know."

"Why didn't you stay with your father?"

"It just worked out that way."

The journalist in her jumped onto the detail. Questions

sprang to mind. Had there been a problem? An estrangement? Some legal issues? Why had Arizona's father let his only child be taken from him and subjected to such an odd upbringing?

"You're going to pursue this line of questioning, aren't you?" Arizona sounded more weary than annoyed.

"Yes. I'm figuring out which way to go."

He didn't answer. Instead he raised his head to the sun. "It's warmer than I thought it would be," he said.

"We're about ten degrees above normal for this time of year."

"I should have dressed for it." He reached for his right cuff and undid the button.

All the questions and strategies about how best to handle the interview fled from her mind. The entire world disappeared as she focused her attention on those long fingers and his casual act.

He finished rolling up the right sleeve and started on the left. She knew what she was going to see there. Despite the fact that she'd only met the man yesterday and that he'd been wearing long sleeves then, too. Despite the fact that none of the photos in her research files showed him in anything but long sleeves. She knew about the scar because she'd seen the man naked in her dreams.

That wasn't real, she reminded herself. It hadn't really happened. So when he rolled up the sleeve, there wasn't going to be a knife scar on the inside of his left forearm. Except she knew that was exactly what she was going to see.

She stopped breathing.

He made one fold of the fabric, then another. The tail of the scar came into view. She told herself this wasn't really happening, except it was and she didn't know how to make it stop.

He caught her stare. "It's not so bad," he said, motioning to the scar. "Want to hear how it happened?"

"I can't," she said, her voice tight. "I can't. I have to—" She couldn't think of a real excuse so she didn't bother making one. Instead she gathered up her notes and her tape recorder and thrust both into her briefcase.

It was too much to take in. The dream and the man and the fact that she'd known what the scar looked like before she'd even seen it.

"I'll be in touch," she managed as she scrambled to her feet and headed for the parking lot.

"Chloe? Is something wrong?"

She held him off with a wave. As soon as she was on the far side of the garden, she began to run. It was only when she tried to fit her key in the lock that she realized she was blinded by tears she could neither explain nor understand. What on earth was happening to her?

CHAPTER FOUR

CHLOE FINISHED STACKING the folders into neat piles. She'd already dusted her computer, rearranged her pencil cup and answered all her messages. Even the boring ones. Still, the busywork wasn't enough to keep her mind from scurrying around like a frantic chicken, scuttling from place to place, or in her case, subject to subject.

She'd tried lecturing herself on the importance of being professional. She'd scanned a couple of articles on maintaining one's cool during interviews. She'd taken countless deep breaths, tried a bit of stretching in the ladies' room and had even sworn off coffee.

It wasn't helping. The truth was she was scared.

Something strange was happening to her. She didn't want it to be true, but she could no longer ignore the obvious. Fact number one. Before yesterday, she'd never met Arizona Smith. She didn't think she'd even seen a picture of him or known who he was. Fact number two. Night before last she'd had a long, detailed, highly erotic dream about Arizona. A dream so intense just thinking about it sent a quiver of excitement through her belly. Fact number three. In said dream, she'd pictured Arizona naked. She *knew* what the man looked like naked. That was fine. All men sort of looked the same without their clothes. The basic working parts had a lot in common. But it was more than that. She knew about his scars. The one on his knee and the one on his forearm. Fact number four. That very morning she'd had confirmation that her dream had some basis in reality. After all, the scar had been exactly as she remembered it.

Fact number five. Maybe she was going crazy.

Chloe folded her arms on her desk and let her head sink down to her hands. She refused to consider insanity as an explanation to her problem. It had to be something else. Something logical. Maybe along with seeing his picture and not remembering it, she'd also read an article that mentioned his scars.

Or maybe the nightgown was real.

That last thought made her shudder, but in a whole different way than when she thought about making love with Arizona. Anything mystic was just too weird for her. She didn't want the nightgown to be real. She didn't want to know her destiny and she sure didn't want to have to get involved with a man like Arizona Smith. He had a woman in every port. He didn't even believe in love.

She straightened in her chair. He was wrong about love. It did exist. Unfortunately it wasn't worth the pain it brought along, but it was definitely real.

"I don't want this," she murmured to herself. "I want my life to be normal, like everyone else's."

She suddenly remembered she was in the office. Talking to herself in the car was one thing, but in front of others, especially coworkers, was quite another.

This has gone on too long, she told herself firmly and silently. She had to pull herself together. She reached for the pad of paper she always kept by her phone and then grabbed a pen. She would make a list. List making always helped.

First, she would pretend the dream never happened. Every time she thought about it, she would push it to the back of her mind. Eventually she would forget. Second, she was going to act like the professional she was. No more personal conversations, no more freaking out because she saw a scar. She didn't even want to imagine what Arizona must think of her.

"Professional," she muttered. It was time to work on her article.

She glanced at the list she'd made, figured she could remember both items on her own and tossed the paper into the trash. Next, she reviewed the background material Nancy had left her. There were a couple of points that hadn't been clear. Chloe picked up the phone and dialed the reporter's home number.

When Nancy answered, Chloe introduced herself and politely asked about her pregnancy. They talked about work for a few minutes, then Nancy mentioned Arizona.

"I've been seeing the man everywhere on the local news. Is he as impressive in person?"

Chloe thought about her own reaction to Arizona and bit back a sigh. "Unfortunately, yes."

The two women laughed.

"Gee, Mark and I have wanted children for a long time, but now I'm feeling a little left out of it. I'm getting stretch marks and a daily afternoon backache while you're out playing with the new guy in town. It's not fair."

"But in a couple of months you're going to have a baby, and all I'll be left with is a story." And a broken heart.

The last thought came without warning and Chloe firmly ignored it. She was not going to get involved enough to get her heart broken. In fact she wasn't going to get involved at all.

"Speaking of the story," she said. "I have a few questions on a couple of your sources."

"I figured you would. My system of taking notes is

tough for people to follow. You'd think after all this time I'd be more organized, but I'm not."

Chloe went through her questions and wrote down Nancy's replies. When they were finished she said, "From what I can tell you were angling your story toward telling about the man and his myths."

"Right, but I was never happy with that. Have you thought of something better?"

"I don't know if it's better, but I have another idea. I'd like to write about the man *behind* the myths. Arizona has traveled all over the world. He has a strong belief in the mystical and spiritual. From what I've seen he has an image the media loves. But who is the man underneath? How does he decide what he's going to pursue? What are his influences now and what were they in the past?"

"I like that," Nancy said. "I think the readers will like it, too. Arizona is getting tons of media attention so there's no point in rehashing old material. Everyone will be tired of it by then. But this is new and fresh. Have you run it by Jerry?"

Chloe glanced at her watch. "I have a meeting with him in a couple of hours."

"He's going to think it's great." She laughed. "Actually what you're going to hear is a noncommittal grunt, which means he thinks it's great. If he hates it, he tells you to your face."

"I know that one firsthand. Okay, Nancy. Thanks for your help." They said their goodbyes and hung up.

Chloe turned on her computer and prepared to type up her notes. Usually she could focus on her work, but today there was a voice nagging in the back of her mind.

"This is too ridiculous," she said softly. "I won't get a moment's peace until I fix this."

With that, she picked up the phone again, consulted a pad of paper and dialed.

"Room 308," she told the receptionist. "The guest's name is Arizona Smith."

She waited while the call was connected. It was possible that he hadn't gone back to the hotel yet. He might be out all day. If that was the case, she would leave him voice mail asking him to get in touch with her. No matter how long it took, she was going to have to talk to him and apologize for her behavior that morning. There was no point in trying to explain—she wasn't about to tell him about her dream or the fact that she'd known about his scar even before he'd rolled up his sleeve. But she at least had to atone for her rudeness in running off.

The receiver was picked up, cutting off her train of thought.

"Smith," he said by way of a greeting.

"Hi, it's Chloe. I'm sorry to bother you."

"No bother."

His voice sounded normal. She took that as a good sign. "I'm calling to apologize for what happened earlier today. I don't know why I ran off like that." She crossed the fingers of her free hand, hoping the superstitious gesture would make up for the small lie.

"I understand. Sometimes I have that effect on women. They lose control and rather than let me see how overcome they are, they run off."

His voice was so calm and serious it took her a minute to figure out he was teasing. She chuckled. "Yeah, right, that was it exactly. Overcome by your substantial charms, I had to retreat to the relative sanctuary of my office so that I could recover."

"Are you better now?" he asked.

"Much, thank you." They laughed together, then she

said, "I'm serious. I don't know what came over me. It was terrible to leave like that. I promise it won't happen again."

"It better not. You won't get much of a story if you keep running out on the interview."

"Can I make it up to you? Would you please come over for dinner tonight?"

He hesitated. Chloe swallowed as her good humor disappeared like feathers sucked up into a tornado. Of course. Why hadn't she thought of that? "You have other plans," she said, making it a statement, not a question. Who was she, this other woman?

"Actually, I don't. Yes, I would love to join you for dinner. However, your aunt already issued the invitation and I accepted."

"Aunt Charity phoned?"

"First thing this morning."

Chloe knew she shouldn't be annoyed at her aunt. After all, Charity called the old Victorian mansion home, and she had every right to invite whomever she liked. But the tension was there all the same.

"That's great," Chloe told him. "I'll see you then. This time I promise not to freak when you show off your scars."

"If you're very good I'll even let you touch them."

She thought about the one on his leg and couldn't suppress a shudder of anticipation. "You've got yourself a deal."

CHLOE PULLED INTO the driveway. Mr. Withers, the seventy-year-old misogynist caretaker sat on his rider-mower, going back and forth on the front lawn.

"Evening, Mr. Withers," Chloe called out as she stepped up to the front porch.

Mr. Withers offered a wave that was more dismissal than greeting and muttered something under his breath. Probably something mildly offensive, Chloe thought with a grin. The old man had been around since long before her mother had been born. He'd always taken care of the house. If either of the sisters dared to try to engage him in conversation they risked being called mindless ninnies. Chloe had always wanted to ask what other kind of ninnies existed—didn't the definition of the insult imply a mindlessness? But she didn't think Mr. Withers would appreciate her humor.

"Have a nice night," she told him as she stepped into the house and was rewarded with another grunt.

She shut the front door behind him, effectively cutting off most of the noise from the power mower. "I'm home," she yelled in the direction of the kitchen.

"It's Chloe!" Cassie came racing down the hall and slipped to a stop in front of her. "I want to hear everything, but so does Aunt Charity so you have to wait until we're all together. But plan on spilling lots and lots of details. Oh, and *he's* coming to dinner. Isn't that great?" She took a deep breath before continuing. "He is so amazingly cool and good-looking. How can you stand it? I mean, spending the day with him. Did he look into your eyes and say something wonderful? Don't you think he's just incredibly interesting?"

Chloe put down her briefcase and slipped out of her linen jacket. After linking her arm with her sister's she led them both to the kitchen. "I don't even know where to start," she admitted. "I swear, Cassie, sometimes you act like you're barely sixteen instead of nearly twenty-five."

Cassie tossed her head, making her short dark hair dance around her face. "I'm blessed with an enthusiastic nature," she said, not the least bit insulted by her sister's comment. "I enjoy life and all that it has to offer. Arizona Smith is a very interesting man and I'm enjoying his company. We can't all be jaded reporters. I'd rather be the romantic dreamer I am any day."

They reached the kitchen. Cassie stepped away and got them each a soda from the refrigerator. Chloe settled at the kitchen table. "Where's Aunt Charity?" she asked.

"Taking a shower. The spaghetti sauce has been simmering for hours." She pointed to a pot on a back burner. She plopped down opposite her sister. "Tell me everything."

Chloe obliged, telling her sister about the gem exhibit and recounting Arizona's stories.

Cassie sighed. "It's so romantic. What a great way to spend the morning. But you probably just sat there taking notes, not even noticing the man. You're hopeless." Cassie tucked her short hair behind her ear. "I swear, when I have my twenty-fifth birthday and I get to wear the nightgown, I'm not going to waste a perfectly good opportunity dreaming about nothing! I plan to have a wonderfully romantic dream."

Chloe smiled as her sister talked. She was glad they were back together again. The three years they'd spent apart in high school had been difficult for them both. She fought against a familiar flash of anger. Their parents should have planned better, she thought for the thousandth time. If they had, the two sisters wouldn't have been separated and put into different foster homes.

She shook off the old memories and concentrated on the evening ahead. She'd promised herself that she would act like a real professional, that she wouldn't let thoughts of the dream interfere.

"What time is Arizona coming over?" she asked.

Cassie glanced at the clock above the stove. "In about an hour."

"I'd better get changed."

Cassie followed her up the stairs. "Are you all right? Is something bothering you? You got a funny look on your face a second ago."

"I'm fine." They reached her bedroom first and both women entered. They sat on the bed facing each other. "I was just thinking that I'm glad we're back together. High school was hard."

Cassie's good humor faded a little. "I know. I hated that the courts forced us to live apart. But we're together now—at least until you run off to the big city to write for one of those New York magazines." Cassie held up her hand. "Don't even say it. I know the drill. This is what you want and you have every right to pursue your dreams. But I'll miss you."

Chloe leaned toward her. "You could come with me. We could rent an apartment together."

Cassie shook her head. "No. I don't want to leave Bradley. I like it here. I adore my job."

"You're a nursery school teacher."

"Exactly, and I love it. The kids are great. I know you don't understand—you want more for me. But this is what *I* want and you have to remember to respect that."

"I know." Chloe sighed. It was a familiar discussion. One she'd never won. "I just think you could do so much more with your life."

"And I think working with children is the most important thing I *can* do. Besides, even if I was tempted to run off to New York with you, which I'm not, I couldn't. What about Joel?"

Chloe forced her expression to remain pleasant and

her hands still, when all she wanted to do was grab her sister by the shoulders and shake some sense into her.

Joel and Cassie had been dating since high school. They had an "understanding" that they would become engaged and then marry.

It was all a quirk of fate, Chloe thought grimly. While she had been sent away to another city when their parents had died and the two girls had been put into foster care, Cassie had stayed in town. She'd gone to the local high school and had started seeing Joel.

"If you can't say something nice," Cassie warned.

"Joel is the most boring man on the planet."

"That's hardly nice."

"You don't know what I was going to say. It's a real improvement."

"Oh, Chloe, we can't all be like you. I think it's great that you want to leave Bradley and make something of yourself. That's your life and you're going to be wonderful. But it's not my life. I want to stay here. I want to have a family. Joel wants to marry me. I love him. I've been dating him for nearly nine years and he makes me happy. Let it go."

Chloe bit her tongue and nodded her agreement. There wasn't anything else she could say. Cassie was right— they each had to live their own lives.

Her sister stood up. "I have to go make myself beautiful for our guest and I suggest you do the same." She paused in the doorway and leaned back dramatically, the back of one hand pressed against her forehead. "Maybe he'll tell us about the time he saved the virgin from the angry volcano by single-handedly fighting off a dozen hostile natives with his bare hands."

"I'm sure that will be the first story to cross his lips."

"I knew it." Cassie waggled her fingers and left.

Chloe stared after her. The two sisters couldn't be more different. Part of the reason, she knew, was because they weren't related by blood. When her mother had had trouble conceiving, her parents had gone on a long waiting list for adoption. As sometimes happened, Amanda Wright had later found out she was pregnant. The doctors had warned her she was unlikely to have another baby, so they hadn't pulled their application. Seven months after Chloe had been born the Wrights received a call telling them there was a one-month-old girl available, if they wanted her.

Growing up, Chloe couldn't remember a time when Cassie hadn't been around. The girls had been inseparable. That had made those three years apart even more difficult.

She stood up and walked to the closet, not sure what she was going to wear tonight. Something pretty, but professional. She was going to ask Arizona questions to make up for her lapse earlier that day. As she studied her wardrobe, she heard Cassie's enthusiastic but off-key singing drifting down the hall. She smiled. Cassie was one of those rare people who absolutely believed the best in everyone and always told the truth. She led with her chin and sometimes she got hurt. But that never changed her feelings about herself or the world.

Chloe wondered what it would be like to have that much faith. She was too cynical to believe in people. Especially those she didn't know well. That's why she was a decent journalist. The thing was if she wanted anyone else to believe that, she was going to have to write a dynamite article. Arizona Smith and the secrets of his life were her ticket out of Bradley.

ARIZONA SWALLOWED A drink of beer and wondered why the sight of an attractive young woman cooing over the scar on his arm didn't do a thing for him. Cassie bent over him and made tsking noises.

"I can see where they first stitched you up in the field," she said. "There are still a few puncture wounds."

Her fingers were cool and smooth as she stroked his skin. He waited, hoping to feeling a tingle or a flicker of interest. Nothing. Less than nothing. He was restless.

Cassie straightened and smiled. "Any other scars?"

She'd noticed the mark on his arm the second he'd walked into the house. As near as he could figure, the sight of it had sent Chloe screaming out of his presence. Funny, he'd never thought it was that scary looking, but then he was a guy. Maybe Chloe was squeamish.

Cassie's gaze was filled with curiosity and good humor. She reminded him of the little sister he'd never had. He couldn't help teasing her a little. "I do have another scar on my leg. I'd show it to you, but I'd have to take my pants off to do it."

"Oh, I don't mind," Cassie said quickly.

Arizona watched her, but there was no guile in her expression. Had she really meant what she'd said?

Footsteps interrupted his thoughts. He looked up and all the attraction that had been missing when Cassie had touched him slammed into him with the subtlety of an aircraft carrier taking out a forty-foot yacht.

Chloe stood just inside the kitchen. She wore a sleeveless dress in pale peach. The soft-looking fabric clung to her curves in a way designed to make a man forget to breathe. Her long hair had been pulled back into a braid. His fingers itched to tug the curls free.

"You might want to rethink your comment, Cassie," Chloe said to her sister. "I believe you just told Arizona you wanted him to take his pants off."

"I do." Suddenly, Cassie seemed to realize the implications of what she'd just said. She blanched, then color flooded her face. "Oh, no. I didn't mean— That is to say, he has a scar and—" She glanced from him to Chloe and back. "I didn't mean anything else. We were talking and—"

Chloe chuckled. "We know what you meant. Just be careful. Not every strange man is going to understand you're not issuing an invitation."

Cassie nodded.

Arizona leaned close to her. "I won't take offense if you'll explain to your sister that I'm not really strange."

Chloe took the seat opposite him. "Yes, you are, and I'll thank you not to corrupt my little sister."

"Little by how much?" he asked. "Charity told me you're about the same age."

"Chloe is six months older," Cassie told him. "I was adopted."

"So I heard." He looked from one to the other.

Charity came into the room and walked to the stove. "The sauce is nearly ready," she said, lifting the cover and stirring. Instantly a spicy tomato aroma filled the room.

"I'll do the garlic bread," Chloe said.

"I'll take care of the salad." Cassie headed for the re-frigerator.

"Should I offer to help or will I be told to just stay out of the way?"

"The latter, of course," Charity told him, her eyes twinkling at him as she glanced over her shoulder.

He leaned back in his chair. It didn't matter how many cultures he visited, or where he traveled in the world. Some customs remained the same. The ritual dance of women preparing a meal was one.

Whether the women were barefoot by an open fire, in a log house, a stone kitchen or a Victorian mansion, they moved with a grace and rhythm that was as old as the species. Conversation ebbed and flowed as they performed their magic. He supposed he enjoyed watching because no one did this for him very often. He was a frequent guest, but never a member of the family.

He caught Chloe's eye and they shared a moment of connection across the kitchen. The rest of the room disappeared until she was the only one left. Then Cassie touched her arm and she turned away from him. He was again on the outside. He envied her the place she held in this special world.

THE DINNER DISHES had been pushed to the center of the table, but no one was in a hurry to pick them up. Arizona tore apart the last piece of garlic bread as Cassie raised her hands in frustration.

"How can you say it's not true?" she asked. "The nightgown has been in the Bradley family for generations."

"It's just a nightgown," Chloe insisted. "How can you say it has magic powers? As I've said before, there is no such thing as magic or destiny. It's all smoke and mirrors."

Cassie shook her head. "Aunt Charity, you talk to her."

"She won't listen to me," the older woman said. "Arizona, you have a go at it. Chloe is our resident cynic."

"I'll try." He leaned forward and stared at the beautiful woman sitting across from him. He would rather carry her up to bed, but that hadn't been offered as one of the options, so he thought about the various feats of magic he'd experienced personally.

"Several years ago I was in India," he began. "A boy had been mauled by a tiger stalking the village. The cat nearly took off his leg. Although the bone wasn't broken, he lost a lot of blood."

He tried not to notice the way her eyes darkened as her pupils widened with the storytelling. He tried to ignore the scent of her body, the slender curves beneath her dress or the way he *knew* how great it would be between them, almost as if they'd been lovers before.

"If he'd been near a hospital, he might have had a chance," he continued. "But the village didn't even have a nurse, let alone medical facilities. My grandfather and I knew the boy was going to die and we could only offer painkillers to ease his passing."

He paused, remembering his own fear from that night. He'd been thirteen or fourteen, and he could relate to the screams of fear and pain from the injured child.

"That night the village performed an old ceremony of sacrifice and worship. They came together to heal one of their own. I wasn't allowed to attend—I was considered too young. But I heard it. The singing and chanting. I smelled the incense. I don't know what they did but it worked. When I went to visit him the next morning, I was afraid he would already be dead. Instead, I found him sitting up. His wound had nearly healed. He was talking and laughing because the pain was gone. Within a week, it was as if it had never happened. Since then, I've witnessed many things I can't explain."

"Wow," Cassie breathed. "That is so cool."

Chloe rolled her eyes. "Every supermarket tabloid has a story about people being abducted by aliens. Do you believe that, too?"

So she was a doubter. Somehow that made the challenge more interesting. "I saw the boy. When I see aliens abducting people from cornfields, I'll believe that as well."

"I want to know what has made you believe in all this."

"I want to know what has made you such a cynic," he responded. "Do you mean to tell me that in all your twenty-five years there hasn't been one incident you can't explain? One event or circumstance that makes no sense, but that you can't deny?"

Their gazes locked. Something flickered in her eyes. Something that called out to him and if they'd been alone...

But they weren't, he reminded himself. They had two very interested onlookers.

"My, look at the time," Chloe said. "If we don't get these dishes soaking, they'll never come clean."

With that she sprang to her feet and started to clear the table. The other two women moved to help her. Cassie shooed Arizona back into his seat when he tried to assist. His gaze followed Chloe. She was hiding something. He could feel it.

There was a mystery behind her pretty face and he had every intention of solving it.

CHAPTER FIVE

"I LOOK like a bridesmaid," Cassie complained.

Chloe fluffed her sister's hair. "You look beautiful. I love that dress."

"It's too young. I should change into something else. Why can't I look sophisticated, like you?"

Chloe faced front and studied their reflections in the mirror. They stood in her bathroom, both ready to go out for the evening. Cassie wore a long-sleeved, silky dress of pale pink that fell to midcalf. Lace edged the oversize collar. Her thick hair had been smoothed away from her face, exposing the gold heart earrings she always wore—the earrings that matched Chloe's locket— a legacy from their mother.

Chloe was willing to admit that while Cassie didn't look like a bridesmaid, there was definitely something virginal about her dress and her expression. She was still untouched by the ways of the world. Chloe thought about her own heartache and figured her sister was lucky to still be so unaware of the emotional pain that awaited her.

Chloe turned her attention to her own reflection. In contrast to her sister's innocence, she looked ready for sin. She'd pulled her long curls up on top of her head, securing them in a large clip. The ends fell to the back of her neck and danced against her bare skin. Her dress was simple. A scoop-neck, long-sleeved velvet dress. The soft burgundy fabric came to midthigh, exposing a lot of leg.

Overtly sexy wasn't her usual style, but then neither
was a man like Arizona. She was attending a reception
in his honor. She figured she needed all the help she
could get just to maintain some kind of power base in
the relationship. If only she weren't so attracted to him,
she might have a fighting chance. But she *was* attracted.
She shivered at the thought of being near him again. Of
seeing him and talking to him. Lord help her if he asked
her to dance. She would probably become a giant puddle
right there on the dance floor.

"I hate being short," Cassie said with a sigh.

"You're five-five. That's average, not short. Besides,
I would love to be petite."

"Me, too." Cassie patted her hips. "Instead, I'm curvy.
You get to be tall and slender and beautiful. If you weren't
my sister, I think I'd hate you. I might just hate you anyway."

Chloe smiled and kissed her cheek. "You know you
love me. I love you, too. So we're even."

The doorbell rang downstairs. Cassie glanced toward
the door. "That will be Joel. You know we're going out to
dinner before we come to the reception, right?"

"Why? There will be food at the party. You can eat
there."

Cassie slipped out of the bathroom. "You know how
Joel is. He's concerned that with Arizona's reputation
and his world travel, the university will be serving something exotic. Joel doesn't eat exotic things. We'll go to
our regular restaurant and join you later."

Chloe resisted the urge to roll her eyes. What on earth
was Cassie doing with Joel? Why couldn't she see she
was simply settling? There was a whole world out there
just waiting to be seen. But instead of speaking her mind,
Chloe forced herself to smile. They'd had this discus-

sion a hundred times. Cassie knew her sister's opinion on the subject, and she was old enough to make her own decisions.

"Don't change your mind about coming," Chloe said. "I really want you there."

"I wouldn't miss it. I promise." She waved, then left to meet her date.

Chloe lingered in the bathroom for a few minutes, touching up her makeup and spraying on perfume. As a rule, she didn't put much on her face during the day. A little mascara, sunscreen and powder. But for events like this, she went all out. At least she had the satisfaction of knowing she looked her best. She would need the confidence to face everyone at the reception.

"It's really dumb to lie to myself," she said, and she collected her tiny evening purse. Okay, she would tell the truth. She wanted to look her best to give herself the confidence to face Arizona...and because she was female enough to want to knock his socks off. It wasn't going to happen, of course, but a girl could dream.

Thirty minutes later, she accepted the car claim ticket from the valet and stared up at the front of the hotel. The welcome reception was being held in the grand ballroom. Bradley wasn't that big a town and most events like this were held here. She knew the approximate layout of the room, at least half the guest list and who was likely to get drunk and embarrass themselves. She was here both as a reporter and as a guest. The former role meant that she would need to spend at least part of the evening talking to Arizona.

"Talk about a hardship," she murmured under her breath. She made a promise to herself that no matter how good he looked in his tux, she would not swoon, then she squared her shoulders and headed for the ballroom.

The huge room was much as she expected. Bright lights glittered from a dozen chandeliers. There were crowds of people in tight conversation groups. Her name was checked against the list of invitees, then she was admitted.

Chloe made her way to the bar in the east corner and ordered a glass of white wine. It was false courage at best, but she had a feeling she was going to need all the help she could get.

As she sipped the tart liquid, she glanced around. While she told herself she was just checking out who was wearing what, she knew she was actually searching for him. *Damn.* She couldn't even pretend she wasn't interested for five minutes. What hope did she have of pulling off the professional act? Well, she was going to have to figure out a way. Maybe if she walked around for a while and chatted with some other people she might figure out how to pull this off. If she—"I thought you were never going to get here."

The voice came from behind her, but she didn't have to turn around to identify the speaker. Even if she hadn't recognized him from how he sounded, her body instinctively knew. Was it his scent, his heat or something more basic than that? She wasn't sure. All she knew was that there wasn't going to be enough time to get her act together.

Fake it until you make it, she told herself as she turned so they were facing each other.

He'd had a recent haircut and shave. She filed the information away as she drank in the sight of him. Strong, handsome features, green eyes that twinkled with amusement and what she hoped was appreciation. He wore a black tux, obviously tailored, and a crisp, white shirt. He was tall, dangerous and too sexy by far. The only thing that gave her hope of surviving the evening without making a fool of herself was the fact that he seemed to be studying her as completely as she had studied him.

"Well," he asked and did a quick turn, like a fashion model. "What do you think?"

"You clean up very nicely, Dr. Smith."

"I could say the same, but it wouldn't do justice. You always look lovely, but tonight you're radiant."

He brought her free hand up to his mouth and kissed her knuckles. The old-fashioned gesture nearly drove her to her knees. She had to consciously remind her body to keep breathing.

"We are," he said as he tucked her hand into the crook of his arm, "a fabulous-looking couple. Everyone will be jealous. It's our duty to walk through the crowd, spreading our attractiveness among them. They will expect it. They might even throw money." He gave her a wink.

His outrageousness made her laugh and his easy smile calmed some of her nervousness. "How noble of you," she told him. "I'm terribly impressed by your concern for the little people."

He leaned toward her. "Seriously, I expect you to protect me. I hate parties like this. Everyone wants to impress me with their exotic travels. Some even bring pictures. I never know what to say. I don't do the celebrity thing very well."

His confession both surprised and pleased her. "I'll do what I can to keep you safe."

They began to circulate through the room. Chloe had been prepared to introduce Arizona to the local dignitaries, but he already seemed to know them. He greeted the mayor and most of the city council by name.

"How do you do that?" she asked when they'd excused

themselves to go sample the food. "How do you know who everyone is?"

Arizona collected an empty plate for each of them and led her to the buffet line. "I met the mayor and her husband at the airport. There was a city council meeting yesterday and I attended."

Chloe glanced at the food spread out before them. There was nothing more exotic than some enchiladas, but Cassie had probably been right to let Joel take her out to dinner. He would have fussed over the fact that there wasn't a steak in sight.

"I have a terrible time remembering people's names," she said as she took some salad. "I keep a detailed card file so I don't mess up at press conferences."

"I'm lucky," he admitted. "It's easy for me to remember names and faces. I only have to meet someone once and I know them. It works. People like to be remembered."

Especially by someone like him, she thought. It wouldn't matter if he was at a dinner at the White House, or in some small village. He would always be the center of attention. Even now, she knew people were watching him, trying to figure out an excuse to talk to him.

The adoration should have made him unbearable, but Arizona handled it with grace and humor. She suspected that was true for most of his life. Was there anything he didn't do well?

"How's the story coming?" he asked as they settled into two chairs to eat. "Are you going to dig up the skeletons in my closet?"

"Do you have any?"

"No, but wouldn't it be fun if I did? Maybe I'm Elvis." He curled his upper lip and tried to look sexy.

She laughed.

He pretended to be wounded. "I wasn't trying to be funny. If there weren't so many people around, I would sing for you."

"I can't wait."

"Dr. Smith?" A beautifully dressed middle-aged woman stopped in front of him. Chloe recognized her as the chairperson of the cultural council. It had joined forces with the university to sponsor Arizona's visit and lecture series. "It's nearly eight o'clock. The university president is about to introduce you and we'd like you to say a few words."

"No problem." He stood up and set his plate on a tray, then winked at Chloe. "You'll be able to tell which one is me up there," he said, pointing to the small stage at the far end of the room. "I'll be the one stuttering."

She smiled. "I'll wave."

"Great." He winked. "Don't go giving all your dances away. I want one."

"No problem," she said lightly, while every cell in her body screamed that he could not only have all her dances, he could have her, too. Anytime, anywhere.

So much for acting professional.

As Arizona was led to the podium, the crowd moved in that direction as well. Chloe found herself swept along. She caught bits of conversation around her. Everyone was talking about him. The men wanted to be him and the women wanted to make love with him. She couldn't blame either group. He was just that kind of man—a force of nature.

She supposed her physical reaction was something to be expected. It wasn't a crush, exactly, but really close. Still, she could control it. At least enough to get her job done. Tonight they would dance together, and she would probably lose her head a little, but in the morning everything would be back to normal. At least that was her fantasy.

The university president greeted the crowd. Chloe tried to listen, but her gaze kept slipping to Arizona. He was tall and powerful as he stood in front of everyone. There was an ease about him. He was the kind of man you could talk to and instinctively trust.

It took her a few minutes to realize that she was the center of some attention and speculation. She heard her name mentioned and when she turned in that direction, the woman who had been speaking blushed and looked away.

Chloe sucked in a breath. People had noticed Arizona with her. Of course. How could they not? He'd been at her side since she'd arrived. They were talking about them. She could *feel* it.

Arizona started to speak. He thanked the crowd for attending and soon had them laughing at one of his stories. Chloe watched him with a combination of trepidation and pride. He was going to come back to her when he was done up there. He'd as much as told her and she believed him. He might have a woman in every city around the world, but for tonight, he would be with her.

He did return, and as he did, the band started playing. He swept her into his arms without asking. She didn't mind. Where else was there to be?

They moved together easily, like an old married couple dancing to a familiar song. There were others on the floor, but she felt as if they were alone. Still, when they circled around, she caught interested stares and heard murmurs of speculation. One woman glared at her in obvious outrage. She wasn't sure if she should be irritated by the other woman's anger or flattered.

"What are you thinking?" he asked.

She wore pumps with two-inch heels. Even so she had to tilt her head to meet his gaze. "That I've never been out with the most popular boy in school before. Some of the cheerleaders are a little cranky."

"I don't believe you didn't date the football captain."

She liked the feel of him next to her. His body was strong and warm. It was also exactly as she remembered it from her dream, but she didn't want to think about that.

"You should," she told him. "I wasn't very popular in high school. I was too tall and too skinny. These things—" she glanced down at her modest breasts "—didn't bother making an appearance until nearly eleventh grade. I didn't think I was ever going to get breasts. Big eyes, big lips, too much hair. I've sort of grown into my looks. But it's a recent thing."

"You've done a fine job."

"Well, thank you, sir. What about you? How does it feel to be the archaeological equivalent of a rock star?"

She thought he might pretend to misunderstand the question, or give her a teasing response. Instead, he looked slightly uncomfortable and asked, "Do you really want to know?"

"Yeah, I do." Even though she found it hard to concentrate, what with them being so close and all. If she closed her eyes, she found herself mentally drifting back to that night in the cave when they'd made love. If she kept her eyes open, she got lost in his dark gaze and never wanted to surface again. It was a tough choice.

He solved her dilemma by wrapping his arm more tightly around her waist and drawing her closer. His cheek rested against her temple.

"Women have always been available," he said. "I don't claim to understand what combination of genes and luck make that true. It started when I was about thirteen and it hasn't let up yet. When I was younger, in my teens and early twenties, I took advantage of that fact."

He pulled back enough for her to see his face. His expression was earnest. "I was smart enough to be careful, so no one got pregnant and I hope no one got hurt. But it wasn't my finest hour. Fortunately, it got old very quickly. I learned it was more fun when I got to know the lady in question and took the time to develop a relationship to her."

He pulled her against him again. She liked being close. For reasons she couldn't explain, being with him made her feel safe.

"A wise old woman, and I do mean that, helped me see the light. She was a shaman and had to be close to a hundred years old. Anyway, this wise old woman once told me that every time people make love, they give away a piece of their soul. If one makes love with the same person again and again, eventually they exchange souls and that is what was intended for married couples. But if one makes love with many people, one will find oneself with nothing left to give to the one who matters. Worse, we end up with no soul of our own."

"I hadn't thought of it that way, but the theory has merit," she said.

"I agree. *Now.* At the time I was all of eighteen, and if I remember correctly, all I could think about was getting her great-granddaughter into bed, so I wasn't the most appreciative audience."

The music stopped. They broke apart and applauded. "Let's go get some fresh air," Arizona said.

She allowed him to lead her to the open patio at the far end of the room.

The night air was clear and balmy. She reminded herself she was working and should be trying to get a story from him. But she couldn't think about anything but the man standing next to her. There was something about him—something that called to her. If she was the kind of woman who believed in destiny, she would be willing to admit he was the one for her. But she wasn't and he wasn't. Still, he was a very good time.

"You're beautiful," he said, leaning against the railing and drawing her against him.

She supposed she could have resisted, but she didn't want to. She wanted to be next to him, to feel his arms around her again. It was almost like dancing, but they were alone in the shadows and the only music came from inside her head.

His face was so familiar, she thought. It was as if she'd known him forever. Had they really made love or had it just been a dream? Did he own a piece of her soul?

"What are you thinking?" he asked. "Sometimes you look at me and you get the strangest expression on your face. I always wonder if I have spinach in my teeth."

"It's nothing," she said quickly. There was no way she could tell him she'd been thinking about that dream. He would want to know the details. He was already intrigued by the story of the Bradley family nightgown and the legend. She didn't dare think what he would make of her story.

"It has to be something," he insisted. His expression turned teasing. "I have ways of making you talk."

"Some spell or curse?"

"Nothing that drastic."

He tilted his head toward her. Instinctively she raised hers. This was not professional, she reminded herself, then she decided she didn't care. They'd been heading toward this moment since they met. She wanted to kiss him. She *needed* to kiss him. She had to know if it was the same as she remembered.

His mouth brushed against hers. They weren't standing all that close. His hands rested on her waist, hers were on his forearms. For a second—as her body registered the sensations of his heat, the firm softness of his mouth—she couldn't do anything more than absorb what was happening.

Then she felt it. The absolute electrical jolt that shot through her. It was hotter and brighter than lightning. It was recognition and need and passion and color, as if every part of her being responded to this man. Even more terrifying, it was familiar.

She knew what he was going to do even before he parted his lips. She knew the taste and feel of him. She knew how his hands would slide up her back, how she would step into his embrace, how their bodies would fit together. The knowledge only increased her desire. She wanted him because being with him was so incredibly perfect, she thought as his tongue slipped into her mouth.

Her breasts swelled, that secret place between her legs dampened. She felt his hardness press against her hip bone. They breathed in sync. She tilted her head one way, he moved the opposite, so they could deepen the contact. Reunited lovers kissing for the first time.

It was better than she remembered, she thought, then wondered how she could remember kissing a man she'd never kissed before. The dream didn't count. It wasn't real. Then she stopped thinking because her brain shut down. She could only feel him next to her, holding her, touching her. Their bodies fit perfectly together. She wrapped her arms around him and buried her fingers in his cool, soft hair. His shoulders were broad, as was his chest. Every part of him had been put together with her pleasure and enjoyment in mind...or so it seemed.

Tongues circled and danced and mated. She wanted more from him. She wanted to feel him inside of her; she wanted him to claim her and mark her in the most primitive, primal way of all.

At last, he drew back slightly, breaking the kiss. His breathing was as labored as hers. He rested his forehead against hers and exhaled.

"Pretty amazing," he said, his voice low and husky. "Even better than I thought, and I thought it would be great."

"Me, too."

He tucked a loose curl behind her ear, then brushed his thumb against her cheek. His eyes were bright with passion. She could feel the need radiating from him. Faint tremors rippled through his hands.

"Chloe, I—"

He lowered his head and she knew he was going to kiss her again. She also knew that this time they might not stop at kissing.

"There you two are. We've been looking everywhere. Isn't the ballroom lovely? They always do such a great job with the decorations."

Cassie's voice cut through the quiet of the night. Instantly, they stepped apart. Chloe touched a finger to her mouth and wondered if her lips were swollen.

"Hi," she managed, hoping that her expression wouldn't give her away. The last thing she needed was Cassie's knowing glances, or getting the third degree when they were both home later.

Cassie gave her sister a quick smile and turned to Arizona. "I wanted Joel to meet you." She looked at her boyfriend. "Joel, this is Arizona Smith."

The two men shook hands. While Arizona looked elegant in his tailored tux, Joel was obviously ill at ease in his too-small navy suit. He had the disgruntled air of a man who would rather be home watching a movie on cable.

Chloe suppressed a sigh. Joel was perfectly decent. A pleasant enough man, with short blond hair and pale blue eyes.

"Did you catch the Giants' score?" Arizona asked. "When I left my room, they were ahead three to two."

Joel's sullen expression eased. "Dodgers tied it up in the eighth, but that was when we got here and had to park the car. I don't know what it is now."

"I'm sure they have a television in the bar," Arizona offered.

"Great." Joel turned his attention to Cassie. "Would you mind if we checked?"

"Of course not." She gave a little wave, then took Joel's hand. "We'll see you later."

"Save me a dance," Arizona called after her.

Cassie giggled.

Chloe watched her go. "It's only the beginning of the baseball season and already he would rather watch a game than anything. What on earth does she see in him?" She leaned against the railing, then straightened abruptly. "Wait a minute. How did you know Joel was interested in sports?"

Arizona shrugged. "Many men are and he looks like the type. I wasn't trying to get rid of him, but I figured if he watched the last inning, he wouldn't sulk when Cassie wanted to dance."

"Good thinking. I wish…" Her voice trailed off.

"That he were a different kind of man?"

"Exactly. She deserves better."

"But he's the one she wants."

"Is he?" Chloe wasn't so sure. "He's the only man she's ever dated. How is she supposed to know what she wants? She should get out there and experience life. She deserves someone who will love her and cherish her. Someone intelligent. Not Joel." She rubbed her temple. "It's an old argument and one I've never won. After all, it's her life."

"You and Cassie are very close."

It wasn't a question.

"We always have been."

"It's none of my business, but why are you so angry at your aunt Charity?"

She couldn't have been more shocked if he'd suddenly grown horns. Her first instinct was to ask him how he figured it out. Her second was to tell him to mind his own business. Her third was to wonder if she was that obvious.

"I don't know," she said at last, glad the shadows on the patio would hide her face. She didn't want him to know what she was thinking. She did know why she was angry with her aunt, but she wasn't ready to deal with it. She might never be ready.

"Want to talk about it?"

His perceptions suddenly annoyed her. How did he always know what she was thinking? How dare he always know the right thing to say or do! "Only if you want to talk about why, if your father is still alive, your grandfather raised you."

"Touché," he said. "I'm sorry. I should learn to leave tender ground alone. I'm sorry."

She ducked her head. "No, I'm being snippy. I'm the one who should apologize."

"Okay."

She looked up at him.

He grinned. "I'm waiting," he told her.

"I apologize."

"That's it? That's all you're willing to say? No declaration of your unworthiness? Of how gracious I am to put up with you? Nothing about—"

She lightly slapped his arm. "Stop it."

He stepped back in mock alarm. "Violence. I don't know what to say. I'd been about to suggest we find a quiet room somewhere and make wild passionate love together, but now I'm not sure I can trust you not to take physical advantage of my person. I guess we're just going to have to dance, instead."

She didn't know whether to laugh, agree to the lovemaking, or slap him again. "You make me crazy."

"That was the plan all along, Chloe."

"I figured as much."

He held out his hand and she took it. Then she followed him back into the main room to have that dance.

CHAPTER SIX

"OH, MY GOODNESS, the man has a fan club!" Cassie said as she pointed at the computer screen.

Sure enough, an Internet search on Arizona's name had unearthed an assortment of references, including a link to a fan club.

"We have to check this out." Chloe clicked the arrow on that entry. She was at her home computer, continuing her research on Arizona, which she was starting to think was just a way of avoiding starting the actual writing. Once she figured out the first sentence of the article, she knew the rest of it would come fairly easily. But so far she was in the dark about her beginning.

Cassie pulled up a chair and sat down next to her. "I can't believe it. I've never known anyone with a fan club before." She laughed and touched her sister's arm. "We could write him a letter. You could talk about how great he dances. Maybe you could talk about the other stuff, too."

Chloe glanced at her sharply. "What other stuff?"

Cassie puckered up her lips and made kissing noises. "I saw what you two were doing out there on the patio last night. I figured we had better come interrupt before things got too hot and heavy. There wasn't a whole lot of privacy."

"Nothing happened. It was just a kiss." She flinched, half-waiting for lightning to strike her down. It had been a whole lot more than the kiss—which was part of the problem. It should have been pleasant or even very nice. Instead it had burned her down to her soul. She wasn't even sure if she was relieved or disappointed that he hadn't followed up that first kiss with a second. Once they'd gone back inside to the reception, Arizona had been swept away by interested guests and Chloe had finally left alone around midnight.

"It looked like some major passion to me," Cassie said, and leaned her elbows on the desk. "I wish Joel would kiss me like that."

"Doesn't he?"

Cassie shook her head. "Joel and I have a very comfortable relationship."

"Comfortable is okay for year thirty of marriage, but you guys are still dating."

"I know." Cassie shrugged. "I don't want to talk about it." She pointed at the computer screen. "Look."

The computer had located the web site for Arizona's fan club. There were photos of him, a bulletin board on which to leave messages, letters to Arizona and a map showing all the places he'd visited.

"Imagine how much money we'd make if we could get a picture of him naked," Cassie said thoughtfully. "We could sell copies. What do you think?"

Chloe laughed. "I think he would probably want to be cut in on the profits. Are you going to be the one to ask him?"

"It might go better if you did that."

Chloe ignored her. She clicked on various pages of the web site and made notes. "These people need to get lives."

"It's romantic. He's a very exciting man. You know, you should post your article here when you finish it. I'm sure they'd really like it." She sighed. "He's just so great. Gracious and funny. I really like him. I think you do, too. Wouldn't you like to travel around the world with him? He's just—" She clapped her hands together. "He's exactly the kind of man I want to dream about when I wear the family nightgown. Don't you agree?"

Chloe felt a surge of irritation. She was having enough trouble controlling her raging desires without her sister throwing logs on the fire. "Number one, you're supposed to be engaged to Joel. Number two, I actually have work to do and that would be a lot easier without your editorial comments."

Cassie stared at her for a second, nodded, then rose to her feet. "Sorry. I leave you to your research." She walked out of the room without looking back.

Chloe returned her attention to the web site, then groaned. She was turning into a witch.

With a couple of clicks, she logged off the Internet and returned to her word-processing program. After saving her work in progress, she rose to her feet and headed down the hall. Cassie's bedroom door was open. Her sister was curled up on the bed reading a book.

Chloe watched her. She didn't know exactly what to say. At this point, she wasn't willing to risk the truth. She didn't want to admit that part of her problem was that she *had* dreamed about Arizona, and it was making her insane.

"I'm sorry," she said at last. "I had no reason to snap at you. I have a lot on my mind and I'm just not myself."

Cassie looked up. "I know. This article is very important to you. It's your ticket out."

Chloe entered the large room with pale pink walls and a lacy bedspread on the full-size mattress. "I wouldn't go that far."

Cassie patted the bed, indicating that her sister should have a seat. "It's true. Come on, Chloe, it's time for you to leave. It's what you've always wanted. Sometimes I think you've stayed because of me, but I'm practically your age and I've been all grown-up for a long time. Aunt Charity and I will be fine without you. Of course we'll miss you, but it's time for you to move on. We can take care of the house until you're ready to come back."

Chloe reached out and squeezed her sister's hand. "You're way too nice a person. Why do you put up with me?"

"Beats me."

Chloe smiled. Then her humor faded as the familiar guilt took its place. She knew that Cassie would take care of the house for her. Cassie wouldn't think twice about it, but she, Chloe, was annoyed that it was an issue. Their parents had been wrong, she thought, as she had dozens of times in the past. They should have left everything to the girls equally. Instead Chloe had inherited the house and a small trust fund. Cassie had inherited a large trust fund—equal in value to Chloe's inheritance—but not equal in spirit. The message had been clear. Their only blood heir had received the family home.

Chloe knew that Cassie put on a brave face; she never said anything. But Cassie was the real traditional one in the family. She was the one who believed in the legend—she was the one who loved the house. It should have been hers. She also knew that on some level Cassie had been hurt by the will. But Chloe didn't know how to talk to her about it.

There was a knock on the open door.

"Chloe, there's a call for you," Charity told her. "It's Arizona."

Cassie made kissing noises again. Chloe rose to her

feet. "I'm ignoring you," she said as she crossed to her sister's desk and picked up the extension. "Hello?"

"Chloe, it's Arizona. I hope I'm not interrupting."

"Not at all." If the nerves soft-shoeing inside her stomach were anything to go by, she was very happy to hear from him.

"Something's come up. I've been doing some research about a lost tribe up in the Pacific Northwest. I just got a call from some friends of mine working up there. They've found something I need to take a look at. The lecture series doesn't start for a few days and I don't have much holding me here, so I thought I would go and see what they've found."

"I see."

He was leaving. She'd always known that he would—it was the nature of the man. But she hadn't expected it to be so soon. The nerves in her stomach fizzled into a cold knot of disappointment.

"I'll work on the article while you're gone and save any questions I have until you get back," she told him, hoping she sounded calmly professional.

"That's one scenario," he agreed. "However, I thought it might be interesting for you to come along. You could observe what I do firsthand."

She wanted to jump up and down shrieking "Yes, yes, oh yes!" at the top of her lungs. Instead she drew in a deep breath. "An interesting idea."

He was probably coming on to her, a voice in her head said. As lines went, it was a good one, but still a line.

"I hope you don't think I've made this up simply to get you alone in the wilderness. Actually I'm just not that creative, otherwise I would have. But the artifact is legitimate. I can give you a number to call to check it out."

He could read her mind. Why was she not surprised?

Of course she wanted to go. Desperately. She wanted to spend as much time with Arizona as possible and she refused to question her motives. "I'll need to run this past my editor," she said. "Can I call you first thing in the morning?"

"Sure. I'll be hoping for a yes."

Me, too, she thought. "I'll be touch. Bye."

When she hung up the phone, Cassie was dancing from foot to foot. "You're going away with him. This is *so* cool. You'll be in wilderness. It'll be romantic. Maybe you'll see him naked and we can get that picture for his fan club!"

Chloe's heart was pounding and she wanted to jump up and down like her sister. Instead she shrugged. "It would be okay to go. I think it will add some dimension to my article."

"Article-smarticle. I'm talking about adding some dimension to your life! Chloe and Arizona sittin' in a tree. K-I-S-S-I-N-G."

"I'm ignoring you," Chloe said as she walked out of the room.

"Confess," Cassie called after her. "You *want* to see the man naked."

"I'm sure he's not that impressive."

"Liar!"

But Chloe didn't know if the accusation came from her sister or her conscience. After all, she *had* seen Arizona without his clothes, and it had worked for her in a big way.

"I'M NOT sure what he's going to look at," Chloe continued nervously. "But I think seeing an archaeological dig and watching him work will add depth to the story."

Jerry didn't even look up from the papers he was reading. Her editor made a grunting noise low in his throat. She wasn't sure what that meant.

"So you want me to go?" she asked.

Finally, he spared her a quick glance. "Yes, I want you to go. Keep track of expenses. The magazine will reimburse you for the reasonable stuff. Don't go ordering any expensive wine with dinner. Don't sit in poison ivy."

"I think I can handle that."

"Good." His gaze narrowed. "How's the guy? Is the piece gonna be decent?"

She thought about telling Jerry all she'd learned about Arizona, about the fan club on the Internet, the inherent charm, the way he actually believed in magic. But she didn't think her boss really cared about the details. He would find all that out when he read the article.

"It's going to be great," she told him.

"Better be." He grimaced. "Nancy said you were on the right track and I trust her. Not that I should. Pregnant. Do you know she actually expects time off after the kid is born? I asked her what for. She says she wants to breast-feed. Can you believe it? Like a bottle's not good enough. What is it with women today?" He shook his head in disgust and glared at her. "Don't you have a story to write? Packing maybe? Get out of here."

"Yes, Jerry." Despite herself, Chloe grinned. Jerry acted so tough all the time, but he would be the first one at the hospital after Nancy gave birth. He would be cooing like everyone else over the newborn.

She made her way back to her desk. She had her permission. She was really going away with Arizona. Out into the wilderness, where anything could happen.

CHLOE STARED AT the clothes folded neatly on top of her bed. "I don't know what to take," she admitted. "I've never been camping."

Cassie sat in the chair by the desk and smiled. "You'll

do fine. Take jeans and underwear. Shirts and sweaters. You'll want to layer if it gets cold, but you won't want anything bulky."

"Arizona says we'll have to hike in the last part, so I have to carry everything with me."

Cassie leaned forward, picked up the blow-dryer and waved it in the air. "In that case, I'd leave this behind. It's big, heavy and you're not going to have electricity."

"I know. I just thought—" She shuddered. "I don't know what I was thinking. It was a hideous mistake to agree to this. I'm completely out of my element."

"You'll be fine. Arizona will keep you safe."

Chloe didn't know whether to laugh or scream. What her sister didn't understand was that Arizona was part of what she was afraid of. But she couldn't say that to Cassie without going into detail. And how was she supposed to tell her sister that she had indeed had a dream the night of her twenty-fifth birthday and that the man in her dream had been someone she'd met the very next day? How was she supposed to confess that every time she was near him her body went up in flames, and that all the time they were apart, he was all she could think of?

Besides, not all of her fears were about Arizona. Some of them were about herself. She didn't know what was wrong with her. She felt herself changing. Nothing was as it should be. She wanted... Chloe sighed. That was the problem. She didn't know what she wanted.

Cassie stood up and walked to the bed. She opened Chloe's cosmetic bag and dumped the contents.

"Toothbrush and toothpaste," she said. She rummaged through the rest of the items, then eyed her sister's long hair. She picked up a wide-toothed comb and a cloth-covered rubber band. "Don't worry about makeup." She fingered a tube of sunscreen. "This has moisture in it."

She added a tiny bottle of shampoo to the small pile. "Arizona will bring soap, I'm sure. Use his."

Chloe stared at the half-dozen items. "How do you know this stuff?"

"I work with preschoolers. If nothing else, I've learned to improvise." She pointed to the piles of clothing. "Want me to do the same on that?"

"Please."

As Chloe watched, her sister sorted through jeans, shirts and sweaters. She picked up a waterproof wind-breaker, a thin, high-tech fabric pullover guaranteed to keep Chloe warm, two flannel shirts, a spare pair of jeans and underwear.

"Take extra socks," Cassie told her. "Your feet might get wet."

"That's it?" Chloe asked.

"It is if you really have to carry it on your back. I know this from personal experience. I've baby-sat too many kids who didn't want me to bring the stroller. I told myself it was just a quick trip to the mall and that they didn't weigh all that much. After about five minutes I learned they got heavy very quickly, and I always regretted my decision."

"I'll take your word for it," Chloe said. "You're obviously the expert."

"I might have some shampoo samples," Cassie said. "You know those little flat packages? Let me check, because they would be lighter than this bottle. I'll be right back."

After she'd left, Chloe looked at the small pile of clothing and wondered what on earth she was getting into. Would she and Arizona be alone for any part of their trip? That thought both terrified and excited her. She didn't know what was going to happen.

Nerves fluttered in her stomach. Actually, that wasn't true. If they were alone together for any length of time, she knew *exactly* what was going to happen between them. Was she ready for that?

She wasn't sure. She thought about her sister and wished she could tell her what was really going on. She would like someone else's opinion on her best course of action. Unfortunately, Cassie was a classic romantic and would only see the potential for love, not the probability of heartache. Chloe might firmly believe that love wasn't for her, but that didn't mean her emotions couldn't be engaged under the right circumstances. So far, Arizona had everything going for him.

She thought about having a few words with Aunt Charity. No, Chloe told herself. That would never work. She couldn't confide in the older woman. Arizona had been accurate and perceptive when he'd picked up the fact that there was trouble in the house. Chloe didn't trust her aunt. Maybe it was childish, but she'd never forgiven her for not being there.

Chloe walked to the window and gazed out at the lawn. There had been a time in her life when she'd wondered if she would ever see this perfect view again. She reached up and fingered the locket hanging around her neck. Her thoughts drifted back to that horrible time when she and Cassie had lost their parents in a car accident. One minute everything had been fine, the next they were alone in the world. They'd clung to each other until the courts, unable to find their legal guardian, had split them up and sent them to different foster homes.

Three years, Chloe thought grimly. The family lawyer had looked for three years until he'd finally found Aunt Charity, their father's sister. As soon as she'd been told what had happened, she'd flown back to America and had brought the girls home. Cassie had been grateful, but for Chloe the rescue had come too late. She'd been all of two months from her eighteenth birthday when she could have returned home on her own.

Chloe knew that logically it hadn't been Aunt Charity's fault that she'd been traveling the world. No one expected her to sit at home in case her brother died unexpectedly. But logic hadn't helped Chloe get through those years apart from Cassie and away from the only home she'd ever known. So even though she desperately wanted someone to talk to, she wasn't about to confess all to her aunt.

So she was going to have to be a grown-up and take care of herself. That or she was going to have to accept the consequences of her actions.

"I knew I had them," Cassie said, walking back in the room. She held out a handful of cosmetic samples. "I found a couple that are face cleaners as well as two shampoo packs, so take them all."

"Thanks. I really appreciate the help. I would have packed all wrong without you."

"No problem."

Chloe looked at her sister. Cassie had a very innocent expression on her face. She stood with her left hand tucked behind her back.

"What have you got there?"

"Nothing."

"Don't give me that. What is it?"

Cassie grinned wickedly. "Well, it won't take up much room in your backpack and it will certainly give you two something to talk about over roasting marshmallows."

She pulled her hand free. A condom rested on her open palm.

Chloe felt color flare on her cheeks. "I didn't know that you and Joel had been intimate."

"Oh, we haven't been," Cassie said easily. "But I do like to be prepared in case we ever decide we're ready. So, do you think one is enough for you and Arizona, or do you want to pack the whole box?"

Chloe stared at the protection and didn't know what to say. It was absurd to assume she and Arizona would become lovers. They hadn't known each other that long. But like her sister, she had been raised to be prepared.

"Nothing's going to happen," she told her sister firmly, even as she took the condom and stuck it in her small cosmetic bag.

Cassie grinned. "If you're very lucky, you just might prove yourself wrong!"

CHAPTER SEVEN

"YOU READY?" Arizona asked.

Chloe glanced back at the four-wheel-drive Explorer heading down the mountain. Then she looked at him. Her expression was two parts apprehension, one part honest-to-God fear.

But she didn't answer him right away. Instead she squared her shoulders, then adjusted her backpack, raised her chin and smiled. "Sure. This is going to be fun."

"Liar," he told her.

Her smile broadened. "Okay, maybe I'm exaggerating. I confess, I do wish there was another way into the site or the dig, or whatever you call it, but I'll survive. I appreciate the opportunity to see what you actually do with your day." She paused. "Also, we'll be able to continue our interview while we're hiking. At least until I'm so out of breath I can't ask questions. But your lecture series starts in three days. Will we be back in time?"

"That's not a problem," Arizona told her while he ignored the flicker of guilt. There *was* an easier way into the valley, but he wanted them to hike in. There was something going on between them—something he'd never experienced before—and he wanted time to explore that. His visit to Bradley was limited already. There were so many drains on his time.

If he were going to be completely rational, he knew there was no point in pursuing whatever attraction might flare between them. There was no way to make a relationship work. He'd sworn off casual affairs and even if he hadn't, Chloe didn't strike him as the type to give herself easily. Logic dictated that he should just answer her questions and ignore the rest of it. However, he'd never been one for logic. The unexplained caught his attention time after time. He wanted to know the whys. He couldn't pass up a good mystery. In this case, there was something between him and Chloe and he was determined to find out what. These couple days alone might be his only chance.

She pulled a small tape recorder out of her jeans pocket. "I'm ready if you are," she said.

"Then let's go."

He checked the placement of the sun and figured they had about six hours of daylight. Chloe wouldn't be able to hike much more than that anyway. Not that she wasn't in great shape. But she wasn't conditioned for long hours on the trail.

There had been a surprisingly long stretch of relatively dry weather, so the ground was only damp underfoot. Towering trees lined the trail. The low-lying plants were bright green. Wildflowers and berry bushes were in full bloom. The air smelled clean and crisp. It was a perfect afternoon.

He started walking nearly due east.

"Where are we going?" Chloe asked as she kept pace with him. At this point the trail was wide enough for them to walk side by side.

"There's a valley on the other side of this low range," he said, pointing ahead. "We'll reach the top of the rise tonight. That will be where we camp. Tomorrow we'll head into the valley. The site is there. Just curious—was that information for you or the article?"

Her brown eyes twinkled. "Both. I have so many questions, I'm not sure where to start."

"Does it matter?"

"I suppose not." One corner of her mouth turned up slightly. "So, Arizona Smith, why don't you wear a hat?"

Involuntarily, he reached up and touched his bare head. "I don't need one here. There's no need to protect myself from the sun."

"I see. I thought all bush types wore hats. They do in the movies." Her voice was teasing.

He shook his head. "That's part of my problem. I wore one nearly all the time. Before." He grimaced. "That movie. It changed everything. After that my lecture series became more popular. I appreciated that, but I hated the billing. A few places advertised me as a 'real-life Indiana Jones.'"

"Did your audiences expect you to show up with a bullwhip?"

"You'd be surprised." He thought about the women who would come to his lectures and sit in the front row. Their adoring gazes had nothing to do with him—who he really was. They were only interested in the persona.

Not like Chloe. He glanced at her. Her stride was long, her posture straight. She was gorgeous. Today she wore her curly red hair pulled back in a braid. She was tall and lean and he wished they were lovers so that he could suggest they stop for an hour or so and make love right here...out in the open.

"Do you have anything in common with Indiana Jones?" she asked.

"Sure. We're both men. His finds are more spectacular. How can anyone compete with the Ark of the Covenant or the Holy Grail? I think I had better luck with women. We're both teachers, although none of my students have ever fallen for me."

"I doubt that," she said. "I would guess more than three-quarters of your students are female and almost none of them are there because they need the class for their major."

He opened his mouth to protest, then realized she was right. His classes *were* predominantly female. "None of them have come on to me." He held up a hand before she could protest again. "Trust me, I would have noticed that."

"I'm sure they were working up to it."

"I hope not. They're a little young."

"You're not all that old."

"Old enough."

Old enough to know what he wanted, he thought. It wasn't just that Chloe was pretty. His attraction to her was as much about the way she made him laugh and her intelligence as it was about her body.

"I assume you know you have a fan club on the Internet," she said.

He groaned. "I might have known you would find that."

"You're not proud?" she teased.

"Of course not. It's humiliating. These people—"

"Women," she interrupted. "They're women, Arizona. I checked the membership directory. We're talking at least ninety-five percent women."

"Great. Men, women, Martians, it doesn't matter. I still don't get it. I'm not brilliant, I'm tenacious. I've studied and I've had some luck. Yes, I've made a few finds, but I'm not going to change the world. I don't know what they see in me."

"Don't you?" Chloe stopped and looked at him. "I can't tell if you're serious or if you're fishing."

"I'm not unaware that some people find me physically attractive," he said formally, wondering if it was possible to sound like more of a jerk than he did.

"Good to know," she said solemnly.

"You're teasing me."

"A little. This is the first time you've ever been pompous."

Pompous? Was that how she saw him? Perfect. He'd sure done a great job charming her. Talk about a crash and burn.

She touched his arm. The light contact seared him all the way down to his knees. His groin ignited. The wanting was as powerful as it was instantaneous.

"I do understand what you're saying," she said and dropped her hand to her side. "Who do you consider a hero?"

"Easy question. Joseph Campbell. He wrote several books, but the best known is *The Hero of a Thousand Faces.* He explored the idea that storytelling is universal to the human condition. All races and cultures have stories about the beginning of the world, the creation of man, stories that tell how boys become men. I was very young when I first read his work. He's the one who got me interested in the mystic."

"I'm not discounting his place," Chloe said. "But what about the things you've found? All those treasures might have stayed hidden for generations."

"Granted, but while I've brought some tangible artifacts to light, he explained why we have the dreams we do. I've visited my fan club web site. It's very flattering, but I'm not the hero in that. They've created a myth about someone who doesn't really exist. In my mind, Joseph Campbell is someone who truly is a hero. His ideas changed lives. I know he changed mine."

He motioned for her to continue walking, then fell into step with her. The air was cool, but the sun warmed them.

"There is a certain amount of fame that comes with some of my discoveries. It's my least favorite part of what I do. I get through it by reminding myself it's fleeting. In a couple of weeks no one will care who I am until the next discovery."

"That sounds cynical, although realistic. Would you rather the world ignored your finds?"

"Good question. The answer is no. I want them to understand and appreciate. I know enough to realize I can't have one without the other."

She looked at him. "Why do I suddenly suspect you like it much better in the bush where no one knows who you are and you're treated like just another visitor?"

"You'd be right. I've traveled all over the world. My best memories are of people I've connected with, not of standing behind a podium talking to a cheering crowd."

"So do the women ever throw you their panties?"

He tugged on the end of her braid. "I'm not the kind to kiss and tell."

She laughed. "I'll take that as a no."

"It's probably best."

"So have they shown up in your room unexpectedly?"

"Why this sudden interest in my personal life?" he asked, although he was pleased that she seemed focused on that. He would hate for the attraction to be one-sided.

"Ah, so that was a yes."

He chuckled. "Yes, once or twice."

"How was it?"

He thought back. "The first time was in a small village on an island in the South Pacific. I was all of eighteen and the woman was at least thirty. Her husband had died and she was about to remarry someone much older. I think I was her last fling."

"And?"

"And what? I was a kid. I had no concept of quality, so I made it up in volume. She taught me they weren't interchangeable."

"I see. And the second time it happened?"

He drew in a deep breath. "I was on a lecture tour in Europe a couple of years ago. There was a particular young woman who developed a crush on me. I didn't encourage her at all, in fact I barely knew who she was. One night I came in late and found her waiting for me in my bed."

Chloe's eyes widened. "What did you do?"

"I explained that I was flattered, but not interested. When she wouldn't leave, I got another room for the night, then in the morning, I changed hotels."

Chloe burst out laughing. "The most trouble I've ever had with the opposite sex is when old man Withers, the seventy-year-old misogynist who takes care of the grounds of the house, calls me a ninny. He calls all women ninnies."

"Are you going to put that in the article?" he asked. He hadn't requested that any part of their conversation be off the record. Perhaps he should have. When he was around Chloe he thought of her as a woman first and someone he would like to get to know second. He rarely remembered she was a journalist.

"I'm not out to make you the bad guy," she said. "I want to show a different side of you and connect that with your work. Neither my editor nor I is interested in a hatchet job."

"I appreciate that."

"I find it interesting you're asking me this after the fact. Isn't that dangerous?"

"Yes."

"You're not concerned?"

"You've just explained that I shouldn't be."

They were still walking side by side. Their hands brushed. Without thinking, Arizona laced his fingers with hers. Chloe stumbled a step, but didn't pull away.

"But how do you know you can trust me?" she asked.

Was it his imagination or was her voice a little breathless? He wanted to know that she was reacting to him the same way he reacted to her. He wanted to know that she felt it, whatever the *it* was, too.

"Gut instinct," he said. "I've met a lot of people in my life and I've learned how to read them."

Her hand was small but strong. He liked the feel of her next to him like this, walking together on the trail. He found himself eager to show her the site, to explain his world to her. He wanted her to enjoy their time together, to be impressed by him, to think he was nearly as exciting as his image.

"Is there anywhere on this planet you haven't been?" she asked.

"If you're talking continents, I haven't been to Antarctica. Otherwise, I would guess I've hit most of the major points."

"Why am I not surprised?" She gave him a quick, sideways glance. "You can be a little intimidating," she admitted. "I've interviewed fairly powerful people in the past. Government officials, celebrities. You're the first one who has made me feel like the country mouse come to town for a visit."

He leaned close. "You don't look anything like a country mouse. In fact, there's nothing rodentlike about you at all."

"Gee, thanks."

Gently, reluctantly, he thought, although that could just be wishful thinking on his part, she pulled her hand away from his. "Back to business," she told him. "I have a lot more questions."

"Ask away."

"About your travels. From what I've been reading, most of them were financed privately. You don't work with a particular foundation or for a university."

"That's true. There's a rather impressive family trust fund that has paid my expenses. I've had opportunities to work for charitable organizations, helping them raise funds. I do that frequently. When I do guest lecture series I tend to donate my fees to the local children's hospital and women's shelters. I've done specific tours for museums, and then they keep the proceeds."

"You don't keep any for yourself?"

"I don't have to." At her look of confusion, he shrugged. "My family has a lot of money. I don't need more so why wouldn't I give some of it away?" He replayed his last couple of comments in his mind and frowned. "I'm not some do-gooder," he said. "I was taught it was my place to give back. But don't make me out to be a saint. I'm very much a man with as many flaws as the next guy."

"I see."

Her words didn't give anything away, and he couldn't tell what she was thinking. He almost didn't want to know. Better to imagine she was thinking about being with him, touching him, holding him close. Because that was what he wanted her thinking. He wasn't willing to explore the realization that it was much easier to deal with Chloe wanting him than her actually liking him.

THEY STOPPED AROUND one o'clock to take a break. Chloe let her backpack fall to the ground, then rotated her shoulders.

"Cassie warned me it was going to get heavier as we walked, but I didn't believe her. I see now I was wrong."

"Sore?" Arizona asked.

"I'll survive."

She watched him release his pack as if it weighed nothing. It had to be twice the size of hers, but then he was not only male and stronger, but used to this sort of thing.

The afternoon was warm, but not too hot. She eyed the clear sky. "I thought the Pacific Northwest was known for rain."

"It is. Looks like we're going to get lucky." He hesitated just long enough for her breath to catch. "With the weather."

"Of course," she murmured. With the weather. What else? Certainly not with each other. It wasn't her fault that she found the man wildly attractive. The more she got to know him, the worse it got. It wasn't enough that he was good-looking. No, he had to be smart, funny and kind as well. She was going to have to be very careful when she wrote her article, or she was going to come off like some teenager with a major crush.

"Ready for lunch?" he asked.

He sat on a fallen log and reached for his backpack. Chloe settled next to him. She had two canteens hanging from her pack. They'd stopped at a rapidly flowing stream about a half hour before and refilled their water supply.

"Here you go." He handed her two protein bars, a small plastic bag filled with what looked like cut-up dried vegetables and fruit, and an apple.

"Goody, five-star cuisine," she said as she eyed what was supposed to pass for a meal.

"Don't wrinkle your nose at me, young lady. There are plenty of vitamins and minerals there, along with enough calories for energy."

"I didn't say anything."

"You didn't have to."

Usually she was more difficult to read. Was she so open around him, or could he just see inside of her? "I wasn't complaining. This is different from what I'm used to. I don't have your 'bush' experience. What with how you grew up and all."

"It wasn't like this," he said as he stretched out his long legs in front of him and crossed them at the ankles. Worn jeans hugged his powerful thighs. "My grandfather didn't believe in living with physical discomfort. We always traveled first-class."

"There are a lot of places you can't get a jet or a limo."

"True. We used carts and camels, boats, whatever was necessary to get us where he wanted to go. But he arranged for the best. Plenty of staff along to handle the luggage and the details."

Chloe tried to imagine that kind of life. On one hand, it sounded very exciting, but on the other she would miss having a place to call home.

"Did you like living like that?" she asked.

"I suppose every kid dreams of running away to live a life of adventure. I did that and more. I have experienced things most people just read or dream about. But there were things I missed."

He stared into the grove of trees, but she knew he was

actually seeing a past she could only imagine. How had his world and his life shaped him? What would he have been like if he'd grown up as the boy next door?

"I never had my own room, so I didn't collect things the way a lot of kids do," he said. "I didn't have a lot of friends. In some places there weren't boys my age around, or if there were, they were busy with school or helping the family. We moved around so much, I would just get to know someone and then it would be time to leave."

"I hadn't thought of that," she admitted. "It sounds lonely."

"Sometimes it was. I had tutors. They were usually with us for a couple of years at a time, so that was something I could depend on." He shrugged. "Growing up like that is all I know. I can't pass judgment on it without something to compare it to. I don't think it was better or worse, just different. I experienced the world from a different point of view. If we planned to settle in one place for a few months, I usually enrolled in the local school."

He looked at her and grinned. "When I was a teenager I used to complain about not having fast food or high school girls around."

"So despite everything, you were very normal."

"I like to think so." His smile faded. "I always wanted a brother or sister. Someone around my own age to talk to and be with. Grandfather tried, but he wasn't a peer. I envy you and Cassie for being so close."

She couldn't imagine anything in her rather dull life that someone like Arizona would be interested in, but the idea of a sibling made sense.

"She's my best friend," she said. "We're so different, we can't help arguing sometimes, but none of that really matters. We love each other so much."

"It shows." He ripped open the protective covering on

one of his protein bars and took a bite. After chewing he asked, "So how are you different?"

She nibbled the dried vegetables and found they tasted better than they looked. "You have to ask? Cassie is a dreamer. She believes in fairy tales and magic."

"That's right. And you're the completely practical one."

"Exactly. She wants a very traditional life. Husband, children, a home." She stopped talking and pressed her lips together. A home. The house. That beautiful Victorian house that their parents had left to her instead of leaving it to the two girls equally.

They'd probably been afraid the sisters wouldn't be able to work out a way to share. No doubt they'd been trying to prevent the house being sold. But their will had reinforced Cassie's feeling of not truly being a part of the family.

"Is there anything wrong with wanting a traditional life?" Arizona asked.

"No, and it makes sense for her. Cassie just wants to fit in. She wants to have roots."

"Doesn't she now?"

"I don't know that she thinks so." She shrugged. "It's complicated. Cassie—" She automatically reached inside the neck of her T-shirt and pulled out the locket she always wore.

Arizona reached over and touched the heart-shaped piece of jewelry. "Connections with the past," he said. "She has the matching earrings. And her memories. Your parents chose her. Isn't that enough?"

His dark eyes saw too much, she thought. She felt as if he could look deep down into her soul and that made her nervous. Was she enough for him? Sometimes she didn't think she was enough for herself, let alone someone else. But then she was used to being confused. It was becoming a constant in her life. She didn't understand her relationship with Arizona any more than she understood why the man had appeared in her dream. She didn't know what she wanted from him, what she felt about him, or what he expected from her.

She jerked her thoughts back to their conversation. "I have the house," she said. "I wish they'd left it to both of us instead of just me."

"So she would have that connection?" he asked.

She nodded.

He touched the locket again. His knuckle brushed against her throat. A warmth flowed through her, just as it had when he'd taken her hand while they'd been on the trail.

"It's not the house," he said. "It's here." He placed his fingers against her forehead, then moved them lower, to just above her left breast. "And here. No one can take that away from her. Or you."

He wasn't talking about the house anymore, she realized. There was something in his eyes, something dangerous and irresistible. She wanted to lean closer. She wanted him to kiss her. She wanted to feel his arms around her, holding her close, making her safe. With Arizona she felt safe…and that had been missing from her life since her parents had been killed.

But instead of leaning toward him, she straightened, putting distance between them. Who was this man who invaded both her dreams and her life? What did he want from her? And how on earth was she supposed to resist him and his power?

CHAPTER EIGHT

STARS FILLED THE night sky. Chloe stretched out on her sleeping bag and stared up at the vast expanse of lights above her head. Bradley wasn't a big town, but it was close enough to Sacramento that the city lights washed out most of the stars, even when the weather didn't interfere. Or maybe her life had gotten so busy, she didn't take time to look at the heavens anymore. She would guess most people suffered the same fate. Now, gazing up and admiring the beauty of the stars, she wondered what other wonders filled what she considered her very ordinary life.

"It's a beautiful night," Arizona said as he stepped back into camp. He dropped onto his sleeping bag only a few feet from her own.

"I was just thinking that," she said and tried to ignore the fact that she was going to have to do as he had done and venture out into the wilderness to do her business.

It was bad enough to have to do that during the day when she could see whatever was lurking around, but at night—she would be defenseless. She didn't want to act all wimpy and girllike, but she couldn't help picturing herself from a critter's point of view. A pale white expanse of tempting flesh just hanging there, begging to be bitten or scratched or…

Stop thinking about it, she ordered herself silently. But

it was one of the few times she envied men their "equipment" that let them pee standing up.

"So what did you think of dinner?" Arizona asked in a tone that warned her he expected a positive response.

"Great," she lied cheerfully. "I had been worried that freeze-dried food would taste gritty and odd when it was mixed with boiling water, but I was wrong."

Actually, it wasn't a lie. The food at dinner had easily been worse than she'd imagined.

"I liked it, too," he said. "Beats grubs any day."

She dismissed him with a wave. "You didn't eat grubs. This afternoon you said your grandfather liked to travel in style. I'm sure he brought along a chef to cook his favorite dishes."

"You're right." His teeth flashed white in the light of the campfire.

"I figured. You thought dinner was pretty gross, didn't you?"

"Wretched comes to mind. I think they forgot to cook the rice before packaging it. Tell you what. When we get back to civilization, I'll take you out for a fancy dinner."

"You've got yourself a deal."

Their gazes locked. Despite the few feet between them, she felt his heat. She was in trouble now.

She forced her gaze away and returned her attention to the stars. "Do you know anything about the constellations?" she asked, hoping he would go along with the change in subject.

"I do now because I've studied them, but when I was a kid, I would make up stories. Sometimes the village elders would tell me what the different stars represented. I learned that all different cultures have their own view of what the heavens mean. I suppose some of that is because the sky looks different in different places."

Chloe told herself she should dig out her tape recorder and turn it on. But she didn't want to break the mood. Besides, she wasn't having trouble remembering anything Arizona said to her. She didn't even have to close her eyes to hear his voice in her head.

"The changing stars can tell about the coming seasons. The harvest sky is different from the planting sky."

He continued talking. She listened to the words and wrapped herself in the stories he wove. He was so different from anyone she'd ever known. And yet the heart of him was familiar to her. Was it the dream? Was it her imagination, trying to create a connection so she could pretend her attraction had some basis in emotion and not just in physical awareness? But it was more, she reminded herself. She didn't just want him...she actually liked him.

There hadn't been many men in her life. Normally she didn't make time for them. She didn't want all the bother of trusting someone only to have him let her down.

"What are you thinking?" he asked.

She inhaled deeply and smelled the wood smoke from their fire, along with the lush scent of the forest growth. "That for me, the sky is always constant. The stars might change with the time of year, but I've never seen a different sky. I've just realized that's the perfect metaphor for the differences between us."

"Is that bad?" he asked.

"No, it's a fact that we can't change, but I don't think it's a value judgment. We don't have anything in common."

"I would disagree with that."

She turned to face him. In the darkness of the night, his body was little more than murky shadow. "I'm surprised you'd think that."

"Why? We're both intelligent, curious about our world.

We both ask questions. We laugh at the same things. We're very much alike."

"I hadn't thought of it like that," she admitted. "I was more focused on our life experiences. For example, the first day of school. I was a very mature five and a half, while Cassie hadn't quite turned five. My mother bought us matching dresses, but in different colors. I've seen the pictures and we were too adorable for words."

Arizona smiled. "I'll bet."

"Bradley Elementary," she continued. "It's built on the site of the original Bradley schoolhouse, founded by my family back in the late 1800s. There's even a plaque by the auditorium. I don't think your first day of school was anything like that."

"You'd be right." He closed his eyes for a minute, then opened them. "I was in Africa and I attended a tribal school. Interesting, but not educational. I didn't speak much of the language. That afternoon my grandfather started making arrangements for me to have tutors."

"That's my point," she said. "Different experiences."

"Even if I'd been living in the States, I don't think I would have been in a matching dress."

She laughed. "Probably not."

He propped his head on his hand. "Tell me about your first kiss."

"Oh my. First kiss. I was fourteen, I think. At a girl-friend's birthday party. Also my first boy-girl party. We were playing Spin the Bottle. His name was Adam. He was shorter than me, but very cute. All the girls had a crush on him. It was brief and not very romantic, but I hugged the memory close for months. And you?"

"Penelope. We were both twelve and in Cairo. Her fa-ther was a peer of the realm, but don't ask me his title. I don't remember. He was in the British embassy. Penny and I met at a very dull party where we were the only children. I remember it was hot and she smelled like roses."

Chloe flopped onto her back. "You had your first kiss in Egypt and I had mine in Cynthia Greenway's basement. What is wrong with this picture?"

"Nothing."

"Easy for you to say. Next you'll be telling me that your first lover was some fabulously beautiful courtesan arranged for you by your grandfather. That she was a Christmas present."

Arizona was silent.

Chloe sucked in a breath, turned back toward him and stared. "You're kidding?"

He cleared his throat. "Actually, it was a birthday present, and courtesan is a strong term. She was experienced."

"How polite. And you were all of sixteen?"

"Seventeen."

"I'll bet you had a really good time."

"I did. I was young and at the time I didn't know there was a difference between having sex and making love. She taught me a lot about mechanics but nothing about the heart."

Chloe was grateful for the darkness. At least Arizona wouldn't be able to see her stunned expression. She didn't consider herself a prude, but apparently she was. This was too far out of her realm of experience. She didn't know what to say.

"You're shocked," Arizona said.

"A little. That sort of thing doesn't happen in Bradley."

"What does happen?"

"Are you asking about my first lover?"

"Yes."

She sat up and pulled her knees into her chest. "I haven't thought about Billy in a long time." Mostly because she didn't let herself think about him.

"You don't have to talk about it if you'd rather not."

"No, I don't mind." Actually, she didn't, which surprised her. Maybe enough time had passed. Maybe she'd finally healed.

"When my parents died," she began, "Cassie and I were sent into foster care. She stayed in Bradley, but I was sent to a family in a neighboring town. They had a son, Billy. He was a couple of years older than me. The first few months I stayed in my room and kept to myself. I'd lost my parents and Cassie. We wrote and saw each other when we could, but it was different. We didn't feel like sisters anymore."

"How was the family you were with?"

"They were very kind to me. They tried to understand what I was going through. They gave me time. Eventually I started participating in family events. One day I looked up at the dinner table and realized Billy was sitting across from me. He smiled and I smiled back. A few pieces of my broken heart mended at that moment."

"Sounds romantic."

"It was fairly typical. We went on dates, then started going steady."

"Did his parents know?"

"Yes. We tried to keep it from them for a while, but we weren't very good at sneaking around. I think the first time Billy and I made love was in the back seat of his car." She smiled at the memory. "It wasn't very comfortable."

"The car or the act itself."

"Both. We didn't know what we were doing. It was quick. The sex itself was always much more for him than me. I liked the holding and being close. It didn't matter if it was physically satisfying because I loved him, so it was perfect."

"I'm sure it got better."

She smiled. "Not much." Her smile faded. "We weren't together long enough for us to get really good at it."

She didn't want to think about that, she reminded herself. So instead she recalled what it had been like to be with Billy. He'd been so attentive and eager—both for her and to please her. He'd always touched her as if she were the most precious creature alive. Perhaps to him, she had been.

But the sex itself hadn't moved her. Perhaps she'd been too young, or they'd been too inexperienced. She'd never felt that ultimate pleasure, either with him, or the two young men she'd been intimate with during college. It was a sad state of affairs that the best it had ever been had been in a dream…with the man just a few feet away from her.

"So Billy was your first boyfriend and your first lover," Arizona said. "Were you in love with him?"

"Yes. Deeply. He stole my heart and I've never been sure I got all the pieces back from him."

Arizona pushed himself up into a sitting position. They faced each other. "So you believe in love, but you won't believe in anything magical or mystical."

"They're not the same. I've experienced love." She might have experienced magic—in the form of her dream—but she wasn't ready to admit that to him.

"I don't," he said flatly.

It was the second time that night that he'd stunned her into silence. He'd mentioned it before but she hadn't really believed him. Everyone had to believe in love. Her mind raced, but she couldn't form any words. Finally she managed to blurt out, "How is that possible? What about all the weird stuff you research? You'll put your faith in a rock or a story, but not in the depth of human emotion?"

"Exactly."

"Are we talking about romantic love or all of it? What about parents caring for their children. Most would die for them. Isn't that a demonstration of love?"

"Yes. I would agree that many parents have strong feelings for their children. In most cases I would be willing to call that love."

His careful qualification of his answer made her curious, so she filed that information away to ask about another time. She didn't want to get away from what they were already talking about.

"So it's just the issue of romantic love you have problems with," she said.

He nodded.

She was still having trouble believing this conversation. Arizona believed in things she couldn't even begin to understand, but not love. But love was a fundamental part of the human condition.

"What are you so afraid of?" she asked.

He leaned toward her. "Do *you* believe in love between a man and a woman?"

"Of course. I plan to avoid it, but I know it exists. I've experienced it."

"With Billy?"

"Yes."

"Anyone else?"

She shook her head.

"So why do you want to avoid loving a man?"

She struggled to find the words to answer his question. "If you don't get close, you can't get hurt. So I avoid getting close."

His face was in shadow. She didn't know what he was thinking about. But she anticipated what he would ask next and braced herself for the pain.

"How did Billy hurt you?"

"He betrayed me."

"With another woman?"

If only it had been that simple. "He died." She wrapped her arms around her knees and pulled them closer to her chest. "It all gets twisted in my brain and I can't figure out what happened when."

She drew in a deep breath. "I went into the foster home when I was nearly fifteen. Billy and I began dating toward the end of my sophomore year of high school. The next fall, he started getting sick. It took the doctors a while to figure out that he had leukemia. He fought it for a long time. They used drugs and chemotherapy. He was in and out of the hospital. He promised to love me forever. He promised to get better. I believed him because I couldn't face the alternative. Then one day, he died."

She closed her eyes against the memories, but that didn't help. Her throat tightened. "I know he didn't die when my parents did. If he had, he and I wouldn't have met. But that's how I remember it. My parents dying, then Billy. All the time he was suffering and slipping away all I wanted was my family. My parents. If they couldn't be there, I needed my sister with me."

She felt the tears on her cheeks. How long had it been since she'd cried over Billy? "I used to pray every night that he would get better, that the lawyer would find Aunt Charity so Cassie and I could be together again. It didn't help. Billy passed away in October of my senior year of high school. He was all of nineteen. I was seventeen. Aunt Charity showed up four months later. Four months too late in my mind."

Maybe it was the tears in her eyes, because she hadn't seen Arizona move, but suddenly he was crouched next to her and pulling her close. She went into his arms. She needed his strength and warmth to chase away the coldness of the past.

"I'm sorry," she whispered. "I don't usually get like this."

"We all have our demons."

"I don't believe in that."

"I'm talking about emotional demons, Chloe. The kind that live inside. We all have them, whether we want them or not."

His arms wrapped around her as he pulled her next to him. She rested her head on his shoulder.

"Do you still love him?" he asked.

"No." Her voice was muffled against his neck. "I did for a while, but we were so young. I don't know that the relationship would have lasted as long as it did if he hadn't been sick. That added a level of intensity that fueled whatever we were feeling. But he was a good person. I admired him, his courage, his determination. I just wish I hadn't believed him when he told me he wouldn't leave me."

"The people who are supposed to love us the best always end up hurting us."

She closed her eyes and focused on being next to him. He smelled of wood smoke and the unique fragrance that was his own. "That sounds like the voice of experience talking."

"It is. When we first met, you asked about my parents. You assumed, because I was raised by my grandfather, that they were both dead."

"You said your father was still alive."

"He is. The reason my grandfather took me is that

my father abandoned me to nannies. He blamed me for my mother's death. Apparently the labor was hard and long, and she wasn't very strong. He couldn't bear to be around me." He took a deep breath. "Emotionally and physically, he turned his back on me. I'm lucky. My grandfather was there to pick up the slack. But I spent the first fifteen years of my life trying to figure out why my father hated me. My grandfather finally took pity on me and explained it."

The ache inside of her deepened. "I'm sorry."

"There's no need for that. I've put it behind me and moved on. But it might make it more clear as to why I'm not a huge believer in love. Even when it comes to parents loving their children. I've seen a lot of neglect in my life, and I've experienced it firsthand."

She raised her head and looked at him. "We are quite a pair, aren't we?"

"It's not so bad."

He shifted until he was reclining on the sleeping bag, then pulled her down next to him. She settled into his arms, her head on his shoulder, her hand resting on his chest. She should have been self-conscious in such an intimate position, but it felt right. Perhaps it was the privacy of being alone together in the middle of nowhere; perhaps it was because they'd both just bared their souls. She didn't care which. At this moment in time, there was nowhere in the world she would rather be than here, with him.

A thought occurred to her. She raised her head and looked at him. "You know everything we've talked about tonight is private. I won't be using it in my article."

He touched the tip of her nose with his index finger. "Yes, I knew that. I trust you, Chloe."

"I'm glad." She settled down again. "So what was it like growing up with your grandfather? Were you close?"

"We were as I got older. When I was a kid I think he thought of me more like a puppy than a person. I know he cared, but he wasn't the most responsible parent. I wanted to be able to depend on him and I couldn't. He would pay attention to me for a while, then ignore me for weeks at a time. At least the staff always took care of me."

"I can't even imagine what that was like. At least Cassie and I had our parents for the first fourteen years of our lives, and we had each other." She pressed her lips together. No doubt all the fans on the Internet and everywhere else thought the same thing she had—that Arizona's life had been like a movie. All good times and laughter, played out in exotic locations. But the truth was different.

"While there are some things I would have liked to change, I don't regret how I was raised," he said. "Like I said before, it's all I know."

"Think of all you missed. Life in the suburbs can be pretty exciting. Barbecues, mowing the lawn, school dances." Her voice was low and teasing.

He chuckled in response. "You make it sound so tempting." He shifted his arm and rested his hand on her head. Long fingers stroked her hair. "I haven't lived any part of the American dream. Sometimes I wonder how I would have been different if my grandfather hadn't come to get me."

"You would be a different person. We're shaped by our experiences."

"The old nature-versus-nurture argument. But you're right. I would be different. How did we get on this topic of conversation?"

"We started out talking about firsts. First kiss, first

love." She frowned. "If you don't believe love exists, then you've never loved anyone."

He stiffened slightly. "I cared for my grandfather very much. He was important to me. I have friendships that matter. But romantic love, no."

He spoke the words so easily, yet her reaction to them was anything but casual. Her heart tightened in her chest and her throat closed. She wanted him to believe in love, which was insane. What did it matter to her? His stay in town was very temporary. Even if it wasn't, she wasn't interested in any kind of entanglement.

"We are a sorry pair," she said lightly, as much to conceal her emotions from him as to convince herself that she was fine. "You don't believe in love. I believe in it, but I want to avoid it at all costs. I refuse to hurt that much again."

"Just think of the heartache we're saving ourselves."

"Agreed. Except…" Her voice trailed off.

"Except what?"

"I can't help wondering what we're missing. Look at Cassie. She's so different from me. She leads with her chin and wears her heart on her sleeve. There are probably other clichés that apply, but I can't think of them right now. The point is she just puts it all on the line."

"Is she happy with her boyfriend?"

"Good question. I don't know. I hope so. I think she's settling for Joel, but then I'm not the one in the relationship."

"Sometimes people would rather accept what they can get instead of spending their time wishing for the moon."

It felt so good and right to be in his arms, she thought. She didn't ever want to leave. If the price of this moment was another day of hiking in the Cascade Mountains, then it was a small payment. She liked the heat of him, the scent of him, the feeling of safety, the way her body was slowly coming alive.

"According to your fan club online, you're something of a superhero, Arizona. Are you telling me you couldn't get me the moon?"

"Hey, I'm just a guy."

"Oh, but what a guy."

She made the statement without thinking. Arizona raised himself up on one elbow and stared down at her. Light from the fire flickered on his face. His gaze locked with hers. Sometimes she didn't know what he was thinking, but this time she had no trouble reading his thoughts.

The heat between them flared instantly as her body went up in flames. She knew what he was going to say even before he spoke.

"I want you."

Those three words stole her breath. Every part of her melted in anticipation.

"I want you," he repeated as he traced a line from her cheekbone to the corner of her mouth.

It wasn't going to mean anything, she told herself. It was impossible that this would be for more than one night. In the end, it wouldn't be more real than the dream. Was that enough for her? Could she live with those rules and not have regrets?

Her first lover had been Billy. Her second, a boy in college. She'd hoped he would help her forget her first love, but the plan hadn't worked. The lovemaking had been disappointing. The only time in her life she thought she might have experienced ultimate pleasure had been during the dream about Arizona. What if reality didn't live up to that billing?

What if it was better?

She continued to look at him as she realized it didn't

matter. She didn't want to be with him because of her body, she wanted to be with him because of her heart. It wasn't love, she reminded herself. She wouldn't do that again. But it was respect and caring. Wasn't that enough?

"I've never made love in a sleeping bag," she said at last.

"Actually, I haven't either, but I understand it can be done. There are, however, certain limitations."

"Like what?"

He smiled. "Let me show you."

CHAPTER NINE

HE BENT DOWN and pressed his mouth against hers. His lips were warm and firm. He moved with a sureness that told her he remembered their previous kiss. The one at the reception. Unfortunately her memories stretched back to another time when they'd made love in a cave on the side of a mountain.

She told herself not to think about that. The dream was just that—fantasy. This was real, this man who held her in his arms and moved his mouth back and forth as if seeking the most perfect fit. But even as she tried to push the past away, it intruded and she wondered if reality could stand up to what she'd experienced that night.

One of his hands moved behind her shoulders. He gently pulled her braid out from under her back, then tugged on the rubber band holding her hair in place. With his fingers, he freed the long curls and combed them into place around her face.

When he was done, she reached up and wrapped her arms around him, drawing him closer. She wanted to feel him press against her. She wanted to absorb his heat and his strength.

He tilted his head slightly, then opened his mouth and pressed his tongue to her lower lip. She instantly parted for him. He slipped inside, a quick, confident movement that made her wonder what else he would do well. Would he know how to touch her? Would he find the right places to stroke and tease, discover the proper cadence to send her soaring into perfection?

She couldn't answer the question and when his tongue touched hers, she didn't care. The warmth flowed through her, as if her body were melting against his. She moved one hand to his head, to hold him in place. His hair was soft and cool beneath her questing fingers. Her breasts swelled, her nipples puckered. An aching tingle began between her legs. She wanted this...wanted him.

He shifted, sliding one leg between hers. His rock-hard thigh pressed against her feminine place. The pressure teased her with promises of what would come later. Gently, slowly, almost as if she didn't want him to notice, she began to rock her hips up and down, sliding herself against him. The action both eased and increased the feeling of tension filling her.

"Chloe," he breathed against her mouth. "I want you so much."

His hands cupped her face. He lifted his head slightly, so they could look at each other. His expression was hard, his muscles tense. His breathing came in heavy bursts. Against her hip she felt the proof of his desire.

A quiet pride filled her. She didn't know why this man wanted her. No doubt he'd met other, more exciting, prettier women. Some probably had been smarter, some funnier, but none of that mattered to her. He was in her arms, holding her close. He wanted to make love with her and she clung to that reality with every fiber of her being.

He kissed her cheek, her jawline, then forged a damp trail to her ear.

"I want you," he repeated. "It's like being a teenager again. I feel like I'm going to explode." He rubbed his hardness against her hip, then groaned. "I could lose control right now."

Boldly, not sure where the courage sprang from, Chloe slipped one hand down his chest to his jeans. She placed her hand flat against the throbbing ridge. He swore once, then bit on her earlobe. Arousal shot through her, brought on by the feel of him against her palm, the word he'd muttered and the sharp nip of his teeth.

"You're going to make me embarrass myself," he told her.

"Then we'll just have to do it again until you get it right."

"That won't be a problem."

His slow, masculine smile made her toes curl. She wondered where on earth she'd gotten the courage to say these things to him. Was it the dream? She wasn't sure and she didn't mind. With Arizona she wanted to be bold—she wanted to be the kind of woman he would want and admire.

He cupped her face in his hands and kissed her again. This time he didn't wait—this time he plunged inside instantly and she was ready for him. Her tongue met his. They brushed against each other, circled, stroking. She inhaled his breath. Her body softened against his hardness, dampening, swelling, readying. She continued to move herself up and down against his thigh. Her panties were wet and she had the feeling that if she could just figure out the right spot or rhythm, something wonderful would happen.

One of his hands moved down her neck to her shoulder. From there he traveled across her chest to her right breast. She arched against him, encouraging him to touch her there. Her skin tingled, her nipple was hard, her body ached with a need that threatened to overwhelm her.

He slid over the curve, then cupped her. Through the layers of her clothing—bra, T-shirt, sweatshirt—she felt him move in a circle, as if discovering all of her. Chloe was pleased with her long, slender legs, could live with her butt and hips, but she'd always felt self-conscious about her small breasts. She thought they were fine, but compared to those she saw in magazines, she knew she was bound to disappoint some men.

But not Arizona. She wasn't sure how she knew this. He didn't say anything and she wasn't sure she believed that she could read his thoughts by how he touched her. Yet the rounded curves fit perfectly into the palm of his hand and she knew that was exactly how he liked it.

His hand moved lower until he reached the hem of her sweatshirt. He tugged on the garment, pulling it up. They broke apart enough to help him free her of the fleece. Her long-sleeved T-shirt followed. Instantly the cool night air nipped at her skin. She shivered, knowing that soon he would be on top of her, touching her everywhere, warming her through to her bones.

He knelt, straddling her legs. With a quick movement, his sweater and shirt joined hers in a pile on his sleeping bag. His green eyes glowed as if lit from within. His breathing was as rapid and ragged as her own.

She gave a nervous laugh. "So what do the forest creatures think about what we're doing?" she asked.

He grinned. "That humans have a funny way of staying warm at night."

He stretched out beside her and pulled her close. Her head cradled in the crook of his arm. Their mouths met. With his free hand, he tangled his fingers in her hair, then stroked her bare shoulder. Shivers rippled through her— shivers that had nothing to do with the air temperature and everything to do with anticipation.

She didn't notice him unfasten her bra, but the undergarment loosened, then fell away. "So beautiful," he breathed against her mouth as he used his index finger to circle the underside of her breasts.

Her nipples puckered and her breath caught in her throat. She wanted him to touch her there on the tight peaks. She wanted to know if it was going to feel as good as it had in the dream.

He broke away from their kiss and moved down her neck. Her upper body arched toward him in anticipation. He didn't disappoint her. His mouth closed over her left nipple.

Soft, wet heat encircled her. He teased the taut bud with his tongue, then gently scraped it with his teeth. A moan escaped her, then another. She grabbed his head, her actions a silent plea for him to never ever stop what he was doing.

His fingers mimicked the action of his mouth, then he switched. As the dampness between her legs increased, her hips began to move with a will of their own. She needed him.

"I never thought—" She began, but couldn't finish the sentence. There wasn't enough air in her lungs. She'd never thought it could be like this. It *was* better than the dream. So much better. And yet it was all familiar.

She didn't want to think about that. If she got caught up in trying to figure out what had really happened the night she'd worn the nightgown, she would miss what Arizona was doing to her now. She didn't want that. She wanted to live in the moment, because life had never been this perfect.

He licked the valley between her breasts. At the same time, he unfastened her jeans. Large hands tugged at the fabric and slowly pulled it down.

She'd taken off her boots when she'd first sat on the sleeping bag, so her jeans came off easily. He tossed them on the growing pile of clothing. He knelt between her legs and kissed her belly. Until that moment, she hadn't realized he'd pulled her panties off, too.

But there wasn't time to worry or protest. Because before she could figure out what was going to happen next, he'd kissed her right on top of the soft auburn curls protecting her femininity. His fingers urged her legs apart, then gently parted her woman's folds. With an unerring accuracy, he touched his tongue to that single point of pleasure.

Chloe gasped and came up into a nearly sitting position. No one had ever done anything like that to her before. She didn't know what to make of it, but she was sure she liked it. Even as she braced her weight on her hands, she parted her legs more.

His tongue was magic. He circled her and danced over her. He began a fast rhythm, then slowed until she thought she might scream. Tension filled her. Tension she'd felt before, but not like this. In the past, she'd experienced mild anticipation. Now she knew she was going to die if he didn't finish what he'd started.

Even as he continued to pleasure her, she couldn't help watching him. His head bent low as he loved her so intimately. The play of the firelight on his bare back. Broad shoulders, long legs tucked under him. Bare feet. When had he taken off his shoes and socks?

Then she decided she didn't care. As long as he never stopped what he was doing. As long as— She collapsed onto her back and exhaled his name. Pleasure raced through her, making her tense more, making her want to plead and demand and scream. All her attention focused on the places he touched. Not only on his tongue teasing her so deliciously, but also on the single finger he'd inserted inside of her.

He went in deep, exploring her, urging her on. Her hips jerked, driving him in more, needing him. His tongue moved faster, then stopped, letting her concentrate just on his finger. In and out, rubbing against her, forcing her to a place she'd never been.

She tried to catch her breath. Her heels dug into the sleeping bag, her fingers grasped at the quilted fabric. More. She needed more.

He read her mind. His mouth pressed against her again. He flicked his tongue back and forth. The finger inside of her circled and plunged. The movements conspired together to force her to the edge. Every part of her body tightened in anticipation. Then he stopped. One heartbeat. Two. She knew he was making her wait, building the anticipation. A whimper escaped her.

He touched her again—in tandem. His tongue, his lips, his hand. And she exploded.

She knew what was happening, but she couldn't control it. The moment was too perfect. She bucked and grabbed his shoulders, begging him not to stop. He continued to move, faster and lighter, drawing it all out of her until every cell of her body had filled itself with the passion and pleasure.

Slowly, very slowly, she relaxed. He pulled his mouth away and sat up. Perspiration coated her body. Her legs trembled. She would never be the same again.

"You are incredible," he said.

She opened her eyes and stared at him. "Me? I was just along for the ride. You're the one who—" She broke off and motioned vaguely with her hand. What did one say at a moment like this?

"You're very responsive." He rubbed his hands along her thighs, then up her belly. "I knew just where you were the whole time. That made it easy to know what to do."

Nice to know, even if she hadn't been doing it on purpose. Definitely better than the dream, she thought as he slipped off his jeans and briefs. Comparing what she'd felt then to what had just happened was like saying a cup of salt water was just like an ocean.

The sight of his arousal springing free caught her attention and forced all other thoughts from her mind. He was exactly as she'd known he would be. His chest, the scar on his forearm—she raised herself on one elbow to look—and the one on his knee. Familiar yet different. She didn't have an explanation and right now she didn't care.

"We have a dilemma," he said as he knelt between her legs again. "I want you very much, as you can tell."

He glanced down and she followed his gaze to his very impressive maleness. The thought of him filling her made her tummy tighten in anticipation.

"I want you, too," she whispered.

He leaned forward and kissed her, then he touched her cheek with the back of his fingers. "I didn't bring you up here to make love with you. I'm willing to admit I'd hoped we might end up right here, but I would have politely accepted a rejection on your part."

"Okay." She wasn't sure what he was getting at. "I'm confused."

He exhaled sharply. "What I'm trying to say is that I want to protect you. I brought condoms with me. But I don't want you to get the wrong idea. I really respect you. I think you're great, and I—"

She pressed her fingers over his mouth and smiled. "No problem. I'm glad that you wanted this to happen. And to be completely honest, I brought them, too."

His eyes widened. "You brought condoms?"

She blushed. Thank goodness it was too dark for him

to see. "Well, it's wasn't exactly my idea. Cassie gave me one."

That satisfied male smile returned. He reached for his jeans and withdrew the square plastic package. After putting on the protection, he pressed the tip of his arousal against her, then leaned down to whisper in her ear.

"Just one?" he said. "That wouldn't have been nearly enough."

Chloe's giggle of delight only increased Arizona's need. He'd hoped making love with her would be terrific, but even his imagination hadn't come up with anything even close to this glorious reality. He'd meant what he'd told her before. He *had* practically been able to read her mind when he'd been touching her. Maybe it was just instinct, but there hadn't been any of his usual concerns when he was with a woman. He'd known exactly where to touch, how fast, for how long. He'd known when she was getting close and what she wanted to make it perfect for her.

Now, even before he entered her, he knew exactly how it was going to be. She would threaten to swallow him completely and he would surrender himself to her.

She reached up and touched his face. "Be in me," she breathed. "Please."

With that, he entered her. He moved slowly, not wanting to hurt her. But she was already so aroused. Her tightness stretched to accommodate him. He had to grit his teeth against the pleasure. All he wanted was to explode right there, but he couldn't. He wanted to make it good for her, too.

He opened his eyes and stared into her beautiful face. Dark eyes stared back at him. She was smiling.

"You feel great," he told her.

"You, too."

He pulled out, then pushed in again. Back and forth, moving a little faster each time. Her eyes widened. She clutched at him.

"It's happening again," she said, sounding shocked.

"It's supposed to."

"I don't—"

Her fingers dug into his back. She raised her legs and wrapped them around him. "Arizona, please!"

He knew what she wanted…what they both wanted. Fast and hard.

He plunged in and withdrew, pumping his hips, taking her with him. She whimpered. Her breathing came in little gasps. He could feel her collecting herself. He swore silently, willing himself to hold back, to give her what she craved.

Suddenly, she dropped her feet to the ground and pushed up against him. He buried himself inside of her. She grabbed his hips and held him in deep.

Her gaze still locked with his, she climaxed around him. Her body rippled, massaging him, drawing him in more, forcing him to give in to the incredible passion surging through him. She milked him until he exploded.

When they had both recovered, he stretched out next to her and pulled her close. He wanted to tell her it had never been like that for him before, but wondered if she would believe him. Even to his mind, it sounded like a line.

The problem was, he meant it. He hadn't felt anything like this before. There had been a connection, a oneness. The words of the old shaman came back to him. "When you mate with a woman, you give away a piece of your soul."

That's what had happened, he realized. He and Chloe had exchanged parts of their innermost selves. He'd never wanted that before—mostly because the thought scared him. But with Chloe, he didn't mind. He liked the thought of having a part of her soul to carry with him, and for reasons he couldn't explain, he trusted her with a piece of himself.

THEY WERE QUIET for a long time. Chloe enjoyed the silence. She needed to catch her breath, both physically and emotionally. She wasn't sure of everything that had happened between them. It had definitely been better than the dream, which was a little terrifying. The good news was, she reminded herself, at least the best it had ever been was now a real-life experience and not something she'd thought up in her head.

"What are you thinking about?" Arizona asked.

Chloe's head rested on his shoulder and her hand stroked his chest. Somehow they'd found their way inside her sleeping bag. "That it's never been like this before."

"For me, too. Pretty spectacular. And that was just our first time out. Imagine what we could do with a little practice."

There was something to think about, she thought. "No, you don't understand. After Billy, there were two young men in college. I'm not a virgin, but I've never climaxed before."

She instantly regretted her confession, but he didn't get all weird on her. The hand stroking her hair never slowed and his breathing remained even.

"I wouldn't have guessed," he told her, "but I'd be lying if I said I wasn't glad. I wanted to make it perfect for you."

"Oh, it was, and then some."

"Good."

She was on her side, facing him. Her right leg rested

on top of his. She bent her knee and rubbed her foot up and down along his shin. Her thigh brushed against a raised ridge in his skin.

"You have a scar." She made a statement rather than asking a question.

"I was cut with a knife when I was about fifteen. We were in India. A man got sick and had a high fever. He was delirious and thought we were trying to take him away. Several of us grabbed him to hold him down, but he got in a couple of good thrusts. I was in the way of one of them."

He spoke so matter-of-factly, she thought. As if that sort of thing happened every day. "I don't have any scars," she told him. "We'll have to bond over something else."

He kissed her forehead. "I think we've done more than our share of bonding tonight."

They had, she thought, realizing he was right. They'd bonded in the most intimate way possible. "I knew it was going to be like this," she said without thinking.

The words hung in the silence of the night. She stiffened, waiting for the inevitable questions, but Arizona never asked. He only held her tighter against him.

I knew it was going to be like this.

The statement filled his head until it was all he could think about. She'd thought about them being together. She'd assumed it was going to be amazing. He didn't know why that should matter so much to him, but it did.

Who was this woman who had made a place for herself inside of him? Was he crazy? They couldn't get involved. She was three different kinds of home and hearth. He'd never lived anywhere longer than six months at a time and he had no intention of changing his ways. He didn't want to settle down. Except for the occasional loneliness, he liked his life. Especially tonight.

He shifted until he was facing her, then he kissed her. The passion flared more slowly this time. Her arms wound around his neck as she opened her mouth to him. As if she read his mind.

Connected, he thought, distracted by the need building. They were connected. Maybe the thought should send him running for cover. It usually did.

"I want you," he murmured against her mouth. "I want to be in you. I want to feel you under me."

Her breathing quickened as her body responded to what he'd said.

They were well matched. She was tall for a woman, and he liked that. He liked the feel and smell of her skin, the brush of her legs against his. He liked her small, tight breasts and the tautness of her nipples. He liked the way her long hair spilled over her breasts, both exposing and concealing them. He liked her.

Something had happened between them. He knew that now. He didn't want to get involved, but he couldn't walk away from her. Not yet. Not tonight and maybe not for a couple of days. He wanted her too much.

As he reached for another condom, he told himself he was risking a lot. Maybe he should back off now.

He tried his surefire method for disconnecting. He pictured Chloe about thirty pounds heavier with a baby in her arms and another clinging to her skirts. He imagined a house, a yard and a minivan in the driveway. In his mind's eye, he saw the suburbs, his nine-to-five job and a medical and dental insurance plan. Then he waited.

But the arousal didn't go away and the vision didn't make him cringe. When she reached her hand between them, he allowed her to guide him inside her. They both groaned as he slid home.

As he began to thrust into her, he moved his hands all

over her body. He liked her like this, but the thought of her with rounder hips, gently aging, didn't distress him as it should have.

He reminded himself that he came from a long line of men who got love all wrong. His grandfather, his father and him. He would never settle down, so this was just make-believe. Not love. Never love.

As her legs encircled him, he told himself this was all he was ever going to have. And for now it was enough.

CHAPTER TEN

DESPITE THE HARD ground, Chloe found herself drifting off to sleep. Perhaps it was a result of the physical exercise from hiking all afternoon. Or maybe it was because her body had been so thoroughly satisfied by Arizona's lovemaking. She decided she didn't much care. As long as he snuggled next to her, his arms around her making her warm and keeping her safe.

She lay on her side with him behind her, spooning against her. One arm rested heavily on her waist. She placed her hand on top of his and savored the feel of him. Her mind drifted and images formed. Images of Arizona. They hadn't know each other very long, but already the man was very much a part of her life.

She slept dreamlessly until well after midnight. Then she sank deeper and deeper into the dreaming place. Unrelated bits and pieces flitted through her mind until they came together to form a picture. Chloe found herself walking toward a vehicle. But instead of her sleek, sporty convertible, she unlocked a Suburban.

"Come on, you two," she called over her shoulder. "We're going to be late." But she wasn't angry as she spoke. The scene had been played out a hundred times before and they'd never once been late, although the children did love to dawdle.

A girl of maybe six or seven and a boy of four trotted

after her, then climbed into the truck. Chloe stepped in after them. She checked to make sure they were wearing their seat belts, then carefully adjusted her own so that it encircled her very pregnant belly.

As she backed out of the driveway, she glanced up and saw the Victorian house where she'd lived her entire life. An upper floor curtain moved and Aunt Charity waved at her. Chloe waved back. Aunt Charity would take care of making dinner tonight, as she had for the past couple of weeks. Chloe was running behind on her book deadline, and she wanted to get the project out before the baby came. Plus there was the party on Friday, for which she wasn't close to ready. Her daughter needed a costume for the school play; she and Arizona had to make plans to celebrate their anniversary. It was overwhelming.

As she turned onto the main street, she found herself smiling. Yes, at times life overwhelmed her, but she'd never been happier or more content. She and Arizona were so right together. As if they truly were each other's destiny.

As she drove into traffic, the two children in the back began to sing. Chloe joined in. The words were a familiar rhyme. Then the sound faded and she found herself drifting out of the dream. She tried to call out a protest. She didn't want to leave. It was perfect there. She wanted it to be real. She wanted him to be her destiny.

Chloe awoke with a start. Cold night air caressed her cheek and for a moment, she didn't know where she was. Something long and strong and warm cradled her from behind, trapping her in an unfamiliar cocoon.

She opened her mouth to scream, then the memories clicked into place. She was fine. She was in the forest with Arizona. They were hiking to an archaeological dig so he could look at some artifacts. They weren't married, she wasn't pregnant. Nothing was different from the way it had been yesterday or a month ago.

Until the last lie, she'd nearly succeeded in calming herself. But now her heart rate picked up and her body trembled. She wasn't the same. Everything had changed since Arizona had dropped into her life. Now they were lovers. How was she supposed to resist him? The way he touched her, the way he made her feel—no woman could walk away from that kind of magic.

She closed her eyes and willed herself to calm down. She was overtired. She was reacting emotionally to a difficult situation. That was what the dream had been trying to tell her—that things were different now. She wasn't really going to marry Arizona, live in Bradley and have three children. That was crazy. She was going to move to New York and write for a major magazine. She wasn't going to get married because loving someone meant opening herself to pain and Chloe had sworn to never do that again. It hurt too much.

"I'm fine," she whispered to herself. "It was just a dream. It's not true."

She repeated the sentences over and over. Slowly, her body relaxed. It wasn't real. He wasn't her destiny. In a couple of weeks he would disappear from her life as abruptly as he'd entered it and she would go on as before.

"There's nothing to be afraid of," she told herself. "Nothing at all."

Arizona shifted in his sleep and pulled her closer. She allowed herself to press against him. Unexpectedly, tears sprang to her eyes. She felt them fill her eyes, then spill onto her temple. What on earth was wrong with her? She was fine. It had just been a strange dream.

And then she knew. The truth dawned and with it

a growing horror. She wasn't crying because she was afraid the dream would come true…but because she was afraid it wouldn't.

THEY WALKED IN to the dig a little after one in the afternoon. Chloe hadn't known what to expect. Her entire experience with archaeology had been a visit to the La Brea Tar Pits in Los Angeles when she'd been ten or twelve. She vaguely recalled some motorized life-size replicas of a woolly mammoth family caught in tar outside, and some fossils on the inside. Behind the buildings was the actual site itself, but that memory was a blur.

Here she'd expected to see a few open pits with college students delicately removing bits of bone using dental instruments. Instead, she and Arizona crested the rise and looked down into an entire village.

To the left were the tents used by the scientists and workers. To the right were obviously ancient stone huts, some reduced to crumbled remains, others standing tall with open places for windows and doors. A couple hundred yards back from the village was an open dirt area with a large circle painted in white.

"What do you think?" Arizona asked.

"It's huge," she told him. "I'd pictured something smaller."

"Most people do. They're studying a society here, not digging up dinosaur bones. Some of the finds are from two or three different Indian tribes. That's what everyone came to study. But about three months ago, they started unearthing a much older civilization…and one that was more advanced. No one knows who they are or where they came from. They're the ones who interest me."

As he spoke, he started down the side of the rise.

Chloe followed him. While she was pleased they'd arrived and she could put down her heavy pack for a few hours, in a way she was sorry to be around other people. Instead, she wanted to be alone with Arizona.

This morning could have been awkward. Between her very strange dream and their physical intimacy, she'd been prepared for stiff conversation and averted gazes. Instead, Arizona had awakened her with a kiss. She'd felt perfectly comfortable lying there in his arms. They'd had breakfast and dressed, but in the process of rolling up their sleeping bags and packing up clothes, they'd become tangled in each other. The lovemaking had been hot and fast, leaving them both satisfied and out of breath. Not a bad way to start the morning.

But all that would be different now, she told herself. There were other people around. She had to remember they were both here to work.

A tall, skinny man with a scruffy beard looked up at their approach. He wore thick glasses and baggy clothes. He had a clipboard in one hand and a handheld tape recorder in the other.

"Arizona!" he called when he spotted them. "I heard you were coming to check out what we found."

"Hey, Jeff. Good to see you." They walked over to him and the two men shook hands. "This is Chloe Wright. She's a reporter."

Jeff shook her hand and winked. "He's all flash, no substance. Don't let him fool you into thinking otherwise."

Chloe found herself smiling at the rumpled man. "I'll do my best to remain objective."

Jeff returned his attention to Arizona. "We've found more artifacts. Some tools, bowls, nothing that will interest you." He slapped his friend's back. "The amulet is in here."

He led Arizona toward one of the larger tents. Chloe fell into step behind them. As they walked, she glanced around and tried to get a feel for all the activity. Long wooden tables had been stacked with bowls, stone disks and knives. There were open crates and two women filling them with the stone objects.

Every time they walked by someone, Arizona called out a greeting. He knew them all by name. He had a few teasing words for each of them. Chloe was reminded of the reception, where he'd known as many guests as she did, and she'd lived in Bradley all her life. She supposed it was just his personality. He enjoyed getting to know people and they wanted to know him.

"In here," Jeff said, motioning them inside one of the largest tents.

Arizona let his backpack slip to the ground before entering and Chloe did the same. There were more tables set up in here, she noticed as they entered. The objects littering the surface were small and delicate. Some were wood, a few cloth. Despite the canvas flaps rolled back to let in both air and light, the area smelled musty.

"We found it in what we thought might have been a wooden box. Unfortunately, it disintegrated when we moved it. But the amulet is intact. There are a dozen or so stone beads. Very round with a tiny hole through the center. We figured it was part of a necklace of some kind. How they made the stones so small and perfect is anyone's guess."

Jeff stopped in front of a table in the rear of the tent. "I've already finished the paperwork. You just have to sign for it and promise you won't lose it."

Arizona smiled. "I'll be careful."

"I know. That's why I'm releasing it to you." He glanced at Chloe. "We have some sandwiches left over from lunch if you want them."

Her stomach growled. "Sounds great."

"Help yourself when you're done." He picked up a rectangular acrylic case that was about six inches square and handed it to Arizona. "Good luck. I'm curious to hear what you figure out." With that he waved and left the tent.

Arizona lifted the cover and stared down at the small round stones. Chloe moved closer. One of the stones was larger than the others, and more oval than round. There was some kind of carving.

"A child sign," he said, and put the oval piece in the center of his palm. "That's a sleeping baby or young child."

She looked down and saw what looked like a cross between a crude drawing of an infant in a cradle board and a baby seal. The ridges underneath looked fluid to her.

"Water?" she asked, pointing.

"Probably. These dots up here—" He indicated the top half of the stone "—are stars. The tiny crescent is the moon. The water indicates a journey or travel. The birth of a baby, or a prayer for a baby to be brought to the family? Maybe a wish for a dying child to have safe passage to the next life." His voice was low and intense. "I'll have to start researching this fairly soon. I'm not going to have much time."

He muttered a few more sentences, then seemed to get lost in what he was studying. Chloe didn't mind. She moved away and bent over a few of the tables, trying to figure out what had been unearthed.

This was, she acknowledged, a different world from her own suburban life. Arizona was unlike anyone she'd ever met. Yet there were many things about him that called to her. His kindness, his intelligence, his humor. She found him physically attractive—she liked the feel of his body next to and on top of hers. She respected him.

She glanced back and saw him carefully weighing the round stones and the amulet itself, then making notations on a card. Their relationship just wasn't about sex—at least it wasn't for her. And that thought terrified her. If it was only physical, it would be so much easier to put into place. As it was, she was confused. What did it mean that Arizona had entered her life? What was she supposed to do now? The obvious answer was that she was supposed to enjoy the fun while it lasted, then forget about him when he left. It made sense. What other choice was there?

But what about the dream? Had that meant anything? Was it a premonition or just wishful thinking on her part?

"I don't want a traditional life," she reminded herself. "I don't want to fall in love again. I don't want to care. If you love people, then they can hurt you."

She'd experienced the latter firsthand. Her parents hadn't meant to die and leave her, but they had. So had Billy. She was tired of caring and then being left alone. She wasn't going to take that kind of chance again.

She heard footsteps and turned. Arizona walked over and gave her a sheepish grin. "Sorry. I got caught up in this." He shook the acrylic box. "Breakfast was a long time ago. You must be starving. Let's go grab a couple of sandwiches."

"Sounds good."

They went outside and found the food. A few of the graduate students came by and talked to Arizona. As expected, he knew all of them by name. When a couple of the young women looked at Arizona with admiring eyes, Chloe had to fight down a surge of irritation. She wanted to slide closer to him and lay claim to him. But she didn't. As far as she could tell, Arizona barely realized they were female, let alone attractive and obviously smitten. For someone who could read a life's story in a single carved stone, he was amazingly dense when it came to women. It was, she acknowledged, a fine quality in a man.

At last, when they were alone, Arizona leaned forward and rested his elbows on the wooden picnic table. "Is it what you thought?" he asked, indicating the site.

"It's bigger and there's more activity. I'm glad you brought me. This will add a lot to my article." She touched the box lying between them. "What are you going to do with this?"

"I'll do some research. Most of what I need is available through Internet links with university libraries. I have to figure out what the carvings mean. Once all this gets dated, I'll look at other cultures from that time. There are often similarities." His eyebrows drew together. "My problem is I don't have a lot of time. Once the lecture series is finished in Bradley, I'm leaving for the South Pacific. I'm doing some work there this summer."

She'd known he wasn't going to stay. Why would a man like him want to spend any time in a small town? But she hadn't really thought much about his going away so soon.

"Are you excited about the island?" she asked, trying to pretend his plans didn't matter to her. After all, she reminded herself, they shouldn't.

"I've been there before. They have a rich oral storytelling tradition and I'll be recording and annotating many of their tales." His gaze lingered on her face. "You'd like it. It's a strictly matriarchal society. The men exist to do the hard physical labor, but all the decisions are made by the women. I find it restful. There aren't any pressures to act macho."

"Oh, right. I would guess you like it because the women there probably wait on you hand and foot."

His smile was modest. "There is that. But it's also very beautiful."

"I'm sure it is." She forced herself to keep smiling. Later, when she was alone, she would try to figure out why her chest was suddenly tight and it hurt to breathe.

"What's next for you?" he asked. "After the article, I mean."

"More work. I've put together some of my best writing. When I finish this story, I'm going to go to New York and see if I can get a job there. At least that's the plan."

"Sounds like a good one."

"I've wanted this for a long time." Chloe frowned. She *had* wanted this for as long as she could remember. Growing up, she'd dreamed about leaving Bradley and making it in the big city. But right now, the idea of being away from everything she'd ever known only sounded lonely.

"Have you ever thought about doing something else?" he asked.

She stared at him. He hadn't shaved that morning and stubble darkened his cheeks. His hair was slightly mussed, his clothes as wrinkled as hers. Yet he was the most handsome man she'd ever met. What was he asking? Was he hinting that he might like her to come along? Would she be willing to do that? What about her career? What about not getting involved?

"I can be flexible," she told him.

"That helps," he said, and though she waited, he didn't add anything.

Chloe fought against the disappointment. She was

being a fool, she thought. Wanting something didn't necessarily make it happen. What was wrong with her? She wasn't usually this scattered. Maybe it was because Arizona had become so important to her in a relatively short period of time. It made everything so confusing.

Jeff sauntered over to the table. The two men spoke. Chloe watched Arizona. When he smiled, her lips curved up. His hands moved as he talked, and she remembered those same hands on her body. She was glad she was with him. She wanted to talk with him, hear his stories, be close.

The realization hit her with all the subtlety of lightning splitting a tree in two. She felt just as ripped apart inside. The reason she felt so confused and unsettled wasn't because Arizona was so appealing, or because the circumstances were new. It was because she'd fallen for him. She, a woman who constantly resisted getting involved, had fallen for a man who specialized in leaving everyone else behind.

A RUMBLE OF a distant engine cut through the silence of the afternoon. Arizona glanced at his watch. Two-thirty. Right on time. Jeff shook his hand.

"Let me know what you find," he said, pointing to the acrylic box. "Good luck this summer."

"You, too," Arizona said, then watched his friend head back to the main part of the dig.

"What's that noise?" Chloe asked. She rose to her feet and stared up at the sky. "A helicopter?"

"It's our ride home," Arizona told her. "The lecture series starts the day after tomorrow. There isn't time to hike out. We should be at the airport in about forty minutes. We're on the five o'clock flight to Sacramento. You'll be home by bedtime."

The noise got louder.

"We could have used a helicopter to get here?" Chloe asked.

"Sure. What did you think that circle was for?" He pointed to the huge white spot on the dirt. "It's the landing pad."

"I see." She turned to him. "So why exactly did we hike in here? I mean, what was the point?"

There was something stiff about her posture. Her face was unreadable.

"Are you angry?" he asked. She didn't answer. He scrambled to explain. "I thought it would be fun."

"For you," she said curtly.

"For both of us. The weather promised to be excellent, it's a pretty easy hike. I wanted to spend time with you. I thought you wanted the same."

He could feel the shifting emotional ground underfoot and struggled to stay upright. It was clear that he'd done something wrong, but for the life of him, he couldn't figure out what.

"Which part was more enjoyable?" she asked. "Was it watching me try to be a good sport my first time camping out, or did you like getting it on better?"

"Chloe, no. It wasn't like that. I enjoy spending time with you. I thought you felt the same. With our schedules, we haven't been able to be together as much as I would have liked. I thought this was a good way to make that happen. I wasn't trying to trick you into anything. I didn't force you last night."

Her expression softened slightly and he saw the pain in her eyes. How in God's name had he hurt her? He took a step toward her. She held up a hand to stop him.

"Don't sweat it, Arizona. You're a hundred percent right. You didn't force me. I practically begged for it."

"Chloe, don't."

"Don't what?" Her dark eyes spit fire. "Don't tell the truth? So I assume you had a radio with you the whole time? You could have called in the helicopter if something had gone wrong."

"Sure. If we'd had an accident."

"Or if I hadn't been good enough in bed."

With that she swung on her backpack and walked away. He collected his belongings and ran after her. The helicopter was on the ground, making it difficult to talk. He grabbed her arm and forced her to stop and face him.

"What's going on?" he asked. "How did we get here?"

"I don't like being made a fool of. You tricked me."

"I'm sorry I didn't tell you about the helicopter, but I'm not sorry about what happened. I don't think you are either." She flinched, but he kept on talking. "Don't make me out to be the bad guy. What we shared out there wasn't just sex and you know it. It was very special. I'm not going to regret that. I'll admit I didn't make you any promises. I don't do commitments, but if I remember correctly, they're not your style either. So why are you so upset?"

Her gaze was steady. Strands of red curls fluttered around her face. "I don't like being the entertainment."

His temper flared. "It was never like that and you damn well know it." He ground his teeth together. "Fine. Let's play it your way. I brought you along to have my way with you. It was great. Thanks, babe. Now can we go home?"

Something dark and ugly flashed in her eyes. Regret came on the heels of his anger and he was instantly sorry. But before he could say anything, Jeff pulled open the helicopter's door and motioned for her to step inside. Arizona followed.

They fastened their seat belts. The pilot glanced over his shoulder and when Arizona gave him a thumbs-up, guided them into the air.

Normally Arizona enjoyed flying. Helicopters hugged the ground, allowing him to see things not visible from planes. But today the scenery didn't interest him. He looked at the woman sitting stiffly next to him. Her gaze was firmly fixed on the window.

"Chloe?"

She didn't respond. It was noisy and she might not have heard him. Or she was ignoring him. Arizona leaned back in his seat and folded his arms over his chest. They were stuck with each other until they arrived back in California. At some point in the journey he would get her attention and explain it all to her.

HE WAITED UNTIL they were seated in the first-class section of the plane. While other passengers were busy stowing luggage and finding their seats, he leaned close and reached for her hand. She tried to pull back, but he wouldn't let her.

"Chloe, you have to listen to me."

She stared out the window. "No, I don't."

"Unless you start humming loud enough to drown out my words, you're going to hear me anyway, so why not listen?"

He took her silence as grudging agreement.

"I'm sorry," he told her. "I was a complete jerk. I should have told you about the helicopter and given you the choice. I really didn't take you out in the woods just to take advantage of you. Obviously I hoped we would become lovers, but my main goal was to spend time with you."

She didn't say anything, but he thought she might have

relaxed slightly. He rubbed his thumb over the back of her hand. "I'm not sorry we made love. I've wanted you from the first moment I met you. You're beautiful and exciting. I'm lucky to have met you. I'm arrogant enough to think you might have wanted me, too. Even if you didn't, the lovemaking was spectacular enough to have changed your mind."

A faint smile tugged at her lips. She turned to look at him. "Even if you do say so yourself."

He shrugged. "You weren't going to say it."

She took a deep breath, then let it out. He squeezed her fingers. "I didn't set you up."

"I know," she said softly. "It's just, when I realized we could have flown in, I felt really cheap and stupid."

"I'm sorry. I didn't want that."

She nodded. "It's okay. How long can I throw stones? I had a condom with me, too."

"I remembered that, but I wasn't going to mention it."

"Probably a wise idea." She studied him. "I'm fine. I understand and I'm not angry."

"Or hurt?"

"That will take a little longer to get over."

"I'm sorry."

"It's okay. You don't have to keep apologizing. I'm fine. We're fine."

But they weren't. He could hear it in her voice. "You're not telling me something. What is it?"

She was silent for so long, he thought she wasn't going to answer. Finally she shrugged. "It's nothing. I just wish…"

Her voice trailed off.

What did she wish for? That things were different? That they were different? Did she want more than he was capable of giving? Women usually did. Normally that made him feel annoyed with them, but with Chloe he felt a sense of panic, that if he couldn't provide what she needed, he would lose her.

But how could he lose what he didn't want and had never had?

"We're fine," she repeated. "We both went into the situation aware that it was temporary. Neither of us wants to get involved and we're not. We had fun. What's not to like?"

She gave him a big smile and squeezed his hand. It didn't work. She was hiding something. But as surely as he knew the sun would come up in the morning, he knew she wouldn't tell him if he asked.

As the plane taxied to the end of the runway, he leaned toward her. Chloe rested her head on his shoulder. He couldn't escape the feeling that he'd really messed things up between them, but for the life of him, he couldn't figure out what...or how. And until he knew that, he couldn't begin to make things better.

CHAPTER ELEVEN

CHLOE PULLED INTO the driveway and stayed sitting in her car. This was *not* how she'd wanted the past couple of days with Arizona to end. She'd hoped they would be fun and pleasant and something she could be excited about remembering. The worst part was she couldn't exactly explain what was wrong.

It was something about the helicopter, she knew. He'd asked her to hike in with him and there had been no need. She understood what he'd told her, that he'd wanted time for them to get to know each other and that they would have a good time together. But…

But why did it hurt so damn much? She rested her head on the steering wheel and drew in a deep breath. She felt stupid. Which didn't make sense. No wonder Arizona was confused—she couldn't make sense of it herself. She'd agreed to go into the wilderness with him. She'd even brought along a condom. So the fact that they'd become lovers shouldn't be such a huge shock. She'd wanted it, too. But telling herself that didn't make the pain in her chest go away.

She got out of the car and pulled her backpack from the small trunk. She'd barely made it to the base of the rear steps when the back door opened and Cassie stepped out onto the porch.

"You're back! I'm so excited. I've been sitting here

waiting. I want to hear every single detail. Start at the beginning and talk slowly."

Chloe stared at her sister's happy face. Cassie grinned like a Cheshire cat. "Was it wonderful?" she asked. "Did you two do the wild thing?"

Without warning, Chloe burst into tears. One minute she'd been fine, but the next sobs choked her as tears poured down her face.

Cassie was at her side in an instant. "Oh, Chloe, I'm so sorry. Come on. Come inside. I don't know what's wrong, but I do know that we can fix it together."

Chloe found herself led into the kitchen. Cassie took her backpack from her and set it in the corner. She settled her sister in one of the kitchen chairs, disappeared for a second, then returned with a box of tissues. While Chloe tried to bring herself under control, Cassie started heating milk for cocoa.

The familiar smells made Chloe want to weep more. Their mother had often made cocoa to help them through life's troubles when they were growing up. It remained a tradition today. Chloe wished that her problems were as simple as they had been all those years ago. The warm drink frequently worked when she'd done poorly on a spelling test or had been teased by a boy in school, but she doubted it was going to help tonight.

Still, she took the mug Cassie offered and when her sister took the seat across from her, she tried to smile. "It's not so bad," she said. "I'm fine."

"Oh, I can tell." Cassie tucked her thick, dark hair behind her ears and leaned forward. "Start at the beginning and tell me what's wrong."

"I don't know where to begin." She took a sip of the steaming liquid. The rich chocolate taste comforted her.

"It's all so complicated. I never meant—" She broke off and glanced around. "Where's Aunt Charity?"

Cassie frowned. She'd never understood Chloe's reluctance to trust their aunt. "She's out with friends. Dinner and a movie. She'll be home late. Quit stalling. What's going on?"

Chloe resisted the urge to unburden herself. "I can't. You'll get angry."

"Why? You haven't done anything to me. I'm your sister, I care about you. I want to help."

"I know, but you'll be hurt and—" She pressed her lips together. She had really made a mess of things. "I never thought it would get so complicated."

"Chloe, you're not making any sense. What is too complicated? I know this is about Arizona, but I don't know how. Did something bad happen? Did he hurt you?"

"No," Chloe answered, knowing what her sister was asking. Arizona had hurt her but not in a way that was anyone's fault. "I want to tell you and I will, but please don't be mad."

Cassie made an X over her heart. "I swear."

As Chloe tried to speak, fresh tears filled her eyes. She wiped them away with the back of her hand, then took a sip of the cocoa. "It's all because of that stupid nightgown," she said at last. "We had sex and it ruined everything." The knot in her stomach tightened. She'd made a complete fool out of herself and she had only herself to blame. What on earth had she been thinking? Why had she given in? He must think… Chloe realized she didn't know what Arizona thought of her, which, in a way, made things worse.

"I don't understand," Cassie said. "What does the nightgown have to do with anything? Did you take it with you and wear it?"

"No." Chloe sniffed. "I lied. The night of my birthday, when I wore the nightgown, I did have a dream. I dreamed about Arizona. It was so incredibly real and passionate. I didn't know what had happened. I couldn't really believe the family legend was anything but a joke. I was embarrassed and I thought it was stupid. That's why I didn't tell you. Then when I saw him on the television, I was so stunned, I didn't know what to say. Since then, everything has been out of control. I'm confused and scared and I'm really, really sorry."

Cassie glanced down at her mug. "I see. You didn't trust me."

Her words and her stiff posture screamed her hurt. The knot in Chloe's gut doubled in size. "I knew you'd be upset. You have every right to be mad at me, Cass. I can't explain what I was thinking except I was stunned by what had happened."

Cassie didn't look at her. She shook her head back and forth, making the gold heart earrings catch the light.

Chloe stretched her hand across the table and touched her sister's fingers. "I never meant to hurt you. You are my closest friend in life. I was very upset by what had happened and I didn't want to talk to anyone about it."

At last Cassie looked at her. "Besides, I was the one so excited about the legend. If I'd known you'd dreamed about Arizona, I wouldn't have been able to keep the information to myself." A smile tugged at her lips. "Imagine if I'd blurted it out that first night he was here for dinner."

"It would have given us something to talk about."

Cassie nodded. "I understand, Chloe. I'm a little hurt, but I'll get over it. Let's talk about you and what happened. You dreamed about him, and then you met him. Was that like the dream?"

"Not the meeting." She quickly explained about going into work that morning and finding out that Arizona was her new assignment. Everywhere she went, pictures of the man stared back at her. She described seeing the scar on his arm in her dream, then finding out he had the same scar.

"How did you know about the scar?" Cassie asked. "What was he wearing in the dream?"

Chloe cleared her throat. She could feel herself blushing. "Nothing. We made love, several times. It was amazing."

Cassie laughed. "No wonder you were stunned the next morning. There's nothing like finding out your fantasy lover is a real person to get your day started."

"Exactly. It was so spooky. You know I don't believe in the legend. I'm a reporter. I want to be able to prove my facts. I couldn't figure out what was going on and it frightened me."

"Plus you wouldn't want Arizona to know too much," Cassie said. "After all, he spends his life exploring the mystic. You couldn't be sure what he would make of the whole nightgown legend once he found out he'd been the subject of your dream."

"Exactly."

Cassie took a drink of her cocoa, then placed the mug on the table and cupped it with her hands. Her eyebrows drew together. "I still don't see the problem. You and Arizona get along well. I think you like him. I know he likes you. You made love and I'm guessing it was lovely. So why are you so upset?"

"Because it's all too strange. Yes, we get along and have fun together. The sex was amazing." She didn't want to think about that, about how she'd felt when he touched her. "That's not the point. It's more complicated. I refuse to fall in love with anyone ever. I won't let myself feel that kind of pain again. Arizona might believe in myths and stories, but he doesn't believe in love, romantic or otherwise. He's the kind of man who wants to spend his life roaming the world. While I want to travel, I do also want to settle down and make a home. Eventually."

"You already have a home." Cassie waved to encompass the kitchen and the entire house beyond. "You have roots. You're from Bradley."

Cassie's tone was light, but Chloe heard the envy in her sister's voice. She never knew what to say about that—about the fact that she'd inherited the house.

Cassie shrugged. "Where you settle isn't important. So he wants to travel, possibly more than you do. Compromise. Couples have been doing that for generations. How do you think marriages last?"

"No one is talking about getting married. That's the last thing I want to do."

"Are you sure?"

"Yes. I refuse to love him. I don't want to get involved with anyone. We're friends and we had a great time together."

"Then why are you crying?"

Chloe couldn't answer the question. Nothing made sense. She wanted to explain about the helicopter and feeling tricked, but she'd had time to think and she didn't believe Arizona had deliberately set out to deceive her. She'd overreacted. Probably because she was feeling a little overwhelmed by her reaction to him.

"I don't know what to think. Maybe if we hadn't made love things would be more clear." She rested her elbows on the table and cupped her head in her hands. "I feel like I'm caught up inside a tornado. Every time it sets me down, I have to get my bearings all over again. Just when I get that all figured out, I'm caught up again, with no control over my destiny."

"Sounds to me like you're falling in love with him."

Chloe sucked in a breath. "No," she said firmly. "That's not possible."

Cassie ignored her. "Of course it is. You've cut yourself off from your heart for so long, you can't recognize the symptoms. Why else would any of this matter?"

"It's not that."

"What else could it be? You're worried about what the man does for a living and how much he travels. If this was just a fling you would be grateful that he was leaving and that you would never have to see him again. Instead it bothers you. You want to find a way to blend your lives. That's what loving someone is all about."

"No. I don't love him. I don't want to love him. I don't want to love anyone."

Now it was Cassie's turn to reach across the table and touch her hand. "Yes, you do. Chloe, it's time to let go of the past. You tend to hang on to things for too long. I miss Mom and Dad, too, but I've let it go. I have the memories. What I learned is that you never know how long you're going to have, so love fully. You learned not to trust them. You probably would have gotten over that if Billy hadn't died and you can't forgive him for being wrong. He was your first love. I remember you told me he'd promised you he would get well, and you believed him. Then he died. It's been nearly eight years and you're still mad at Aunt Charity. It's not her fault that she wasn't in the country when her brother was killed. Was she supposed to live next door all those years, just in case?"

"Of course not." Chloe knew her voice was stiff, but she was having trouble speaking past the tightness in her throat. "I'm not a closed, unforgiving person."

Cassie's fingers squeezed her own. "That's not what I meant. You're a wonderful person and I love you very much. But sometimes, you're so stubborn I just want to shake some sense into you. Let the past go. Look forward for once. Don't lose this wonderful opportunity with Arizona. When are you going to meet someone like him again?"

"You make it sound so simple."

"It can be, if you let it."

Chloe looked at her sister. She wanted to believe her, but she couldn't. Cassie was right—after nearly eight years, she *was* still angry at Aunt Charity. The woman should have known that her brother had died. There was no excuse for staying out of contact for more than three years. If not for her, Chloe and Cassie wouldn't have been sent to foster homes. They wouldn't have been separated. She wouldn't have met Billy.

Chloe stiffened. *She wouldn't have met Billy.* Was that what she wanted? To never have known him?

She turned the thought over in her mind. She regretted his death. It had hurt to love him. But even knowing he was going to die, she wasn't sure she would have wished him out of her life. She'd learned a lot from him. She'd learned about courage and dignity. She'd learned about giving her whole heart and she'd learned about pain.

"What are you thinking?" Cassie asked.

"That this is all so complicated. I should have been more like you and gotten involved with someone like Joel."

"He could never make you happy."

Chloe wanted to ask if he made her happy, but this wasn't the time.

"What are you going to do now?" Cassie asked.

"I don't know." Chloe gave her a smile, squeezed her

hand once, then rose to her feet. "I can't make any decisions until I've thought this through. I'm not going to call him or anything. I'll let him make the next move."

"You need to distract yourself." Cassie glanced at her watch. "It's not that late. Do you want to go to a movie or something?"

"Not tonight. I think I'll try to work on my article. I won't be able to get Arizona out of my mind, so I might as well take advantage of that."

She headed for the stairs, then paused and faced her sister. "Thanks for listening to me. I appreciate it."

"That's part of the job." Cassie grinned. "At least there's good news about the situation."

"What's that?"

"Now that you've slept with him, you really will be able to write an 'intimate' portrait of the man."

ARIZONA LEFT THE hotel bar and headed up to his room. He wasn't much of a drinker, but one beer didn't go very far to help him forget his troubles.

As he left the elevator and started toward his room, he wondered again what had gone wrong with Chloe. Okay, he should have told her about the helicopter, but he really didn't think it was that big a deal. If she hadn't been receptive, he wouldn't have tried anything. It wasn't as if he'd had to talk her into making love with him.

He hated feeling like this—knowing that she was upset and not being able to understand why. It made him crazy that even though they could both agree on the facts and the blame, he still couldn't understand why she was so hurt by everything. It was, he decided as he used the card to unlock the door, a chick thing. Men and women were incredibly different creatures. It was amazing that the species hadn't died out several millennia ago.

The first thing he noticed when he walked into the room was the blinking message light on his phone. Chloe. She'd called! He cursed himself for not coming directly to his room. What if she wanted to see him? What if she was on her way over? She could be sitting by the phone right this minute, assuming his silence meant he was angry with her.

After tossing his backpack on the floor, he picked up the receiver and punched the numbers so that he could listen to her message.

But the voice he heard after the computer instructed him to punch "1" to hear his messages wasn't Chloe's but his father's.

"Hello, Arizona. I've been reading about the gem find and your lecture series in the paper. I wondered how you were doing. I thought I might come out to California to sit in on a couple of your talks. Please give me a call when you have a moment."

Arizona angrily hit "3" to erase the message, then sank onto the blue sofa. He swore under his breath. As if he didn't already have enough trouble in his life.

He didn't want to call back. For several minutes he thought about ignoring the message and all it implied. But he couldn't. However, he could tell the old man to get off his back.

He dialed the area code for Chicago, then the number he'd known all his life. His father answered on the first ring.

"Yes?"

"It's Arizona."

"Son, thanks for calling."

Arizona flinched. He hated being called "son" almost as much as he hated the pleasure in the older man's voice. Grant Smith had finally decided to recognize his only child's existence about thirty years too late for Arizona's taste.

"How are you?" his father asked.

"Fine."

"The series going well?"

"It starts day after tomorrow, but I'm sure it will be fine." He knew his voice sounded stiff, as if he were talking to someone he didn't really like. In a way he was. His father was a stranger. The fact that he now wanted a relationship with his son didn't change the fact that he'd abandoned his son the day he'd been born.

"I've been reading about it here. There's quite a bit of coverage. You know the sort of thing. Hometown boy does good and all that. I'm very proud of you."

Arizona made a noncommittal sound low in his throat. "How's the weather in Chicago?" he asked.

"Still chilly. Listen, son. I was thinking of flying out for a few days. I would like to listen to your series."

"That's not a great idea. I'm only in town until the lectures are finished. The next day I leave for the South Pacific."

"One of those small islands with no electricity or phones?"

"Exactly. I'll be there for three months. Besides, you know you hate to travel. Why put yourself out?"

"Because I want to see you. It's been nearly a year."

"Compared to the first twenty or thirty years I was around, we're doing much better," he said dryly.

There was a moment of silence. His father exhaled into the phone. "Is that why you're making this so difficult? I just want us to spend time together."

"Why? We don't have a whole lot to talk about."

"We're the only family we have left, Arizona. You're my son. You matter."

"You know, Grant, you waited too long to figure that out. I needed you when I was growing up."

"My father took excellent care of you," the older man said stiffly.

"He did the best he could, which is more than we can say for you. But you know what he was like. I can't tell you how many times he forgot I was along and left me behind in some village somewhere. But you never cared about that. You were too busy trying to forget I was alive. Just because you've finally remembered doesn't mean I have to give a damn."

"We're family," his father repeated. "I'm not going to give up on you."

"That's your choice. But I'm not going to change my mind."

"I can be as stubborn as you. Perhaps that's where you get it from. Have a good trip, Arizona. I'll be in touch when you get back in the fall. I love you, son."

Arizona hung up without saying goodbye.

He stared at the phone, hating both his father for wanting back into his life after all this time, and himself for being such a bastard. If only he could just turn his back and have it not matter. Unfortunately it did matter. Too much. To add insult to injury, he almost understood the old man.

Grant Smith had loved his wife with a passion that lasted more than thirty years past her death. Arizona didn't understand that kind of devotion, but he respected it. If only his father had been able to turn a little of that devotion toward his son. But he hadn't. Instead Grant had hired a series of nannies to take care of the boy. He'd left the infant and the staff in the large house by the lake and had moved into a small apartment on his own.

Once his grandfather had shown up and claimed him,

he'd traveled with the old man from then on. Arizona had been twenty-five the first time he'd met his father.

He leaned back on the sofa and groaned. He couldn't do this tonight—he couldn't deal with these demons, too. He didn't want to be alone. But he was in a strange city and he didn't have many friends here. The truth was there was only one person he wanted to see right now.

He glanced at the clock. It was nearly ten. Too late to be calling her. Besides, she was still furious with him. Even so, he picked up the receiver and dialed.

She answered the phone on the first ring. "Hello?"

"It's Arizona. I—" What was he going to say? In the end, there was only the truth. "I need you. It's not what you think," he added quickly. "My father called. He wants… Hell, that doesn't matter. It's just I never know what to say to him. I was a complete idiot. I'm stuck in this hotel room, I'm alone and lonely and I didn't know who else to call. I just want to be with you. I want to see you and hear your voice. We're friends, right? Or did I mess that up, too?"

She didn't answer. If he hadn't heard her faint breathing, he might have thought she'd hung up on him.

"It's not about sex," he told her. "I swear."

"Oh, Arizona, you make it so hard to stay mad at you. Yes, we're still friends. Yes, I'll come over. I want to talk, but I'd be lying if I didn't tell you that I *want* it to be about sex, too."

CHAPTER TWELVE

ARIZONA LEANED BACK against the sofa and sighed with contentment. The remnants of their room service meal had been put out into the hallway. There was still wine in the bottle sitting in the ice bucket and two servings of chocolate mousse waiting for them. This, he thought, was how it was supposed to be. These were the moments that made up a good life.

It wasn't all about the food either, he reminded himself as he glanced to his left and saw Chloe curled up on the sofa next to him. Before coming over she'd showered and changed into a pale green sleeveless dress. The filmy fabric flowed over her body. She'd tucked her bare legs under her and left her long curls loose around her shoulders. She looked different from the sensibly dressed companion he'd had the previous day on their hike. He liked how she changed to fit the circumstances. He'd thought she was as beautiful yesterday as today and he still believed that.

But what took his breath away wasn't her attractive features or tempting body—it was the fact that she was here…in his room. He rarely invited women to his room. Because of his travel schedule, he didn't make a permanent home anywhere, so his hotel and motel rooms were his sanctuary. When he was intimate with a woman, they generally went to her place, or they were somewhere in the wilderness where rooms didn't really matter. Still it felt right to have Chloe here, with him. She was more completion than intrusion.

"You're looking pensive about something," she said, her voice low. "Want to talk about it?"

He shrugged. "It's not important. I was just thinking that I never invite women up to my room. I prefer to keep all this private."

"And the outdoors is neutral," she said.

He glanced at her, but she didn't look angry. "Exactly."

"Then I'm honored, both that you would trust me not to violate your space here, and because you called me when you needed a friend." Her gaze was steady. She took a sip of her wine, then tilted her head slightly to the left. "Tell me about your father."

Arizona knew the conversation couldn't be put off forever. No doubt he would feel better *after* talking about it; he just didn't want to talk about it now. Unfortunately he couldn't think of a good excuse to put Chloe off.

"It's not a nice story," he warned her.

"Are you afraid I'll think less of you as a person?"

"The thought did cross my mind."

She put her wine on the coffee table. "I could tease you and promise that wasn't possible, but that would be taking unfair advantage." She paused for a second. "Whatever has happened between us, however complicated it gets, I've enjoyed knowing you. You're different from anyone I've ever met, but that's just on the surface. Underneath all the travel and the unusual experiences, you're very familiar to me. I think we have a lot in common and I believe we can be friends for a long time. I'll try not to judge you."

"I guess I can't ask for more than that." Their gazes locked. "Thank you," he added. "I want us to be friends, too."

A smile tugged at her lips. "Tell you what. When you're done talking about your father, I'll think up something equally slimy in my life and share it with you. Then we'll be even."

"Sure." But he doubted she could match his story. He drew in a deep breath. "My mother died when I was born. Apparently she and my father were deeply in love. They'd put off having children for several years because they just wanted it to be the two of them. But when she found out she was pregnant, I guess they were both happy. After her death, my father withdrew. He hired a nurse and a couple of people to take care of the place, then he moved out. I never saw him. He provided a staff and paid all the bills, but he was not a part of my life."

He tried to tell the story without thinking about it. He didn't want to get buried in the details, he didn't want to think about what it had been like all those years.

"As I told you before, my grandfather showed up when I was three and took me away with him. When I was about fifteen, he answered questions I had about my family. He never used the word 'blame' but I understood the subtext of what he was saying. If it hadn't been for me, my mother would still be alive."

Chloe shifted closer and took his hand in hers. She squeezed his fingers. "That's a lot for an adult to understand. It must have been an impossible burden for a teenager."

"Agreed. When I was growing up I used to make up stories about my father—exotic tales in which he came to his senses, realized none of this was my fault and showed up begging for my forgiveness. Every night I prayed he would come for me, but he never did." He cleared his throat. "I really cared about my grandfather. He did the best he could and I had some great experiences as a kid, but there were times I longed for a normal family. I wanted to have my own room, toys, friends, and wake up in the same bed for a few weeks. Then I outgrew the dream. I stopped praying my father would come for me. At times I forgot he was alive."

"I don't believe you gave up the dream," Chloe said. "I think you still have it, but now you're an adult and it's more complicated."

"Not at all. In fact—"

She cut him off with a shake of her head. "Sell it somewhere else, Arizona. Of course you wanted your father to come rescue you. We all want to be loved. But you stopped wishing because it hurt too much to always be disappointed."

He wanted to tell her she was wrong, but he couldn't. "How the hell do you know so much?"

"Things are always clearer to those on the outside. Don't worry, your secret is safe with me."

"I never doubted that for a moment."

He wanted to pull her closer. He wanted to feel her heat next to him, to wrap his arms around her and find comfort in her nearness. He didn't. Not because he was concerned she might reject him, but because the need was so intense, it alarmed him. He wasn't supposed to need anyone. If his past had taught him anything, it was that. He'd grown up in such a way that his dependence had been burned out of him at an early age. Needing someone meant having expectations. That only gave that person the opportunity to let you down. He didn't need Chloe—he didn't need anyone.

"What happened next?" she asked.

"He contacted me when I was about twenty. I was in London. He wanted me to come to Chicago and meet with him." He tried to ignore the hurt and anger welling up inside of him.

"You refused." It wasn't a question.

"Yes. He was stubborn and kept talking away. I guess I get that trait from him."

"Did he apologize for what he'd done?"

"In a manner of speaking. He said that he'd been keeping track of me for years, that he'd wanted to get in touch sooner, bring me home, but I was doing so well with my grandfather that he decided not to upset my life twice."

"Sounds reasonable."

"It does, doesn't it." His tone was sharp.

She squeezed his fingers gently. "You didn't believe him then?"

"Of course not. He was taking the easy way out. I exploded. I told him that he was about twenty years too late to be a part of my life. I wasn't interested in him as a father or a friend. As far as I was concerned, he should never contact me again. But he kept at me." He sighed heavily before continuing. "Finally, I told him what life with my grandfather had been like. I told him about the times I'd been injured or put in dangerous situations. I detailed how my grandfather had often left me behind in strange villages or towns with minimal supervision while he ran off and explored something he considered too dangerous for a child. I told him that I'd been left in the outback with a guide who disappeared and left me, that my grandfather had forgotten where to find me and that I nearly starved to death. I told him there weren't any words to make up for that. I said I didn't want to see him or hear from him ever again. Then I hung up the phone."

He felt uncomfortable with what he'd told her, but there was no way to recall the words. "I did warn you it wasn't going to be pleasant."

She ignored that comment. "What happened when he called back?"

"How do you know he did?"

She looked at him. "What else would he do? He called and apologized for all of that. What did you say?"

"That it was too late."

She didn't say anything for a while, then she pulled her hand from his. The rejection stung. Arizona had thought she might be upset or disappointed, but he hadn't expected her to simply turn away.

He shifted to push off the sofa, but before he could, her arms came around him. She moved close and rested her head on his shoulders as she clasped him around the waist.

"You were so young to be dealing with all of that," she said, her voice muffled against his neck. "Twenty isn't really grown-up. You had more life experiences than most kids your age, but I doubt you were any more emotionally mature. He'd hurt you for so many years. You just wanted to hurt him back."

Her understanding loosened the tight band around his chest. He hugged her back. "Thank you," he murmured.

"No problem. To be honest, I'd imagined something a lot worse."

"Like what? Felony convictions in several states?"

She smiled. "Something like that." She kissed his jaw. "I appreciate you sharing this with me. I just have one question. When are you going to let it go? You can't stay angry at him forever. Yes, it hurts him and in a way you still want that, but it hurts you, too."

Arizona straightened and pushed her away. "Thanks for the junior psychology analysis, but it's not necessary." Irritation battled with disappointment. He'd thought she would understand, but she didn't.

"Why are you upset?" she asked. She slid away a couple of feet and stared at him. Her eyebrows drew together. "You wanted to talk about this. If you hadn't, you wouldn't have asked me to come over. You know me well enough by now to know I'm not going to keep quiet, that I'm going to express my opinion. Isn't that what you wanted?"

She made sense and that really annoyed him. "Maybe I just wanted to get you into bed."

He'd expected her to flinch. Instead she shook her head. "If that was true, you would have made your move before now. I've been here two hours and you've barely touched me." She drew in a deep breath, then tucked her hair behind her ears. Her mouth straightened. "Hasn't it occurred to you that the reason I can understand your situation with your father is that I'm facing something similar myself? You're not the only one caught up in the past. You're not the only one who is angry. You think I don't feel the same way? It's hard, Arizona. You want to reconcile with your father, but you don't know if he's suffered enough. I want to forgive my parents, and Billy, and even Aunt Charity, but the pain and anger are all I have. If I let that go, will I lose the last little bits of them and myself that I have?"

"You're making sense," he grumbled. "I really hate that."

"It's hard," she told him. "I am so furious at my parents. I hate them for dying. I hate them for naming Aunt Charity as our guardian. Because of that Cassie and I got split up. I hate that they left me the house. I'm their daughter by birth and the house has been in the family for generations, but it was still wrong." Anger flashed in her eyes. "People matter more than things and they should have recognized how their actions would hurt Cassie.

She has always felt like an outsider. Her only goal in life is to belong. To find roots. That's why she desperately wants the family legend about the nightgown to be true. So she can wear it on her birthday and dream about her fantasy man."

Arizona cupped her cheek. Chloe leaned into his touch. "I'll never forgive Billy for dying after he promised he wouldn't," she continued. "I'm enraged at Aunt Charity for being gone. I know, she had her own life. No one expected her to stay home in case her brother died without warning. I know it, but I can't make my heart believe it. I live with this pain and rage and so do you. But I'm starting to see that we have to figure out a way to let it go. We both hurt, Arizona. But if the wound stays open too long, it gets infected and then we die. I'm not talking about real death, but emotional death. Isn't that worse? Is that more tragic?"

"I don't know."

He held his arms open and she came into them. They hugged each other. He'd felt close to her from the moment he'd met her. Their lovemaking had only cemented the strange bond he couldn't explain. But that was nothing when compared to what he was feeling now. He'd never felt this connected to another person in his life. They came from completely different backgrounds. They believed different things. Chloe was a realist and he made his living searching for the mystical. Yet underneath, they were exactly alike.

"See," she whispered, her breath coming in short puffs against his chest. "I'm a horrible person."

"No, you're a very honest one and I admire that."

"Were you listening? I can't believe it's been eleven years and I'm still mad at my folks. I've got to learn to let that go."

"Hey, it's been more than thirty years and I still don't like talking to my father. I'm much worse."

"No, I am."

He chuckled. "Interesting argument that for reasons I can't explain I feel compelled to win. When I was ten and we were in Africa, I sneaked into the tribal elder's tent and stole a pipe. I got all the other boys to smoke it with me and we all ended up sick."

"Not bad. When *I* was ten, Cassie got a new dress for some reason, and I didn't. I was so furious, I threatened to hold my breath until I got one, too. My mother wasn't impressed. Unfortunately for her, I actually did hold it until I passed out. I really scared her. Once I learned the trick, I kept doing it for about six months. I thought she was going to kill me."

He smiled and kissed the top of her head. "I stole an elephant."

"Goodness. Where on earth would you hide it?"

"I didn't. I took it for a joyride. Well, sort of. We didn't go very fast."

She laughed. "I convinced Cassie to surprise our parents by scenting their bedroom. I had her pour perfume on the bed and the carpet. The stink would not go away. They ended up getting a new mattress and carpeting."

"I don't know if I can top that one," he told her.

Her laughter was soft and sweet. He liked this, he realized. Being with her, holding her, laughing together. He felt safe talking about his past. Even if Chloe didn't agree, she wouldn't judge him. She might speak her mind and say some things he didn't want to hear, but that was a small price to pay for acceptance. Besides, he liked that she was honest.

"It's good that we're spending time with each other,"

she said. "I doubt anyone else would want to put up with us."

"You know that's not true."

She tilted her head back and looked at him. "You're right, I do. But it's fun to pretend." Her humor faded. "I'm glad we talked about all of this. Our conversation has shown me that it's time to let go of the past."

"Are you ready?"

"I think so." She pulled back and gave him a rueful smile. "I don't mind forgiving my parents or Billy. It wasn't really their fault they died. But not being mad at Aunt Charity is going to be harder. I didn't get it until just a few moments ago when we started talking about all this, but I finally understand what's been going on with her. By staying angry, I didn't have to worry about her getting too close. If she died or left, I wouldn't miss her. This has all been a way to protect myself from getting hurt."

"I'm impressed," he said, and tapped the tip of her nose. "That's very insightful."

"I don't mind being insightful, but I really resent having to act on what I've discovered. Still, I'm a strong person and keeping her at arm's length out of fear is the coward's way out. I'm going to have to make peace with her and deal with the consequences."

"I'm sure she's going to live a long life and you won't have to worry about losing her anytime soon."

"I hope you're right, but it doesn't matter. I can't spend the rest of my life avoiding caring about someone because I'm afraid they're going to leave me or run away."

She raised her chin in a gesture of strength and defiance. He respected both her decision and her fearlessness. Self-examination was never easy. He knew that firsthand. But if Chloe hadn't gone easy on herself—could he do any less?

He looked at the phone. He knew what his father wanted and why. Was that enough? Could he let go of the past and forgive an old man who had been driven by pain and loss? The adult side of him was willing to give it a chance, but the hurt child inside wanted restitution. Unfortunately there was nothing his father could do to make up for hurting him.

"Only if it feels right," Chloe whispered.

It did.

He picked up the receiver and dialed the number from memory. His father answered on the first ring.

"It's Arizona."

"I didn't expect to hear from you, son." His father sounded surprised, but pleased. There was no wariness in his voice, no attempt to protect himself against possible attack.

Arizona glanced at his watch. "I didn't realize the time. It's after midnight. I'm sorry if I woke you."

"You didn't. That's one of the ironies of old age. I have less to do with my day than ever before, yet I need less sleep. I could have used this time twenty years ago but that's what happens."

"I'm sorry I was such a jerk when you called earlier."

The older man sighed heavily. "Don't apologize. You have every right to be furious with me. What I did…I won't try to excuse it. I was wrong. I've realized that over the years. I should have known that you and I could help each other out. But I was too caught up in my pain. I was so selfish."

"I understand."

"You don't have to, son. Your mother—" His voice broke. "She was my world. When I lost her, I wanted to die, too. I didn't care about anything or anyone. I'm so sorry about that. Even as I left you alone, I knew it was wrong. I knew she would be disappointed in me if she ever knew. But I couldn't stop myself."

"It's okay." He cleared his throat. "Dad, really, it is."

Dad. He'd never said the word before. He'd always used "Father" or "old man." Nothing friendly or personal.

Chloe moved close to him. He put his arm around her and squeezed. She was his lifeline in this unfamiliar sea of emotion.

"I should have come after you," his father continued. "I didn't want you to go away, but it was also easier to try and forget with you out of the country. I didn't know about all you went through," he said quietly. "With your grandfather. I thought he would take better care of you. I should have realized the truth. I'm sorry about that, too."

Arizona suffered through a flash of guilt. "There were some tough times," he said. "But it wasn't all bad. I learned a lot. I wouldn't be doing what I do today, if I hadn't traveled all over the world."

"I appreciate you trying to make me feel better, but I know what I did and didn't do. I was never a father to you. But if it's not too late, perhaps we could get to know each other and become friends."

Arizona thought of all the times he'd refused the older man's invitations. Of all the times he'd sworn at him, hung up on him or ignored him. Yet his father was still trying, still asking to see him. His father was the only family he had. Why was he willing to let that bond stay broken?

His chest was tight and it was hard to speak. Even so he forced himself to say, "I'd like that. I'm going to be busy until I leave for the island, but we could get together when I get back."

"Could I come see you this summer? On the island?"

Despite the emotion flooding him, Arizona couldn't repress a grin. How would his banker father, a man who had only ever loved one woman in his life, who had mourned her for more than thirty years, survive in a society run for and by women? Visitors were often seduced by widows and unmarried females. Arizona had been in a couple of difficult situations himself until the shaman had taken him under her wing and offered protection.

"That might not be a bad idea," he said. "I'll get together some literature and send it along to you. If you decide you want to make the trip, you can let me know and I'll meet you in Guam."

"I'd like that, son." His father cleared his throat. "It *is* late and I should probably let you go. Thanks for giving me another chance."

"You're welcome. Thank you for not giving up on me."

"I love you, son."

Arizona sucked in a breath. "You, too, Dad. I'll talk to you soon."

He waited until his father hung up the phone before he replaced the receiver. He glanced at Chloe and saw tears on her cheeks.

"That was so great," she told him. "I'm so glad you called him and talked to him. How do you feel?"

"A little strange. Relieved and nervous, I guess. I'm not sure about him visiting me." He told her a little about the culture on the island. "My father is nearly seventy. I think he might be threatened by the ladies wanting to take his equipment for a test-drive."

Chloe wiped her face with the back of her hand and smiled. "It might be just the thing he needs to give him a new lease on life."

"I hadn't thought of that. You're right. He might enjoy

the challenge." He closed his eyes and rubbed his temples. "How does everything get so complicated? These familial relationships get twisted and broken and yet we stumble on. My grandfather abandoned his own wife and child to travel the world. He was an adventurer at heart. He told me once that he never should have married, but when a girl from a good family turns up pregnant, there's not much a man can do."

"Your father grew up without *his* father?" Chloe asked.

Arizona nodded. "He swore he would be different, that he would marry for love and never leave her side. Which was true, even in death. But he also abandoned me as he had been abandoned."

"So he only learned part of the lesson."

He shrugged, not sure what his father had learned. Maybe they were all doomed to repeat each other's mistakes.

"You break the cycle by not believing in love and I assume as a by-product of that, not marrying or having children," Chloe said, as if she could read his mind.

"Something like that."

"It is one way to deal with the problem."

"Not one you approve of?" he asked.

"It's not my place to approve or disapprove," she told him. "I'm just glad you want to work things out with your father and that you're going to see him soon."

"Me, too." He wanted to say more. He wanted to tell her that she was so incredibly beautiful, sitting there in the lamplight. He wanted to tell her that he appreciated the fact that she'd agreed to talk with him tonight, to be a friend when he needed one. Her support had given him the strength to do what was right.

But he couldn't find the words. He could only look at her and want her.

Something must have shown on his face because she smiled faintly, then leaned close. "Fine," she whispered, her breath soft and sweet against his face. "Change the subject if you have to. I don't mind."

Then she kissed him.

His body responded instantly. Even as Arizona moved his mouth against her, heat filled him as blood rushed to make him ready to take her. He was hard and aching in less than ten seconds.

There was little time for tenderness. They touched each other everywhere. Even as he tried to slow down, Chloe tugged at his clothing and whispered words of encouragement, telling him how much she needed him to be in her. When he touched her panties, he found her ready for him. He slipped past the elastic band and pressed a finger deep inside of her. She surged against him. As he kissed her, he cupped a breast with his free hand and toyed with the tight nipple. He moved his finger in and out of her. Within seconds he felt the rhythmic pulsing of her most feminine place surging around, drawing him in deeper. She broke the kiss enough to gasp out his name as her pleasure continued.

From then on it was a blur. One minute they were still half-dressed and on the sofa. The next they were on top of the bed, their clothes forming an untidy trail on the carpet. He plunged into her and felt her climax again. There was no way to stop either of them, he realized. The passion burned away social convention and left them only with driving need.

He dug his fingers into her hair to hold her still. She grabbed his hips and forced him in deeper. Their kisses were hot and wild and when she bucked against him in yet a third release, he exploded into her.

They clung to each other as the fire cooled. They were

both slick with sweat and panting. Arizona slid out of her and settled next to her on the bed. Chloe came into his arms and they snuggled in a position that had so quickly become familiar.

Holding her felt so right, he told himself, and it was the last thought he had that night.

HE FELT HER stir sometime well before dawn. Arizona turned onto his side and squinted as she clicked on the lamp on the nightstand.

"Good morning," she said softly, her eyes still heavy with sleep and her hair mussed. "I'm sorry to wake you, but I have to get to the house."

He nodded. "I didn't mean to fall asleep. Sorry." He motioned to his hotel room. "I know it wouldn't do for someone to see you sneaking out of my room in the middle of the morning."

"There would be talk," she agreed with a smile. "I have to go home and work on my article, but why don't you try and get some sleep? You start your lecture series tonight."

"I just might do that."

He watched as she pulled on clothes. When she was dressed, she crossed to the bed and kissed his cheek. "I'll see you tonight."

He grabbed her hand. "Dinner? After the lecture?"

"I'd like that. Thank you."

He squeezed her fingers. When she pulled away, he didn't want to let her go. He wanted to tell her something, but the words eluded him.

Don't go.

Was that it? Did he want to keep her with him? But before he could figure it out, she'd stepped into the hall and quietly closed the door behind her. He rolled onto her side of the bed. The sheets were still warm from her body and they smelled of their lovemaking. But it wasn't enough. The room had grown cold and empty without her presence. As perhaps, he thought grimly, had his life.

CHAPTER THIRTEEN

CHLOE STARED AT the pile of notes sitting on the corner of her desk. She had too much material. It was, she supposed, the problem to have. After all, too *much* to work with meant she would only be using the very best of what she had instead of scrambling for things to fill the pages. Unfortunately, she was having trouble figuring out what to cut and what to keep. She wanted to keep it all. The article was about Arizona and she thought he was pretty wonderful.

"Not that I'm biased in the least," she said aloud, then shifted in her seat. Her insides still felt a little squishy from their lovemaking the previous night. What a way to go to sleep. If only they could do that every night.

She smiled at the thought and had a bad feeling that she was glowing with happiness. As long as the glow wasn't the least bit magnetic, she wouldn't hurt her computer. Unfortunately, she also wasn't in the mood to get any work done, either.

On a whim, she closed her word-processing program and logged onto the Internet. She found her way to Arizona's fan club. She'd noticed an icon for a bulletin board. Feeling more than a little foolish, she wrote a quick post saying that while the man was completely brilliant, he was also a hunk and wasn't that just as important as his work?

Giggling softly, she posted the message, then went

to check her E-mail. After responding to her mail, she returned to the bulletin board to see if anyone had read her comments. She was stunned to see several replies. Two women agreed completely and went on to describe him in such detail that Chloe wondered if she should feel jealous. Then a third message appeared, this one berating Chloe for her shallowness. That the wonder of Arizona Smith wasn't in his physical appearance, but in the magic of his work. He was more than just a man. He was a symbol for the mystic world. He was a true hero.

She logged off the Internet. She didn't want to talk about Arizona with people who had never met him. She wanted to talk about who he really was and how he made her feel.

He *was* amazing—she could concede that with no problem. He was intelligent, gifted, motivated, kind. But like everyone else, he had his faults. He was a little self-centered and he could be stubborn. He wasn't perfect, but he was someone she could...

He was someone she could love. Someone she did love.

Chloe placed her elbows on the desk and rested her head in her hands. Love? No, that wasn't part of the plan. She wasn't supposed to love him. She was supposed to find him interesting and entertaining, nothing more. Not love. That was too dangerous. She'd learned her lesson. She didn't want to go there again. Because of her past, she'd been avoiding love for a long time. This situation with Arizona had pain written all over it.

"Why me? Why now?"

But there weren't any answers. Maybe it was the luck of the draw, or just her time. She thought she'd been so careful to hide her heart away. But she hadn't. At least not this time. She'd been so stunned when she'd first met him. Because of the dream, she reminded herself.

"So much for the magic nightgown," she said as she straightened in her chair. Didn't the family legend promise a lifetime of happiness? But that wasn't possible with Arizona. He wasn't a man who would be content to stay in one place for very long, and she was the kind of woman who needed a home. There would be no happily-ever-after for her. The only guarantee she had was that he would leave in just a few days and she would be heartbroken.

"I don't need this," she told herself. Not again. She didn't want to love him but it was too late. Love him she did.

A knock on the door interrupted her thoughts. She glanced up and saw Aunt Charity standing in the doorway. The older woman wore tailored slacks and a shirt, the conservative clothing emphasizing a figure that had stayed trim all her life. Her long dark hair was up in its customary French twist. She offered a smile.

"It's nearly lunchtime and you never even bothered with breakfast. I've brought you a snack." She placed the tray on the desk.

Chloe glanced at the pot of tea, the sandwiches and bowl of fruit. "Thank you," she said, forcing her voice to sound soft and grateful. Her natural tendency was to be belligerent with her aunt. Her conversation with Arizona about letting go of the past was still fresh in her mind. "You went to a lot of trouble and I appreciate that."

"You're welcome." As always, Charity's smile was open. "You've been working hard on your project. How is it going?"

"Very well. My biggest problem is that I have too much material. I've made an outline of the topics I want to cover. Now I have to start eliminating the nonessentials. Unfortunately, Arizona is so interesting to write about that I want to include everything."

"That's even before you hear his lecture series."

Chloe nodded. The series started that night. "I've included a section for them, but I don't know how long it's going to be. One of the things I want to focus on is the man rather than the myths about him. I mean, the information about the fan club is fun and I enjoy teasing him about it, but he's more than just that."

Charity placed her hands in the front pockets in her slacks. "I remember the first time Arizona and I met. As I recall, he was surrounded by a group of young women. It was in India—the outskirts of—"

She paused, then sighed. "Never mind. It's not important. I should let you get back to your work. I didn't mean to interrupt." She turned to leave.

Chloe pressed her lips together. Had she really been shutting her aunt out so very much, she didn't feel comfortable telling a story about Arizona? The truth made her flush with embarrassment and shame. She rose to her feet.

"Aunt Charity, wait."

The older woman paused expectantly. Chloe tried to figure out what she wanted to say. She wasn't feeling very brave right now, but she reminded herself that Arizona had been able to make peace with his father and their history had been a lot more complicated and difficult than hers with her aunt. All she had to do was speak from her heart.

"I'm sorry," she began. "I've been a real brat and a pain. I have no excuse. I'm twenty-five, which is plenty old enough to act like an adult. I even had the fantasy that I was being subtle, but I haven't been, have I?"

Charity shrugged. "Only if you secretly think I'm a wonderful person."

"Actually, I do. I just didn't realize it until recently.

You came to Cassie and me as soon as you found out what had happened. You made a home for us, and you've stayed here all these years, even though we would be fine on our own. You'd spent your whole life seeing the world, yet in the past seven and a half years, I don't think you've as much as left the state. I never realized that before. I never thought about what you'd given up to be with us."

Her aunt stepped toward her and cupped her face in her hands. Chloe allowed the physical contact, then found, much to her surprise, she didn't mind being touched.

"You don't have to apologize. I understand," Charity told her. "You had lost your parents and were separated from your sister. It was a difficult time."

"You lost your brother," Chloe pointed out. "I never thought about that, either. We'd had three years to get over the pain of missing them, but you only found out a few days before. I was so angry and hurt, and that was all I could think about. I'm sorry."

"Let's both agree to stop blaming and stop apologizing. We can start over."

"I'd like that," Chloe said, suddenly feeling shy. She motioned to the bed and when Charity sat on the mattress, she took her seat at the desk and swiveled to face her aunt. There were still things to be said between them.

"Cassie and I appreciate all you've done for us, but you've given up enough. Don't you think it's time you started living your own life?"

"Are you throwing me out?" Charity asked, a smile softening the question.

"Of course not. This is your home. At least I hope you think of it that way. But you've always traveled. Don't you miss that? Don't you want to get back out in the world?"

Charity paused to consider the question. Her dark hair was sleek and the color reminded Chloe of her father.

He'd been a handsome man and his sister was equally attractive.

"That's an interesting question," Charity said. "I'll admit when I first moved to Bradley, I didn't think I could survive in this small town. While I loved you two girls and was pleased to help in any way, it was difficult knowing that I couldn't pack up and move on whenever I wanted. But gradually, I began to fit in. I'm not sure I could travel the way I did before. Of course there are a few trips I would like to make, but none of them are pressing."

Chloe leaned forward. "Then stay. When you're ready, make plans. Cassie and I are completely capable of handling things on our own."

Charity nodded. "I've known that for a long time. You're both very responsible." She shook her head. "I'm glad we had this talk, Chloe. I've wanted to get this settled for a long time, but I was never sure what to say. Which is so unlike me. I usually have a sense about these sort of things. But then I didn't know about my brother's death, so maybe I've outgrown the gift."

Chloe grinned. "I've heard these stories before. How you always just kind of *know* things. You can probably convince Arizona and Cassie, both of whom want to believe, but I remain a skeptic. I'll agree we can all have a gut instinct about things, but actual intuition…no way."

"Oh really. Is that a challenge?"

Chloe was enjoying the conversation with her aunt. Fierce regret filled her. If only she'd been willing to talk to her like this before. They could have been friends for years. "If you think you're up to it, yes."

"The stories I could tell you," Charity said. "I wouldn't want to shock you."

"So far all I'm hearing is cheap talk. Do you have at least one example?"

"Of course." The older woman crossed her legs, then gave Chloe a knowing look. "You dreamed about Arizona Smith the night you wore the family nightgown. Before you ask, no, Cassie didn't tell me after you finally confessed everything to her."

Chloe hadn't known what to expect. She'd thought her aunt might bring up some minor transgression from high school. Something that she, Chloe, had thought she'd gotten away with. She hadn't expected this—that her aunt had known the truth all along. Or had she?

"When did you figure it out?" she asked.

Charity's dark eyes were kind, her expression loving. "The next morning. It was so obvious from the look on your face that you'd dreamed about someone interesting. Then you heard the television and glanced at the screen. For a second I thought you were going to faint. Your reaction to Arizona that night merely confirmed my suspicions."

Suddenly a few pieces of the puzzle fell into place. "Did you invite him here deliberately so that I would meet him?"

Charity placed her hand flat against her chest. "Would I do that? Of course not. I had always planned to invite Arizona over during his visit. I'll admit that seeing your reaction to him sped up the timetable a little, but that's all."

"Oh, that's all." Chloe didn't know whether to laugh or bury her face in her hands. She'd been set up. No wonder she'd had the feeling that she couldn't escape the man. Fate might have conspired when she'd been given the article assignment, but it hadn't been working alone. Aunt Charity had been a willing accomplice.

"I'm impressed," she admitted. "You do know things."

"I know something else."

"I'm almost afraid to ask, but here goes. What?"

"You're in love with him, but you don't want to admit it."

Chloe slumped back in her chair. "I know. I am, at least I think I am. I've been fighting it for a while. I don't want to love anyone else. It always hurts."

"Honey, if that's the lesson you learned from your parents' death, then you learned the wrong lesson. Yes, they were taken far too soon, but they still lived. They had each other and you girls. They were happy and they were wonderful people. You should be grateful you had any time with them, not bitter because it hurt when they were gone. If it hadn't been painful, then they wouldn't have been worth loving."

Her words almost made sense. Chloe backed away from the truth. "It's not just them. I've had other heartache."

"I know about the young man you fell in love with in high school. Cassie told me."

"He died," Chloe said firmly. "He was my life. I was seventeen and I loved with my whole heart. One day he was just gone."

Charity's mouth twisted down. "Would you rather have played it safe? Knowing what you know now, if you could turn back time, would you not have loved him?"

The question stung. Chloe sucked in a breath as pain shot through her chest. Knowing what she knew now, could she walk away from Billy? She'd wrestled with this question before.

She pictured his face in her mind, remembered the feel of his hand as he held hers. She thought about the whispered promises they'd made when they thought they had forever. They had been so in love with each other, so convinced that they would never need anyone else.

Those were magical times, she admitted to herself. They'd been so young and yet it had felt right. Would it have been better to play it safe?

"No," she whispered, answering both Aunt Charity's question and her own. "I would still have loved him. I would still have wanted to be there at the end, holding his hand." She blinked back the sudden tears. "Those last months were horrible. The family tried everything, Billy fought against the cancer, but in the end, it won. He wanted to die at home, so he did. We were all there, all trying to be brave for him. I remember he kept saying it was okay to cry."

She brushed at the tears on her cheeks. "He told me I had made his life worth living."

"I'm sure you did," her aunt told her. "That has value... for both of you."

Chloe nodded. Her throat was tight. "I remember his last breath. He exhaled and then was very still. We all waited, willing him to take in another breath, but he was gone. I thought I was going to die. I prayed to go with him so that we could always be together, just like we'd promised each other."

"But your life had a different path than his."

"I know that now, but at seventeen I was devastated."

Chloe thought about all her aunt had asked, all she'd asked herself. "I can't regret loving Billy," she said slowly. "Knowing what I know now, I would do it all again. I would love him and I would sit next to him on the bed and watch him die."

"We aren't always guaranteed a happy ending," Charity said. "But that doesn't mean we are allowed to stop loving. That is our purpose. Our great gift and sometimes the source of our sorrow. The world has much to offer, but first we must be willing to accept what is given. Love doesn't come for free, but it's always worth the effort."

"You're telling me not to be afraid to love Arizona."

"I'm telling you that you'll regret turning your back on the gift, if that's what's offered. But there are no promises, Chloe. You know that."

She didn't know. That was the problem. "In some ways we're so much alike, but in others…" She shook her head. "I've been thinking about what I've been doing. Here in Bradley, I mean. In my life. I keep telling everyone, including myself, that when I have the right number and types of articles, I'll go to New York and find a job with a big magazine. Isn't that the craziest thing you've ever heard?"

"No. You're very talented."

Chloe smiled. "Thanks, Aunt Charity, but that's not what I meant. I've been sitting here wondering what I'm waiting for. Why do I need the perfect article? If I can't get a writing job, I'll bet there's something I can do at a magazine. I can intern, or be an assistant for a while. I already work for a reputable publication. I know the industry. But I've been waiting for exactly the right circumstances."

Her aunt nodded. "You're starting to wonder if that's a symptom for something else."

"Exactly. I'm starting to think I don't want to leave Bradley. That I love this old house and this town. My family, my job, my friends. Somewhere along the line I got the idea that to be a 'real' writer, I had to go somewhere else. Otherwise, I didn't really have a dream. But my dreams can work here just as well. I don't have to move away and I'm starting to think I don't want to."

"Then don't. No one is making you go. I'm sure your

editor at the magazine right here would be thrilled to know you were staying."

"But what about Arizona?" Chloe asked softly. "I've just figured out that all I want in life is right here in my own backyard. Just like in the movies. There's no place like home. But the man I've fallen in love with doesn't have a real home. He travels the world."

"I see your point. It's an interesting dilemma."

Chloe rubbed her temples. "He's not perfect. In fact, I'm very clear on his flaws. He can be stubborn and he does impulsive things that make me crazy. But he's a good man, with a kind heart. He's not perfect, but he's exactly right for me." She looked at the older woman sitting across from her. "I don't know what to do."

"That's easy. Follow your heart."

"But it's not saying anything. I'm torn. On the one hand I want to stay in Bradley. On the other, I love Arizona. I don't see how I can win. Even if I asked him to take me with him and he agreed, I'm afraid I wouldn't be happy."

"There's another solution. Ask him to stay here."

Chloe shook her head. "That's not possible. You know him. He would hate being tied down to one place. All he knows is traveling. He's not interested in putting down roots."

"Maybe he's tired of what he's been doing and wants to try something else. What does it hurt to ask?"

"No," Chloe said firmly, wishing it could be otherwise. "He's not that kind of man. He doesn't even believe in love." She tried to make herself smile and had a feeling that it came out all wrong. "I would need him to love me and I don't think he can. So there's no point in asking him to stay. Letting him go is the right thing to do."

Charity rose to her feet. "At the risk of destroying our

newly found rapport, your logic is completely flawed. Frankly, I think you're afraid. If you don't ask, then he won't say yes and you don't have to put anything on the line."

"That's not true. How can you say that? By not asking, I'm guaranteeing myself that I'm going to get hurt. Do you think I want that?"

Charity stared at her. "It's not that simple. If you don't ask him to stay or even hint that you have strong feelings for him, then Arizona is probably going to leave. While you won't be happy with that, at least you'll be safe. You already know you're going to feel pain when he's gone." She reached out and grasped Chloe's hand. "You're trying to maintain control. If you confess your feelings, then you don't know what you two will decide. You don't know how much you might hope and then be disappointed. Or worse, that he might agree and then you're stuck with him. What then? You might have to actually deal with loving him. You're afraid. It's easier to let him go than to put yourself on the line and ask for what you want. The real terror isn't that he would say no…it's that he would say yes."

CHAPTER FOURTEEN

"SO THERE I was, up to my knees in mud in the pouring rain, staring directly at the white sapphire." Arizona paused long enough to motion to the beautiful gem displayed in a lit glass case at the front of the lecture hall.

The video camera panned to follow his gesture. Instantly the picture on the screens on both sides of the huge, filled-to-capacity lecture hall changed from a silver screen-size view of Arizona's handsome features, to a close-up of the gem.

"I knew if I could just reach a couple more inches, I would hold it in my hand." He smiled. "Talk about living a fantasy."

He paused for effect and gave Chloe a quick wink. She blushed and made sure the camera was still pointing at the gem. As she was in the front row and directly in Arizona's line of vision, he could see her easily. She didn't mind if the people around them noticed the wink, but she didn't want it on the videotape or broadcast to the large crowd. Cassie nudged her, then gave her a knowing smile.

"I would guess he's completely smitten," her sister whispered.

Chloe's only answer was a shake of her head, but she knew her blush gave her away. Whether or not Arizona was smitten, *she* was head over heels for the guy. She'd attended every one of his lectures over the past week. She could listen to him talk forever.

"I leaned forward," he continued. "Then I felt it. The steady pressure of the anaconda going past me, then turning so it was between me and my prize."

The audience gasped. Chloe found herself also caught up in his story. It had been like this each of the previous nights. Arizona wove fabulous stories from his life. They were made all the more enthralling because they were based on truth. But it was more than that. He had a way about him, about his speech patterns and word choices. While other lecture series could inform and even intrigue, his brought the audience right to the moment. He was a born storyteller in the great oral tradition. Had this been a hundred years ago, he would have plied his trade around campfires. Considering all the places he went to, he probably did.

"You can imagine what I was thinking," he said. "That this seems like a great time for a break!"

There was a moment of stunned silence, then a burst of laughter. Everyone applauded.

As the crowd began to circulate through the room, Arizona moved to the stage stairs. Chloe, Cassie and Charity stood up. Chloe glanced toward Arizona, but before she could move toward him, he was surrounded by adoring fans.

It had been like this every night since the lecture series began. The giant ballroom filled to capacity, the mesmerized audience, Arizona the center of attention. Last night, after the lecture, when he'd led her to his bed and held her gently, he'd asked if she was angry with him.

"I don't mean to ignore you," he'd told her.

She'd explained that she understood completely. When he made the audience laugh or gasp or applaud spontaneously, he was just sharing his gift. She wasn't thrilled with the pretty young women who seemed to stand so close, but there wasn't much she could do about that. He'd responded by tickling her until she begged for mercy, all the while telling her she should know better than to think he would be interested in anyone but her. They'd ended up lost in passion.

Later, alone in her own bed, she'd thought about what he'd told her. She wanted to believe him. She wanted to think he wouldn't be interested in anyone but her. However, she had her doubts.

"I'm going to force my way into that crowd," Cassie said as she eyed the group of people around Arizona. "Tonight is the last night of the series. I want to tell him how much I've enjoyed myself. He's leaving in a couple of days and I might not get to see him again."

"I'll join you," their aunt said. "What about you, Chloe?"

"No, thanks. I think I'll head the other way and get something to drink."

She started to make her way through the crowd. As she did, bits of conversation drifted toward her.

"Oh, John, he makes it sound so exciting. Do you think *we* could go to South America?"

"Of course, Lily. Let's call the travel agent first thing in the morning."

A little farther down she heard another couple planning a photo safari to Africa. So it went until she broke free of the crowd and found herself in the relative calm of the ballroom's foyer.

When she was in front of the bar, she reached for her small handbag.

"Can I buy you a drink, pretty lady?"

She spun toward the familiar voice and saw Arizona standing next to her. Despite all the time they'd been spending together and the fact that she'd been seeing him every day for more than two weeks, he still had the ability to make her toes curl.

"How did you escape?" she asked. "Last time I saw you, you were holding court with at least a dozen loyal fans. Including my sister and aunt."

"I spoke to them, told everyone else I needed a couple of minutes to rest, then used a side door to sneak down the back corridor away from the crowd." He nodded at the bartender. "What would you like?"

She gave her order. He took a glass of water for himself, then led her over to a couple of chairs in the corner of the foyer.

"I think it's going well," he said.

She resisted the urge to roll her eyes. "There's an understatement. You have them completely in the palm of your hand. But that's not a surprise. I've seen it happen every night." She met his gaze and smiled. "I'm impressed, as usual."

"Thank you. I've been to some interesting places and people like to hear about my adventures. I'm lucky."

It was more than luck, she thought. "You don't just tell them what happened to you, you also inspire them. I would say at least half the people in that room are talking about taking a trip somewhere they wouldn't have gone before hearing you. Maybe you should talk to the airlines about getting a finder's fee or something."

He chuckled. "Like a travel agent. There's a thought." He shifted his chair closer to hers and slipped his arm around her. "The truth is many of them will change their minds when they find out how much it's going to cost, or when they get the list of vaccinations required for the travel. But some will go and seeing the world will change their lives."

"Always a good thing," she said, then wondered if

she was wrong to want to stay here, in Bradley. Had she discovered her true self or was she simply afraid? Aunt Charity had called her a coward. She didn't want to believe that about herself, but what other explanation was there?

"It's not just travel that changes a person," he said, then leaned toward her and kissed her cheek. "You've changed me. I'm a better man for having known you."

His words warmed her down to her soul. "I would like to say the same thing, but I'm not a better man. In fact I'm not a man at all."

"Brat." He grinned, then squeezed her once and stood up. "I have to get back. We're on for later, right?"

She nodded. They'd had a standing date for after the lectures ever since the talks had started.

"Good." He took a step away, then returned and kissed her on the mouth. "I hate how little time we have left. I want to spend all of it together." He kissed her again. "I wish I could talk you into coming with me. Ah, well, another time."

And with that, he was gone.

Chloe slowly made her way back to her seat. Her head was spinning. Had he meant what he'd just said? Did he plan to ask her to go with him? No, he wouldn't. They got along well, he cared about her and he would miss her. But that's all it was. Arizona wasn't about to fall in love and she...

Chloe settled down next to her sister and aunt and tried to pay attention to the rest of the lecture, but for once, Arizona's wild tales couldn't keep her attention. Her mind raced around as she tried to figure out what was right for her...for both of them. If the truth were told, she *would* like to travel some, see parts of the world. But she wouldn't want to live somewhere else for any length of time. She wouldn't want to be a nomad. She needed roots and family around her. Arizona—what did he need? Was she wrong not to talk about this with him? Maybe Aunt Charity was right about her being a coward. Maybe she should try to figure out a way to explain the situation so they could look for a compromise.

The rest of the lecture passed in a blur. Afterward, the three women made their way to the reception. Aunt Charity and Cassie would stay an hour or so, then leave. Chloe would be there until Arizona told her he was ready to duck out, then together they would head over to his hotel.

She'd just filled her plate from the buffet line when one of the administrators from the university came up beside her.

"Ms. Wright, isn't it?" the elderly gentleman asked. "I'm Dr. Grantham, a vice president at the university."

"Nice to meet you," Chloe said, not quite sure why she was being singled out. "Yes, I'm Chloe Wright."

"Please." He motioned to a table off to the side. "If you have a moment, I would like to speak with you."

"Sure." The hair on the back of Chloe's neck prickled. She had a sudden premonition that she wasn't going to like what this man had to say. She glanced around, then spotted Cassie and motioned that she would be joining her shortly.

When she and Dr. Grantham were seated, he gave her a disarming smile. He was older, with white hair and thick white eyebrows. He looked like an English peer.

"Yes, well, this is a bit of a delicate thing. I hope you don't think I'm intruding or prying. This is about our mutual friend, Dr. Smith."

Chloe put her plate on the table. Her stomach tightened around the knot forming there.

"What about Arizona?" she asked.

"The university has offered him a full professorship. We think a man of his experience and talent would be a great addition to our faculty. We included a generous package with plenty of time off so he could continue to explore the world." Dr. Grantham's mouth straightened. "Much to our disappointment, Dr. Smith turned us down."

Chloe told herself to keep breathing. That the tightness in her chest and throat was just shock and not an actual seizing of her body. She wasn't going to die…it just felt like it.

"You offered him a job?"

"Yes. He was very polite, but said he wasn't interested in settling in one place." Dr. Grantham gave a humorless laugh. "I can only imagine how many other institutions have offered him as much or more. I don't suppose we ever really had a chance, but we had to try."

Chloe nodded. They had to try. They'd failed. Just as she would fail if she asked him to compromise so they could maintain their relationship.

Relationship! What relationship? She was simply a convenience to him.

"I was hoping," Dr. Grantham continued, startling Chloe, who had nearly forgotten the other man was still sitting at the table, "perhaps you could have a word with him. I've noticed you two seem to be particular friends. You might be an influence."

Chloe bit back a choked gasp. Particular friends. It was a gentle phrase from another time. She was willing to admit that she and Arizona were friends. Of course they were. They had fun together. They were lovers. She was *in* love with him. But she had no influence over him. Nor did she have the courage to tackle the subject. Not now. Not when she'd just found out that he'd been offered a chance to stay in her world and that he'd refused it. He couldn't have spoken more clearly. When his time here was up, he wanted to leave her.

She didn't doubt that he cared...in some way. In *his* way. After all, he'd warned her from the beginning that he didn't believe in love. She shouldn't be surprised that nothing had changed. She'd been the one to break the rules, not him.

"I don't think I can help you," she said stiffly as she rose to her feet. "Arizona is his own man."

"I see." The elegantly dressed Dr. Grantham suddenly looked like an old man.

Chloe fought against guilt. Wasn't it enough her heart was breaking? Did she have to be responsible for the university, too? She sucked in a breath. "I'll do what I can," she said. "I'll say something to him. But don't expect a miracle."

Dr. Grantham beamed and shook her hand. "We'll appreciate anything you can do." Then he rose and left her.

Chloe stared after him. She would keep her word and mention the offer to Arizona, but she knew it wouldn't matter. Nothing mattered except the fact that in two days, Arizona would be out of her life forever.

"Dr. Smith, my wife and I have enjoyed your lecture series so much," the older man was saying. "You bring your experiences alive. We feel as if we'd been there, don't we, honey?"

His wife smiled. "Yes, indeed. William and I were just saying that we should travel more. Maybe Egypt or Africa. What do you think, Dr. Smith?"

"There are advantages to both," Arizona told them. "Go through a reputable travel agent and confirm everything in advance."

The couple nodded eagerly and started talking about pyramids versus photo safaris. Arizona felt his attention drifting as he glanced around the room. He knew what he was searching for...make that *whom*. Chloe. Always Chloe. Normally he enjoyed the "meet and greet" part of the evening, but for the past couple of nights he'd wanted to run out directly after his lecture, grab Chloe and escape to his hotel room. He wanted to be alone with her, not talking to all these people.

He tried telling himself it was just sex, but he couldn't buy it. He'd had lovers around before and he'd always been able to focus on what he was doing. In fact if Chloe told him they couldn't make love that night, he would still be as anxious to get her alone. Yes, he wanted to touch her and hold her, but he also wanted to talk with, spend time with her. Be in the same room, listen to her laugh, watch the light in her eyes.

He scanned the line for the buffet, then saw Cassie and Charity sitting at a table. Chloe wasn't with them. He frowned and continued to search, at last spotting her in the company of Dr. Grantham. The courtly older gentleman had approached him just yesterday, offering him a position at the university. The offer had been generous, and were he a different kind of man, he might have considered taking it and settling down here.

The long line moved forward a little and he greeted the next couple. They had a few questions about his lecture. He answered them easily and again found his attention wandering.

Chloe was so damn beautiful, he thought. Tonight she wore a simple black dress. Short sleeves, scooped neck. The style didn't hug her body, but it was formfitting enough to be a distraction. She was shaking hands with Dr. Grantham, then returning to her sister and aunt.

He watched her walk across the room, her hips swaying gently, her body calling to his. What was there about her that drew him? Why did he have the feeling that leaving this time was going to be more difficult than in the past? He knew he couldn't stay. He came from a long line of men who abandoned those they were supposed to love. First, his grandfather had walked out on his wife and son to pursue a life of adventure. While they had never wanted for material things, they'd been denied a husband and a father.

The pattern had continued in his life. While his father had loved his mother to the point of obsession, he'd allowed his only son to be raised at first by strangers, then by the man who had abandoned him. Their family tree wasn't a shining example of healthy family relationships.

So where did that leave him? Wasn't he smarter to avoid that which he couldn't do well? After all, it had taken nearly thirty years for him to forgive his father. They had made tentative peace, but that wasn't the same as actually making the relationship work.

"So you really believe in all this magic nonsense?" a gruff man was asking.

"Of course," Arizona replied easily. "How can we not? There are many things on this earth that can't be explained."

The other man grunted. "I'll admit you tell a good story, but you're not going to make a believer out of me. I believe in what I can see, touch, taste or smell."

"Oh, Harry," his wife said, then tapped his arm. "That's ridiculous and you know it. You believe in God."

"That's different." Harry stiffened slightly. "A man's supposed to believe in God. It's in the Bible."

"My point exactly."

"Not the same thing at all," Harry told her.

"You believe in love," Arizona said. "You love your wife and your children."

"Of course." Harry narrowed his eyes. "What kind of man would I be if I didn't love them?"

"But you can't see, taste, touch or smell love," Arizona pointed out.

"Touché, Dr. Smith," Harry's wife said, then linked her arm through her husband's and led him away.

Arizona stared after them. He'd met many men like Harry in the course of his travels. Men who wouldn't believe in what they couldn't prove. But magic and the unexplainable were everywhere. One only had to be open to the idea.

How can you claim to believe in magic, when you ignore the biggest magic of all—the love people have for each other?

He tried to dismiss the voice in his head along with the question. That was different, he told himself, and knew he sounded just like Harry.

He sucked in a breath. Was that what this came down to? His belief in love? Was that what was happening with Chloe? Was the reason he couldn't forget about her and always wanted to be with her because he cared about her? Was it growing into more than caring?

The reception line finally ended. Arizona headed over to the bar and got himself a drink. As he sipped, he looked for Chloe. But instead of seeing her, he saw the people in the room and realized most of them were couples. What was it that bound two people together for a lifetime? The concept of marriage was as old as man. He'd traveled enough to know it was fairly universal. He'd seen dozens of couples who had faced great odds to be together, who were *still* together after several years.

"You're looking pensive about something," Cassie said as she, Chloe and Charity joined him.

"I'm fine."

"Good." She gave him her pretty, open smile. "The lecture tonight was even better than last night, and I didn't think that was possible. You're really gifted. Do you ever speak at schools?"

"Frequently. Kids are the best. They always have at least one question to stump me."

Cassie giggled. "I know what you mean. At the preschool where I work, every kid's favorite question is 'why?' Sometimes I can't think of an answer. I don't know why water is wet or dogs aren't bendy when you pick them up like cats are."

"Cats are superior animals," Charity said.

Cassie shook her head. "They are not. Dogs love people, cats tolerate them."

Arizona turned toward Chloe and found her watching him. He wanted to get lost in her dark eyes and never find his way out again. He wanted to tell her all he'd been thinking and find a solution together. Which was crazy. He refused to get seriously involved, and Chloe didn't want to put herself on the line again. So there was no need to talk about anything.

Except when he thought about leaving Bradley, he thought about a beautiful woman with a giving soul and a stately Victorian house that one could easily call home.

THEY WERE THE only people in the elevator. Even though Chloe had been to Arizona's room dozens of times, she found herself oddly nervous. Which was crazy.

"Come here," he said when the door closed and they started their ascent.

She stepped into his embrace and welcomed the feel

of his mouth on hers. Instantly, her body was ready for him. Heat filled her as her breasts swelled and that secret place between her legs dampened in readiness.

"You're amazing," he murmured as the door opened on his floor and they broke apart. "I can't get enough of you."

If only that were true, she thought. Then he wouldn't leave. But there was no point in wishing for what could never be.

"Cassie was right," Chloe said as she stepped into his suite. "Tonight's lecture was better than last night's. I don't know how you come up with so many entertaining stories."

"It's a gift," he said as he turned on several lights. "I don't think I can take credit for it. I've always told stories. The difference is this time I'm at a podium instead of sitting around a campfire."

His description matched what she'd been thinking earlier that night. They had much in common—they even thought alike at times. In many ways, she knew him better than she'd ever known anyone before.

She opened her mouth to tell him that, but what came out instead was not what she'd had planned. "I spoke with Dr. Grantham," she told him.

"I saw you two talking," he said as he crossed to the small refrigerator and pulled out a bottle of white wine. "We had lunch yesterday. He's quite the scholar. I liked him very much."

No surprise there, she thought. They would have a lot in common. "He told me they'd offered you a job."

Arizona had reached for a wine cork. Now he placed both on the coffee table and crossed to stand in front of her. He took her small handbag and put it on the sofa, then linked his fingers with hers. He was tall and hand-some. His green eyes glowed with fire and with concern.

"We should probably talk about that," he said.

"There's nothing to say, is there? After all, you turned him down." She tried to keep her voice steady, her tone light. She didn't want him to know she was starting to hurt. At first she'd been numbed by confusion, but now the pain filled her. He was really going away and there was nothing she could do to stop him.

"It's not that simple, Chloe. You know that. There are a lot of reasons I would like to stay…"

"But more reasons to go," she said, finishing his sentence.

His mouth twisted. "Yes." He raised one hand and cupped her face. "You are so beautiful. I've enjoyed all our times together. If I had ever thought about staying, it would be now. With you."

His words were a cold comfort. She had to clear her throat before she could speak. "But you can't."

"No, I can't stay." He pulled her hard against him. His arms came around her body, and she clung to him.

"Please understand," he said. "It's not about you. I come from a long line of men who leave and I don't know how to do anything else but what they've taught me. I don't make promises I can't keep. I'm not sure I believe in love."

She told herself that he'd progressed from definitely not believing to not being sure, but it wasn't enough. "I don't believe in magic," she whispered against his shoulder and closed her eyes as tears blurred her vision.

"We have tonight," he said. "And the time until I leave. Is that enough or do you want to go now?"

She wished he wasn't a gentleman. At least then when he was gone she could try to hate him. But he was. He reminded her he couldn't give her more than a temporary relationship, then offered her a chance to leave if she had to.

Chloe supposed that pride would insist that she stalk out with her back straight and a few stinging words to reduce him to dust. But she couldn't. He'd never lied to her. From that first day, she'd known their relationship was only temporary. Nothing had changed...except for her feelings. But then falling in love with him had been her own stupid fault.

So instead of leaving, she rose on tiptoe and pressed her mouth to his. If they only had a short time to be together, she would savor every second, commit it to memory and live on it for the rest of her life.

CHAPTER FIFTEEN

THE LAST SHUDDER of his release ripped through him. Arizona groaned out Chloe's name, then rested his head against her shoulder. Their breathing came in rapid gasps; they were both slick with sweat and tangled together. He wanted to stay like this forever.

She ran her hands up and down his back. "Thank you."

He raised himself up on his arms and gazed at her face. "Thank *you*. I have to admit, we seemed to have discovered a new level of intimacy. It's almost as if we're communicating with our bodies."

Her smile was content. "Isn't that how it's supposed to be?"

"Maybe, but I've never experienced it before." He was doing a bad job of telling her what he felt, but how was he supposed to explain the sensation of his heart and mind being opened to her? That for those few minutes, when he was inside her and she clung to him, that they really were one…just like all those old sappy songs promised.

"It's amazing," he said at last, knowing that didn't come close to what he meant.

"Well, you're the one with the expertise. All those women in your background. I'll just have to bow to your superior knowledge."

Her expression remained innocent, but the teasing in her voice gave her away. "You think you're very smart, don't you?" he asked.

"No. I don't think it. I know it."

"Oh, really. So what do you know about this?" He reached one hand down and started tickling her bare side.

"No, Arizona, don't!" Chloe wiggled and tried to get away, but she was pinned beneath him. She writhed. "Stop. You have to stop."

"Not really."

He shifted his weight all back on his legs so he could sit up and attack her with both hands. She retaliated, but he wasn't feeling especially ticklish that night. He squirmed under her wiggling fingers, but didn't have to pull away.

She laughed louder, then shrieked, "Stop! Please."

He released her. "Only if you—"

But she wasn't listening. Instead she took advantage of her freedom to lunge for his feet. Arizona scrambled to get out of her way. He knew he was definitely ticklish there.

He grabbed her around the waist and turned so he could fall backward on the bed, pulling her with him. She kicked out and tried to escape, but he held her fast. She spun in his arms so that she was on top of him, facing him.

Her long curly hair tangled around her face. They were breathing as hard as they had been a few minutes ago, but this time for an entirely different reason.

"Ready to give up and play nice?" he asked.

She blew the hair out of her face. A strand drifted up a few inches, then fell back across her nose. "I'll never give up."

He began tickling her sides. "If you insist."

She shrieked again. "No, you win. I'll be good."

"Promise?"

She nodded.

He gently rolled them both onto their side. They were facing each other. He tucked her hair behind her ears, then rested his hand on her waist.

The position was familiar. They often ended up this way after making love. They would talk for hours before she returned to her house. They only had a couple more nights together. He wished she would spend this night with him, but he understood that she didn't want to be seen leaving his hotel first thing in the morning. But tonight, more than any other time, he didn't want to fall asleep without her.

He supposed he should be used to it. After all, except for the night they'd camped out, they'd never slept very long together. He realized he wanted that. He wanted to see her first thing in the morning. He wanted to shower with her, then watch her get ready for her day. He wanted to learn what she was like in all her moods—sleepy, playful, even cranky.

Despite the airline ticket in his briefcase, he didn't want to leave her in less than seventy-two hours.

The information wasn't a surprise, he told himself. He'd been wrestling with it for the past couple of days. The question was what was he going to do about it?

She drew her index finger down his nose and his lips to his chin. There she stroked the stubbly skin. "All kidding aside," she said. "It's never been like this for me, either. I didn't know passion like this existed."

"Come with me this summer," he said without thinking.

Her eyes widened. "What?"

Arizona was a little stunned himself. But now that he'd asked, he didn't want to call the words back. "I'm serious. Come with me to the island. It's only for three months. You'll have plenty of time to write, although they don't have electricity, so you can't bring your laptop. But I'll bet you'd still get a lot done. It would be a great experience. And we'd get to be together longer."

"I could write a book about the mating customs in a matriarchal society."

"Exactly."

He tried to read her expression, but he couldn't. He didn't know what she was thinking. Would she consider it or was this too insane?

"At the end of summer…where do you go next?" she asked.

"Siberia, I think. We're still getting the details ironed out. I'll probably stop in Chicago first and visit my father. But there's always somewhere else I need to be going."

"I'm sure."

Chloe studied his familiar face. It would be easy to say yes. To pack up a couple of suitcases and go with him. It was just for the summer. Arizona was right—she could work, writing longhand. Maybe start a book of some kind. Even the one she suggested, on the matriarchal culture he was visiting. She could write down his stories and they could edit them together. Or…

Chloe kissed his mouth, then rested her head on the pillow. "I'm tempted," she confessed.

"I hear a 'but' in your voice."

"But—" The truth. It always came back to the truth. "That's not my style. I would never be happy just tagging along."

He frowned. "It wouldn't be like that."

Not at first, she thought. But eventually. Because she knew herself. The summer wouldn't be enough. If he let her, she would continue to follow him around the world. She would create work so that she could be with him. But then what? She not only needed more, she deserved more. Her own life with her own purpose. In a perfect world, their two very different lives and purposes would blend together, but life was far from perfect.

They had just made love and laughed, now they were holding each other. *These are the moments,* she thought. This was the perfection everyone sought. This was what it was about. The only rude intrusion was the pain in her chest that warned her it was going to be impossible to forget him.

"I can't," she said. "I need roots. I thought I was waiting until I had the right article before I went to New York. Or maybe I thought I was waiting until Cassie got married and I knew she was going to be all right. But it's not about any of that. Cassie's a grown-up and she's been capable of taking care of herself for years."

His green eyes darkened. "What were you waiting for?"

"Nothing. I thought I should go, but that was about expectations, not about what I wanted. I belong in Bradley. This is my home. I'm not saying I don't want to see parts of the world. I think most people would like to travel, but I'm not like you. I couldn't be happy with your lifestyle. At least not for any length of time."

And you couldn't be happy here, she thought. But there was no point in saying that—they both knew the truth.

She could read disappointment and hurt in his expression. "You're telling me no." It wasn't a question.

She ran her hand up and down his strong back, as if she could memorize everything about him. Later, the remembering was all she would have.

"I'm telling you that you belong out there. You're different from the rest of us, truly larger than life. Go find your magic, Arizona."

"What will you find?"

"What I've had all along. My roots. Just like Dorothy learned in *The Wizard of Oz*. For me, there is no place like home."

She thought about telling him that she loved him, but she was afraid. What would he do with the information? Besides, she couldn't bear to have the words hanging in the silence. Knowing that he wasn't going to say it back wouldn't be enough to keep her from hurting when he didn't respond.

"I don't like what you're saying," he told her. "Unfortunately I can't seem to muster a good argument against it." He kissed her. "I'll miss you."

"I'll miss you, too. More than I should."

He hugged her close. "Maybe you should ask me to stay here. Then we would have each told each other no."

The last little corner of her heart shattered. Until he'd said the words, she'd allowed herself to hope. That maybe he would offer to settle here, at least for a while. But that had never been his intention. Maybe Aunt Charity had been right and she was a coward for not asking, but at least she had the rather empty satisfaction of knowing that she'd been right.

They were silent for a long time. Finally, he reached up and clicked off the light on the nightstand. She stiffened. "I have to be going," she told him.

"Don't," he said in the darkness. "If you won't give me the summer, then just give me one night to sleep in your arms."

She didn't have to think it over. It was what she wanted too. She knew she wouldn't sleep, but at least she would be able to feel him next to her. More memories to have for later.

"I'll stay," she whispered.

"Good." He shifted to get more comfortable. "I should probably warn you that I think I snore."

"I know that from last time."

"Oh. Well, I also sleep like the dead. If you have to wake me up for something, don't bother shaking me. I've slept through hurricanes, earthquakes, not to mention several alarms. I don't even bother with a wake-up call. I never hear the phone. Just turn on the light. That one always gets me. Unexpected light, and I'm instantly awake."

"I'll remember," she promised. And she would. She would think about that small detail and wonder how it would have affected their lives together...if they'd had a future.

You're getting way too weepy, she told herself. *You're with him now. Enjoy this time. Save the suffering for later. There's going to be plenty of it.*

Chloe tried to take her own advice. As Arizona drifted off to sleep, and as promised, began to snore, she relived all their time together. Everything from her stunned amazement at finding him in her kitchen, to their lovemaking just a short time earlier that night.

She must have dozed for a while because when a sharp noise woke her, she wasn't sure where she was.

The phone rang again. Chloe blinked and everything came into focus. Arizona snored on, oblivious to the sound. As she reached for the receiver, she glanced at the clock. It was a little after two. Had something happened to his father?

"Hello?"

"Good afternoon. This is—" There was a sharp gasp of air. The woman on the other end of the line made a soft moaning noise. "Oh, no. You're in California, aren't

you? I'm terribly sorry. It's afternoon here in Sydney. I
can't believe I woke you up."

"It's all right." Sydney? As in Sydney, Australia? "Can
I help you with something?"

"What? Oh, of course. The reason for my call. I'm Jan.
I'm with the travel agency Mr. Smith uses for his South
Pacific travel. He'd called us a while back to have us put
him on a waiting list for an earlier flight. I wanted to let
him know a first-class seat just became available. He'll
be leaving tomorrow." She giggled nervously. "Technically, that's later today, isn't it?"

Chloe sat up in bed. Arizona was still snoring. A couple of seconds ago she'd had trouble focusing her eyes
in the dark room, but now her head was spinning. He
wasn't leaving in a couple of days. He was leaving in a
few hours. He'd arranged for an earlier flight. All this
time she'd been thinking about how much she was going
to miss him while he couldn't wait to get away.

"Give me a minute," she said. "I'll have to write the
information down."

She supposed she could have tried to wake up Arizona, but the truth was, she didn't want to face him. Not
now, not like this. He would be able to read everything
on her face. He would know how much his leaving was
going to hurt her. He would pity her. Lord help her, he
might ask her to go with him again and she didn't think
she could refuse him a second time.

She squinted at the two-line phone and realized there
was a hold button. After pushing it, she set the receiver
back in place, then made her way into the living room.
Once the bedroom door was closed, she turned on a light,
found paper and a pen, then released the call.

"I'm ready," she said.

"Great. He's on Singapore Airlines."

The travel agent gave her the flight information. Chloe wrote it down, then read it back to confirm that she had it right. Then she hung up and slumped back onto the sofa.

Now what? She stared at the paper in her hands and wished it could be different, but it wasn't. He was leaving and she couldn't go with him. Even if she hadn't already figured out her life was here, she could not follow a man around the world, simply to be with him. She needed more for herself.

None of which answered the question of what she should do now. The obvious answer was to get back in bed and try to sleep. In the morning, she and Arizona could talk.

"About what?" she asked in a whisper. "Gee, maybe I could ask if the service on Singapore Airlines is as fabulous as everyone claims. Or discuss ways of handling the jet lag when one crosses the international date line."

The note began to blur. Chloe brushed impatiently at the tears. "What am I crying about? I knew he was leaving. I've expected this from the beginning. Nothing has changed except for his departure date."

But that was part of it. That he was leaving early. How could he do that to her? To them? He was supposed to care, at least a little. But to be leaving *early*.

She sat there for a long time trying to make sense of it all. In the end, she knew she couldn't. She wrote a quick note explaining that the travel agent had called, then gave him the new flight information. Then she turned off the light in the living room and let her eyes adjust to the dark.

When she could see well enough to find her way back to the bedroom, she did so. Her clothes were on a chair by the dresser. She collected them, put the note on her pillow, then left the room.

Dressing took all of two minutes. Chloe stood there,

purse in hand, but she wasn't ready to leave. There was still something left to be done. She crossed to his computer and turned it on. After searching for a couple of minutes, she found the program to access the Internet and went on under her own account number. After getting into the newspaper's system, she accessed her computer there at the office and downloaded her article. She'd finished it yesterday. In a few hours she would be putting it on her editor's desk. She also wanted Arizona to have a copy.

She flipped on his printer and waited while the article came out, a page at a time. When that was finished, she logged off the computer, wrote a note on the last page of the article and returned to the bedroom.

It was after three and from Arizona's body position and loud snoring, he'd barely stirred in the past hour. She put the loose pages under the information from the travel agent, then walked around to his side of the bed.

In the darkness she couldn't make out individual features, but she knew every inch of him. She could predict his moods, recognized his voice and his laughter. He touched her as no one had before. Not just physically, but also in her heart and her soul.

It hurt so much, but knowing what she knew now, she wouldn't change anything. He'd reminded her that loving was a part of her life. That she'd been empty for a long time. She didn't think she would ever get over him, nor was she likely to give her heart to anyone else, but they had had a brief, joyous time together. They'd had a miracle and how many people could say that?

She bent over and kissed his cheek. He stirred slightly but didn't wake.

"I love you, Arizona," she murmured.

"Chloe. I dreamed about you."

She stiffened, then relaxed when she realized he was talking in his sleep. "I dreamed about you, too," she said. "I dreamed about you the night I wore that stupid nightgown. I guess now that I know its power, I have to stop calling it names. You are my destiny, Arizona Smith. If you ever decide to settle down, come back to me."

Then she left the room without once looking back.

AS HE DID every morning, Arizona woke with the first light of dawn. He stretched, then rolled over to snuggle against Chloe.

"What the—"

She wasn't here. He felt under the covers, but her side of the bed was cold. A quick glance confirmed that her clothes were gone, so she had probably left sometime in the night.

The disappointment cut through him. Why? All he'd wanted was one night so they could wake up in each other's arms. Was that asking too much? They only had a couple of days together until he left.

If he left.

Arizona stiffened. Where had that thought come from? Of course he was leaving. He had work to do, a life. He wasn't going to stick around in some small town. What for? Chloe? So they could be together?

He couldn't do it, he admitted to himself. He couldn't take the risk and stay. With his family history, with his poor relationship skills, there was no way he could make her happy. He was bound to blow it and then where would they be?

He cursed loudly, then flopped back on his pillow. As he did, he heard paper crinkle. When he turned he saw a handwritten note and a thick sheaf of papers. Chloe's article?

He read the note. As her words registered, a knot of pain formed in his gut. He swore again, louder and longer this time, then crumpled the note and tossed it on the floor. The change in airline reservations. He'd completely forgotten that he'd called about three hours after he'd arrived in Bradley. At the time, he hadn't wanted to spend more time here than necessary. As soon as he'd found out the date of his last lecture, he'd gone on the waiting list to leave right after that. But since then, everything had changed. He wanted to be with Chloe right up until the last minute.

What must she be thinking? he wondered, then groaned. Probably that he was using her then abandoning her at the first opportunity. No doubt she thought he would take off later today and never give her another thought.

He rolled over and reached for the phone. But before he picked up the receiver, he glanced at the clock. It wasn't quite six in the morning. If Chloe lived alone that wouldn't be a problem, but his call was going to wake up Charity and Cassie, too.

That can't be helped, he thought. But before he could grab the phone, it rang.

"Hello?"

"Good morning. I can tell by your voice I didn't wake you."

Arizona sat up and clutched the receiver. "Chloe? It's not what you think."

"I know."

She sounded all right, but he wasn't sure he could believe that. He had to make sure she understood. "What do you know?"

"That you made the reservation before we got involved. At least that's what I'm hoping."

He breathed a sigh of relief. "Of course it is. I forgot I'd requested an earlier flight. I'm going to call them right now and tell them I want to keep on the original schedule." Or maybe go later, but before he could add that, she sighed.

"Don't," she whispered.

The knot of pain returned, and with it a tightness in his chest. "Don't what?"

"Don't change the flight back. You're leaving. Whether it's today or in a couple of days, you're still going to be gone. Last night was terrific. I don't think we could top it, so why not let that be our last memory?"

Because I want to see you again. I want to hold you and hear you laugh. I want to figure out a way to make this work.

But he didn't say any of that. She sounded so calm and controlled. Maybe this hadn't mattered to her as much as he'd hoped. If she really wanted him gone, then he would go. But he made one last attempt. "Are you sure? I would like to see you again."

"Arizona, I—" Her breath caught and then he knew. She wasn't calm or unmoved by their conversation. She was clinging to composure by a thread.

"Chloe, don't make me do this. Let me stay a couple more days."

"No. It will only hurt more. I need to start getting over you and today is as good a day as any. Just promise me one thing."

"What?"

"Promise me you won't read the article until you're on the island."

His body felt strange. All tight and hurting. He wanted to beg her to come with him. He wanted… That was the problem, he realized. He didn't know what he wanted.

"You're just afraid I'm going to be critical," he said, hoping his voice sounded at least close to normal.

"That's it exactly. Promise?"

"I give you my word. I won't read it until I'm on the island. Of course I'll have to read it during the day, what with there being no electricity and all."

She made a noise that sounded more like a strangled sob than a laugh, but he let it go.

"I'm going to miss you," he said.

"Me, too. So much. You've been wonderful. All of it."

He cleared his throat. "Maybe I could come back. You know, at the end of the summer. Just to say hi and see how you are."

"I don't think that's a good idea. I won't be over you enough by then."

"Chloe?"

She exhaled sharply. "Don't ask me what that means, okay? Just accept it as the truth. I can't promise very much right now. It's j-just—" Her voice cracked. "I guess this is harder than I thought."

"Chloe, I want to see you before I leave."

"You can't. I have to go to work. Jerry's going to read the article this morning and we'll be editing it all afternoon. Your plane leaves around one, right? So there's no time."

"I'll make time. I'll keep the original flight." He wasn't sure why, but he suddenly had a sense of urgency about seeing her. That if he didn't, he would lose something very precious and important.

"Why?" she asked. "Nothing is going to change. You're still going to be leaving and I'm still going to stay here. It would hurt, too much." She paused. "Tell you what. Call me when you get back from your island. If things have settled down and you still want to see me, maybe we can work that out. Okay? But you don't have to. I mean, if you've met someone else, I'll understand."

"There's not going to be anyone else. You're the one—" He stumbled verbally. "I really care about you."

"Thank you for saying that. Look, Arizona, I have to go. Have a safe trip."

She hung up.

He stared at the phone a long time before replacing the receiver. Something was wrong. He could feel it. This wasn't right. Usually he was itching to leave, but this time he wanted to stay. What did that mean?

He would call her back, he decided. Then the voice in his head asked, "And say what?"

He didn't have an answer to that. What would he say? That he cared about her? He did. But that wasn't enough. He knew that now. Chloe wanted and deserved more than the temporary relationship he could offer her. She deserved a commitment.

He glanced around the hotel room, which was exactly like a hundred others he'd called home over the years. What did he know about commitment? His entire life had been devoted to wanderlust. The only thing he'd ever committed to had been getting his various degrees and those had been acquired at an assortment of universities around the world. Stay in one place? Be with one woman? Whom was he trying to kid?

Determined to put this behind him, Arizona got up, pulled his suitcase from the closet and began to pack.

CHAPTER SIXTEEN

CHLOE WAITED NERVOUSLY while Jerry finished up his phone call. He'd kept her waiting nearly ten minutes, which wasn't all that long except her nerves were shot. She'd had nearly no sleep the previous night and she didn't know how she was going to get through the day... let alone the rest of her life. She'd let Arizona go. She glanced at the clock and realized he would already be in San Francisco to catch his flight. It was too late to change her mind, too late to offer to go with him, too late to ask him to stay. Too late to realize she might have made the biggest mistake of her life.

Her editor put down the phone and looked at her. His gaze narrowed. "It's too long and too emotional," he said without even a greeting to start the conversation. "You got too close to your subject. Didn't they teach you anything at college?"

Chloe willed herself to stay calm and keep from flushing. She'd tried so hard to be impersonal as she'd written the piece. Obviously, she'd failed.

Jerry leaned back in his seat and tucked his hands behind his head. "It's also about the best damn article I've read in years. It's powerful, both in the images you invoke and in the story itself. I'm impressed as hell."

She felt heat on her cheeks, but she no longer cared. "Really?"

"Yeah, really. You're a decent writer. Of course, I

knew that all along. That's why I wanted you for this assignment."

Chloe pressed her lips together to keep from smiling. This was not the time to remind Jerry that he hadn't chosen her at all. She'd been handed the job after Nancy had turned it down because of her pregnancy.

"You know," he continued. "You could write a book on this guy. Not that I'm giving you any ideas. I don't want you to think you can parlay this article into a different career. And don't even think about leaving Bradley and heading off for New York."

"Actually, I have no intention of leaving," she told him. "My home is here."

Now it was Jerry's turn to look surprised. He straightened and slapped his hands on his desk. "Who would have thought? I figured a smart young writer like yourself would be heading off to the Big Apple at the first chance she got." He tapped the pages in front of him. "This is your ticket in. You know that don't you?"

"I know, and there was a time I was interested, but not anymore. I belong here."

"Great." He handed her the article. "I've made notes in the margins. I want the changes back to me by the end of the week. This will be the cover story, so get yourself a professional publicity photo. We'll need it for the byline."

Chloe swallowed hard. While she'd had bylines before, the magazine had never run her photo. The cover story! "Thank you," she managed.

"Yeah, yeah." He pointed to the pages she now held. "We can talk about anything you don't agree with. I doubt you can change my mind, but you're welcome to try. Now get out of here."

She clutched the sheets to her chest and made her way to the door. Her head was spinning. So much had happened so quickly. First Arizona leaving, then Jerry telling her she was going to have the cover.

"Oh, and Chloe?"

She glanced at her boss over her shoulder. "Yes?"

"I'm promoting you to the senior writer level. You'll only be working on features now. The new title comes with a raise and an expense account." He waved his hand. "Yeah, yeah, you're so grateful, you're speechless. Now get out of here, kid. Go home, celebrate the rest of the day and in the morning get your butt in the chair and make those changes."

"Thank you," was all she could manage. She stumbled her way back to her desk and collapsed into her chair.

She'd been promoted. She was really succeeding here at the magazine. There were only two other feature writers and they had both been working here much longer than she had. She'd impressed her boss.

She laughed out loud. With a little luck, she might even get a bigger cubicle, or maybe even an office of her own. Excitement and happiness bubbled inside of her. Without thinking, she reached for the phone and punched in the number for the hotel where Arizona was staying. When the operator answered, reality hit and with it a gut-twisting pain.

"May I help you?" the woman asked again.

"I'm sorry," Chloe whispered. "I have the wrong number."

She hung up. All her excitement and happiness vaporized, leaving her feeling as if she had just swallowed poison. Her body stiffened and her chest tightened. She couldn't call Arizona and share the news with him. He was gone. She had sent him away and he wasn't the kind of man who was likely to bother coming back this way again.

CHLOE WALKED INTO the kitchen and set her briefcase on the table. She'd taken Jerry's advice and had left early. But she had no plans to celebrate her promotion. She knew that in time she would be thrilled with the opportunity. She was a good writer, and she would excel at her new position. But for now none of that mattered. There was only the pain. How long would it take to forget him? Lord help her if souls really were reincarnated because she had a bad feeling it was going to take more than one lifetime to get over him.

"You let him go."

Chloe glanced up and saw her aunt standing in the doorway. Charity's hair was pulled back into its customary French twist. Her tailored slacks and fitted blouse highlighted her attractive figure. She was a familiar anchor in Chloe's suddenly storm-tossed world.

As the tears formed, she walked to her aunt. The older woman embraced her, holding her close. Chloe cried, hoping the release of tears would ease some of the pain. Sobs racked her body. She felt the physical rending as her heart tore in two.

"I h-had to," she managed between sobs as she tried to catch her breath. "I couldn't go with him, and he doesn't belong here."

"Foolish girl. Of course he does."

Chloe sniffed and straightened. "What are you talking about?"

Charity led her to the table, then started the kettle for tea. While the water was heating, she settled in the seat opposite Chloe's and handed her niece several tissues.

"You dreamed about him, Chloe. He's your destiny. You should have asked him to stay."

Hopelessness churned with the pain. "That's just some stupid old family legend. You know that."

"Fine. Ignore the dream, but what about everything else? What about the fact that you love him and you let him go without telling him?"

Chloe blew her nose. Her body ached as it did when she had the flu. "I told him. Sort of."

"He didn't know it when he called."

Her head came up and she stared at her aunt. "Arizona called? Here?"

"About an hour ago. He was in San Francisco. His plane was about to take off, and he wanted to talk to you."

She opened her mouth, but there weren't any words. She'd missed his call? It was too devastating to consider. "I just—"

"Oh, Chloe. Why didn't you fight for him?"

"He doesn't belong here. The world is his home."

"Home isn't a place, it's a state of mind. I think he wanted to stay, but wasn't sure he would be welcome."

Chloe turned that thought over in her mind. "He never hinted that he did." She swallowed. "I've been over this a thousand times. The truth is I love him, but I couldn't ask him to stay. I don't know if that makes me a coward or not. Everything happened so fast. It's hard to have him gone, but I believe we need the time. I'm sure of my feelings, but I don't think he's sure of his. I think he's afraid of being abandoned again, so he always does the leaving. And I can't be with a man who won't trust me."

"So what happens now?" her aunt asked.

"Now I wait. You're wrong. I did tell Arizona how I felt. I told him if he wanted to come back to me, I would be waiting. So it's up to him. I'm giving him time to figure out what he wants. He has to come to me freely, Aunt Charity. He has to believe."

Her aunt studied her face. "You've become a wise, mature woman, Chloe. Your parents would be very proud of you. *I'm* very proud to have you as a part of my life."

"I don't feel very wise. I feel broken and empty."

"I understand." She squeezed her fingers, then stood up to make the tea. "What are you going to do?"

Chloe had figured that one out on the drive home. "I'm going to spend the rest of the day in bed feeling sorry for myself. Tomorrow, to quote my editor, I'm going to get my butt in the chair and make the changes he wants on my article."

"He liked it?"

"Yeah." Chloe brushed away the tears that continued to fall. In a couple of days she would share the news of her promotion with her family, but she couldn't talk about it now.

Charity looked at her. "Honey, go on up to bed. I'll bring you the tea."

Chloe nodded, then did as her aunt bade. As she headed for her room, she reminded herself she was doing the right thing. She and Arizona needed time. It was the old cliché about setting something free. If he came back to her, then they would be together. If he didn't, he had never really wanted to be a part of her life. Unfortunately, the cliché didn't give any advice about getting through the waiting period or knowing when it was time to give up hope.

THE AIR ON the island was thick and humid with a sensual lushness that never failed to make Arizona feel like a nonbeliever entering a sacred temple. This small paradise off to one corner of the Pacific Ocean had always been one of his favorite places. Yet as he stepped off the boat onto the soft sand, he couldn't shake the feeling that everything was wrong.

For the first time in his life, he didn't want to be here. He didn't want to be anywhere but back in Bradley. What was the point of seeing the world if he couldn't also see Chloe's face, hear her laugh, touch her?

He shook off the thoughts, telling himself it was little more than jet lag. Something that was to be expected after traveling nearly forty-eight hours straight. He would get over being tired and slightly off balance, just like he would get over missing Chloe.

Several women waited for him. He waved. Nada, the high priestess and ruler of the island, came toward him. Some of his pain eased as he felt genuine gladness at seeing her.

"Welcome back, Arizona," she said in her oddly accented voice. Nada had grown up on the island, but in her late teens, she'd been sent to England. She'd stayed there nearly fifteen years, studying and learning customs of the West. Some women whispered she'd even taken an Englishman as a husband. If that were true, Arizona had never seen any sign of him. When he'd asked about that he'd been told that her husband had wanted to rule her head as well as her heart so she'd cut out *his* heart and eaten it for dinner.

"That showed him," Arizona had replied before pointing out that the people of the island weren't the least bit cannibalistic, and Nada had always frowned on violence of any kind.

True, he'd been told, but it made for a great story.

Nada walked toward him. She was tall and regal. He didn't know her age, but guessed she had to be close to seventy or eighty. She wore her hair long—to her waist—and there was little gray in the shining black strands.

He bowed to the island princess and offered her a thin gold bracelet as a sign of affection and respect.

"Thank you," she said. "But did you bring books?"

He grinned. "Two suitcases full. Romances and mysteries."

Nada smiled at him. "We do like a good bit of death to mix with our love stories," she admitted. "Come, everyone is waiting."

He left his luggage by the boat, knowing that it would be placed in his hut for him. As usual, when he walked through the village, only the women came out to greet him. The men were too busy with their chores. Besides, it wasn't correct for them to speak with strangers. On this island, men were to be seen and not heard. Which reminded him of something.

"I might have a visitor," he said.

"No, you won't." Nada spoke with the confidence of one who often viewed the future and was rarely wrong. She wore a sarong-style garment that trailed onto the ground. Her stride was long and sure.

She glanced at him. "Who did *you* think might come out to the island?"

"If you know I'm not going to have a visitor, then you should be able to figure that out on your own."

Her silence was a clear indication of her displeasure at his impertinence.

"I'm sorry," Arizona said quickly. "I didn't mean to be rude. I—" What was his excuse? He knew better. "I have a lot on my mind."

The night moved in quickly as it always did in the tropics. Torches had been lit to illuminate the path. The lush plants crowded around so that he had to push against them as he followed Nada to the ceremonial grounds.

"My father," he said at last when they stopped in the center of the open area. "We talked before I left California, and he said he would like to visit me."

"I would make your father welcome," the high priestess promised.

Arizona bit back a groan. He knew exactly what that meant. "He's pretty old and he doesn't get out much."

Nada flashed him a smile. "I would be very good for him. I would help him forget. When you go back, tell him to come without you."

Arizona knew better than to ask how she knew his father had anything to forget. Nothing about Nada surprised him. She probably would help his father to forget...if the excitement of the event didn't kill him first.

As if sensing his exhaustion, Nada kept the welcoming ceremonies brief. As she escorted him to his hut, she didn't even make the courtesy offer of one of the young women in her court. He was grateful not to have to politely turn down the gift. He had a bad feeling that tonight he couldn't have thought of anything pleasant to say.

As he stretched out on his cot, he willed himself to sleep. But instead of oblivion, he saw Chloe. Forty-eight hours and half a world later, he realized he should have stayed. Even for a few days. They still had so much to say to each other. There were many things he didn't understand. If only he'd told her...

Told her what, he asked himself? What was the mysterious message? That he would miss her? That he cared about her? But caring wasn't love and Chloe deserved more than he had to offer.

He fell asleep still wrestling with the problem and awoke at the first light of dawn, still exhausted and restless. As he rolled over on the cot, he saw Nada sitting in the only chair in the room. For all he knew, she'd been there all night.

"Good morning," she said.

"If you've come to take advantage of me, I'm going to be a disappointment," he teased.

"I am not your destiny, Arizona Smith."

There was something strange about her voice. Not just the accent, but also the tone and power. For once he had the feeling he wasn't speaking to Nada, his friend, but instead Nada, high priestess and ruler of this land. Someone privy to mysteries and secrets he would never know.

He pushed himself into a sitting position. "I'm listening," he said quietly.

"I dreamed about you, Arizona," she said. "I dreamed when you would arrive and when you would leave. I dreamed that this trip was wrong, that you were leaving behind something very precious."

Could everyone see the truth but him? he wondered. "A woman," he admitted. "Her name is Chloe."

"And?"

"And nothing. We were together for a while." He ran his hands through his hair. "It's so damn complicated. I love my life. I travel the world, I do what I want. No responsibilities, no ties. But she lives in this small town. Her family has owned her house for a hundred years. She belongs there."

"Where do you belong?"

A simple question. The answer came instantly and with it a painful insight into the blackness of his heart. "Nowhere," he said softly. He had never belonged. His father had abandoned him, his grandfather had dragged him from place to place, at times even forgetting about him. He didn't dare risk caring about people or places because he knew he would soon be ripped away from them. All he knew was being left, so he'd learned early on to do the leaving first.

"Yes," Nada told him. "But you are not that little boy

anymore. You're a strong and powerful man. You can choose to stay with her. You can choose to accept your destiny."

She leaned forward and held out her hand, palm down. Without being told, he held out his hand, palm up. She placed something warm there. He tightened his fingers around the object without looking at it.

"See with me," she whispered.

He closed his eyes and then he knew. Images flashed through his mind. Chloe, always Chloe. He saw them laughing together, talking. He saw himself teaching. He saw their three children playing together.

How could he have walked away without telling her how he felt about her? He loved her. He'd never loved anyone before, but she was everything he'd ever wanted. With her, he could risk putting down roots. She would never abandon him. Look at how she'd always cared for the people in her life. She was his perfect other half.

He rose to his feet. "I have to get back to her."

"I know." Nada stood. "The boat will be here shortly." She gave a self-satisfied smile. "I arranged it last night."

He kissed her smooth cheek. "When will we be back?" he asked.

"In two summers. But your father will have visited me before then. In fact, he might decide to stay here."

Arizona laughed. "Great. Just be gentle with him. It's been a long time."

Nada's smile faded. "I will not be taking your mother's place."

Arizona wrapped his arms around her and hugged her close. "I know. But thank you for worrying about that."

She patted his face, then swept out of the hut. Then she glanced back over her shoulder. The Cheshire-cat smile had returned. "Congratulations."

He waved, thinking she meant on his upcoming marriage. Good news. At least with her blessing, he was reasonably confident Chloe would say yes. Maybe he *hadn't* blown it completely.

But that wasn't what she'd meant at all. When Arizona turned to pack the few things he'd taken out of his suitcase the previous night, he remembered the small object Nada had pressed in his hand. He uncurled his fingers. Instantly his throat tightened as wonder filled him.

The small stone statue was old, weather-worn and had probably been carved a thousand years before the birth of Christ. But he could still recognize the crude rendering of a woman. He rubbed his thumb over the round mound that was her belly and knew what else Nada had seen in her vision.

Her congratulations hadn't been about his upcoming marriage, they had been because Chloe was pregnant.

THE OPERATOR WAS very apologetic, but she couldn't seem to make the connection. Arizona thanked her, then slammed down the pay phone. He didn't know what was going on. He'd never had trouble making a call from Guam to the States before. He had the oddest feeling that fate was conspiring against him speaking to Chloe before he could actually see her in person.

He glanced at his watch and swore. His plane would be boarding in less than fifteen minutes. He didn't have time to keep trying a call that was obviously not going to go through. He closed his eyes and tried to think. Then it came to him. He sprinted across the terminal and raced up to a window.

"I need to send a telegram," he said, and began frantically writing the message.

Thirty minutes later he was in his seat on the plane,

refusing the offer of something to drink before they took off. From Guam he would fly to Hawaii with a five-hour layover, then on to San Francisco. This wasn't the most direct way back, but it had been the best he could do on such short notice. At least Nada had arranged for the boat to return for him. Otherwise, he would have been stuck on the island an extra week.

Thinking of Nada made him think of Chloe, but everything did these days. He pulled out the small statue and closed his fingers around the worn stone. He doubted she knew about the tiny life growing inside of her. He hadn't decided if he should tell her or let her figure it out herself. Maybe he should just propose and then wait for her to tell him about the baby. He didn't want her thinking he was only interested in her because of the child. Even if he and Chloe could never have children, he would still want to be with her. She was the very best part of him. He ached for her the way a swimmer staying underwater too long ached for air.

He tucked the statue back in his pocket, then opened his briefcase. He might as well try to work on the long flight. He doubted he would be able to sleep.

He pulled out a folder and saw a thick stack of papers underneath. Chloe's article. He'd been too caught up in missing her when he'd been flying to the island to read what she'd written. Now he wanted to see what she had to say. Maybe reading her words would make him feel connected to her.

The article opened with a quote from him. "I'm no one's idea of a superhero. People who are heroes change the world for the better. Gandhi, Joseph Campbell, Mother Teresa…these people are heroes. I'm just a stubborn man who does his research and occasionally gets the opportunity to find something fantastic."

Chloe went on to say that there were those who would disagree with the idea that he wasn't a hero. She hadn't made up her mind, but from all that she'd seen, he was, at the very least, a good man, and how often could that be said about someone these days?

She wrote about his background, mixing humor with the sad image of a little boy often left alone in strange places. She explained how those experiences had molded him into a unique person. She detailed the myth behind the man.

Arizona didn't know whether to be thrilled or embarrassed. She made him sound like a really great guy. He liked that, but he was also aware of his limitations. Then he turned the page and froze.

"The first time I saw Arizona Smith was in a dream." She went on to tell about the family legend, the magic nightgown, and how on the night of her twenty-fifth birthday, she'd worn the nightgown and he'd appeared before her. She talked about meeting him the next day, of how he was exactly as she'd dreamed…right down to the scar on his arm.

Arizona didn't know how long he sat there, dumbfounded by the revelation. Everything fell into place. No wonder she'd acted so odd when they'd first met. She must have been terrified and confused. After all, Chloe didn't believe in magic. He closed his eyes and tried to remember all he could from the family legend. A smile curved his mouth. The fact that she'd dreamed about him meant they were—if he recalled correctly—destined for each other. It confirmed what Nada had said…and what his own heart had finally told him. They belonged together. For always.

He read through the rest of the article. Chloe's style was clear and concise. He could see her visual images clearly. As he turned to the last page he wondered if she would consider collaborating on a writing project with him. Something about his travels. Then he noticed a handwritten note at the bottom of the page.

"I couldn't let you go without telling you the truth. I love you. You don't have to do anything with that information. I don't expect you to say anything back. I know that we have very different lives and goals. At first I told myself it was enough that I'd known you and we'd had a short time together. But now I want more. I want to know if there is a way to find a compromise between our worlds. Please use your time on the island to think about this. At the end of summer, if you find you want me, I'll be waiting."

It had been there all along. Her confession. If only he'd read it that morning, or on the plane. He closed his eyes and shook his head. Or maybe it was supposed to have been this way. Maybe he had to leave to know what he'd lost.

He pulled his telegram out of his pocket and read the first two lines.

I COULDN'T LET YOU GO WITHOUT TELLING YOU THE TRUTH. STOP. I LOVE YOU. STOP.

They'd used exactly the same words.

He leaned forward anxiously, then realized that he couldn't make the plane go faster, no matter how much he willed it. So he forced himself to relax and to wait.

He would call her from Hawaii. This time he would get through. He had to. He loved her.

ARIZONA PRESSED THE receiver harder against his ear. The noise in the terminal was deafening. "Chloe, is that you?"

"Yes." Her voice sounded strange.

"Are you okay?"

"I'm fine. I sound funny because I'm crying."

His chest tightened. "What's wrong?"

"Nothing, silly. I'm crying because I'm happy. I got your telegram. I'm sorry you had to cut your trip short, but I'm glad you're coming home. I love you, Arizona."

"I love you, too." He practically had to shout, but it was worth it. They were actually talking to each other. "I missed you."

"I've missed you, too." She cleared her throat. "Are you sure you want to do this? I mean with your work and everything, are you sure you want to give up the travel?"

He understood that she was asking for him—wanting him to make sure that he wasn't going to regret his decision later. "I have two things to say about that," he told her. "First, I'm going to take the job at Bradley University. Their offer gave me plenty of time to travel in the summer, along with scheduled sabbaticals. I sort of thought you'd go with me."

"Of course. I'd like that. First class all the way, right?"

"Sure. I'll get you the best camels and carts around."

She laughed. "I do love you. What else?"

"I sent the telegram before I read the article, Chloe. I sent it before I knew what you'd written on the last page."

He heard her breath catch. She was crying again.

"Chloe, don't."

"I can't help it. I'm so happy."

He looked at the crowds in the terminal. The public-address system announced the first boarding call for his flight. This was not how he'd wanted to do it, but he didn't have a choice.

"I have to go," he said. "But first I want to ask you something."

She sniffed. "What?"

"Will you marry me?"

"What?"

The terminal suddenly got very quiet. Arizona looked up and saw several dozen people staring at him. He waved, then turned his back on them. "Will you marry me? I love you and I want us to be together for the rest of our lives. We'll make it work. I know we can do that."

"I know we can, too. Yes, I'll marry you, Arizona. I'll also be waiting at the gate in San Francisco. I'll rent a room down by the waterfront and we can spend the night drinking champagne and making love."

He thought about the little statue in his pocket and knew they would have to pass on the champagne. But the rest of it sounded perfect.

"I'll see you in about five hours," he said. "I love you. I can't wait to see you."

"Fly safe. 'Bye."

He hung up the phone and picked up his carry-on bag. The crowd around him burst into applause. He was still grinning when he took his seat.

"SPARKLING CIDER?" Chloe asked, as she handed him his glass.

Arizona raised himself up on one elbow to take the fruit drink and smiled. "I wasn't in the mood for alcohol. Thanks for indulging me."

She slipped into bed and snuggled close. "Right now I would do anything for you."

She would, too. It felt so right to be back together with him. Letting him go had been difficult, but in her heart Chloe knew she'd made the right decision. Maybe Arizona had needed to go away to figure out where he really wanted to be. She didn't know if it was fate, the nightgown, the stars or just luck, but they were together and they were going to stay together. She couldn't ask for anything more.

Arizona leaned over, put down his glass and grabbed a pad of paper from the nightstand.

"What's that for?" she asked.

"A list. Eventually we're going to leave this bed and head back to Bradley."

"Probably," she teased.

He kissed her, then returned his attention to the paper. "This is everything we have to do in the next few days. First, I have to call and accept the job offer at the university."

"I made an appointment for you with Dr. Grantham. It's on Friday at ten." She winked. "I know your style. You would want to see him as soon as possible."

He grinned. "We're going to be great together. Okay, that's done. Second, I have to call my father. Nada, the woman I was telling you about, wants him to come visit her."

"I'm sure he'll enjoy his time there." Chloe glanced at the fat little statue he'd brought her. It sat on the dresser, its unblinking eyes seeming to see everything. "There's something strange about the shape of that thing," she said. "I just can't put my finger on it."

"We need to set a date for the wedding."

She considered that. "I don't need anything fancy, so we can have it quickly, if you would like to."

He kissed her again. "I would like to very much."

"Good, I—"

But instead of pulling back, he deepened the kiss. Chloe leaned close to him. "What about your list?" she asked.

He tossed the paper and pen onto the floor. "It can wait. I think we have a little more catching up to do."

He lowered her onto her back and slid his hand over her body. Chloe arched into his touch. His warm fingers lingered on her belly, stroking the smooth skin there. Without meaning to, she opened her eyes and saw the little stone statue. How odd, she thought. If she didn't know better, she would swear its little face was smiling. Then Arizona's fingers slipped lower and she couldn't think about anything except how wonderful it was to be back where she belonged…where they both belonged.

She closed her eyes as he entered her and for that brief second, she thought she felt straw under her back, as if they were in the cave again. Just like in the dream. As passion carried her higher and higher, she realized that nothing about life with Arizona was ever going to be completely normal, but it was always going to be wonderful and exciting. They could give each other everything and accept everything in return. They were bound by forces they couldn't see or understand, caught up in the tide of love. After all, they were each other's destiny.

* * * * *

DREAM GROOM

CHAPTER ONE

"HE HUNGRY," said twenty-six-month-old Sasha solemnly, her large blue eyes darkening with the first hint of worry. "He want peanny butter."

Ryan Lawford glanced from his niece to the "he" in question. Unfortunately the hungry creature wasn't a baby brother or even a pet. It was, instead, a beeping fax machine. Crumpled paper jammed the feed, gooey peanut butter covered the keys, while a sticky spoon sat where the receiver should be. His fingers tightened around the ten-page report that he was supposed to be faxing to Japan in less than twenty minutes.

"Me hungry, too," Sasha announced. "Me want es-ghetti."

"Sure," Ryan said, his teeth clenched, his blood pressure climbing toward quadruple digits.

Spaghetti—why not? He could just whip some up, maybe a nice salad and some garlic bread. Red wine for himself, milk for his niece. There were only two things standing in his way. Make that three things. First, unless the meal came in a little plastic dish with instructions on how long to heat it in the microwave, he wasn't going to be much help in the kitchen. Second, last time he'd checked, the only food in the refrigerator had been a half-empty jar of peanut butter that the fax machine had just consumed. Third, what the hell was he doing here? Children and their needs were beyond him. Helen and John had been crazy to make him Sasha's guardian.

He spun on his heel. "I'll be right back," he said, in an effort to keep Sasha from following him. Ever since he'd arrived at the end of last week to help with the funeral arrangements for his brother and sister-in-law, the kid had been dogging his every footstep.

Sasha wasn't deterred. Still clutching the jar of peanut butter to her chest, she trailed after him. "Unk Ryan? Go see Mommy?"

The phone in his makeshift office began to ring. He headed toward the back of the house. Sasha hurried to keep up.

"Unk Ryan? Me want M-Mommy."

Her tiny voice cracked. He didn't have to look at her to know that tears had started down her face. In the background the fax machine continued to beep. His phone rang again. As he reached for it, he eyed his computer and figured he would scan the pages and send them out using the modem.

He picked up a receiver and barked "Hello?" into it.

The jar of peanut butter dropped to the floor. Mercifully it didn't break, but now Sasha's tears began in earnest.

"Mommy," she sobbed as if her baby heart were breaking. Ryan grimaced. It probably was. Her chin wobbled, soft dark curls clung to her forehead and her tiny hands twisted together.

One of his staff members began discussing a difficult problem. Ryan couldn't concentrate. "Hold on," he said, set down the receiver and started toward Sasha. Before he could reach her, the doorbell rang.

He clamped his lips down on the curse waiting to slip out. What else could go wrong today? he wondered, then mentally banished the question. He didn't need to tempt fate to try harder to mess things up. Life was complicated enough.

He picked up the phone. "I'll call you back," he said and hung up before hearing a reply, then turned to Sasha. "We'll talk about your problem in a minute. I have to get the door."

The little girl sniffed. "Mommy," she whispered.

Ryan swallowed another oath. How was he supposed to tell a toddler that neither her mother nor her father was going to come home? For the thousandth time in less than a week, he cursed his brother for making him the sole guardian of his only child.

He crossed the wood floor of the foyer and jerked open the front door. "What?" he demanded.

A young woman stood on the porch and smiled at him. "Hi, Mr. Lawford, I'm Cassie Wright. We met after the funeral, but I don't expect you to remember me."

She carried two bags of groceries in her arms, one of which she thrust at him. He had a brief impression of average if pleasant features, chin-length thick, dark hair and big eyes.

"It's been nearly a week," she said as she stepped past him into the house. "I figured you would probably be pretty frustrated about now. Sasha's a sweet kid, but the terrible twos are called that for a reason. I knew you didn't have any kids of your own. Your brother's wife talked about you some when she was at the school. So here I am."

She'd kept moving during her speech, and by the end she was standing in the center of the kitchen, surveying the disaster that had once been a pleasantly decorated room. Dishes and microwave-safe containers filled the sink, along with every inch of counter space. There were spills on the floor from his attempts to feed Sasha at the table, before he'd figured out that she was too small and, despite her claims to the contrary, really *did* need her high chair.

Cassie Wright turned in a slow circle, then faced him. "I brought food, but a cleaning crew would have been a better idea."

Ryan didn't like feeling inadequate, but he was not equipped to take care of a child. "It's been a difficult few days."

"I'm sure." Cassie's friendly expression softened into sympathy. She set her bag of groceries on a chair, which, except for the floor, was about the only free space.

He looked at her, then at the bag in his arms, then back at her. "Who are you and why are you here?"

Before she could answer, he heard a soft shriek from the hallway, followed by the sound of small feet racing toward the kitchen. "Cassie!" Sasha called in obvious pleasure. The toddler barreled into the room as fast as her short legs would allow. She threw herself at the strange woman.

"Hey, Munchkin," Cassie said, crouching down to collect the child in her arms. She straightened and hugged Sasha close to her chest. "I've missed you. How are you doing?"

Sasha gave her a fierce hug, then rested her arm around Cassie's neck and gave her a wide grin. "Me help Unk Ryan."

Cassie looked at him. "Uh-oh. Sasha's heart is in the right place, but her helping tends to create disasters. You have my sympathy."

"The fax machine needs it more. She tried to feed it peanut butter."

Cassie winced. "Did you do that?" she asked Sasha

as she wiped drying tears from her face. "Did you give the fax machine dinner?"

Sasha nodded vigorously. Her dark curls danced with her every movement. "He hungry. Me help."

Ryan stared at the young woman in front of him. She was comfortable with Sasha, and the kid obviously knew her. So he was the only one out of the loop. "Who *are* you?" he asked.

Cassie set Sasha on the floor, then smoothed her palms against her skirt. She took two steps closer to him and held out her right hand. "Sorry. I should have been more clear. I'm Cassie Wright. I'm a teacher at Sasha's preschool. I've known her for about a year, and she's been in my class for the past six months." She met his eyes and her voice softened. "I'm so sorry about your recent loss. I thought you might be having some trouble adjusting to life with a two-year-old, so I came by to see what I could do to help."

The feeling of relief was instant. He gripped her hand as if it were the winning lottery ticket, and he smiled at her. "This is great," he told her. "You're right. I don't have any kids, and I don't have any experience with them. I've been trying to do work, but Sasha follows me everywhere. It's nearly impossible to get anything done."

He released her hand and glanced at his watch. "I need to fax something to Japan. It's already late and I have to scan it into the computer before I can send it. Would you watch her? Just for a couple of minutes. I'll be right back."

He edged out the door as he spoke, then disappeared into the hall before she could refuse him.

His prayers had been answered, he thought as he saved the scanned documents into a file, then prepared to send them via modem. If Cassie whatever-her-last-name-was knew Sasha, she could be a great resource. He hadn't yet figured out what he was going to do about his niece. While he wanted to get back to San Jose as fast as he could, he didn't think that was going to be possible for a while. As if his own company didn't keep him busy enough, he had John and Helen's affairs to settle. He had to decide what to do about the big Victorian house his brother and sister-in-law had recently purchased. There were a thousand details he had neither the time nor the inclination to take care of. Unfortunately, there wasn't anyone else.

Cassie could help him with Sasha. Maybe she could baby-sit, or recommend someone who could move in full-time. That was what he needed, he decided. A nanny. Like Mary Poppins.

Thirty minutes later, Ryan made his way back to the kitchen. He wasn't ready to face Sasha again, but he knew he couldn't leave her alone with Cassie forever, despite the temptation to do just that.

Sasha sat at her high chair. As she was literally up to her elbows in a red sauce, she'd obviously just finished eating an early dinner. Cassie stood with her back to him as she bent over to fill the dishwasher.

He froze in the doorway. While he'd seen this exact domestic scene a thousand times on television or at the movies, he'd never experienced it in real life. There was something vaguely unsettling about having a woman and a child in his house, he thought. Of course this wasn't his house. If anyone was out of place in this scenario, it was he.

Cassie glanced up and saw him. "Did you get your papers sent?"

"Yeah. Thanks for looking after her."

As he glanced at Sasha, she gave him a big smile, then

picked up her plastic-covered cup in both hands and carefully brought it to her lips. She managed to drink without pouring more than a couple of teaspoons. He winced quietly as he remembered the first time he'd given her a glass of milk…in a real glass…about ten ounces. The cold liquid had ended up down the front of her pajamas, over and in his shoes, not to mention coating the kitchen floor. He'd cleaned up as best he could, but his shoes still smelled funny.

Sasha set her cup back on her high chair tray and wiggled in her seat. "Down," she announced.

"Okay, but let's get you cleaned up first," Cassie told her. She dampened a paper towel and wiped off Sasha's face and hands. Then she untied the bib and set the little girl on her feet.

Sasha dashed over to him and wrapped her arms around his right leg and stared up at him. "Esghetti."

"For dinner?" he asked. When she nodded he glanced at Cassie. "I'm amazed. That was her request."

Cassie grinned. "Don't be too impressed. I feed her lunch nearly every day, so I know what she likes. It was just a matter of picking it up at the store."

"I see." He untangled himself from Sasha and walked to the kitchen table. Cassie had cleared off the chairs. He took the closest one and indicated that she should take the one across from his.

She crossed the floor toward the seat, pausing long enough to collect Sasha in her arms and bring her along, too. When Cassie sat down, she settled the toddler in her lap.

There was a moment of silence as he tried to figure out where he should begin. "This has been very difficult," he started, then paused as he wondered if she would think he was talking about his dealings with Sasha or the death of his brother.

"I'm sure it has been," Cassie said, before he could explain himself. "Everything was so sudden. The police came to the school to tell us. I took Sasha home with me those first couple of nights, until you could get here."

He blinked at her. He'd never given it a thought, he realized. When he'd received the phone call informing him that his brother and sister-in-law had been killed, he'd had to wrap up as much work as possible, then drive over to Bradley. Sasha hadn't been at the house when he'd arrived. Until she'd been placed in his arms, he'd nearly forgotten about her existence.

"The woman who returned her to me was…" His voice trailed off.

"My aunt Charity," Cassie said. "I was working that day." Her gaze settled on his face. "You didn't visit your brother and his family much."

He couldn't tell if she was stating a fact or issuing a judgment. "I run a large company in San Jose," he told her, even as he wondered why he cared what a nursery school teacher thought of him. "I have a lot of responsibilities."

She wrapped her arms around Sasha and kissed the top of the girl's head. "This pretty girl looks small on the outside, but she's going to be one of your biggest."

He didn't want to think about that. A child. "I'm not parent material," he said. "I don't know what John was thinking."

"You're family," Cassie reminded him, as if that explained everything. "Who else would he trust with his only daughter?"

"Someone who knew what he was doing. Someone in a position to take care of his child." Anyone but him.

He didn't want the responsibility. Worse, he didn't know how to handle it. Work was his life and he preferred it that way. If only John had left a dog instead of a kid, things would have been a whole lot easier.

"You'll struggle at first," Cassie said, "but that won't last long. They look really breakable, but actually children are tough. All they need are attention and love." Her mouth curved up in a smile. "The occasional meal helps, too."

"What this child needs is a nanny." He looked at her. "Would your aunt be interested in taking on the job for a couple of months? I'll be in Bradley about that long. I have to straighten out John and Helen's affairs while I'm figuring out what to do with her." He nodded at Sasha, who was happily playing with a spoon she'd discovered on the table.

"Aunt Charity isn't the nanny type." Cassie studied him for several seconds. "If you're only talking about a couple of months, I could do it."

His luck wasn't usually that good, he thought. A young woman who worked in a preschool and was familiar with Sasha. What could be better? "You already have a job," he reminded her.

"I know, but because the school year has just started, my boss won't have any trouble getting replacements for me." She smiled at what he guessed was his look of confusion. "The university has a large child development department, and all the students are required to work several hours a week with young children. The preschool always gets many more applicants than we have openings. The students work part-time so it takes two or three of them to make up for one full-time employee, but with the semester just beginning, that isn't a problem."

Perfect, he thought. "When can you start?"

She raised her eyebrows. "You'll want to check my references, first. I don't have a formal résumé with me, but I can leave names and phone numbers with you."

"Yes, of course."

Ryan knew he was going about this all wrong. He knew he had to check on Cassie Wright and make sure she would take good care of Sasha. He just didn't have any experience in this sort of thing. "Assuming everything checks out, can you begin in the morning?"

She thought for a moment. "I'll have to make some arrangements with the preschool, but I believe that would be fine. Do you want me to live in, or just work days?"

"Live in. The house is huge and there are several guest rooms. You can have your pick and—"

Sasha threw back her hands and released her spoon. The piece of flatware sailed straight into the air. Cassie reached up and grabbed it. As she did so, he caught a glint of light from her left hand. A ring. He should have known. Of course it wasn't going to be this easy to solve his child-care problems.

"I doubt your husband will appreciate you staying in the house," he said, trying not to sound like a kid who just had his bike stolen. "Perhaps you can fill in during the day until I can find someone to live in."

Sasha wiggled to get down and Cassie helped her to her feet, then smoothed her skirt back in place. She frowned. "I'm not married."

He pointed to her left hand. "You're wearing a ring."

She glanced down, then extended her fingers toward him. "It's not a wedding band, it's a promise ring. I'm engaged to be engaged. Joel and I have been dating for years."

As she looked to be in her early twenties, he doubted it had really been years. A promise ring. He'd never heard of that. He leaned forward to study the slender band. There was a mark in the gold. "It's scratched," he said, pointing to the indentation. "Did you hit it?"

"It's not a scratch, it's a diamond." She sighed. "Well, a diamond chip, rather than a real stone."

He leaned a little closer, then took her hand in his so he could study the diamond chip. It looked like a speck of lint, but if he turned her hand back and forth it *almost* caught the light. Looked like Joel was not much of a spender.

"It's very nice," he told her.

"Thank you."

He released her hand and straightened in his chair. "If you'll leave me the phone number of your employer, I'll call and check the reference. Then I can phone you later and confirm our arrangements for tomorrow."

He sounded so formal, Cassie thought as she resisted the urge to smooth her hands against her thighs. Her fingers were still tingling from where he'd touched her. She didn't want Ryan to guess that she was nervous. Fortunately he couldn't hear the jackhammer pounding of her heart or know that her knees were practically bouncing together like bowling balls.

She'd never seen a man like him before. Of course she wasn't around that many men in the course of her day. Harried fathers picked up their children from the preschool. There was the UPS driver, although the new one was a woman. All in all, except for her sister's husband and Joel, she lived in a world of women.

Ryan was talking about the terms of her employment. He'd named a generous salary that far exceeded what she earned at the preschool, and was explaining that because her employment was for only two months there wouldn't be a benefit package, although he would be happy to re-imburse her for her medical coverage during that time.

She nodded her agreement because it was a little hard to talk, what with her throat closing up and all. He was so incredibly sophisticated and worldly. Helen, his sister-in-law, had often talked about Ryan's business, his early success, how driven he was. He'd always been too busy to visit, even after Sasha was born. He was the younger of the two brothers, but older than Cassie, probably by eight or nine years. At least she'd thought ahead enough to wear her best summer dress, even if it was doubtful he'd noticed anything about her other than her ability to care for Sasha.

"I believe that's everything," he said. "If you can write down the phone numbers."

She did as he requested, all the while telling herself not to stare. She didn't usually have problems around people she didn't know, but Ryan was different. Part of the rea-son was he was so good-looking. He had a strong-jawed face with perfectly chiseled features. She could barely bring herself to glance away from his dark green eyes. It had been hard enough to maintain her equilibrium when they'd met at the memorial service, but at least there she'd had lots of other people to distract her. But here there was only Sasha, and the two-year-old was no match for her dreamboat uncle.

Cassie finished writing out her phone number and handed the paper to Ryan. She knew she was behaving like a schoolgirl with her first crush, maybe because he *was* her first crush. After all, the only boy she'd really noticed was Joel and they'd been dating forever.

"I'll call you this evening," he said in his well-mod-ulated voice.

She had to fight back a sigh. Between his handsome

face and his smooth-as-Godiva chocolate voice, he could be on television or in the movies. But instead he was in Bradley and she was going to work for him.

Sasha had wandered into the living room and was watching a video. "I'll just slip out," Cassie said quietly, as they passed in front of the open door. "I don't want to upset her by saying goodbye."

Ryan looked relieved. "The tears are the worst part."

"They pass quickly and then there are lots of smiles."

He didn't look convinced.

When they reached the front door, she thought about risking a second handshake, but the first one had about made her swoon, so instead, she waved. "I'll talk to you soon," she told him and walked quickly down the front stairs.

FIFTEEN MINUTES LATER she let herself in through the back door of her house, an equally large Victorian mansion in the small town of Bradley, California. Unlike the house Ryan's brother had bought three years before, this one had been in the family since it was built in the late 1800s.

Cassie made her way up to her room without encountering her aunt. Normally she loved to talk with Aunt Charity, but for once, she needed to be alone.

When she reached her bedroom, she moved to the window seat and sat down on the thick cushion. It was too dark to see the well-manicured backyard, but she wasn't staring out the window for the view. She didn't see the lace curtains that matched her bedspread, or her own reflection in the glass. Instead she saw Ryan Lawford, tall, broad, handsome. The perfect hero.

She drew in a deep breath, then released it as a sigh. If only someone like him could be interested in someone like her. The thought made her smile. She might be the romantic dreamer in the family, but she wasn't a fool. She was too young, too unsophisticated, too ordinary. Men like him fell in love with fashion models, or at the very least with beautiful, charming women like her sister, Chloe. Besides, she had Joel. While it was fun to fantasize about Ryan, she knew it was just a game. She loved Joel as much today as she had on their first date, nine years before.

Enough daydreaming, she thought. She should really start packing. After all, she knew exactly what Ryan was going to hear when he checked her references. Actually what she needed to do was call her boss and tell her that she was taking a two-month leave of absence from her job. Mary, her boss, wouldn't be surprised. They'd discussed Ryan's situation several times since they'd heard the news about Sasha's parents' death. They'd known that a single man was going to need help learning to deal with a toddler. Mary had been the one to encourage Cassie to visit him in the first place.

Cassie made the call and laughed when Mary told her that Ryan had already checked her out. "I gave you a glowing report," Mary said. "He's never going to want to let you go."

"I doubt that," Cassie said.

They chatted for a few more minutes, then hung up. Cassie crossed to her closet and pulled out her suitcase. She would take a few things in the morning, then come back for more clothes as she needed them.

As she reached for her makeup bag on the closet shelf, her hand bumped against a flat box. She caught it before it could tumble to the ground, then carried it over to her bed.

She didn't have to open the box to know what was inside, but she lifted the lid anyway, then stared at the familiar ivory nightgown. It was beautiful and old-fashioned with long sleeves and a high neck. Lace edged the cuffs and collar. She rubbed her fingers against the soft, aged fabric. Six weeks, she thought. Six weeks until she knew if the legend would come true for her.

She placed the lid back on the box and forced away the twinge of longing that threatened to overcome her. All she'd ever wanted was to belong, to have a place in the family history. The town of Bradley had been established by Cassie's mother's family. Bradley was Cassie's middle name, but only by law. Not by birth.

She reminded herself that being adopted meant that she'd been chosen. They'd really wanted her. But the familiar words didn't help very much. Chloe was their child by blood—they'd made that clear when they'd left her the family house in their will. Cassie's inheritance had matched in money, but not in legacy.

"Maybe with the nightgown," she whispered to herself, wishing it could be true for her, but fearing she wanted the impossible.

Legend had it that a family ancestor had saved an old gypsy woman from being stoned to death several hundred years ago. In gratitude, the women of the Bradley family had been given a nightgown said to possess magic powers. If they wore it on the night of their twenty-fifth birthday, they would dream of the man they were going to marry. If they married him they were guaranteed great happiness for all their days.

Nearly five months before, Chloe had worn the nightgown and dreamed of a handsome stranger. She'd met him the next day and they'd fallen in love. Cassie desperately wanted the nightgown to be magic for her, too.

She twisted the promise ring on her finger. Her dreams weren't fair to Joel, but he swore he didn't mind. They'd talked about the nightgown several times. She'd told him that she didn't want to get engaged until after her twenty-fifth birthday, now just six weeks away. He always told her he wasn't in any hurry, that he knew she was going to dream about him and waiting was just fine.

Cassie told herself she should be grateful. Not many men would be so patient. But sometimes she got tired of his patience and his willingness to wait. She wanted to be swept away by passion. She wanted to be overwhelmed. She wanted to feel the magic.

"Not tonight," she told herself as she returned the nightgown to the closet. The good news was that in the morning she was going to move in with an incredibly handsome man who made her whole body tingle just by being in the same room with her. The fact that he barely knew she was alive was a small detail, something she would deal with another time.

CHAPTER TWO

CASSIE PULLED INTO the driveway of the Lawford house at exactly 8:25 the next morning. She assumed that Ryan would expect promptness on her part and she'd promised to arrive by 8:30. After parking her car to the left of the garage, she popped the trunk and pulled out her suitcase, along with a bag of toys she'd borrowed from the preschool. She'd stopped by there on her way over to pick up a few of Sasha's favorites.

I can do this, she told herself as she stared up at the imposing facade of the house. *I can get through the next several weeks without making a fool of myself.*

Cassie smiled. Of course she *could* get through her period of temporary employment without doing something completely humiliating. The real question was *would* she? She started up the walkway. She didn't really have a choice in the matter. She'd said she would help and she would. The fact that Ryan made her want to hyperventilate when they were in the same room was something she was going to have to deal with on her own time.

She was still ten feet from the door when it was flung open and the man who had haunted her thoughts, and humiliatingly enough, her dreams for the past fourteen or so hours, appeared on the porch.

"Thank God," he said, hurrying toward her and taking her suitcase. "I didn't think you'd ever get here."

She glanced at her watch. "I'm on time."

"I know. It's not that." He hesitated before stepping back into the house, as if he were an escaped soul being forced to return to hell. "We're not having a good morning."

Cassie gave him a quick once-over to check out his appearance. The poor man did look a little harried. There was a juice stain on his light blue shirt, one of his athletic shoes had come untied. He'd cut himself shaving and his hair was mussed. All this and it was still relatively early in the day.

"A problem with Sasha?" she asked sympathetically, knowing the toddler was thirty-plus pounds of pure energy and motion.

He closed the door behind her and set down her suitcase. "The worst. She's been crying."

Cassie had to bite her lower lip to keep from laughing. While she was sorry that Sasha was having a tough start to her day, Ryan had uttered the statement with all the solemnity and worry of a man talking about flood, famine and pestilence.

"It happens," Cassie said, working hard to keep her expression serious.

"But how do you make it stop?" He ran his hand through his hair and shook his head. "I'm completely at a loss. She looks at me with those big tears rolling down her face and I panic. I've told her I'll give her anything she wants if she just stops crying."

"You might want to rethink that philosophy," Cassie said. "It could get expensive in years to come. Plus it's never a good idea to give away power in the parent/child relationship. They're going to learn fifty different ways to play you as it is. Trust me on this."

His green eyes darkened. "She's asking for her mother."

Cassie's good humor faded. "I'm not surprised. This is a difficult time for both of you."

The previous day she'd seen Ryan as a cool, sophisticated businessman, but now, standing in the foyer of his late brother's house, he just looked confused. "What am I supposed to say?" he asked. "How do I tell her that her mother isn't coming home and I'm all she's got?" His mouth twisted. "They screwed up big time leaving that kid to me."

"No, they didn't. If leaving her to you had been a mistake, you wouldn't be worried about her feelings. You'd just be going on about your day and not giving her another thought."

His gaze locked with hers. "Then I'm the biggest bastard in town because that's exactly what I want to do."

She read the pain in his face, the questions. Having kids around could be difficult under the best of circumstances, but Ryan didn't even have the advantage of experience. He and Sasha were strangers.

"It doesn't matter what you *want* to do," she said quietly. "We all have thoughts we're not proud of. Fortunately we're judged on our actions, not our fantasies."

He didn't look convinced. "Will she get over losing her parents?"

Interesting question, Cassie thought. "Yes, but not in the way you think. She'll eventually stop asking for them. We can try to explain what happened in simple terms and she'll accept it. But she'll always carry an empty space around inside of her. She'll always wonder how it would have been different if her parents had lived."

"You sound like you know what you're talking about."

"I do. I'm adopted. It comes with the territory." She forced a lightness into her voice. "Everything will be fine. You'll see. Look at how great I turned out."

His gaze lingered on her face. "Thanks for listening. I don't usually dump on relative strangers."

She had a feeling he didn't talk about his emotions with anyone, but she didn't say that. "No problem. The advice is worth about what you paid for it."

"No, it's worth a lot more than that." He motioned to the family room off to the right. "She's watching a video. What did parents do before VCRs?"

"I have no idea."

"Thank God for technology." He picked up her suitcase. "I'll take this up to your room. I've put you across the hall from Sasha. I hope that's all right. The room is pretty big and it has its own bathroom. Everything is clean. From what I can figure out, a cleaning service comes through about once a week."

"I'm sure the room is fine," she said, as he headed for the family room. She wished there was a way to prolong their conversation. Ryan's confession of his feelings had only added fuel to the fire that was her infatuation. After all, now he was more than a pretty face—he was also emotionally tortured. How was she supposed to resist that? It was just like a scene out of *Pride and Prejudice,* she thought dreamily as she walked into the family room. Ryan was Darcy, proud and standoffish. She was plucky Elizabeth. In time he would realize that she was the—

"Cassie!" Sasha shrieked in delight when she saw her. The toddler grinned, then pointed at the television. "Toons."

"I know. Are they fun?"

Sasha nodded, her short curls flying up and down with the movement of her head. Cassie could see the lingering trace of tears on the child's face and resisted the urge to pull her close and hug her. There was no point in upsetting the little girl's happy mood. There would be plenty of tears later for her to cuddle away.

She settled on the floor next to Sasha and listened to her chatter about the video. While the fact that Ryan was handsome and sophisticated added a little spark to her temporary job, she knew she would have taken it even if he'd been an old man, or even a woman. Because no matter how she daydreamed about her boss, the reality was she'd committed herself to Joel. Even more important than that, Sasha needed her to help her through this difficult adjustment. Cassie had a big heart and there was more than enough room for one little girl to slip inside.

RYAN HAD GOTTEN so used to the noise drifting in from different parts of the house that he wasn't sure at first what had broken his concentration. Then he realized it was the silence. He leaned back in his chair and turned to stare out the window at the well-manicured grounds around the Victorian house.

"Peace and quiet," he breathed with something close to awe. It was a sound he hadn't heard much of since Sasha had returned home after the funeral last week, especially not during the day. This was something else he had to thank Cassie for.

He'd gotten more work done in the past—he glanced at his watch—five hours, than in the previous five days. He didn't mind the sound of running feet or the bursts of laughter, the slamming doors or the clatter of toys falling somewhere in the house. None of that bothered him, mostly because his office door was closed and he knew that as long as Cassie was around, no pip-squeak with big eyes was going to come interrupt him. Until this moment, he'd never really appreciated the sound of silence.

He drew in a deep breath, reveling in the freedom of

not being completely responsible for Sasha. Someone else would take care of feeding her and dealing with her tantrums and her tears. If he could keep full-time help around, the kid might not be so bad.

There was a light knock at his door. For a second he panicked, then he realized that Sasha was not one to ask politely for entrance. Instead she seemed to feel that the entire world existed for her pleasure.

"Come in," he called.

Cassie opened the door and stepped into his office. "Hi, do you have a minute? I need to talk to you about a couple of things."

"Sure. Please, have a seat."

He motioned her to the chair that sat on the opposite side of his desk. As she crossed the room, he took in her appearance. Yesterday he vaguely recalled that she'd worn a dress when she brought over the food. Today she was in jeans and a long-sleeved green T-shirt. She was of average height, maybe five-five or five-six, with short dark hair and a pleasant face. If he'd seen her on the street, he wouldn't have bothered looking at her a second time, but here in his brother's house, taking care of his brother's child, Ryan thought she was an angel.

"Is everything all right?" he asked, suddenly nervous that she was having second thoughts about the job. "If you need any supplies or want me to buy anything, I'll be happy to take care of it. Just say the word."

She smiled and held up a hand to stop him. "It's okay, Ryan, you don't have to offer me the world. I promise not to cry, or quit."

"Good." He rested his hands on his desk. "Then what can I do for you?"

"I have a couple of questions. I just put Sasha down

for her nap. She resisted me a little, but fell right asleep as soon as I got her quiet. Has she been sleeping okay?"

He stared at her blankly. "Nap? The kid is supposed to take naps?" He thought about the long afternoons when his niece had gotten more and more cranky. "No wonder she was difficult," he muttered more to himself than Cassie. "Shouldn't children come with instructions or something? How are people supposed to know this sort of thing?"

"They learn by doing," Cassie said with a straight face, although he caught the slight quivering at the corner of her mouth.

"You're laughing at me. You work in a preschool, you're around children all the time. I've never been around them. Not since I was one."

He thought about his childhood, how his mother had been always pushing him to make the most of his time. He'd been the younger of the two brothers and there hadn't been many other children in their neighborhood. Now that he thought about it, except for school and his brother, he'd never been around kids.

"I swear I'm not laughing," Cassie said. "You're right, I do have more experience. I have a degree in child development. I'm sure if you put me into your world of business and computers, I would be just as uncomfortable. And to answer your question, yes, Sasha still needs a nap. At the school all the children have to rest for at least half an hour every afternoon." Noticing his blank look, she continued her explanation. "The littler ones like her have a separate room and they generally sleep for at least an hour. She'll still need a good night's sleep, but the nap will make her easier to deal with in the late afternoon and early evening."

He grabbed a notepad and scrawled the word *nap*. He

couldn't imagine how many other things he'd been doing wrong. "What else?" he asked.

Cassie wrinkled her nose. "I know that Sasha's your niece and that you need to spend time getting to know each other. However, I wondered how you would feel about her going to the preschool a few mornings a week."

He didn't say anything because all he could focus on was the sense of relief, followed by a flash of guilt. He knew it was wrong not to want to take responsibility for Sasha. He supposed he must have a defect in his character or something because a normal, caring uncle would be thrilled to take charge of his family. But Ryan just wanted to pack up and head back to San Jose. He wasn't proud to admit it but, given his choice, he would dump Sasha with Cassie indefinitely. However, no one was offering him that as an option.

"I know what you're thinking," Cassie said quickly, as if she was afraid he was going to protest. "It seems a little soon."

"Actually, that wasn't what I was thinking," he admitted.

"Good. I believe that what will help Sasha the most is to get back into her old routine. She needs her life to return to normal as much as it can. She has friends at the preschool, other teachers whom she really likes. I think a couple of hours three or four days a week will make her feel more secure."

"That sounds fine," he told her. "You're the expert."

"You're her family. I don't want to interfere."

He leaned forward. "Cassie, until last week, I'd never seen her. I don't know anything about raising a child. To be honest, this was not part of my game plan, but Helen didn't have any family and John only had me, so the buck stops here. I would appreciate any suggestions or thoughts you might have on the best way to handle any situation with Sasha."

"All right. Thank you for your candor."

Dark eyes regarded him appraisingly. He wondered what she was thinking about him. No doubt she found him highly lacking in paternal skills and feelings.

"How has she been eating?" Cassie asked. "I didn't notice a problem at dinner last night, or at lunch today."

She might as well have asked his opinion on the viability of a Mars colony in the next twenty years. "I have no idea how she's eating," he said wryly. "Sometimes she gets the food in her mouth, and sometimes she's more interested in getting it on me and everything around her."

"Oh." Cassie smiled. "You're right. You wouldn't know what is normal and what isn't. I'll watch things and let you know." She paused. "What about at night? Has she been having nightmares?"

He thought about the past few nights. "I think so," he told her. "Sometimes she cries out. I've had to go in and rock her a couple of times. She just curls up in my arms and cries."

He pushed those memories away. He didn't want to have to think about that.

"Are you surprised?" Cassie asked.

"No. I guess not. I wish this hadn't happened."

"Give her time," she said. "The same time you're going to need. I suspect her pain will come in waves, then disappear for a while. She'll probably make up stories about her parents to comfort herself. A lot of children do that when they've suffered this kind of loss."

"Is that what you did?" he asked, then wondered if the question was inappropriate. But, he reminded himself, she'd been the one who had told him she was adopted.

"I didn't make up stories because I didn't have anything to remind me of my birth parents. Sasha will have photos, and you'll talk about them. I don't think she's going to have memories, though. She's pretty young." She shifted in her chair and tucked her hair behind her ears. "I grew up knowing I'd been adopted, just as Sasha is going to know she lost her parents. I was always grateful that the Wright family had wanted me in their life. Sasha is going to be pleased to have her uncle Ryan to look after her."

He didn't know about the latter, but he nodded as if he did.

"You don't believe me," she said.

Her perception startled him. "I didn't know you were a mind reader as well as being a genius when it came to kids."

"I'm not, but it's obvious you're uncomfortable with Sasha. You're feeling out of place, so the rest of it makes sense. It's going to be okay, Ryan. In time you'll be as thrilled to have her around as she is to have you around. Sometimes the family we have to earn can mean more than the family we're given." A warm glow filled her eyes. "My sister and my aunt are all I have left of my family and both are precious to me. Chloe, my sister, has always been there, but Aunt Charity is a relatively new addition. I treasure her all the more for being an unexpected bonus in my life." She flashed him another smile. "You're going to have to trust me on this."

"I guess you're right."

Her gaze dropped from him to his desk. "I see you have a lot of work to do, so I'll leave you to it. Thanks for taking the time to talk with me."

"You're welcome."

She rose to her feet and quickly walked out of the

room. Ryan stared after her until the door closed and he was again alone, then he turned his chair and stared out at the unfamiliar view of manicured lawn and trimmed hedges.

He'd never met anyone like Cassie. There were some who would say that her views of family were old-fashioned. Actually, he would be one of the first people in line to say that, but he was starting to wonder if maybe he was the one out of step. Just because everyone he knew, including himself, was driven by career rather than a personal life didn't mean it was right.

He grimaced. "Who are you trying to kid?" he asked aloud. Yeah, family had its place, but everyone knew that getting ahead was the most important thing in the world. His own mother had spent her life dedicated to that philosophy.

He remembered all the times after he'd finally found success, when he'd wanted to give his mother something nice. Even though both of her sons had been secure in their careers and anxious for her to take it easy, she'd insisted on working two jobs, taking cash from her employers instead of vacation time. She'd always turned down their offers of nice clothes or a better house, urging them instead to invest the money. She'd been poor and hardworking for too long to believe it was okay to accept a "freebie" from anyone…even her children.

Now, when he thought about those years, he felt sad. She'd died without ever once taking time for herself, or time to enjoy all she'd earned. Her entire life had been a quest to have enough, and once she had enough, to have more.

Somewhere between her world and Cassie's lay what was normal. At least in his opinion. But for now, he was weeks behind on his work and with full-time help to take care of Sasha, his days could finally return to something close to productive.

CALLIE AND JAKE moved closer to the crib. "What do you think is in there?" Callie asked, her little pink nose all wrinkled and her white whiskers quivering.

"I don't know," Jake answered as he put first one paw up on the edge of the mattress, then the other as he tried to see. "It makes a lot of noise and it smells funny. I'm scared."

The calico cat and the marmalade cat looked at each other. Something strange was going on in their house and they weren't sure they liked it.

Cassie stopped reading aloud and pointed to the pictures in the children's storybook. "Can you see the kitties?" she asked Sasha.

The toddler cuddled against her as they moved back and forth in the rocking chair in Sasha's room.

"Cat!" Sasha announced proudly as she pointed to the color drawing of the two cats cautiously investigating the new crib in their home.

"That's right. Two cats. The calico one is Callie. She's a girl cat. The orange cat is Jake. He's her brother."

"Cat!" Sasha said again.

"Two cats. Can you say two?"

"Two!"

"Very good."

Cassie kissed the top of the little girl's head and inhaled the baby talc scent of her. After dinner she'd given Sasha a bath, and now they were reading a story before bedtime. As far as first days went, it had been successful. At least in her eyes.

Sasha stretched and yawned, then pointed at the book. "Read," she ordered. "Read cat story."

So Cassie read about the two kitties who were scared of the stranger in their house. How they didn't like the noises or the smells, but when they saw the baby for the first time, they got a warm feeling in their chest that made them purr. And how when the neighbor's dog got inside by accident, they both stood up to the larger creature and protected the baby. The last picture showed the infant on its mother's lap with both cats curled up next to her, ever watchful over their new charge.

"The end," she said, and closed the book. "Time for bed."

"Gen...read story gen."

Cassie put the book down and carried Sasha to her crib. "Not *again*. Not tonight. You have to sleep." She set her on the mattress, then pulled up the blanket and kissed her cheek. "Night, muffin. Sleep well. I'll see you in the morning."

Heavy-lidded blue eyes blinked slowly. "Read peas. Not tired."

Cassie chuckled. "Liar. You're exhausted. You're going to be asleep in less than two minutes."

The sound of murmured conversation carried to Ryan as he stood in the shadowy darkness of the hall. He told himself he should go in and say good-night to his niece. Maybe pat her shoulder or something. But the thought made him nervous. He wasn't good at all the parenting stuff. Cassie was obviously a capable woman and Sasha was better off in her care.

So instead of joining them, he walked to his office and closed the door. But for once the silence and solitude didn't invigorate him, and the thought of working didn't inspire him. For the first time in a long time, he wanted something more than his computer and some time in which to concentrate.

It was that damn kid, he thought resentfully. She was going to change everything and he didn't like it. No wonder he felt unsettled.

He sure could relate to those cats in that dumb story. He didn't like the smells and the noise either. But when he looked at Sasha *he* didn't want to purr...he wanted to run.

He wasn't very proud of himself these days, but he didn't know how to change. Worse, he wasn't sure he wanted to change.

He turned and looked at the portrait hanging over the fireplace in the makeshift office. It showed a laughing couple holding their baby daughter close. It had been done about a year before, when Sasha had been about a year old.

Ryan took in the man's features, which were so similar to his own. His throat tightened. "Dammit, John, what do you want from me?"

Of course there wasn't any answer. He hadn't been expecting one.

"I wish..." he started, then his voice trailed off. He coughed to clear his throat. "I wish you hadn't died. I miss you."

Then, because he was a busy man who didn't have time for all the emotional nonsense in his life, he turned his back on the portrait and settled down in front of his computer.

CHAPTER THREE

"ME HELP," Sasha informed Cassie as she banged the wooden spoon on the inside of the pot.

"I know," Cassie said and smiled down at the toddler sitting by the kitchen table. "You're a big girl and you help me a lot."

The praise earned her a big grin. Sasha was such a sweet child, she thought as she turned back to the stove and checked on the meat loaf. A glance at the timer told her the main course still had about forty minutes to cook. Time for her to get started on the potatoes.

She collected a half dozen and began peeling them. Sasha sang tunelessly in an effort to accompany herself on her pot banging. Cassie wondered how far the noise would travel in the big house and if Ryan was having trouble concentrating.

This was her third day working for him, taking care of his niece. They'd all settled into a routine fairly quickly. She took care of Sasha while Ryan hid out in his office. He made occasional appearances, but most of them occurred after the toddler was in bed. Still, despite his lack of participation in the day-to-day events, Cassie knew he was in the house with her. There was something oddly domestic about the arrangement. While she liked it, the situation also made her a little nervous.

On occasion, she allowed herself to imagine everything was real. That this was her home, Sasha her child.

By default, of course, Ryan was the adoring husband and father. It was like being a kid again and playing house, she thought. Only this time she couldn't walk away if she got tired or wanted to play something else. There was also the added twist of hormones. Hers were still deeply infatuated with Ryan.

The mental image of microscopic hormone-filled cells swaying in time with some love song from the fifties caused her to chuckle out loud.

"What's so funny?"

The unexpected male voice made her jump. Cassie spun and saw Ryan standing in the doorway to the kitchen. He propped one shoulder against the door frame and crossed his arms over his chest. As usual, he wore jeans and a long-sleeved shirt rolled up to the elbows. Today that shirt was blue.

There was something so incredibly masculine about him. While she knew in her head that Joel was also male, he seemed to have nothing in common with Ryan. It was as if the two men were two completely different species.

"I, um, was just thinking about some things," she said when he continued to look at her expectantly. She could feel a flush heating her cheeks and she hoped that if he noticed, he would assume it was from the oven or the exertion of cooking.

"I see."

She couldn't tell if he was letting her off the hook because he was being polite or because he had figured out what had been on her mind and he didn't want to talk about it. Please God, let it be the former.

"Unk Ryan!" Sasha waved her wooden spoon in the air. "Me help."

"You're like the drum major for a marching band," he said. "I'm sure Cassie appreciates you setting the beat."

Sasha frowned in confusion, returned to her pot and began banging against the side and singing. Ryan winced at the noise, then moved into the kitchen.

"What are you cooking?" he asked, raising his voice slightly to be heard over the noise.

"There's a meat loaf in the oven. I'm going to make mashed potatoes and green beans." Cassie paused, then lowered her voice as Sasha got caught up in the play of light on the pot lid and stopped banging. "I never thought to ask what you liked to eat. I generally fix simple things like this or spaghetti. Roast chicken, that sort of stuff. But if you have a preference, I can see what I can do."

He tucked his hands into his jeans pockets and looked at her. "You're not here to cook for me. You're Sasha's nanny." He glanced around the kitchen. "I should have hired someone to take care of meals. I never thought about it."

"It's all right. I don't mind. In fact, I sort of like cooking."

His green-eyed gaze settled on her face. "Practice?"

His features were strong and so perfectly proportioned, she thought as she stared back. She'd never met a man with such gorgeous eyes before and she found that she really liked how they looked. He didn't smile much, but when he did she could feel it all the way down to her toes. And his voice. Smooth and low, his voice belonged on the radio, or maybe recording books on tape.

"Cassie?"

"Huh? Oh, um, practice." That had been the last thing he'd said, right? At least she thought so. "Practice for what?"

He pointed to her left hand. "When you get married. I was asking if you were seeing what all that would be like. This is a great simulation."

Yeah, she thought dreamily, except they weren't simulating the good parts.

"I hadn't thought of it that way," she forced herself to say, because he seemed to expect a response from her.

"You're a natural. Your boyfriend is a lucky guy." He smiled.

On cue, her toes curled, her stomach dove for her knees and her mouth went dry. The man had a smile that could change carbon into diamonds. Boyfriend, she thought vaguely. Oh, yeah, Joel.

Joel! Yikes, what was she doing? She was practically an engaged woman. Cassie stiffened her spine and forced away all warm and yummy thoughts about her employer. She was wasting her time daydreaming. He was not for her. The man was successful, probably rich and definitely older by at least seven or eight years. She didn't usually act like this. What was wrong with her? She forced her attention back to the potato she was supposed to be peeling.

"Thanks," she said and was proud when her voice came out sounding completely normal. "I'll tell him you said that the next time he and I are together."

"You do that."

"Unk Ryan, up!"

Sasha had abandoned her pots and spoon and now stood in front of her uncle. She raised her arms toward him. "Up," she repeated.

"What does she want?" Ryan asked.

"Just what you think she does," Cassie answered, not sure how it was possible to misinterpret the toddler's request. "She wants you to pick her up and hold her."

"That's what I was afraid of."

He mumbled more than spoke the comment as he bent over and reached for his niece. Sasha smiled broadly as he picked her up and held her in front of him. But when he didn't move her close to his body, but instead kept her nearly at arm's length, her smile faded.

Cassie dropped the knife and potato onto the counter, then moved next to him. "You've got to hold her so she feels safe," she told him. "Sasha wants to snuggle. Rest her on your hip."

She put her hands on the toddler's waist and supported her while Ryan awkwardly shifted the child to his left. Only he didn't have the same naturally curved hips that women had, Cassie realized a half second later as Sasha started to slide down.

"Wrap one arm around her waist and pull her to your chest. She can put her arms around your neck."

She stepped back to give them room to maneuver, but it was too late. Sasha struggled to break free of him. "Down," she said forcefully.

Ryan set her on her feet and shifted awkwardly. "I'm not around kids much."

"It will get easier," Cassie assured him, hoping she was telling the truth.

Sasha stared at her uncle with a hurt look of betrayal on her face. Tears were only a couple of seconds away, Cassie realized and moved to the silverware drawer.

"Can you help me set the table?" she asked, then handed the little girl three spoons. "Will you please put these on the table?"

Sasha sniffed twice, then took the spoons and carried them over to the table. She pushed them up onto the wooden surface, then took one back and returned her attention to her uncle.

"I'm not like you," Ryan said, barely noticing the child. "I don't have any natural ability in this arena."

Sasha carried the spoon over to her uncle. She thrust it toward him. He glanced down at her, then at Cassie.

When she nodded encouragingly, he took the spoon and patted the top of Sasha's head. She beamed.

It was sad, Cassie thought as she watched them. If only Ryan had spent a little time in his niece's company, he wouldn't be feeling so out of place now. But he hadn't and they were both paying the price. Every situation seemed so forced between them. She wished there was a way to make it easier...for both of them. The only solution was for them to spend more time together, but Ryan didn't seem willing to pursue that option. He passed through their day like a ship's captain checking briefly on the passengers before returning to more important duties.

"Be back," Sasha said, then trotted out of the room.

"Was that a request or information?" Ryan asked.

"I think it was information."

Cassie finished peeling the potatoes. She sliced them, then dropped them into the pot and set it on the stove.

"Do you want me to finish setting the table?" he asked. "You can probably trust me with the forks and knives."

"Sure," she told him. "Thanks."

While he pulled out napkins and place mats, she went to work on the green beans. After a couple of minutes of silence, she began trying to think of something clever to say. When she failed on witty, she went with the obvious.

"How are you adjusting to working here?" she asked.

"I'm doing better." He set out two place mats, then collected Sasha's high chair from the corner and brought it over to the table. "I can do nearly everything I need to via conference call or through the modem. I might have to take a couple of trips back to San Jose, but they would be pretty short."

Sasha raced into the kitchen and handed Ryan one of her dolls. He stared at it for a couple of seconds, then finally took it from her.

"Thank you," he said.

Sasha grinned and raced out again.

"What am I supposed to do with this?" he asked.

"Just hold it. She'll be back shortly and it will hurt her feelings if you've put it down."

"Great." He looked at the doll. "I'm not much into redheads."

"Maybe you should let her know," Cassie said. But what she'd wanted to ask instead was how he felt about brunettes. Ah, she had it bad, she thought with resignation. But at least she would probably get over him just as quickly. Crushes didn't usually last…at least she didn't think they did. She didn't have any personal experience with the subject. Maybe she should phone her sister and get some advice.

Sasha returned to the kitchen and skittered to a stop in front of Ryan. This time she held out a battered, flop-eared bunny.

"You are too kind," he said.

Sasha giggled, clapped her hands together and made another mad dash out of the room.

"Looks like she's going to empty her toy box just for your pleasure," Cassie said. "You might want to get comfortable."

The toddler returned with a book. This time, instead of just thanking her, Ryan reached into his pocket and offered her a penny.

Her rosebud-shaped mouth fell open as her eyes widened. "Money," she said with all the reverence of clergy addressing God. She held it out to Cassie.

"Wow. Look at what you've got."

Sasha clutched it to her chest as she ran out of the room.

"You've made a friend now," Cassie told Ryan.

"I wasn't sure she would know what it was."

"I doubt she knows the value of a penny over a quarter, but she has a slight grasp of the concept. I don't think she would be as thrilled with bills as she is with coins, though."

"So she's a cheap date."

A rattling sound warned them of Sasha's approach. This time she carried her Mickey Mouse bank in her arms. When she stopped in front of Ryan, she set the bank on the floor, sat beside it and carefully placed the penny inside.

Cassie applauded. After a half-second delay, Ryan did the same. Then he reached into his pocket and pulled out another coin. Sasha took it and again slowly slid it inside. When it clinked against the other coins, she laughed.

They continued the game until Ryan held up his hands in mock dismay. "I don't have any more change, kid. Sorry."

"'Kay," Sasha said in an attempt to reassure him.

Cassie checked on the dinner, then glanced at the picture uncle and niece made. Handsome, businesslike Ryan sat on a kitchen chair with a red-haired doll and a worn stuffed rabbit tucked into the crook of his arm. Sasha sat at his feet, leaning against him, currently mesmerized by the laces on his athletic shoes.

His hair was lighter than Sasha's curls; their eyes were different colors. But Cassie saw some family resemblance between them. She caught it in a glance, the curve of a smile. She suspected they would look more alike as Sasha grew from a toddler to a little girl and her features became more defined.

The oven timer buzzed. Sasha straightened. "Food," she said.

"That's right. The meat loaf is done and the potatoes

will be ready in about five minutes. It's time to wash up so we can eat." She pointed at the toys in Ryan's arms. "Will you please take those back to your room for me?"

"I'll do it," Ryan told her as he stood. "I'm heading back to my office anyway."

Cassie tried to ignore the flash of disappointment that raced through her. He wasn't going to eat dinner with them? She wanted to pout like Sasha, thrusting out her lower lip and threatening tears if she didn't get her way. Instead she asked, "Aren't you hungry?"

He looked down at his niece, then at the set table. "Not right now. I'll grab something later."

Then he was gone. Cassie stared after him and wondered what had happened to chase him away. Her gaze moved to Sasha who was looking down the hall with the most forlorn expression on her face.

"I know just how you feel," Cassie told her. "I wanted him to stay, too. And not just for me, but also because you two need each other. Unfortunately I don't think your uncle has figured that out yet."

"So TELL me what to do," Cassie said as she leaned forward and rested her elbows on the kitchen table.

Aunt Charity poured coffee into her mug. "I'm sure it's frustrating."

"Exactly," Cassie said, relieved to finally have a chance to come home and talk with her sister and her aunt about Ryan Lawford. The old Victorian house was similar in size to Ryan's, but had a completely different floor plan. Here Cassie knew every room, every picture. She was familiar with the sounds and smells. Who would have thought that just a week away would have left her homesick? She'd even been pleased to see Old Man Withers sitting on his power mower as he trimmed the lawn. Even though the old goat did little more than insult any woman who made the mistake of offering him a friendly greeting.

"Sasha and I see Ryan less now than we did when I first arrived."

Her aunt looked at her sister. They were, Cassie realized, a study in contrasts—these three women who had, for a time, lived in the same house. Her aunt was slender with dark hair pulled back in a neat chignon. Her tailored clothing emphasized the youthful shape of her body, despite the fact that she was well into her fifties. Chloe was beautiful, as always, but especially radiant at nearly six months pregnant. Her curly red hair tumbled down her back in loose disarray. If Cassie hadn't loved her sister so much, she could have easily hated her for being so darned attractive. As it was, she depended on her. Chloe was her best friend and had been so all of her life.

"I don't know what to do," Cassie continued as she settled her hands around her mug. She glanced at the clock over the stove. She only had a short time until she had to pick up Sasha at the preschool. "It's not that he's hostile. I don't think he dislikes her as much as he's uncomfortable being around her. A few days ago he came in the kitchen while I was fixing dinner. Sasha was bringing him toys. He seemed fine with that. He even gave her a penny, which sent her racing for her Mickey Mouse bank. They seemed to be having fun together, but then he just left."

She looked at the two women she cared about most in the world. "I'm completely at a loss."

"How is Sasha doing?" Chloe asked. She was drinking a warm glass of milk instead of coffee, having given up caffeine for her pregnancy.

"Pretty well, considering everything she's been through. She has her spells when she wants her mother.

I hold her when she cries and, after a time, it passes. We haven't really talked about her parents going to heaven and not coming back. I don't know how to do that." She drew in a breath. Despite her degree and her experience working at the preschool, at times she had no idea how she was supposed to help Sasha deal with her loss. Sometimes all she had to go on was what her gut told her to do.

"She's sleeping and eating?" Aunt Charity asked as she set out a plate of cookies, then took the seat opposite Cassie's.

"Yes. That's all fine. I'm sure being in her house with her room and her routine is helping her. Ryan said he didn't want to deal with the issue of moving her just yet and decided to stay for a few more weeks." She pressed her lips together. "It's not that he's mean or rude. I think he forgets that she's around."

"Hard to imagine a toddler being quiet enough for that to happen," Chloe said wryly.

Cassie smiled. "Okay, maybe forget is too strong a word. I think he has a fabulous ability to focus on his work and he can ignore her for long periods of time."

"If he's never been around children, I'm not surprised by any of this," Chloe told her. "You shouldn't be either. How many times have you gotten frantic calls from fathers left with their kids for the first time? If you don't know how to deal with kids, it can be traumatic."

Aunt Charity pushed the plate of cookies closer. "This withdrawal might be his way of dealing with the loss of his brother."

Cassie took a chocolate chip cookie and nibbled on it. "I hadn't thought of that, but you could be right. The question is, what do I do about it?"

"You're going to have to remind him of his responsibilities," her aunt told her. "He's using you as a buffer and that's fine for now, but you're not always going to be there."

Cassie sighed. "I know," she said, even though she didn't want to agree. The thought of having that conversation with Ryan put a knot in her stomach. "He hadn't even met Sasha before the funeral," she said. "I don't understand families spending that much time apart."

Chloe touched her hand and smiled. "Not everyone is like us. Some siblings don't get along."

"What a waste." Cassie couldn't imagine living in a household like that. She returned her attention to the problem at hand. "I guess I'll say something to him. I'm just not sure what."

"How is Sasha acting around her uncle?" Chloe asked. "Is she frightened of him?"

"Not at all. She keeps including him in things. She often wants him to pick her up, but he doesn't know how to do it. He's too stiff, which scares her. It's never a positive experience for either of them. But Sasha is a sweetie and very forgiving. Ryan has a long way to go before he chases her off."

"That's something," Chloe pointed out. "She can be your ally in all this."

Cassie smiled at her aunt and her sister. "Thanks for the advice. That's why I came here. I knew you two would be able to steer me in the right direction."

Chloe sipped her milk, then smiled. "Our pleasure. And speaking of men who don't have a clue, what does Joel think about all this?"

"Don't insult Joel," Cassie said automatically, stalling for time, even though she knew what her sister was asking. She did *not* want to have this conversation with Chloe.

"Okay. What does Joel think about your new living

arrangements?" her sister asked. "Is he concerned that you're staying alone in a house with a good-looking, older man? Someone sophisticated enough to sweep you off your feet?"

Chloe's words were close enough to Cassie's own fantasies that she was afraid she would blush. "Joel doesn't think anything about it. We've spoken on the phone several times. He knows what I'm doing and why, and he's very supportive. He's not the jealous type."

She made the last statement with a note of defiance in her voice, even though she wasn't feeling especially pleased with Joel's actions...or lack thereof. In truth she would have liked him to be a *little* concerned about her close proximity to another man. After all, Ryan was everything Chloe had said and then some. Ryan was handsome and brilliant, and while she didn't know him that well, she could easily imagine him to have other fine qualities, qualities that every woman looked for in a partner. What she did know was that he was smart and driven about his work. She wasn't so sure about his humanity, though. He wasn't an obviously warm person, although she'd caught glimpses of humor now and then.

"It's very nice that Joel is being understanding," Aunt Charity said, and shot Chloe a warning look.

Chloe ignored it. "Joel doesn't have the sense God gave a turnip. I can't believe he's just sitting back and letting you do this without protesting."

"That's not fair," Cassie told her sister. "If Joel had gotten all macho on me and insisted I not live there, or if he'd been otherwise concerned, you would have called him a bully. You're not going to let him win either way."

Chloe had the good grace to look a little uncomfortable with her sister's words. "I would not," she said, but without much conviction.

Aunt Charity patted Cassie's hand. "You're going to be fine. I'm sure Joel feels a little jealousy. What man wouldn't? But he doesn't want to show it. As for Ryan and Sasha, it seems to me that you're on the right track. Be patient. It will all work out."

"I hope you're right," Cassie said.

The three women chatted for a little longer, then Cassie got up to leave. Chloe walked her to her car.

"You're glowing," Cassie said as they paused in the driveway. She had to speak up to be heard over the lawn mower. Old Man Withers was still out doing his weekly round over the grounds.

Chloe pressed her hand against her bulging tummy. "I don't know about glowing but I do know that I'm very happy." Her smile was tender. "Being in love will do that to a woman."

Cassie searched her face. "No regrets? It happened so fast. One minute he was a stranger, the next you were involved."

"I know. When I think about how quickly we found each other, I have trouble believing any of it is real." She smiled. "But the more we're together, the more I'm sure this is exactly right. Arizona isn't the perfect man, but he's perfect for me. We understand each other so well, it's almost scary. It must be the magic nightgown."

"Must be," Cassie agreed, trying not to be envious of her sister's happiness. Despite being a nonbeliever, Chloe had worn the Bradley nightgown when she'd turned twenty-five and she'd dreamed about Arizona Smith. They'd met the next morning and sparks had started to fly instantly. They'd had passion…they still did.

"You'll get your chance in a few weeks," Chloe reminded her. "Are you excited?"

Usually, she was, Cassie thought with surprise. But

not today. "I'm not a real Bradley," she said. "Even if I was, there's Joel."

Chloe gave her a quick hug. "You're a Bradley in your heart and I'm sure that's all that matters. As for Joel…" Her voice trailed off. "I swear, Cassie, you make me insane with your devotion to that man. What do you see in him?"

For once Cassie couldn't answer the question. "We're going to have to agree to disagree on this one."

"I know. I'm sorry. You have enough going on in your life without me making trouble with this old argument. I'll be good."

"Thanks."

They said their goodbyes. Cassie got into her car and started driving toward the preschool to pick up Sasha. She had to wrestle with an unfamiliar emotion—guilt. She didn't want to envy her sister's happiness, but she did. She didn't want to feel unsettled about Joel, but she did.

It wasn't fair to him, she reminded herself. He hadn't changed. He was exactly the same man she'd fallen in love with nine years ago. He was kind and gentle and caring. Okay, maybe he wasn't flashy and he didn't have a high-powered career or a lot of ambition, but he was good and decent. Wasn't that more important?

"What about passion?" a little voice whispered.

Cassie tried to push it away. There was more to life than sex. She should know. She'd gone her whole life without once experiencing what it would be like to be with a man. She knew that in time, if things continued on their present course, she and Joel would marry. They would become lovers. She was sure that their physical intimacy would be as pleasant as the rest of their relationship.

"I don't want pleasant," she muttered rebelliously. "I

want fire. I want to be swept away by needing someone. I want to feel alive."

She was being foolish, she told herself. Her priorities were messed up and the quicker she got them back in order, the happier she would be. But the traitorous thoughts wouldn't go away, and deep in her heart, she wasn't sure she wanted them to.

CHAPTER FOUR

"I'M GONNA get you!"

Cassie's voice drifted down from upstairs, followed by Sasha's laughter. The sound of thundering tiny feet accompanied the giggles. Earlier Ryan had heard running water, then splashing, so he assumed that Cassie had given his niece a bath before getting her ready for bed.

Over the past week, his life had taken on some kind of order, the movement of the hours marked by Sasha and Cassie's comings and goings to preschool, followed by the excitement of lunch, early-afternoon reading time, the quiet of his niece's nap, the preparation for dinner, evening playtime, then bath and bed. Despite his attempts to distance himself from the child as much as possible, he was still aware of what went on in her day.

He'd assumed that as he got used to being in the house with her and as he developed a routine, he would find her easier to forget. He could go for long stretches of time without thinking about her, but then she appeared in his mind without warning. He would think about how she smiled at him as he passed her and Cassie in the hall, or the way she liked him to read her at least one story before dinner each evening. He didn't understand her need for him to be there, but he found himself showing up before he was asked and lingering in the room until Cassie had prepared dinner, even though he rarely ate with the two of them.

One of the things that startled him the most about Sasha was her blind trust. Not so much of him as of Cassie. The toddler simply expected Cassie to be there to take care of her. If she had a need, she expected it to be fulfilled. If she wanted a hug, she asked and expected to receive affection. He couldn't imagine trusting another person so completely.

It was a curious situation, he thought as he returned his attention to his computer and buried himself in his work.

Sometime later he noticed the silence in the house and knew that Sasha was asleep. Peace reigned again. But before he could focus on his work, there was a knock at his door.

"Come in," he called and gave Cassie a welcoming smile as she entered his office. Except for seeing her with Sasha a couple of times a day, they were rarely together. He didn't know anything about this young woman who took care of his niece and quietly brought him food on trays so he could continue working through the day.

She moved across the floor toward him, then paused in front of his desk. "I have a couple of things I would like to talk to you about," she said. "Is this a convenient time?"

"Sure. Have a seat."

"Thanks." She settled in the chair across from his.

He leaned forward. "Before you start, I want to tell you that you're doing a terrific job with Sasha. She seems very happy these days. You've got her on a schedule, the house is in order. I really appreciate that."

"You're welcome." Cassie tucked a strand of dark hair behind her ear. "To be honest, it's easy duty. Your niece is a very happy little girl. She's intelligent and fun to be with." She paused and cleared her throat. "Although we talked about salary when I was first hired, we never discussed time off."

Ryan stared at her for a couple of seconds. He opened his mouth to respond, then closed it. "You're right," he said at last. "I'm sorry. I should have thought of that and I don't know why I didn't." He shrugged. "Evidence to the contrary, I'm not usually a slave driver when it comes to my employees. What seems fair to you?"

"I don't need that much," Cassie told him. "I have some time to myself when I drop her off at the preschool. They invited me to come back to work for those few hours each morning but I told them I had my hands full already. So I'm able to get any personal things done then. What about two evenings a week, and one full day every other week? Just to make it easy on you, I'll arrange day care for the full day. You should be fine on your own in the evening. Sasha sleeps soundly through the night."

He felt a faint whisper of panic at the thought of being left alone with his niece again. Their first few days together hadn't gone well. But, he reminded himself, Cassie was right. Sasha slept through until morning. As long as he wouldn't have to deal with her during waking hours, he would be all right.

"When did you want to start your nights off?" he asked.

"Tonight."

He heard the words as she spoke them but it took a little longer for the meaning to sink in. Great, he thought grimly. He was being thrown into the fire without warning. "That will be fine," he told her, careful to keep his voice and his expression neutral.

She continued to stay in her seat, but instead of sitting quietly, she fidgeted slightly. Obviously she had more on her mind.

"What else did you want to talk about?" he asked when it became clear she needed prompting. He could only hope it wasn't another bombshell about leaving him alone with Sasha.

She touched her right heart-shaped earring, then laced her fingers together. She was nervous about something, he thought as warning bells went off in his head.

"It's about Sasha," she started.

Despite the fact that he didn't want to hear anything negative she had to say on that topic, he told her to continue.

"She's your niece," Cassie continued.

"Surprisingly enough, I'm aware of that."

She gave him a brief smile. "I know it's hard for you to connect with her. You haven't been around children much. Your work is very demanding. Adding to the stress in your life is the fact that you recently lost your only brother and you've had to temporarily relocate to a new town."

Ryan wasn't sure where all this was going, but he knew he wasn't going to like it when they got there. "None of this is news to me."

She squared her shoulders and met his gaze. "You can't ignore Sasha forever. She's not going away. If it's difficult for you to deal with the loss of your family, imagine how she feels. She's too young to understand anything except that her parents—in essence her entire known family and her whole world—are gone. She's scared and alone and she's barely two years old. She needs you to be around more. She needs to know she can count on you."

Ryan wasn't ready for a child to count on him, nor was he any great prize in the family or responsibility department, but one look at Cassie's determined expression told him he wasn't going to get away with saying that to her.

"I'm not going anywhere," he said at last, when it became obvious Cassie was waiting for a response. He was stuck, even if he didn't want to be.

"I appreciate that, and I'm sure if Sasha was old enough to understand, she would appreciate hearing that, too. But right now actions are going to speak louder than words for her." Her eyes darkened with compassion. "I know this has been terrible for you. Losing your brother and Helen, taking responsibility for Sasha. While it might make sense for you to hide out until you feel as if you've started to heal, it would be so much better for Sasha if you could allow yourself to need her, at least a little. She needs *you* so very much."

He didn't need Sasha, he thought. He hadn't needed anyone since he was seven or eight years old. His mother hadn't only taught him the power of hard work, she'd also taught him self-reliance. But he couldn't tell that to Cassie; she wouldn't understand. Besides, there was an odd knot in his stomach when he thought about his niece and he had a feeling that if he examined the sensation too closely he would find it was fueled by guilt.

Cassie was right—he couldn't ignore Sasha forever. Even though a part of him wanted to. Even though he was the wrong person to raise her and he didn't know what the hell he was supposed to do with her. But his only brother had entrusted him with Sasha and he couldn't turn his back on that trust.

In truth he'd been hoping the problem would go away by itself. He wanted to remind Cassie that he'd relocated to Bradley, had moved into his brother's house, and wasn't that enough? Why should he have to do more?

"I see your point," he said quietly. "What do you want me to do?"

"Nothing that scary." She tilted her head and smiled.

"Just get to know her. Pretend she's your new neighbor. How would you meet someone like that?"

"I wouldn't." At her look of surprise he found himself adding, "I'm not a very social person."

"Why would you choose to spend your life alone?"

No one had ever asked him that before, but he didn't have any trouble with the answer. "It's easier."

"Not getting involved?"

He nodded. "Things are a lot more tidy when people don't get involved."

Her dark brown eyes seemed to be staring into his soul. "Sounds lonely."

"Sometimes, but it's a small price to pay for autonomy." He drew in a breath. For some reason, Cassie's questions made him uncomfortable. He decided to shift the conversation back to something safer. "If I wanted to get to know my neighbor, I would say 'hi,' strike up a conversation in the elevator, that sort of thing."

"It's not so different with Sasha," Cassie told him. "You need to spend more time with her. Get to know her in her world."

"She's two."

"She still has a world of her own. It's a little different from yours but it's not so very foreign."

"You want me to play dolls with her?"

Cassie grinned. "I was thinking more of spending time with her at meals, maybe reading to her at bedtime, going for walks. Although if you like the idea of playing dolls, go ahead."

"Gee, thanks." He shifted in his seat. She made it sound so simple, but it wasn't. At least not for him. "I'm not dismissing your advice, but I feel awkward around her. She's so small. I'm afraid I'm going to step on her or something. Worse, I don't understand half of what she's saying."

"Oh and I do?"

He stared at her. "You don't?"

"Of course not." Cassie leaned toward him. Her mouth curved up in a smile. "She's doing great on her verbal skills, but she's not ready for the debate team. Some of what she says is hard to interpret, but if you pay attention to her facial expressions and her body language, you can usually understand what she's asking for or telling you. Sometimes, though, you've just got to nod and act interested even if you don't have a clue."

"You make it sound simple."

"It is, Ryan. You're a smart man and this isn't going to be that hard for you. I'm not asking you to take over all her care." Her smile turned impish. "After all, that would mean I would lose my great job. But you need to be with her more each day. Start slowly. That's how everyone does it. Most parents get to begin in the baby stage, where they're caught up in crisis management all the time and there isn't so much communication involved. By the time their child is a toddler, they've grown to understand her. But I think you're more than capable of figuring this all out."

He gazed at her speculatively. "*I* think I'm being given a snow job."

"Excuse me?"

"All those compliments you're throwing my way—I think they have a purpose."

"Is that bad?"

There was a teasing quality to her voice. Something completely feminine and intriguing. As he stared at her, taking in the thick brown hair that moved with each movement of her head, her big eyes accentuated by light makeup and her generous smile, he realized he'd never seen her before. Oh, of course he'd physically noticed her presence in his house. But he'd never noticed she was a woman.

It just went to show what bad shape he was in, he thought as he stared at the faint color on her smooth cheeks and the generous curves of her breasts. Tonight she wore a long-sleeved cream-colored dress with high heels. Heart-shaped earrings dangled from her ears. He vaguely recalled that she'd worn a dress on their first meeting and jeans ever since. He'd catalogued her presence, the sound of her voice, her competence, but he'd never *seen* her. Dear Lord, there was an attractive young woman living in his house. She'd been there an entire week and he'd just got the message.

"Who are you?" he asked without thinking. "Where are you from?"

Her smile widened. "Practicing your skills on me? The questions are a little complicated for your niece."

Perhaps, he thought, but he wasn't interested in Sasha's answers. He already knew those. He wanted to know about Cassie Wright. How old was she? She'd told him, he remembered that. Twenty-three, maybe? Twenty-four? How could he not have been paying attention? Maybe it was because she was so different from all the other women in his world. Those he worked with he acknowledged as female, but only in the most superficial way. Long ago he'd found life much easier if he viewed all his colleagues the same way. The women he dated were usually smooth, sophisticated career types who wanted the same things he did and clearly understood how it was all to be played. Cassie didn't even know there was a game in progress.

Her smiled faded. "That was all I had to talk about," she said. "I don't want to keep you from your work."

She was going to leave. He stiffened as he realized he didn't want her to. He searched his mind for some excuse to keep her sitting in place. "Where are you off to tonight?" he asked.

"Joel and I are going to a movie."

Joel? Ah, the boyfriend. His gaze strayed to the slender band on her left hand. Joel of the diamond-lint promise ring.

"Tell me about Joel."

"Joel is, well, Joel." She frowned slightly as if not sure what kind of information to share. "He works long hours. You two have that in common."

At least Joel dated, he thought grimly as he tried to remember the last time he'd been out with one of his female friends. It had been months. Lately he'd spent all his time at the office. Maybe because most of the women of his acquaintance had started to all sound the same.

"What does he do?"

"He's the assistant manager of Bradley Discount Store." She fingered the promise ring. "His is a very responsible position. He's going to be manager in a couple of years, and when that happens he'll be their youngest manager ever. He's worked there since he was sixteen."

"Sounds like they appreciate him," he said, wondering why he'd thought Cassie would be dating a lawyer or a doctor.

She nodded. "He's done well. He takes management classes at the community college. One day he'll be able to transfer to the university." She paused, then added, "He's very nice."

"I'm sure he is."

"He's nothing like you, of course." Her voice sounded defensive.

He raised his eyebrows. "Because I'm not nice?"

Cassie opened her mouth, then snapped it shut and closed her eyes. A bright flush swept up her cheeks. "I didn't mean that the way it came out," she mumbled.

He'd been interested before, but now he was intrigued. Not only by Cassie and her faux pas, but by the differences between himself and Joel. "So Joel and I don't have much in common?" he asked in an attempt to rescue her.

She shot him a look of gratitude. "Not really. He's lived in Bradley all his life. You're a lot more sophisticated. Then there's the age difference. He's only a year older than me. We're just the country mice here, while you've been all over."

He thought about telling her that the big world beyond Bradley wasn't as wonderful as she made it out to be, but doubted she would believe him. "How long have you two been dating?"

"Nine years."

He blinked…twice. "I'm sorry, did you say *nine* years?"

Some of the color had faded from her cheeks. It returned now, although she didn't turn from his incredulous gaze. "Yes. I started dating Joel when I was in high school."

"And you're not married?"

"No."

"You're not officially engaged?"

"No."

"But you've been dating for nine years?"

"Why is that so hard to understand?"

"I've never known anyone who has done that," he admitted. "I doubt I've dated anyone for nine months, let alone that long." He couldn't imagine any situation in which that made sense. Of course his personal life had never been all that important to him.

She shrugged. "We don't want to make a mistake. Getting married is a serious commitment and we want to be sure."

Ryan didn't think they could be any *more* sure, unless they were planning to experience old age together first, to see what that was like.

He had several other questions he wanted to ask, but before he could, the doorbell rang. Cassie shot out of her chair.

"I'll get that," she said quickly and practically ran from the room.

Ryan followed. While he didn't really have the right to intrude on Cassie's private time, he couldn't help wanting to get a look at the young man who had dated Cassie for nine years without "being sure" of his commitment. He walked into the foyer just as Joel stepped in from the porch.

The two men stared at each other. Joel was a few inches shorter, maybe five-nine or -ten, with wavy blond hair and glasses. He was slight, dressed in freshly pressed khakis and a blue, long-sleeved shirt.

Joel blinked first. He stepped forward, offering both his hand and an easy grin. "You must be Ryan Lawford," he said. "Cassie has told me a lot about you. She's really pleased to be able to help out. She's the best," he added, a note of pride in his voice. "Great with kids." His smile faded. "I was real sorry to hear about your brother and sister-in-law. It's a tragic loss."

Until that moment Ryan hadn't realized that he'd wanted to dislike Joel, or at least have the kid show up with hay in his hair, dressed like some hick out on the town for the first time in a year. Instead, Joel was exactly what Ryan should have expected. A nice, sincere young man with prospects.

"Thank you," Ryan said, shook Joel's hand, then stepped back.

Cassie moved to her boyfriend's side and gave him a quick hug. "Hi," she murmured.

They didn't kiss, or show any outward affection, but Ryan figured that was because he was there, cramping their style. No doubt they would be more intimate later, maybe going back to Joel's place and making love. There was a definite connection between them. He could see it in the shared glance, the way they stood so close together. He'd thought he would feel superior and a little worldly when compared with Joel and Cassie, but instead he felt inadequate and out of place.

"Enjoy yourselves," Ryan said as Joel held the front door open for Cassie. "You've got a key, right?"

She gave him a quick smile over her shoulder. "Yes, you gave me one last week. Don't worry, Ryan, I'll be back before midnight."

"You don't have to be."

Her dark eyes slipped away from his, as if she had something she was trying to hide. "I know, but it's a weeknight. Joel and I both have to be up early in the morning."

She gave him a quick wave, then they were gone and he was alone.

Ryan stood in the foyer until he'd heard Joel's car pull out of the drive and the silence settled around him. Silence and loneliness. He was in a strange place and the only person he knew in town had just left for the evening.

Maybe he could call a friend and talk, he thought, then dismissed the idea. He didn't have the kind of friends he could just call. Guys didn't just call; there had to be a reason. Except for his brother. He and John had talked on occasion. But his brother was gone…forever.

Ryan stiffened as he realized, perhaps for the first time since the funeral, that John was never going to be coming back. The last of his family had died.

Except for Sasha. His gaze turned toward the stairs. Toward the toy-filled room on the second floor. He remembered Cassie's comments that he had to take more time to get to know his niece, that they only had each other now. As she'd talked, he'd wanted to protest the additional responsibility, to tell her that he wasn't interested. But now, alone in the too-quiet house, he thought it might not be so bad. Tomorrow he would start getting to know his niece a little more.

For some reason the plan cheered him. He returned to his makeshift office and got back to work. As he did, he suddenly realized that the quiet didn't seem so lonely after all.

CHAPTER FIVE

CASSIE SIPPED HER soda and tried to think of something to say. Although it was nearly ten in the evening, the restaurant bustled with an after-movie crowd. As usual, Cassie and Joel's midweek date had consisted of going to a movie, then stopping for pie. Their other favorite date was to go out to dinner.

It was all just too exciting for words, Cassie thought sarcastically, then scolded herself for being critical. In the past she'd been very happy with her and Joel's dating routine. The sameness had made her feel safe. But not anymore, she realized. Now she just felt trapped.

"The new shipment was just as bad," Joel was saying. "Nearly all the lamps were broken. I called the distributor. I asked him what I was supposed to do with a hundred broken lamps. The very same lamps that are featured in the Sunday newspaper circular." Joel paused to chew another bite of chocolate cream pie. "I told him that if he couldn't get me a hundred perfect lamps by Saturday morning, I wouldn't be doing business with him again."

"Do you think he'll deliver the lamps?" Cassie asked.

"Sure. He doesn't want to lose the Bradley Discount Store account. It's one of his biggest."

None of this was fair, Cassie thought sadly. It wasn't Joel's fault that he wasn't the most interesting guy on the planet. He started another story about yet another crisis with the delivery of merchandise. She tried to pay attention, but her mind wandered…about five miles east to the Lawford house on the other side of Bradley. What was Ryan doing now? Was he still working? Had he gone to bed?

Stop thinking about him! she told herself firmly. It was wrong to be on a date with one man and dwelling on another. If only things were different between her and Joel. If only there was more spark.

She studied her boyfriend's face, the blue eyes, the wire-rimmed glasses, the freshly shaved jaw. He was a good man; nice-looking and kind. There was a time when she'd thought they would spend the rest of their lives together. What had changed?

She wanted to blame it all on her blossoming feelings for Ryan, but she knew it wasn't about him at all. She'd felt restless and trapped for several months. For a while she'd thought the feeling would pass, but now she wasn't so sure. Joel was steady, hardworking, honest and funny. They enjoyed each other's company. She wanted to tell herself that was enough. She wanted to believe that craving more was just plain greedy. Unfortunately, she wasn't sure.

"So you didn't like the movie," Joel said.

Cassie blinked. "What?" Hadn't he just been talking about work? "The movie was fine." They'd seen a spy thriller with a strong romance woven through the action scenes. Something for both of them.

Joel finished his pie, then pushed his plate away. He took a sip of his coffee and looked at her. "What's wrong, Cass? You're not really here tonight, are you?"

She shook her head. She wasn't surprised by his observation. After all, they'd been together nine years. Of course Joel knew her.

"I have a lot on my mind," she told him, then cleared her throat. "Actually, I've been thinking about Ryan."

He nodded as if he'd suspected as much. "He's an interesting man. What does he do?"

She was a little surprised he wasn't angered by her confession. "Ryan owns a computer software design firm. They put out a few games of their own, but mostly they do subcontract work from large companies. He started it himself when he was barely out of college."

She paused as she wondered if she should tell him that she'd actually learned all this during the past year, from Helen, Ryan's sister-in-law, rather than from the man himself. In the week she'd been working for him, she and Ryan hadn't had a personal conversation. Nearly everything they talked about revolved around Sasha.

Joel frowned. "This has to be a really tough time for him, what with losing his brother and all. I'm sure he appreciates your help." He reached across the table and squeezed her fingers. "*I* appreciate that you were willing to drop everything and move in there to lend a hand. It shows the kind of person you are."

Cassie wanted to scream. "I'm not a saint," she said testily. "Sasha is a sweet little girl and I like taking care of her. Looking after one child is much easier than watching six and Ryan's paying me a lot more than I make at the preschool. There isn't much that's noble or self-sacrificing about what I'm doing."

"You're too modest. Most people wouldn't have bothered to offer their services in the first place."

"I know, it's just…" She glared at him. "Aren't you the least bit jealous or concerned about the situation?"

Joel released her hand and straightened in his seat. "What situation?" he asked in genuine bafflement.

His confusion only added fuel to her temper. "I'm living with a very attractive, very single man. He and I are alone in that house, day after day. A twenty-six-month-old toddler isn't much of a chaperon."

Joel stared at her for a couple of seconds, then started laughing. At first it was just a chuckle, but the sound grew. He slapped both hands on the table. "Jealous? Oh, Cass, don't worry about that at all. It's nice that you're concerned about what I'm thinking, but don't be."

She thought about strangling him but knew she didn't have the physical strength. There weren't any weapons close at hand, not even a fork—the waitress had cleared away Joel's plate and flatware. Which left her glass, a straw, his cup and a spoon. Nothing lethal there. She settled on glaring.

Finally he stopped laughing enough to give her a lop-sided smile. "Really. I'm not worried. A man like Ryan would never be interested in a woman like you."

It wasn't anything she hadn't told herself a dozen times in the past week. But whispering it in the quiet of her mind was very different than hearing someone else say it out loud.

"I see," she said sharply. "So I'm not sophisticated enough. My job isn't intriguing, and I don't go to the right parties or know the right people." *I'm not pretty enough,* she thought, but she couldn't bring herself to say that one aloud.

"Exactly."

She looked away and concentrated on keeping her hurt from showing. She knew she wasn't anything like the women in Ryan's world. If she were more like her sister, the situation would be different. Chloe was tall and beautiful. As a journalist, she had a glamorous pro-fession. She could talk to anyone in any situation. She wasn't a preschool teacher whose idea of a hot night on the town was a movie with her boyfriend of nine years.

"Cassie, what's wrong?"

"Nothing." Blinking back tears, she kept her gaze firmly on the collection of plants in the bay window to her right.

"I can see you're upset. Did I say something?"

She turned back to face him. "Nothing but the truth. You're right—a man like Ryan wouldn't be interested in me. I know that, but it's not the point."

He looked bewildered. "Then what is?"

"You're supposed to be worried," she told him. "You're supposed to care that I'm living with another man, that we're in close proximity all day long. You're supposed to think that I'm special enough to tempt anyone. But you don't."

The last three words came out softly as she tried to control her suddenly quivering lower lip. He stretched his hand across the table. "Cassie, don't. I think you're very special. You're a wonderful young woman and I'm lucky to have you."

She waited, but he didn't say anything about how a man like Ryan could be interested in her. Obviously he hadn't changed his mind on that one. He didn't see the problem and she wasn't going to explain it to him.

"Are you angry?" he asked.

She shook her head. "It's late. Let's go."

The drive back to Ryan's was silent. Cassie saw Joel darting her little glances as he tried to assess her mood. Part of her felt guilty for being angry with him, while the rest of her felt it was justified. She didn't understand what was going on or what she was feeling. She just knew she wanted things to be different.

When they pulled into the driveway of the old Victorian house, he put the car in Park and looked at her. "Do you want me to walk you to the door?" he asked, his tone cautious.

She shook her head. "Don't worry about it."

He leaned close and kissed her cheek. "I had a good time tonight. I hope we can get together soon. I miss you."

The streetlight didn't offer much illumination and she could barely make out his familiar features. *Do you really miss me?* But she only thought the question instead of asking it. She wasn't sure anymore.

"Why don't you ever just take me?" she asked suddenly.

"Take you where?"

She nearly groaned in frustration. "Sex, Joel. I'm talking about sex. We never do more than kiss and most of those are chaste. Don't you ever want to rip my clothes off and do it right here in the car?"

He glanced at the narrow bucket seats, then at her. "There's not much room."

She made a low strangled sound in her throat. "Never mind."

But he grabbed her arm before she could reach for the door handle. "What's going on? Are you unhappy with me or the relationship?"

"I don't know."

He stared at her. "I thought this is what we both wanted. I thought we agreed to take things slowly."

"It's been nine years. You've never even touched my breasts. Does that seem natural to you?"

Joel shifted until he faced front. He tightly gripped the steering wheel. "I respect you. Of course I've thought about us…well…being together…that way. After we're married. I am more than just my animal passions. I thought you were, too."

She ignored the judgment inherent in his comment. "Not all the time. Sometimes I want to be swept away and I've always wanted you to be the one doing the sweeping. Please, Joel."

He swallowed hard. "Please what?" He sounded faintly panicked.

"Just kiss me like you mean it. Please."

"All right."

He turned toward her and drew in a breath. They reached for each other, but their arms tangled, and with the awkward angle, not to mention the hand brake between them, they couldn't find a comfortable position. Finally Cassie simply grabbed the front of his jacket and hauled him close.

"Kiss me," she ordered.

He pressed his mouth to hers. She angled her head and parted her lips. He neither moved more nor responded to the invitation. Instead he froze in place, not kissing her back, not putting his hands on her body, just sitting there. Like a fish, she thought sadly and slowly straightened.

"Enough?" he asked.

At first she thought he was being sarcastic and punishing her, but then she remembered this was Joel and that wasn't his style.

"Thank you," she whispered. Sadness swept through her and she knew tears weren't far behind.

"It's better this way," he said kindly. "We really should wait."

"I know," she said as she collected her purse and opened the car door. "Good night."

She stood on the porch and watched him drive away. What had seemed so right for so long now felt very wrong.

It wasn't that she objected to waiting to make love.

She thought it was important to choose one's partners carefully. Given the choice, she would rather just have one lover for her whole life. But she wanted passion in addition to affection and respect. Was that so wrong?

She also didn't remember talking to Joel about putting off intimacy until after marriage. From what she could recall, he'd made that decision all on his own. She wouldn't mind so much if only she could be sure it was all going to work out when they finally did it. But she wasn't sure. Shouldn't they be having trouble keeping their hands off each other? Shouldn't they be breathless and aching with desire? That's what she'd always read about. That's what Chloe talked about when she shared bits and pieces of her relationship with Arizona.

Cassie unlocked the front door and stepped into the silent house. Ryan had left on a light by the stairs. She moved toward it and sighed. Maybe passion wasn't in the cards for her. Maybe she was better off settling. Joel loved her and she loved him. Maybe it was wrong to look a gift horse in the mouth.

But in the darkness of her bedroom, she searched her heart and found that this was too important an issue on which to compromise. She deserved more than just settling…and so did Joel.

THE NEXT MORNING, Ryan hurried down to breakfast. He told himself he wasn't actually interested in Cassie, and he certainly wasn't going to ask about her date, except in the most general, socially correct way. A pleasant "how was your evening?" was expected, even welcome, in most work situations.

He entered the kitchen and paused, taking in his niece and Cassie along with the swept floor, the clean counters and empty sink. Except for the bits of hot cereal on

Sasha's face, hands, arms and the front of her bib, not to mention the tray of her high chair, the room was perfect. Nothing like the disaster he'd been living in before Cassie had shown up to straighten out his and Sasha's lives.

He stood in the doorway unobserved. Cassie was back in jeans and a sweatshirt. Her thick short hair swayed with every movement. She'd pulled up a chair next to Sasha's high chair and encouraged the child to keep eating, all the while sipping on a cup of coffee.

She'd come in much earlier last night than he had expected. It had been barely ten-thirty. Not that he'd been watching the clock, he assured himself. He'd just happened to go up to his room to read, and had heard the front door opening. He had thought she would stay out much later. Not that he cared, of course. His was only the most passing of interest in a trusted employee's well-being.

Ryan grinned. Even he was having trouble buying that line. Okay, he could admit it to himself. He was dying to know if Cassie and Joel had made love last night. Probably because it had been so long since he'd had the pleasure of being with a woman, he told himself. He was intrigued by Sasha's nanny. But just because he'd finally noticed her didn't mean—"Unk Ryan!"

He glanced up and saw Sasha had spotted him. Her baby face split into a grin and she waved her spoon at him.

"Hey, kid."

Cassie turned. "Good morning," she said as she rose to her feet. "The coffee is fresh."

"Thanks."

He quickly glanced at her face, but couldn't see anything lurking in her eyes. No shadows to indicate a restless night, no telltale love-bite marks on her neck.

Sasha held out her cup. "Mill," she said.

He'd already figured out that "mill" really meant milk. "Is she offering me some of hers or asking for more?"

Cassie poured his coffee and grinned. "Why don't you find out?"

He'd actually been hoping for a recap of last night, not a lesson in child rearing, but she'd been right when she told him he was going to have to figure out how to get along with his niece. Tentatively he moved close and took the offered cup. He shook it; it was empty.

"More milk," he said and walked to the refrigerator.

When he handed Sasha back her cup, she beamed at him. Her slight "t" sound could have been an expression of pleasure or thanks. He found he didn't really mind which. With Cassie around to protect him from making a hideous mistake, he sort of liked being with the kid.

"What can I get you to eat?" Cassie asked as she set his mug on the table. "We have cereal and fruit. There are frozen waffles, or I could make you eggs or even pancakes."

Tentatively, prepared to spring up at any moment, he took the seat next to Sasha's high chair. She gave him another grin, then dropped her spoon into her cereal and began eating again.

"You don't have to feed me," he said, not taking his gaze from his niece. She wasn't exactly coordinated, he thought as a bit of cereal went flying, but she got the job done.

"I know it's not technically one of my responsibilities," Cassie told him, "but you have to eat something. Not only is breakfast the most important meal of the day, but Sasha is going to mimic just about everything you do. If you refuse food, she's going to do the same."

There was no fighting a woman when she'd made up

her mind about something. He'd learned that lesson early and well. "Cereal," he said. "With a banana. And after today I'll get my own breakfast."

"Whatever you'd like. You're the boss."

Her tone was sweet, but he didn't buy it for a second. She was in charge here, and she knew it.

As Cassie prepared his cereal, Sasha finished hers. Every couple of bites she offered him the spoon. He finally figured out she wanted him to feed her. "Okay, I can do some of the work."

He scooped out a small amount of the warm, rice cereal. Sasha opened her mouth, then looked at him as if to say "Aren't I too clever for words?" He found himself smiling at her. If it had been this easy when he'd first been alone with her, he wouldn't have panicked so much.

When she'd finished eating, she drank the last of the milk, then said, "Down."

Ryan looked at Cassie. "She wants out."

"If she's finished eating, that's fine."

He glanced from her back to Sasha. That hadn't been the answer he'd expected. He'd thought that Cassie would come over and take care of things. Okay, so she was giving him practice. He could handle this.

He crossed to the sink and fished a clean dishcloth out of the drawer, then dampened it and returned to the high chair. After removing the bib, he cleaned the toddler's face, hands and arms, then unhooked the tray and put it on the table. Sasha held out her arms.

Ryan bent over and lifted her from the seat. But instead of leaning down toward the ground, she pressed a wet, cereal-scented kiss on his cheek. "Unk Ryan," she explained.

"Yes, I know," he said, somewhat at a loss as to his

next move. Finally he set her on her feet. She giggled once, then scampered out of the room.

"You've won her over." Cassie set his breakfast on the table. After picking up the dirty high chair tray, she carried it to the sink.

"I don't think it was the clear victory of the campaign," he admitted, "but it was a pleasant encounter."

"If this is a campaign, then you must be the general in charge?" she asked.

"You have to ask?"

"Five-star?"

"If they come with that many, sure."

She smiled at him as she returned to the table and took the seat opposite his. He glanced at his cereal, the neatly sliced banana and the plate of toast sitting together on the place mat.

"Thanks for doing this," he said. "I meant what I said. I'll take care of it from now on."

"Whatever you'd like."

He started his breakfast, all the while trying to ignore the unusual domesticity of the situation. He rarely had women over to his place because he wasn't comfortable with them spending the night. Actually it wasn't the nights he minded as much as the awkward mornings. So he did his thing and escaped as gracefully as he could. Besides, the women of his acquaintance had to be at work as early as he did, so there was no time for idle chitchat.

It occurred to him that Cassie was *already* at work and that for her, this was simply a part of her job. The thought unsettled him although he couldn't quite say how.

Sasha ran into the room and handed him a red ball. He took it, but before he could say anything, she was gone again.

"Oh, we're going to play that game again," he said and patted his front pockets. "I don't have any spare change."

"There's some over here," Cassie said, rising to her feet. She crossed to the counter and pulled a white envelope out of a drawer. "It's the remaining grocery money." She fished out several pennies and two nickels. "This should keep her happy." She placed the money next to him and took her seat.

Morning light spilled in through the big, lace-covered window. Cassie looked freshly scrubbed and well rested. Except for the heart-shaped earrings she usually wore and her promise ring, she didn't have on any jewelry. Her clothes were as casual as his. Yet there was something about her...something sexy.

He cleared his throat. "So, how was your evening?"

Her gaze lowered. "Very nice. We went to a movie, then stopped and had dessert."

"Were you out late?"

He was a fraud, he thought even as he asked the question. He knew exactly what time Cassie had gotten home. With a quick calculation of the time needed to drive to the theater, watch the movie, then order and eat dessert, unless they did it in less than fifteen minutes, it was unlikely Cassie and Joel had made love the previous night.

The realization pleased him and he refused to consider why.

"I think I got back about ten-thirty," she said.

"Oh. I was reading in my room last night. I didn't hear you." The lie slipped easily off his tongue and he had a moment of guilt. Then Sasha returned with her favorite stuffed bunny and distracted him. He gave the girl a penny, which she took with a squeal of delight, then raced out of the room again.

"So you had fun?" he asked, not sure why he was pursuing this particular topic.

She hesitated. "Of course."

"You must be very comfortable with Joel. Having dated him for so long. I mean that in a good way," he added quickly when she glanced at him.

"We're…" She hesitated. "Can we change the subject?"

"Of course. I didn't mean to pry."

"It's not that. It's just I have lot on my mind."

What? he wanted to asked, but knew it wasn't his business. Still, his mind raced. Was it Joel? Had they fought? Were they—Sasha came back, this time carrying a long, pink dress. Instead of offering it to him, she held it up in front of herself. "Kern," she said, her expression serious. "Unk Ryan, me kern."

He turned to Cassie. "This would be an excellent time for you to translate."

"There's a big assumption there," she said. "I'm not sure what she's asking. Sasha, what's that you're holding?"

Sasha came around to her side of the table and held out her dress. "Oh, it's your dress for Halloween." Cassie motioned to the garment. "Sasha is going to be a princess, aren't you, honey?"

Sasha nodded vigorously. "Me kern."

"Kern," Cassie repeated thoughtfully.

"Isn't a kern a kind of bird?"

"Maybe, but I doubt that's what's on her mind." She leaned toward the toddler. "What's a kern, sweetie? What do you want?"

Sasha huffed out a breath. "Kern," she repeated and patted her head. "Pincess kern."

Ryan searched his memory for something like a kern,

then got it. "She means crown. She wants a crown so she can wear it with her princess dress."

Sasha rushed to him and chattered on about kerns and pincesses and Lord knew what else. Ryan felt as if he'd just aced an IQ test. He stroked the girl's hair, then touched her cheek. "We'll get you a crown. The prettiest crown ever." He glanced over at Cassie. "Do they sell them?"

"No problem. I'll take her by the party-supply store on our way back from preschool. She can pick out her own. They're made out of cardboard, so they're easy for the kids to wear."

"When is Halloween?" he asked. He hadn't thought of that particular holiday in years. His condo was a secure building, so they didn't get any foot traffic, and it wasn't the kind of place that welcomed children.

"Monday. I haven't bought any candy. I'll do that when I do the grocery shopping."

Ryan reached into his back pocket and pulled out his wallet. He passed over one of his credit cards. "Use this for anything you need. Expenses for the house, whatever. Does she need clothes?"

"Not right now. She doesn't seem to be in a growth spurt, so we're fine. However, kids her age can shoot up, almost overnight, so I'll let you know if anything gets small or tight."

She nodded at Sasha who had left her dress draped over Ryan's lap and was quietly playing on the floor, between her uncle's feet. "You're doing well with her."

"Thanks." He fingered the soft cotton of the princess dress. "You were right last night. I *do* need to spend more time with her. I appreciate you caring enough to say something."

"Just doing my job."

"It was more than that. I'll admit to being a little nervous about the whole thing, but I'm determined to give it my best shot."

"She can't ask for more than that." Cassie paused. "It would be great if you took Sasha out trick-or-treating on Halloween."

"Sure, if you'll come with us."

"No problem. I can ask my sister to hand out candy here while we're gone. She and her husband are going to a party, but that's not until later in the evening. Sasha won't want to go to more than a dozen or so houses. When she gets tired, we can come back here, then she can give out candy."

"Sounds like a plan."

Cassie glanced at the clock above the stove. "Sasha, time to go to school. Let's put your toys away really fast, then we can leave, okay?"

The toddler scrambled to her feet, then bent over and grabbed her bunny. Ryan handed her the dress. While Cassie took care of his niece, he took his dishes to the sink.

He listened to the sounds of them getting ready. He'd grown accustomed to the chatter of voices and the thumping footsteps. Maybe this wasn't going to be so terrible, he thought. Maybe John hadn't made as huge a mistake as Ryan had first thought.

It was Cassie's influence, he realized. She was very special. Honest and giving, an old-fashioned sort of woman.

She stuck her head into the kitchen. "We're outta here. See you later." She hesitated. "You have the most peculiar look on your face. Is something wrong?"

"Not at all." He couldn't tell her what he'd been thinking. She wouldn't understand and he didn't want to do anything that would make her uncomfortable. "I was thinking that Joel is a very lucky man."

Her smile faded slightly and her eyes took on a haunted quality. But before he could ask, her expression returned to normal. "Thanks. I'll be sure to tell him the next time I see him."

CHAPTER SIX

CASSIE GREETED HER sister at the front door. Chloe handed her a large paper shopping bag, reached down and grabbed two more from the porch, then stepped into the Lawford house.

"I don't know why I thought this was going to be a great idea," Chloe said and laughed. "It didn't seem like such a big deal to show up at the party in costume. I conveniently ignored that step in the middle, the part where I actually had to put it all together." She bent forward, her round belly making her awkward, and gave her sister a kiss on the cheek. "I really, really appreciate you offering to help me with this."

"My pleasure." Cassie closed the door behind her and led the way to the kitchen. "I thought we could work in here. Sasha is down for her nap. Apparently they played outside at preschool, so she's exhausted from all the running and jumping. I figure she'll have about an hour and fifteen minutes of honest sleep, then maybe she'll spend another thirty minutes quietly playing in her bed."

Cassie set the shopping bag on a chair and began emptying the contents. "To try and stack the odds in our favor, I went to her room a couple of minutes ago and put her favorite doll in with her."

"Clever," Chloe said as she, too, dumped yards of green, yellow and white fabric onto the table. "I like that in a woman. Now if only you can be equally creative with this mess."

She dug around until she found several of the larger pieces that she'd already sewn together. "Where's Ryan? I don't want to expose my pregnant self to him. I think the poor man is probably traumatized enough in his life."

"Don't give me that," Cassie told her sister. "You look amazing. The problem wouldn't be Ryan, who would be instantly smitten, it would be your husband's insane jealousy."

Chloe tossed her head, causing her ponytail to dance. "Arizona's not insanely jealous. He just keeps a close eye on me when we're out."

"That's because he knows you're the most beautiful woman in the world and he desperately wants you."

Chloe's smile was content. "I don't know about thinking I'm that beautiful, but he does like to keep me around."

"An intelligent man."

"Obviously."

The two sisters laughed. "Do you want something to drink?" Cassie asked. "I have milk and juice."

"Milk would be great." Chloe rubbed her belly. "I'm trying to get all my calcium naturally, which means at least two glasses of milk a day, sometimes more. So while the baby is growing, leaving less and less room for my bladder, I'm drinking more and more. I swear, there are some days I just want to set up my laptop by the bathroom to save myself the time of walking back and forth." She took the glass Cassie offered. "It's only going to get worse before it gets better, too."

"But it will be worth it."

"I know."

Cassie looked at her sister, noting the glow to her skin

and the light in her eyes. Chloe had always been the tall, slender, pretty one, but now she was radiant. Arizona's love filled her with a joy she'd never known before. Pregnancy agreed with her, she was working hard on a book about her husband's travels, and she'd never been healthier or happier.

"I'm glad for you," Cassie said, meaning it with all her heart. She believed there were enough good things out in the universe for everyone. The fact that Chloe had found what she wanted in life meant that it was possible for Cassie, too.

"So Ryan's working?" Chloe asked.

"Yes, and unlikely to surface anytime soon. You're safe."

"Good." Chloe unbuttoned the oversize shirt she'd worn that afternoon. Underneath she had on leggings and a sports bra. "I can't get any part of this costume to work," she said as she slipped into the long green sleeves. "If you could just help me pin it together, maybe baste it in a few key spots, I can sew it when I get home."

Cassie stepped back and appraised her sister's attire. The invitation to the university's Halloween party stated that attendees were to dress like famous couples in literature. Chloe's advancing pregnancy had prevented her from wearing anything formfitting. She'd toyed with the idea of Romeo and Juliet, but she'd decided that was too obvious. Not to mention the fact that Arizona had refused to wear tights.

"I think you two are going to be the hit of the party," Cassie said as she found the layered front of the costume. Chloe had sewn yellow on the lower part of the belly, with white up by the throat. "The crocodile and Captain Hook are perfect."

"Like I said, I thought it was brilliant until I realized I

didn't know how to sew a crocodile costume. I want the puffy-out belly part to skim over my stomach. At least then the pregnancy won't be obvious, but I'm not sure it's going to work."

Cassie stepped close and held up the midsection. "It's not sticking out enough," she said. "And the pocket for your tummy has to be lower. Let me rip out the center seam and insert about six more inches of the yellow cloth. Then we'll use ribbing to give it a little more shape on the side."

"Is that what's wrong?" Chloe asked, then shook her head. "I should have asked for you to help me from the beginning. You always were better than me at this domestic stuff. I've been tearing up pieces for a week and getting nowhere."

"We have different talents," Cassie said as she started separating the layers of fabric.

Growing up, she and her sister had sometimes sewn dresses, but usually Chloe didn't have the patience. She'd always been going and doing. Cassie was the one who liked to stay home and take care of things there. They were so different, Cassie thought. Probably because they had different biological parents. Being raised in the same home could only do so much.

As she worked, Chloe talked about her life. Cassie listened and tried to ignore the faint whisper of envy that drifted through her. She was glad for Chloe and her happiness, and she reminded herself there was still plenty of time for her own dreams to come true.

"Arizona is completely crazed about the plans for next summer," Chloe was saying. "He's received invitations from all over the world. Everyone wants him to come speak. The baby will be six months old, so I told him my requirements were for a relatively short flight, decent facilities and no luggage restriction." She rolled her eyes. "Do you have any idea how much stuff babies require? The more I read about that, the more it amazes me."

"So you'll be staying in the country?"

"Maybe. I don't know." She spread her arms so Cassie could pin on the modified front panel. "Two universities in England have made fabulous offers, so he's talking about lecturing for a few days in New York or Washington so we get adjusted to the change in time and the plane ride isn't too awful. Then we would take the Concorde to England and spend the summer there."

"Sounds like fun."

"I hope so." She looked sheepish. "He's already talking about a second baby, timing it and everything so that we're always free to travel in the summer. He's very concerned that I don't get overwhelmed with all of it and—"

Chloe pressed her lips together. "I'm sorry. You don't want to hear about all this."

Cassie stopped pinning and stared at her sister. "Why not? I *want* you to tell me about your plans. Just because you're married doesn't mean we've stopped being friends."

"I know. It's just I feel as if I've gotten everything and you don't have…as much."

Cassie knew the pause had been because Chloe had started to say "anything."

"I appreciate your concern about my feelings," she said. "But I do have a lot. Maybe it doesn't seem like it to you, but you and I have never wanted the same things. You're a great reporter and a terrific writer. You've always wanted to travel and you've married a wonderful man who adores you and wants to show you the world. Everything is working out. That makes me happy. But my path is different."

"I know." Chloe touched her arm. "I'm not being critical. In the past we've argued about your career choice, but I finally understand." She rested her hand on her stomach. "When the baby kicks, I can feel the life growing inside of me. Until that happened I didn't know why you would want to 'waste' your life with children. Now I see it's the most amazing thing you can do with your time. I respect that and I admire you for realizing it before you had a child of your own."

Cassie was a little embarrassed by the praise. "Wow, you make me sound like a saint or something. I'm not."

"Hey, I know that—I'm your sister, remember. But you're a good person who pays attention to what is right. I just wish…"

Her voice trailed off. She fingered the front of her costume. "I think this is going to work, don't you?"

As subject changes went, it wasn't a very smooth one. Cassie knew what her sister had been about to say. "You just wish I would break up with Joel."

Chloe drew in a deep breath. Her mouth twisted down on one side. "You've tried to explain it to me a dozen times and I still don't understand what you see in him. Yes, he's very nice and he's honest and hardworking, but Cass, you could do so much better. You're bright and funny, you care." Her tone softened. "I want you to find a man who understands that you're an amazing prize and that he's lucky as hell to have you. Not some guy who thinks of you as little more than a housekeeper and broodmare."

"You're not being fair to Joel," Cassie said, but her reply was automatic. She was too conflicted about her feelings to try and explain them to her sister.

"Does he make you laugh?" Chloe asked. "Does he make your heart beat faster just by walking in the room?

Does he have a certain way of looking or smiling or have a phrase that makes you realize that if you never heard it again or saw it that you would just die?" She caught her sister's gaze. "Do you think about spending the rest of your life with him and know, deep down in your heart, that if something happened to him, you would be happier being alone rather than trying to find someone else?"

Cassie dropped the pins onto the table and sank into a chair. "I don't know," she said quietly. "I just don't know anymore. I wish I could tell you yes to all of those questions, but I can't."

Chloe took the chair next to her and placed a hand on her shoulder. "I'm sorry. I didn't mean to upset you."

"I'm not upset, I'm confused. I used to be sure. I thought that Joel was exactly right for me, but something's different. I don't know if it's him or me or circumstances." She looked at her sister. She had to know. Of all the people in the world, she knew that Chloe would tell her the truth.

"Is passion real?" she asked. "Is it like in books and movies? Can it really sweep you away until you can't imagine anything else ever being so wonderful?"

Chloe stared at her for a long time. Finally she nodded. "It's exactly like that."

Cassie hadn't realized she was holding her breath until she released it. "I was afraid of that." Her shoulders slumped forward. If passion was real, then she and Joel were doing something very wrong. Maybe they weren't right for each other or meant to be together. As much as she wanted to believe otherwise, she doubted it was suddenly going to flare between them. So she had to decide if she could live her life without experiencing that kind of fire, or if she had to leave the security of the only man she'd ever dated.

"You have to be sure," Chloe told her. "It's been nine years, so it's not going to hurt if you wait a little longer until you get engaged to Joel, but please promise me you won't settle. If you think it over and believe in your heart that Joel is the man who is going to make you happy for the rest of your life, then I swear I'll be the sweetest sister-in-law ever. But don't make a mistake. Marriage is tough enough, even with love."

Cassie looked at her sister, at the affection and concern on Chloe's face. "I appreciate the kind words and the fact that you worry about me. You're the best sister ever."

"I know," Chloe said and laughed. She stood up and put her hands on her hips. "Enough of this emotional nonsense. Let's get this costume finished."

"Absolutely." Cassie picked up the pins and went back to work.

"How's Ryan doing with Sasha?" Chloe asked as she raised her arms so Cassie could pin the front panel to the sleeves.

"Better. Obviously it's going to take time, but our talk went really well. He seems to intuitively understand how Sasha needs him. They're spending more time together. He joins us for breakfast, he's reading to her before she goes to bed. Considering their shaky start, I'm impressed. Ryan's a quick study and the situation is helped by the fact that he's bright and has a great sense of humor. All important factors for good parenting. Plus, he's kind. He makes me feel like part of the family."

Cassie finished pinning and stepped back. The top and bottom of the costume were unfinished, but there was definitely a crocodile-like shape to the strips of yellow and white down the front. "Maybe a clock," she said, half to herself as she eyed her sister. "Hadn't the crocodile in *Peter Pan* swallowed a clock? We could make the face of a clock out of fabric and sew it on in front. Or maybe you could find a pocket watch somewhere. There's always…" Her voice trailed off as she realized her sister was staring at her.

"What?" Cassie asked. "You've got this weird look on your face."

Chloe broke out into a smile. "Cassandra Bradley Wright, you have a thing for your boss! Why didn't you tell me?"

Cassie desperately wanted to deny her sister's claim, but she could already feel the heat crawling up her face. She ducked her head. "I do not." The statement sounded lame, even to her.

"You do. I can't believe I didn't get this before. Is there anything going on?" Her teasing tone grew serious. "He's not taking advantage of you or the situation, is he? Geez, Aunt Charity and I should have checked the guy out before letting you come stay here. Has he—"

Cassie raised her hand to cut off her sister. "Stop right there. Don't get all worked up about nothing. I swear Ryan isn't taking advantage of me." Not that she would mind if he did, a little voice whispered in her head. Cassie tried to ignore it and the faint warmth that swept over her at the thought.

"Are you sure?" Chloe asked, sounding skeptical.

"Taking advantage of someone requires knowing that person is alive. While I don't doubt that Ryan is aware of my existence, as far as he's concerned, I'm just a helpful household appliance. He has no clue I'm female."

Chloe looked at her and shook her head. "I can't buy that. You're very pretty."

"Get real. I'm a good person, I'm amusing when I'm in a situation where I'm comfortable, I'm reasonably intelligent and I'm honest and have a way with kids. But I'm not his type. Why do you think Joel isn't jealous, and please don't say anything cruel about him. The truth is, a man like Ryan could never be interested in a woman like me."

"Why on earth not?"

Cassie was so startled by the question it took her a minute to figure out how to answer. "There's the age difference," she said at last.

"What is it, five years?"

"Almost nine. He has a successful business, and as you so like to point out, I work in a preschool. What would we talk about?"

"What do you talk about now?"

"Sasha."

"So you have *something* in common."

Cassie reached for the bag and fished out the long length of fabric that would serve as Chloe's tail. "You're pushing this because you think it might be a good way to get me away from Joel."

"Is that so terrible?"

It could be if the crush became something more, Cassie thought. She wasn't looking to get her heart broken. "Maybe," she said, then stopped when she heard footsteps in the hallway.

Chloe glanced toward the door and groaned. "This is *not* how I planned on meeting your boss."

"You look cute," Cassie told her and knew she was telling the truth. Chloe had pulled her dark red curls into a ponytail at the top of her head. Makeup accentuated her big eyes, while pregnancy added a glow to her cheeks. She looked like what she was—a radiantly beautiful woman in the prime of her life.

"Cassie, is there…" Ryan's voice trailed off as he entered the kitchen and saw her company. "Sorry, I didn't mean to interrupt." He glanced over the partially completed costume and raised his eyebrows. "So people *do* dress differently in Bradley than in other parts of the country."

Cassie smiled. "Not exactly. Ryan, this is my sister, Chloe Smith. Chloe, this is Ryan."

The two shook hands. "You have me at a disadvantage," Chloe said, motioning to herself. "I don't like making a first impression in costume." She told him briefly about the party she and Arizona were to attend, then rested her hand on her stomach. "I figured my choices were limited if I didn't want to spend the night as 'pregnant' Cleopatra and Mark Antony, or 'pregnant' Scarlett O'Hara and Rhett Butler."

"It's very original. I suppose pregnant Wendy was out of the question."

Chloe laughed. "I thought about it, but my husband refused to consider anything that involved wearing tights."

"Smart man," Ryan said. "I can't say that I blame him."

Cassie smoothed the tail to pin it in place, but Chloe stopped her. "I'll have to do that at the last minute. Aunt Charity can help me. Otherwise, I'll never fit everything in the car."

"I hadn't thought about that." Cassie turned to Ryan. "My sister drives a little BMW Z3 roadster. Cute car, with absolutely no trunk."

"Very little room for my tummy, either." When Chloe indicated she needed to step out of the costume, Ryan politely turned his back. "I'm going to have to start trading cars with Arizona so that there's room between me and my steering wheel."

Cassie folded the fabric. "Are you sure we did enough? I don't mind working on this some more."

"It's fine," Chloe told her. "If I have any trouble, I'll

call you to come rescue me." She waved goodbye to Ryan and left.

Ryan waited in the kitchen while Cassie walked her sister to the door. When she returned, he pointed to the scraps of material on the table and floor. "I didn't know you could sew."

"I used to do it more. When I was in high school, I made a lot of my clothes. Not because we couldn't afford to buy them but because I couldn't always find things I liked." She shrugged. "I can handle most of the domestic arts. Cooking, child rearing, sewing. I'm a decent baker and pretty handy in the garden, but I don't like cleaning. Given the choice, I would rather pay to have someone else do it." She glanced at him out of the corner of her eyes. "Most women are well versed at several of these same activities. You don't have to act surprised that I've conquered them."

"It *is* surprising," he told her as he leaned one hip against the kitchen counter. "At least for me. The women I date are more interested in their careers than what they plan to serve for dinner. I'm not saying either is right," he added quickly, not wanting her to think he was judging.

"Agreed," she said. She finished picking up the scraps and carried them to the trash. "Times have changed, but what about when you were growing up? Did your mom bake or sew?"

He shook his head. "She put on patches when we tore out the knees of our jeans, but that was about it. As for baking—" He tried to remember coming home to the smell of brownies or a cake. On birthdays she'd usually bought something day-old from the bakery. "She worked two jobs. There wasn't a lot of extra time."

Cassie's expression softened with compassion. "It must have been really tough for her, having to work so much and still try to raise you and your brother. I'm sure she was really conflicted about the situation."

Ryan couldn't answer that. If his mother had had doubts, she'd kept them to herself. "She taught my brother and me to be hard workers, like she was. She always told us that rich was better than poor. That we were to get good educations and work hard. I've respected that."

"You've done both," Cassie told him.

"Agreed. On the down side, she never spent much time with us. Some of it was because of her long hours at work. For the rest of it, I'm not so sure." He wasn't about to tell Cassie that he'd always felt his mother had seen her children as getting in the way of her goals. That if she'd been alone, she would have done much better. Still, he couldn't fault her on her day-to-day care, or for inspiring John and him to get ahead. That had to count for something.

"There wasn't much fun in our house," he said at last. "No money and not enough time."

"You can have fun with Sasha," Cassie told him. "Little kids need lots of attention and lots of fun."

Her smile was easy, her posture relaxed. She was completely comfortable with him, and very pretty, he thought, wondering for the thousandth time how he'd managed to not notice her for nearly a week. Now he was having trouble being in the same room without finding something new about her that appealed to him. Sometimes it was her laugh, sometimes a comment she made. Once he'd been caught up in the play of light on her thick, shiny hair.

Telling himself she was completely wrong for him didn't help. Reminding himself that she was not only his employee—and therefore deserving of his respect—but also involved and committed to another man, only intrigued him. He couldn't remember the last time a woman had haunted his thoughts and he found he liked having something other than work on his mind.

Cassie glanced at the clock. "Sasha should be waking up soon," she said. "I have just enough time to get the cookies in the oven."

With that she walked over to the refrigerator and pulled open the door. Ryan was about to excuse himself when she bent over and retrieved a bowl sitting on the bottom shelf. He told himself he was worse than a kid in high school, but he couldn't help looking. Her jeans tightened around her rear end, making him want to go over and pull her close against him. He could imagine how she would feel next to him, under him, naked and....

"Ryan?" Cassie asked as she straightened and caught him staring. "Are you all right?"

"Fine," he said, sounding only a little strangled. "I, um, I think I'll go back to my office." He turned away quickly, hoping she hadn't noticed the rather obvious manifestation of his wayward thoughts.

He was slime, he told himself. Lower than slime. He was the single-celled creature that slime fed on. Because even though it was wrong, even though he was violating fifteen different kinds of moral conduct, he liked that she turned him on. Being around Cassie reminded Ryan that he was alive.

"THAT ONE," Sasha said as she pointed at the candy. "This one, too."

Ryan obligingly picked up the two pieces of candy in question and dropped them into the small, clear plastic bag decorated with grinning pumpkins. "She's a tyrant," he complained good-naturedly.

"You're the one who told her she could pick what to put into the bags," Cassie reminded him as she slid ghost-shaped sugar cookies onto the cooling rack. "Don't come crying to me, now."

"I know. How many of these bags do we need to do?"

She settled the last of the cookies in place, then put the empty sheet into the sink. After removing the oven mitts from her hands, she crossed to the kitchen table.

It had been a very good few days, Cassie thought happily. Ryan had responded well to her suggestion that he spend more time with his niece. They were getting to know each other and finding pleasure in each other's company. On a personal level this meant she also spent more time with the man, but she wasn't about to comment on that. Despite her crush, she knew that Sasha was the important one around here.

She counted the filled plastic bags. "You've done eighteen. We need twenty-four." She bent down and hugged the toddler. "Are you helping?"

Sasha nodded, then pointed at Ryan. "Work!" she commanded.

He laughed. "Yes, ma'am. Gee, give the woman a little power and she's ready to take over the world."

"Must be genetic," Cassie said casually, then laughed and jumped back when Ryan glanced at her sharply.

"Are you saying I'm a tyrant?" he asked, his gaze narrow in mock anger.

"I've heard bits of your phone calls, when I've brought you dinner," she said. "You like ordering people around. I think it's in the blood."

"Did you hear that?" he asked Sasha. "She's called us bossy. I don't think that's true. Just because we know what's best for everyone. Right?"

Sasha blinked a couple of times, then planted her hands on her hips and looked at Cassie. "Right!"

"I've been outvoted. Fine. I'll start making the icing for the cookies."

As she collected ingredients, she had to hold in a sigh of contentment. Sasha and Ryan were doing great. She was thrilled that he'd offered to stay in the kitchen after dinner and help with the Halloween bags needed for the party at Sasha's school. She ignored the fact that his actions played into her private fantasy that this was all actually real. It wasn't, of course. It was play, and as long as she didn't forget what was going on, she was allowed to enjoy pretending for as long as the situation lasted.

Abruptly, Ryan pushed back his chair and rose. "I've got work in my office," he said without warning and left.

"Unk Ryan?" Sasha slid off the seat onto her feet and started after him. "Unk Ryan? Back! More work."

Cassie put down the bowl she'd been holding and hurried to the toddler. She caught up with her in the hallway. Sasha stood staring at her uncle's closed office door.

"He's busy," Cassie said quietly. "He'll help us again tomorrow." She glanced at her watch. It was nearly bedtime. "Let's go give you a bath, then I'll read you two stories."

For a second Sasha's lower lip quivered and Cassie was afraid she wasn't going to allow herself to be distracted. But she finally held out her hand and Cassie led her away.

Two hours later it was Cassie's turn to pause outside Ryan's closed door, but unlike his niece, she knocked once, then entered. Ryan stood in front of the window, staring out into the darkness of the night.

There were several lamps on in the room and they reflected in the glass, creating a mirror effect. She could see his face, the pained expression and his closed eyes.

She hesitated, not sure what to say.

"I'm sorry," he told her, his voice tight.

"What happened?"

"Nothing. I had to leave. I'll explain it to Sasha tomorrow." He opened his eyes and met her gaze in the window. "Is she all right?"

She nodded. "She's asleep. I told her you were busy."

"Thanks."

He looked away as if expecting her to leave.

"What happened?" she repeated.

"I'm fine."

She drew in a deep breath. Was she crossing the line? Did it matter? After all, she wasn't about to back down. "I'm not going away."

He turned toward her. "You never told me you were stubborn."

"You never asked."

He nodded, then motioned for her to take the seat opposite the desk. She did. He settled into his chair. "It's going to sound really stupid," he warned her.

"I doubt that, but I promise to listen anyway."

He leaned back and stared at the ceiling. "It was Sasha. She tilted her head a certain way and in that split second, I saw my brother in her."

"She's his daughter. Why does that surprise you?"

"Because I never got it before. I knew in my head that she was John's child and my niece, but I hadn't internalized the information. I'd always thought of her as a person in her own right."

His gaze slid down until it met hers. "I never bothered to come visit them," he said quietly. "They lived less than two hundred miles away, but I was always too busy. I thought there would be time. So birthdays and anniversaries and Christmases went by, all without me. And now it's too late."

Cassie's heart ached for him. He'd finally realized

his brother was really and truly gone. "I'm sorry," she murmured.

"Thanks." He paused. "I wish I'd done things differently."

The light from the floor lamps added depth and shadows to his strong face. His eyes were haunted by the pain of actions that would never be.

"You still have Sasha," she said, knowing it was a small comfort, although it was the only one she had to offer.

"I know. I still don't think I'm the right choice, but I'm glad they didn't leave her to anyone else. She's all that's left of my brother."

"No," Cassie told him. "You have all the memories you carry around inside yourself. Those will always be with you."

He leaned forward. Some of the tension left his body. "You're right. I hadn't thought of it that way, but it's true." He smiled. "Thank you, Cassie. You're very insightful."

It was, she knew, her cue to leave. So she wished him good-night and walked out. After closing the door behind her, she leaned against the thick wood and reminded herself it was just a crush. Nothing else. But at this moment, still feeling empathy for his pain, it felt like much, much more.

CHAPTER SEVEN

"CAN YOU smile?" Ryan asked as he adjusted the focus on the camera.

Sasha obliged him by placing one hand on her hip, gazing up at him and giving him a big grin.

"Very nice," he told her. "You're a beautiful princess."

Sasha twirled around, then settled to the floor in a cloud of pink fabric. "Pincess! Me pincess."

"Yes, you *are* a princess," Cassie said, moving forward and straightening Sasha's glittery cardboard crown. "The loveliest princess who ever graced a Halloween evening. Look at Uncle Ryan. He wants to take more pictures."

Instead of following instructions, the toddler held out her arms for a hug. Cassie knelt down and gathered her close. "You're going to have fun tonight," she told the child.

Ryan looked through the viewfinder of the camera and took three quick photos, then chose not to look too closely at his motives for doing so. Why would he want photographs of the nanny? Except he knew deep down inside that Cassie was more than that. Over the past few days, she'd also become a friend.

His conscience battled it out over conflicting needs and moral obligations. As his employee, Cassie was entitled to his consideration. As a friend, the same rules applied. The fact that he saw her as a desirable woman put a difficult spin on everything. He still respected her and wanted to pay attention to what was right, but he couldn't stop noticing her, thinking about her, *needing* her.

She didn't wear perfume, but a soft, clean feminine scent clung to her and drove him crazy. During the day he could hear her moving around the house and he wanted to go find her and be with her. He thought about her when he was supposed to be concentrating on work. The more he tried to dismiss her from his mind, the more she seemed to invade his every thought.

If she'd been just a pretty face, he probably could have forgotten about her fairly easily. But she wasn't trying to get his attention. Most of the time he figured she thought of him as *her* uncle Ryan, as well as Sasha's. She treated him like a much older, distant relative. Obviously the nearly nine-year age difference meant a lot more to her than it did to him.

So even as he took a couple more quick pictures of her, he told himself he had to let this fantasy fade. It was nonproductive and only left him aroused and restless.

"Where's your pumpkin?" Cassie asked as she pulled Sasha to her feet and gave her costume a quick once-over. "Wasn't it right here?"

Sasha frowned. "Pun'kin?"

"Yes, the plastic pumpkin Uncle Ryan bought you so that you can take it when we go trick-or-treating and get candy. It's about this big." Cassie demonstrated the size with her hands.

"Me know," Sasha said, then dashed out of the room.

Ryan lowered the camera and stared after her. "Do you realize I've never seen that kid walk? She runs and skips, sort of, and races everywhere."

"Excess energy. Too bad we can't suck a little of it out of her each morning. Think of how much work we could both get done that day."

"Interesting thought." He returned his attention to her. Cassie had dressed in black jeans and a multicolored sweater. Her usual heart-shaped earrings dangled, catching the overhead light.

"You look nice," he told her.

She glanced at him. A slight flush climbed her cheeks. "Thanks. I wanted to be warm. It's going to be cool tonight. I knew that Sasha wouldn't want to wear a coat over her costume so I put her in two long-sleeved T-shirts and long pants underneath her dress. She's a tad bulky to fit in with the royal set, but otherwise, she's the perfect princess."

She didn't quite meet his gaze as she spoke and the flush lingered. He made her nervous, he thought with some surprise, incredibly pleased by the fact. Maybe Cassie wasn't as immune to him as he'd first thought. Then she raised her hand to tuck her hair behind her ear and he caught sight of the ring on her left hand. Joel's ring.

She was already committed to someone else, he reminded himself. He had no right to mess with her life.

He set the camera on the counter. "You don't have to come trick-or-treating with us tonight," he told her. "You haven't been out with Joel in several days. Don't the two of you have plans?"

She shook her head. "Bradley Discount is having a big celebration, with candy for kids and several departments offering special sales. Joel is in charge of all that, so he couldn't get away. Besides, I *want* to come out with you and Sasha. I doubt she remembers last year, so this will practically be her first time. She's going to have fun."

"If you're sure."

Her gaze met his. "I am."

He was too, sure that he wanted her. He could feel the

heat rising inside him, the need growing. One of these days he was going to have to start dating again, he told himself. He couldn't keep having fantasies about inappropriate women—they were starting to interfere with his work.

Sasha raced back into the kitchen. She held out her plastic pumpkin and grinned. "Me find!" She handed the container to Cassie, then walked over to her uncle and raised her arms. "Up."

Ryan bent over and gripped her, pulling her into the air and toward him in one, smooth motion. Her little arms went around his neck. He settled her at his waist, his forearm supporting her butt.

"Hey, kid, you ready to go out trick-or-treating?"

Sasha nodded. "Me pincess."

"You're right. I shouldn't have called you a kid. Are you ready to go trick-or-treating, your highness?"

The toddler giggled.

The doorbell rang and she pointed. "Go see."

"Oh, so I'm transportation now, am I?" Ryan asked, although he didn't really mind. He liked that his niece was comfortable with him and that he enjoyed being around her.

Cassie beat both of them to the door. She pulled it open, allowing her sister, in crocodile costume, and a man dressed as a pirate to enter. Sasha took one look at them and buried her face in Ryan's shoulder.

"It's okay," he said softly as Cassie greeted her sister and brother-in-law. "You know Chloe, don't you? Cassie's sister? You like her. And that man is her husband. I'm sure he would really like to meet a real princess. Especially one as pretty as you."

Sasha raised her head slightly, gave a squeak and hid

away again. Cassie smiled at him. "She's gone shy, has she?"

Chloe glanced down at herself. "Do you blame her? I think the theory of the crocodile costume was a good one. While I don't look hugely pregnant, I also don't look much like a normal crocodile. Maybe one that has pigged out over the weekend and is a little bloated."

"You look spectacular as always," her husband said. He glanced at Ryan. "I'm Arizona Smith. You must be Ryan. I've heard a lot about you."

They shook hands.

"Great costume," Ryan said, motioning to the other man's black wig, fitted blue jacket with a matching hat and the fake pistols strapped to his waist.

"I left my hook in the car. I thought it might scare Sasha. I see we did that anyway." He touched the child's arm. "Sorry, little one. Adults are strange creatures and you're going to have to get used to that."

She raised her head slightly. Arizona gave her a big smile, then an exaggerated wink. Ryan felt her relax in his arms.

"You're a very beautiful princess," Arizona told her.

Sasha nodded, as if to say she already knew that much and did he have anything new to tell her. Cassie and Chloe laughed.

If Ryan hadn't known Cassie was adopted, he would have wondered how the same family could have produced two such dissimilar daughters. Chloe was tall and elegant, even pregnant and dressed as a crocodile. She had the kind of sparkle about her that caused men to drop what they were doing just to watch her walk by. Cassie was several inches shorter, curved where her sister was lean, with a quieter beauty that Ryan found all the more appealing for its subtleties.

"We really appreciate you doing this," Cassie told her sister. "We won't be out long. Sasha will get tired pretty quickly."

Sasha began to wiggle. Ryan set her on the ground. She walked over to Cassie and put her hands on her tiny hips. "Me not tired."

"I know, sweetie. You're a big girl. You're going to have a lot of fun." Cassie straightened her crown, then returned her attention to her sister. "The candy is there," she said, pointing to a bowl on the table by the front door. "As I said, we'll be back in plenty of time for you to head out to your party."

Ryan glanced at his watch. "If you want to leave before we're back—"

Chloe cut him off with a shake of her head. "The university party doesn't start for over an hour and it goes practically all night. Take as long as you'd like." She touched her stomach. "Arizona and I are thinking of this as practice for the coming years."

"Absolutely." Arizona stepped next to his wife and put his arm around her. Chloe shifted closer.

They stood together as if they'd been a couple for decades instead of less than a year. Their love for each other was as obvious and real as their costumes. Ryan felt a twinge of envy inside. Was this what his brother and Helen had experienced in their marriage? He'd never been around them enough to notice, and even if he'd visited, he doubted he would have bothered to pick up on the small signals all couples sent and received.

What a waste, he thought grimly. He could have been a part of a very special family…his family. Instead he'd wasted his time with too much work.

"Then I think we're ready," Cassie said. "Oops, Sasha's pumpkin is in the kitchen. I'll go get it."

She walked down the hall. Sasha trailed after her.

"So what do you think of Bradley?" Arizona asked.

"It's a great town," Ryan told him and knew that wasn't the question Arizona really wanted to ask. He decided to make it easier on the other man. After all, he was looking out for a family member. Ryan respected that.

"I regret that it took a tragedy to bring me here," he said. "Without Cassie's help, I wouldn't have made it through these past couple of weeks. She's terrific with Sasha and a wonderful person to have around. I have the greatest respect for her."

"We think she's special," Arizona said, his gaze steady.

"As do I. It's fortunate that she has family close by. If anything were to happen, she would have plenty of support."

"I'm glad you recognize that," Arizona said.

Cassie and Sasha returned to the foyer. "We're ready." She paused. "What are you two talking about?"

"Nothing special," Ryan told her. "Let's go."

They called out their goodbyes and stepped into the clear, cool night. When the door had closed behind them, Cassie looked at him. "You're not getting off that easily. I could smell the testosterone in the air. Was that some kind of male dominance contest?"

"Not at all." He bent down and smiled at Sasha. "Would you like me to carry your pumpkin for a while?"

Sasha nodded. He took it from her, then held out his hand to his niece. Cassie took her other one and they walked to the sidewalk and turned right. Already there were dozens of children and adults out for the festivities. As they passed a group of boys dressed like monsters, Sasha shrank against Ryan. He squeezed her hand reassuringly, then continued his conversation with Cassie.

"Your sister and brother-in-law are concerned about your safety while you're living alone in my house. They wanted to make sure that I understood they were looking out for your interests. I assured them that I respect you as a person and would never do anything to make you uncomfortable."

"I'm impressed you two got all that said. After all, I wasn't gone that long."

"Guys read between the lines. He understood, as did I."

"If you say so. You would have more experience with the guy thing than me." She paused. "Why wouldn't they trust you? I do."

His first thought was to tell her that was because she was so young. She didn't have enough life experiences to know that she should be wary. But then he realized it wasn't about age at all. It was about Cassie. She was one of the most open people he'd ever met. She would be this trusting at eighty.

"You take the world at face value," he said. "That's not always a good thing. Be grateful you have family watching out for you."

They'd reached the first house. Cassie dropped to one knee and straightened Sasha's crown. "Do you remember what we talked about this afternoon?" she asked. "About trick or treat?"

Sasha nodded.

"Okay, then all you have to do is walk up to that door and knock. When the people come out, hold out your pumpkin, say 'trick or treat' and they'll give you candy."

Sasha hesitated.

"We'll go up with you," Ryan assured her.

With Sasha leading the way, the three of them moved

toward the front door. The porch light was on and more light spilled from the open windows.

"Go ahead and knock," Cassie said.

Sasha stood immobilized.

"I guess this is a bigger moment than I'd realized," Ryan said. He leaned forward and rapped his knuckles on the door.

When it opened a large, older woman peered out. "Oh, look, Martin, this one is so precious. Aren't you just the prettiest thing." She beamed at them all. "What a lovely family. Can you say 'trick or treat'?"

Sasha opened her mouth, but there wasn't any sound.

"Next year," the woman said kindly. "She'll be demanding seconds for sure. Here you go, hon." She dropped a small candy bar into Sasha's pumpkin. "You have a good time tonight and don't eat too much sugar."

They thanked the woman and left. As they walked down the path, Sasha fished the candy out of her pumpkin and held it up to both of them. "Look," she said.

"I see." Cassie took it from her and put it back in the container. "We're going to wait until we get home before we eat any. You want to go to another house and try again?"

"More," Sasha said.

Ryan smiled at Cassie over the girl's head. "I think she's getting the hang of this."

At the next house they had to wait while the group in front of them collected candy. Sasha held out her pumpkin. She still didn't say "trick or treat," but she managed a faint "tank you" when a candy bar was placed in her container.

"More!" she called out. "More and more and more."

"Ah, the greed is setting in," Cassie said with a laugh. "It sure doesn't take long." She bent down and swept the girl into a hug. "Yes, we'll get you more. Unfortunately you won't eat very much of it, so that means I'll have to help. Like I need more chocolate decorating my hips, thank you very much, young lady."

Against his will Ryan found his gaze focusing on Cassie's hips. They were round and womanly. Did she really think there was something wrong with them? He loved the shape of her hips. He'd spent many pleasant moments thinking about touching them, of having her on top of him and grabbing those perfect hips to guide her up and down on his....

"Unk Ryan, there." Sasha pointed to the next house.

"As my lady wishes," he said, forcing his mind away from his passionate, albeit inappropriate, thoughts.

This time Sasha raced up to the house and eagerly knocked on the door. When it opened she held out her pumpkin. "Candy," she said.

The man at the door laughed. "Not the traditional greeting, but it gets the point across." He dropped two wrapped pieces into her pumpkin.

Sasha smiled at him, set her container on the ground, then carefully took out one candy bar and handed it back to him. He took it and winked.

"You don't have this thing figured out yet, do you?"

"Candy!" Sasha said loudly. "Candy, candy, candy. Tanks!"

With a little wave, she turned and headed for the street.

"What about this?" the man asked, still holding the treat she'd given him.

"I think she wants you to have it," Ryan told him. He took Sasha's free hand. "How long do you think she'll hold out?"

They ducked around Darth Vader, a ghost and a kid in a really ugly slobbering-monster mask.

"I thought we'd go to the end of the block," Cassie said, pointing to the stop sign three houses up. "We can cross over and come back on the other side of the street. She should be tired by then."

They continued to walk from house to house. Sasha collected more candy than she handed back. Around them the sidewalks filled with more families. Ryan saw parents with their children, groups of kids alone. Several people stopped to tell Sasha that she was a beautiful princess. The child beamed with each compliment and Ryan felt an odd sense of pride, even though he had nothing to do with Sasha's appearance.

He felt a sense of community that was as tempting as it was unfamiliar. He wanted this all to be real. For the longest time he'd thought his brother was a fool, that John had sold out for something insignificant and that he would live to regret cutting back on his hours so that he could spend time with his wife and daughter. Now Ryan knew that John had made the right decision. He'd had no business judging his brother's actions.

Cassie and Sasha chatted with each other, occasionally drawing him into the conversation. But he was content to mostly listen while he mulled over his own thoughts. They turned up another walkway. Sasha was a couple of steps ahead when Cassie tripped over an uneven flagstone. Ryan grabbed her around the waist to keep her from falling. She clutched his arms.

Their combined actions brought her up against his chest. He felt the pressure of her breasts against him. One of her thighs slipped between his and bumped his rapidly swelling arousal.

The need was as instant as it was unexpected. One minute they'd been talking about upcoming movie releases for the holidays and the next she was in his arms.

It took all his self-control to keep from hauling her closer and kissing her until they both forgot all the reasons they had to maintain distance in their relationship.

"Ryan?"

It was too dark for him to read her expression, but he heard the question in her voice. What the hell was he doing?

"Are you okay?" he asked, trying to sound casual. He released her and, when he was sure she'd regained her balance, stepped back a few feet. "You nearly took a header there. That path is pretty rough. Watch your step."

She drew in a shaky breath. "I will. Thanks."

For a second he thought she was going to say more, but thankfully she turned away. "Sasha?"

The little girl had paused halfway up the path. Now she waved and headed toward the front door. "Candy," she called over her shoulder.

"That's right," Cassie told her. "You can…" She groaned. "Sasha, wait. Don't go there."

Ryan heard the concern in her voice. He scanned the front porch and saw what had alerted Cassie.

Fake cobwebs hung from the eaves of the porch. Candles flickered on the porch railing and in the corner two masked kids giggled together as they watched Sasha approach. Spooky music rose to a crash of cymbals, drowning out Cassie's plea that they not scare the little girl as she approached.

Unsuspectingly, Sasha trotted right up the front steps and headed for the door. Ryan raced after her, passing Cassie in three strides. Even so, he was too late.

Sasha innocently reached for the bell beside the door. As she did so, the two monsters sprang toward her, yelling and waving their arms. Sasha let out a screech that took ten years off Ryan's life, dropped her pumpkin and fled down the stairs. In her haste, she lost her balance. Ryan scooped her up before she tumbled to the ground.

"Hush, sweetie, it's okay," he said.

Sasha screamed and sobbed, clinging to him. Cassie rushed over and hugged the child. The three of them stood huddled together, the two adults murmuring promises that nothing bad was going to happen to her. Ryan could feel the tremors rippling through her.

"We're really sorry," a young voice said. "We were just playing. We do this every year. Most people know to keep the little kids away if they get scared. We're sorry, mister."

Ryan saw the two "monsters" in question had pulled off their masks and were maybe eleven or twelve. The boys looked as shaken as Sasha, probably because they were under orders not to frighten small children. One of them held out Sasha's pumpkin.

"Here's her candy. We gave her a couple of extra pieces."

"Thank you." Cassie took it, then smiled at the boys. "It's not your fault. She's only two and doesn't really understand what's going on. We know you didn't scare her on purpose." She kissed the top of Sasha's head. "Let's go home."

Ryan nodded. The toddler's tears had slowed, but she still trembled. "I'm glad you spoke to those two boys. I wanted to blister their hides and I would have overreacted."

"I don't think they were being deliberately cruel. I saw the cobwebs and candles when we were walking toward the house. I should have realized what was going on."

"It's not your fault," Ryan told her. He shifted Sasha. "Should you be holding her instead of me? I mean, I got to her first, that's why I grabbed her."

In the dim light from the streetlamps, he saw her smile at him. "She's *your* niece. You should be the one holding her. I think it's great." She turned her attention to the child. "Better?" she asked.

Sasha nodded. "Bad boys," she said.

"Not bad, just playing. I'm sorry you got scared. But you're safe now and we're not going to let anything happen to you. Okay?"

Sasha nodded.

She was so damn small, Ryan thought as he carried the toddler the rest of the way home. The world was a large and difficult place. He would have to protect Sasha as much as he could, all the while teaching her how to survive. The enormity of the responsibility made him shudder, but he couldn't back away from it now—he was all Sasha had.

When they arrived at the house, they said quick goodbyes to Chloe and Arizona. The doorbell rang again and again as more children stopped by for candy. With each cry of "trick or treat," Sasha clung tighter to Ryan's neck.

"She's not having much fun anymore," Cassie said. "Why don't you put her to bed while I man the door."

"Me?" Ryan shook his head. "You know how to do that stuff. I'll—"

Before he could finish his sentence, Sasha raised her head and looked at him. "Unk Ryan," she said. Tears stained her face; her eyes were puffy from crying.

How was he supposed to say no to her?

"You need to do this," Cassie told him. "She doesn't need a bath. I even brushed her teeth before we went out and she hasn't had anything to eat since, so don't worry about that. Put her in a nightgown, get her in bed, then read to her. She looks tired and I'm sure she'll fall asleep fairly quickly."

He wanted to protest that he wasn't ready to handle this sort of thing. Instead he nodded and carried his niece upstairs to her room. It only took a couple of minutes to get her out of her costume and put her into her pink kitten pajamas. Then she was tucked in bed and he was searching for the right story.

"Unk Ryan?"

He looked up from the bookcase. Sasha's big blue eyes were filled with tears again. "Me don't like monsters."

"I know, sweetie." He sat on the edge of the mattress and pulled her close. "I'll protect you. I promise to check the whole house tonight. Every closet, every door. You'll be safe. Uncle Ryan will keep you safe."

He didn't know how much she actually understood. At first he thought he'd gotten through to her because she was quiet, but then he realized she couldn't talk because she was crying too hard. He drew her up onto his lap and rocked her. She cried as if her little heart was breaking. Finally she murmured a single word.

"Mommy."

Now Ryan felt tightness in *his* chest. None of this was fair.

"I know," he murmured. "I know you miss her. I know I'm a poor substitute for both your parents. I wish I could offer you more, but I'm it. I don't know how to do things, and to be honest, kid, there are times when you terrify me. But I'm not going anywhere. We'll figure this out together." With a lot of help from Cassie, he reminded himself. He wouldn't have survived this without her.

Sasha continued to cry and he continued to hold her. Eventually she fell asleep. Carefully he lowered her into her bed and pulled the covers up to her chin. Then he sat in the darkness and wondered what the hell he was supposed to do now.

CHAPTER EIGHT

THE LAST OF the trick-or-treaters had rung the doorbell about a half hour before. Cassie moved restlessly in the living room and wondered what Ryan was doing. He'd been in with Sasha for so long that if he hadn't had to come down the stairs—which she could see clearly—she might have thought he'd slipped into his office. But he hadn't. He was still with his niece.

She moved to the front door and stared out through the beveled glass. The darkness seemed thicker than it had before when costumed children had brightened the sidewalks. She sank onto the wooden bench there, then sprang back to her feet. She wanted to be doing something, but she wasn't sure what—nothing felt right.

Part of the problem was her concern for Sasha. The poor girl hadn't needed a scare like the one she'd experienced. It wasn't a fun way to end her night. Cassie knew the boys had only been playing, but Sasha was too young to understand. At least she would probably forget between this year and next.

The good news was that in her time of need, she'd turned to her uncle and Ryan had been there for her. Slowly, uncle and niece were forming a family.

This was what she wanted, Cassie reminded herself. This was what she would have chosen for Sasha. She was pleased and relieved. At least she wasn't going to have to worry when Ryan took the girl back to San Jose, or whatever he decided to do with her. But the knowledge that they were bonding also left her feeling like an outsider.

Cassie leaned her forehead against the cool glass. Telling herself that everything was happening the way it was supposed to didn't help. Everything was mixed-up. She knew in her head that Ryan and Sasha had to form a family unit. Originally she'd been concerned that he would simply ignore the toddler and not want anything to do with her. But when she'd reminded him of his responsibilities, he'd come through like a seasoned parent.

So what was the problem? Maybe it wasn't about Ryan and Sasha at all, but about Ryan himself. The man had no flaws. Oh, he could get caught up in work and he liked to think he was the center of the universe. On a good day, he wanted to be treated as such, but Cassie wasn't talking about the details. She meant the inner being that made up the essence of Ryan Lawford. He'd resisted dealing with Sasha, but when push came to shove, he'd been there. Now, only a few short weeks into the relationship, he was terrific with her: patient, caring, making the little girl feel that she was the most important part of his life. Acting as if she was. How was she, Cassie, supposed to resist that?

It's just a crush, she reminded herself. Her feelings, whatever they were, had no basis in reality. In fact— The sound of footsteps broke through her thoughts. She turned and saw Ryan heading down the stairs. He looked tired and drawn.

She crossed the foyer and touched the curving end of the banister. "Is everything all right?" she asked. "Did Sasha have trouble falling asleep?"

Dark emotions filled his green eyes. "At first she was worried about the monsters. I told her I would protect her, but I don't know if she understood what I was trying to say. Then—" He cleared his throat. "She was asking about her mother."

His expression turned haunted and he swore under his breath. "How am I supposed to deal with that? I can't fix her problem. There's nothing I can say or do to make it better."

"You're right," Cassie said gently. "You can't fix it. No one can. You can only be there to help her get through the tough times."

"Maybe." He shrugged. "I held her. I rocked her in my arms and let her cry her little heart out. I thought I was going to go crazy listening to the sobs. I didn't know what else to do. I'm useless."

"No. You're exactly what she needs."

"Yeah, right. What with all my experience with kids." His mouth twisted. "I'm screwing this up."

His pain called to her, making her want to step closer and offer him comfort. Knowing that he would refuse, she held back. "You're doing everything exactly right. There *are* no set rules. Every parent has to find his or her way in the dark. Sasha isn't going to understand any complicated explanation about what happened to her folks. She only knows that she misses them deeply. Most of the time, when she's happy, she's fine, but when something rocks her world, she cries out for them. That doesn't mean you're doing anything wrong."

"I guess." He sank onto the bench by the front door. A bowl of candy sat on the small table next to him. He reached in and pulled out a small candy bar, then held it out to her. "Want one?"

"Sure." She took it, then settled into the seat opposite his.

Ryan unwrapped a piece of chocolate for himself and

ate it. When he was done, he leaned forward and rested his elbows on his knees.

"I didn't think it would be like this," he said. "Dealing with Sasha, I mean. When I found out John and Helen had made me her guardian, I was annoyed and frustrated, but I never got how big a responsibility it was."

"It's a challenge," she agreed. "But it's worth it."

He raised his head and met her gaze. "I didn't understand that part, either. But I do now. She's kind of like a tick that burrows under the skin. First you notice a bump and don't think much about it. The next thing you know, you've got a raging infection all through your body."

He grinned. "Sorry, that was kind of gross, and I didn't mean it in a bad way. It's just that for the first couple of weeks, I thought of Sasha as a responsibility I didn't want to deal with. I was very happy to pass her on to you. Now I look forward to spending part of my day with her. The little kid has gotten under my skin."

His words created a warm feeling in Cassie's stomach. Ryan had come to care about his niece. They would do well for each other, she thought, pleased that the sweet child would always have a family of her own. Someone who knew her history and could, in later years, tell her about her parents. Roots were important—Cassie knew that firsthand.

Ryan fished another candy bar out of the bowl. He offered it to Cassie, but she shook her head. He opened it and took a bite. After he'd swallowed he said, "I was thinking about my brother earlier. He was about ten years older than me. We had different fathers, but that didn't matter to us. We were really close. Apparently my mother had bad taste in men because neither of our dads bothered to stick around long enough to see us born."

He made the statement lightly, but Cassie caught the

tension in his body. She knew exactly what it felt like to be abandoned by a parent, but she kept her compassion to herself. She had the feeling that at this moment in time Ryan needed to talk more than he needed to listen.

"Our mother worked hard." He shrugged. "She was always urging us to get ahead. John became a doctor." He gave her a quick smile. "Mom was really proud of him. I was, too. It's tough to get through all the training but he did it. Then he turned around and paid back his loans in record time."

He straightened on the bench and leaned his head against the wall. "About five years ago John called me to tell me he'd met Helen and they were getting married. I was a little surprised. In our family we were big on work, but relationships had never been that important. When I pointed that out John said he didn't care. He'd fallen in love and he wanted to get married. He told me that he and Helen had also talked about starting a family. That one really threw me."

"You've never thought about doing that yourself?" Cassie asked before she could stop herself.

Ryan shrugged. "Not really. I never saw the point. There have been women in my life, but no one I wanted to marry."

Cassie wasn't sure what to make of that statement. He'd had women. Did that mean they'd all been lovers? Did he take women to his bed for a few times, then send them on their way? Or was it a mutual decision? Was that what other people did? She couldn't even imagine.

"He told me he wanted to slow down," Ryan continued. "I remember staring at the phone not believing what he was saying. I'd just started making a success of my own company and I was working eighteen-hour days.

Who had time to slow down? I couldn't believe he meant it. Worse, I thought he was selling out."

He drew in a deep breath, but he didn't speak. Cassie observed him, watched the play of light on his strong face, the twitch of a muscle as he clenched his jaw. At times she still didn't understand Ryan, but right now she knew exactly what he was thinking.

"You understand now," she murmured. "His actions didn't make sense five years ago, but you're starting to understand what he was trying to tell you."

He nodded slowly. His gaze was steady and direct. "What I remember most about my mother is how hard she worked. She'd been poor for a long time and I understand that it's difficult to let go of the past, but the last few years of her life, she could have slowed down some. She had two sons who were sending her money every month. But she wouldn't spend it. We sent her nice clothes and things for the house. When she was gone, we found all of them, still in their boxes. She never wore them or used them. I don't understand that."

Cassie didn't either. "Do you think she was saving them?"

"I don't know. Sometimes I think she forgot what she was working for. The process became important and she lost sight of the goal." He shook his head. "Or maybe it's something else entirely. All I know is that she died too young, surrounded by lovely things she wouldn't let herself enjoy."

He paused. "I wish…" His mouth twisted and he avoided her gaze.

"What?" she asked.

"I wish I'd spent more time with John. He and Helen kept inviting me here for holidays or just a weekend and

I kept putting it off. I didn't think it was as important as my work. I thought we'd have more time."

Her heart ached for him. He was in as much pain as Sasha, but in a way Ryan suffered more. He wouldn't cry out or allow himself to be comforted.

A vague feeling of disquiet settled over her. This was dangerous territory for her. Ryan the remote, successful man at the other end of the house was safe. She was allowed to have a crush on him without having to worry about getting into trouble. But this man was someone different. He wasn't remote or hard to understand. If anything, she felt they had a lot in common. They talked and laughed together easily. She couldn't have a crush on this Ryan because he was real. Once he was real, then her heart was at risk.

Don't be a fool, she told herself. *He* might be more real to her, but *she* was still just the nanny to him. He never thought of her as a woman, someone who might interest him.

Ryan glanced out the window. "I guess we're done with Halloween for this year." He looked at his watch. "It's after ten. I should probably let you get to bed."

She nodded, thinking that she should make her way upstairs. Morning came early when there was a two-year-old in the house.

"I don't suppose you'd care to join me for a quick drink," he offered.

Cassie opened her mouth to tell him that wasn't a good idea. Not with the way her body had gone on alert, every cell tingling with breathless anticipation. But her legs were suddenly heavy and the stairs looked too tall to climb right now. It was just a drink, she argued with herself. What could it hurt?

"That would be nice," she said.

He rose to his feet, then started toward the study he'd taken over as his office. "I think there's some brandy in here," he called over his shoulder.

Cassie trailed after him. It was just a drink, she repeated silently. Nothing significant. It didn't mean his feelings about her had changed. Oh, but she wanted it to mean something, she thought to herself as heat and excitement raced through her. Brandy. They were going to have a glass of brandy together. She thought people only did that in the movies.

She followed him toward the back of the house. While he opened the sliding doors that concealed the bar area in the study, she settled onto a corner of the dark blue leather sofa against the wall opposite the bay window.

A large desk dominated the room. Ryan had brought in a new fax machine, a printer, some other computer equipment she didn't recognize and three filing cabinets. There were thick overnight envelopes on his desk and stacks of paper on nearly every free surface.

Ryan poured brandy into two glasses, then carried them over to the sofa. "I haven't had this before," he said as he handed her the quarter-full snifter. "But John always had excellent taste. I'm sure you'll like it." He touched his glass to hers.

He acted as if she did this sort of thing all the time, she thought with some amazement. No way she was going to tell him that she was more of a beer and white wine kind of girl. Cassie didn't think she'd ever tasted brandy before in her life. While Ryan sat down on the opposite end of the sofa, she took a first, tentative sip.

The liquid burned her tongue and her throat, but not in a bad way. It really was exactly like what she'd read about in books—she *could* feel the fire all the way down to her stomach.

"What do you think?" he asked.

She gave him a smile. "I like it." She took another sip and tried to act as if she did this regularly.

Ryan set his drink on the glass coffee table in front of the couch. "I have something I've been meaning to mention before, but there hasn't been a good time until now."

He paused and Cassie's stomach sunk like a stone. What? Was he going to tell her he was dissatisfied with her work? Did he know about her infatuation and did that make him angry? Was it—"It's about Joel," he said.

She blinked. "Joel?" That didn't make sense. "What about him?"

Ryan angled toward her and rested his hand along the back of the sofa. "You don't see him very much. I'm concerned that your job is interfering with your relationship." He leaned toward her slightly. "I appreciate how great you are with Sasha. You obviously adore her and the feeling is mutual. You work long hours. Again, you have my thanks, but I don't want your personal life to suffer." He gave a quick smile. "If I'm saying this all wrong, please forgive me. To be honest, I've never had this conversation with an employee before in my life."

She wasn't sure what to say. Part of her thought it was really nice that he was concerned about her relationship with Joel. An equal part of her was annoyed that he was concerned about her relationship with Joel. Couldn't the man have even the tiniest hint of jealousy or envy? She sighed. As everyone had pointed out to her, she wasn't his type. He saw her as the hired help, someone to keep happy and treat fairly.

"You're very sweet to worry," she said calmly, knowing he would be confused if she told him what she was thinking. Maybe confused was putting it mildly. He would probably be stunned…and not in a good way.

"But there's no reason for alarm. I've been seeing Joel as much as ever."

He frowned. "You've only gone out a couple of times a week since you've come to work for me."

"I know. That's all we ever see each other."

"But it's been nine years."

"We don't need to spend every minute together." She kept her tone pleasant, even though she was feeling vaguely attacked. "This works for us."

"If you're finding each other boring before you get married, then you two are in trouble."

His voice was teasing, but Cassie couldn't smile. Ryan spoke something she hadn't dared to think to herself, but that she could no longer avoid. She stared at him helplessly, not sure what to say, then faked a chuckle as coldness enveloped her, chasing away any lingering warmth from the brandy. Was that what was wrong? she wondered. Did she and Joel already find each other boring?

She dismissed the sense of foreboding that swept over her. It was the night, she told herself. Or maybe the man. None of this was real.

They sipped their brandy in silence. Ryan told himself it was getting late and that he should send Cassie upstairs, but he didn't want to. Not only did he not want to be alone, but he enjoyed her company. She made him laugh; she reassured him; she reminded him that he was alive. And if he was honest with himself, he would be willing to admit that he also wanted *her,* which was completely different from not wanting to be alone. The ache inside of him was very specifically for the woman sitting at the other end of the sofa. He couldn't call one of his female friends and have her stop by to fill the void… not this time.

Unfortunately, the only woman he wanted was the one woman he couldn't have.

He looked at her. The light from the floor lamp reflected on her gleaming, dark hair. She took another sip of brandy. "You're staring at me. Do I have a smudge on my cheek?"

"Sorry." He forced himself to look away. "Not at all. I was just wondering about you. You're very different from anyone I've ever met."

She wrinkled her nose. "I know what that means. I've always been the country mouse. I guess I always will be."

There was nothing mouselike about her, but he couldn't admit that. Not with the night closing around them and his wanting growing…along with other parts of him. If he inhaled deeply, he could almost catch the sweet scent of her body. He wanted to know what she would feel like in his arms. He wanted to explore her generous curves, touch her soft face, kiss her and taste her and…

He had to clear his throat before he could speak. "I meant 'different' in a good way," he told her. "While you've chosen a perfectly respectable path, it isn't one designed to provide you with material benefits."

She chuckled. "That's a polite way of saying I'll never be rich working in a preschool." She shrugged. "I know that, but making lots of money isn't important to me. I grew up in a typically middle-class town. We didn't have tons of money, but there was always enough. When my parents died, they left me a trust fund. While it isn't millions, if I had to, I could live off it for several years. As it is, I'm just letting the proceeds reinvest."

She took a sip of her drink. "I always knew that I wanted to work with kids. I love their energy and enthusiasm. They're so honest with their feelings. Sometimes

I wish I could be more like my sister. Chloe wanted a career and made that happen."

"You have a career," he reminded her.

"It's not exactly the same." She stared into her glass. "Chloe always wanted to get away from Bradley and I always wanted to stay. When she met Arizona she realized that she had everything she needed right here, which is nice. I enjoy having her close. But it *is* ironic. I mean I'm the one who cares about genealogy and the history of the family and the town, but she's the real Bradley. I'm just adopted."

She said the words easily, as if they were simply information. But Ryan sensed something underneath, something hidden. The truth, he suspected, hurt her. She wanted to belong as much as her sister did. But by a quirk of birth, she never would.

"John and I grew up in a series of small apartments," he said. "It must have been nice to have a house that had been in the family for generations."

She flashed him a quick smile. "It was. Our mom would tell stories about the founding of the town, along with tales of the different Bradley women." Her smile faded. "It's been nearly ten years and I still miss my mother. I suppose that's one of the reasons I understand Sasha so well. I know what she's going through."

He nodded. "I suppose there's good and bad to being older when one loses a parent. You remember the good times, but you also remember the loss. Sasha isn't going to have any memories of John and Helen."

"There's no good time to lose one parent, let alone both," Cassie said, and Ryan remembered too late that Cassie had lost family before. Her birth mother had given her up for adoption.

"I'm sorry," he said quickly.

"Don't be. I don't mind talking about this." She looked at him. "Sometimes I think the worst part of our parents' death was the fact that Chloe and I were separated for nearly three years. Aunt Charity was left as guardian, but she was traveling and the lawyer couldn't find her. So Chloe and I were put into different foster homes. I stayed in Bradley, but she was sent to another town. I think meeting Joel is what saved me."

"Joel?" What did he have to do with anything?

She nodded. "He and I went to the same high school. We met our sophomore years. At first we were just friends, but then we started dating." She held up her hand. "Please spare me the psychobabble on what that means. Chloe has been over it a dozen times."

She piqued his curiosity. "What's Chloe's theory?"

"Chloe thinks I'm settling. That I suffered a traumatic loss at a formative age and Joel got me through it. Therefore I have misplaced loyalty toward him. She thinks that marrying Joel would be a mistake."

Chloe was a very sensible woman, Ryan thought, not daring to question his reasons for suddenly liking Cassie's sister. "What do you think?"

He'd expected a quick response, either telling him that none of this was his business, or saying that Joel was the love of her life. Instead she leaned back into the corner of the sofa and stared at him.

"I don't know anymore."

Her words hung in the silence. Inside he felt a quick jolt of pleasure, which he instantly told himself he had no business feeling.

"Sometimes it feels so incredibly right," she said. "We've known each other for years. There aren't any surprises, but that's not always a bad thing. We get along, we respect each other. It's comfortable." She drew in a breath. "But sometimes I want the fantasy."

He knew he probably shouldn't ask, but he couldn't help himself. "What fantasy?"

"No, you'll laugh."

"I promise I won't."

Her gaze skittered away from his and he sensed her sudden tension. More intrigued than he had the right to be, he leaned toward her and pressed for a reply. "I really won't laugh. Tell me. What is your fantasy?"

She drew in a deep breath. "The Bradley family has this magic nightgown."

Ryan stared at her, certain he'd misunderstood. "A what?"

"A magic nightgown. A long time ago, there was this gypsy woman. She was being attacked by a mob of drunken men."

He listened while she explained the legend of the nightgown. "I don't know what to say," he told her when she'd finished. "I've never heard anything like this before."

"I know it sounds strange, but I can show you the nightgown."

"No, that's not necessary. I'm sure it exists."

She ducked her head. "At least you didn't laugh."

He didn't know about spells and gypsy promises, but he did know that Cassie had just shared something very important to her. "Why would I? Just because I don't have a similar family tradition to tell you about doesn't mean that I'd make fun of yours. So you're counting on this legend?"

She nodded quickly. "I want the legacy to be true for me. I want to wear the nightgown on my twenty-fifth birthday and I want to dream about the man I'm supposed to marry. Chloe wore it and dreamed about Arizona. They met the next day and if it wasn't love at first sight, it was the next best thing. I want that, even though I'm afraid it's not going to happen."

Magic nightgowns and a promise of happily-ever-after. She really was an innocent. "Why wouldn't it happen for you?"

"I'm not a real Bradley," she reminded him. "I'm adopted. I have high hopes, of course, and Aunt Charity says believing is enough, but I don't know."

He wanted to tell her it was going to be fine, that she would have her special dream on her special night and everything would work out the way she wanted. But what did he know?

"What does Joel think about all this?" he asked, wondering how any fiancé would feel about the possibility of being usurped by a mystery suitor.

She finished her brandy and placed the snifter on the coffee table. "Not much. He's very low-key about the whole thing. Joel believes I'm going to dream about him. I suppose he's right, but sometimes I wish…" Her voice trailed off.

Ryan knew exactly what she was thinking. "Sometimes you wish he would be a little worried, and other times you wish you could dream about someone else."

Her eyes widened. "How did you know?" She leaned forward and covered her face with her hands. "I don't want to know what you're thinking. I know that's horribly disloyal and makes me an awful person."

He moved toward her and placed his hand on her forearm. "Don't think that for a second, Cassie. You're a sweet, good young woman. Why shouldn't you have a few dreams? You said yourself that you and Joel were waiting until you were sure. Doesn't that mean consider-

ing other possibilities? Besides, it's not as if you're acting
on these thoughts. I don't see you out dating other men."
Even though you should, he added silently, thinking that
he would like to go to the top of that list.

He pushed the inappropriate desire away. "Don't feel
guilty about what you want. You haven't done anything
wrong."

She raised her head and looked at him. Her smile trembled a little at the corners, but it was still pretty. She had
a lovely smile. Had he noticed that before?

"Thank you," she told him. "You're very kind."

Kind. There was a word every man was just dying to
have applied to himself. Kind. Maybe she could throw in
loyal and trustworthy. Then he could feel really macho.

This was a mistake, he thought grimly. He was getting
involved in something that didn't concern him. Cassie
was his employee, nothing more. They shouldn't be having this personal conversation.

"Have you ever been married?" she asked.

He'd been about to stand up and excuse himself, but
her question was as effective as a seat belt at keeping him
in his chair. "No," he told her.

"Why not?"

"I never wanted to."

She looked shocked. "Are you saying you've never
fallen in love?"

The truth was, he hadn't. But admitting that made him
feel that there was something wrong with him. "I never
had the time," he answered instead. "I was too involved
with work, then with starting my company. There was
no room for much of a personal life."

"I see." Her gaze was steady on his face and he wondered what exactly it was she saw.

"That's going to have to be different now," she said.

"I'm not suggesting you marry for Sasha's sake, but you are going to have to be around to spend time with her."

"I know." Everything was changing—he could feel it. Somehow when he wasn't looking, his life had taken an unexpected turn. "What about you?" he asked. "What's next? Marriage to Joel? To be honest, I'm surprised he's been willing to wait so long. If I were him I would be worried about that magic nightgown and I would want to sweep you off your feet."

"As nice as that sounds, Joel isn't the sweeping kind."

She made the statement matter-of-factly, but Ryan thought he could read between the lines. Perhaps Cassie wasn't waiting for her twenty-fifth birthday and the promise of the family legend as much as she was waiting for romance. She wanted Joel to want *her* enough to be unhappy about any delay. How else was Joel letting her down?

Ryan remembered her few dates with Joel since she'd been in his employ. She'd been back before eleven each time. It wasn't his place to speculate and he was probably wrong about everything, but he couldn't help wondering what that meant. Didn't Joel know what a prize he held? On the heels of that thought came the realization that he would side with Cassie's sister any day. To his mind, Cassie was settling.

"You've been with Joel for years," he said. "You were very young when you started dating him. Maybe you should go out and explore the world before getting married."

"You don't actually mean the world," she said. "You think I should date other men."

"I think you should be very sure."

She rose to her feet and crossed to the bay window. The lights from the room made the glass reflect images like a mirror. He could see her face, her thoughtful expression. She folded her arms over her chest as if to protect herself from danger.

"I've had this exact conversation with myself," she admitted. "Sometimes I'm completely sure and others..." Her voice trailed off.

"How do you know?" she asked softly. "I love Joel, but I don't know what kind of love we share. He's easy for me to be around. I like him. I respect him. But sometimes I'm afraid I love him more like a brother than a husband." She drew in a breath. "We're long on conversation but short on passion. I tell myself that shouldn't matter, but I'm just not sure."

Ryan felt vindicated. So he'd been right about Cassie's feelings of uncertainty. Unfortunately, he didn't have an answer to her dilemma.

"I tell myself there's more to life than passion," she continued. "Do I have the right to want more? Who am I to think I deserve it all?"

Ryan stood up and crossed to stand behind her. Their gazes met in the reflection of the window. "Everyone deserves it all," he said. She more than most, although he wasn't about to speak the last part aloud.

She turned to face him. "I want to believe you. Sometimes I feel so guilty for not being more grateful to have Joel in my life."

"You like and respect him. That's what we're supposed to do with friends. But you don't have to pretend to love him if that's not what you feel. You don't have to marry him if you're not sure."

They were standing too close, he thought suddenly. He could inhale her sweetness and feel the heat from her body. She wore a sweater over jeans, but somehow the simple clothes had become provocative, calling to him, making him want to touch her. Dear God, what was he thinking? This was all wrong.

He told himself to back off. Cassie wasn't interested in him that way. She saw him as an old man…or at the very least an *older* man. She worked for him. He had no right to want her, to want to take her in his arms and kiss her.

Cassie raised her chin slightly. "I'm not sure," she whispered.

He'd waited long enough. Whatever control he'd had disappeared. There was only the night, the woman standing so close to him, and his need. Telling himself it was wrong didn't help. Telling himself she deserved better than he could ever offer was completely true, but it didn't give him the strength to turn away.

"Cassie, I can't—"

His sentence ended in a strangled sound. Cassie stared at Ryan. He was obviously trying to tell her something, although she couldn't figure out what. She wasn't even sure it mattered. After all, fire filled his magical green eyes. A fire that burned so hot, she felt herself going up in flames.

She told herself she should be afraid, that Ryan wasn't like Joel and that she had somehow become tangled in a situation she had neither the experience nor the skills to handle. But she didn't care. This was Ryan and she trusted him as much as she'd ever trusted anyone. Besides, she couldn't move even if she wanted to. Something had happened to her will. Her legs were too heavy to carry her away. She couldn't think, she couldn't move, she could only wait helpless for something to happen… something wonderful.

He placed his hand on her shoulder. "You should head up to bed."

She nodded. "I should." But she wasn't going to. Not

until…well, she couldn't say until what, but she wasn't leaving anytime soon.

"I mean it, Cassie. If you stand here any longer I'm going to have to—" He broke off and swore under his breath.

"You're going to have to what?"

He placed his free hand on her waist and drew her closer. So close that her thighs brushed against his. Instantly heat poured through her. Her legs went from heavy to melting. Her breasts ached and swelled and pushed against her bra. She raised her hands and rested them on his upper arms. She could feel the tension in him, the rock-hard strength of his muscles.

"Ryan," she breathed. Dear Lord, if she didn't know better, she might think the man was going to kiss her. Right here in his office, in front of a window, on Halloween. It was magic. It was perfect. *He* was perfect, trying to warn her away and all. Even now she could see the conflict in his eyes as he attempted to talk himself out of the moment.

It surprised her that there was even a question. After all, she wasn't like Chloe. Men had never found her irresistible. But she loved the fact that Ryan, of all men, seemed to think her so. His breathing was harsh, his body tense, his eyes questioning.

She thought about raising herself on tiptoe, just to take enough of the initiative so that he didn't have to feel badly about what he was doing. But she didn't want to. This was her fantasy, after all, and in all the books she'd ever read, the guy was the one who kissed first.

So she waited…and waited…until it seemed as if he was never going to do it.

Finally, when she was sure he was going to come to his senses and realize who she was and know that he could never really want her that way, he lowered his head to hers.

"Tell me to stop if you don't want this."

Those were his last words. She vaguely heard him utter them and had a split second in which to think that was *so* not going to happen. Then his mouth touched her lips and she couldn't think at all.

For a heartbeat there was nothing. Just the sensation of his skin against hers. Then it hit. The heat, the need, the hunger, the incredible desire to be closer, to have their mouths forever joined.

He kept the contact light, which drove her crazy. His hands didn't move. He continued to touch her shoulder and her waist, while a voice in her head screamed for him to put his hands everywhere. Tremors started at her neck and worked their way through her body. Her nipples tightened and ached, while between her legs damp heat made her fear she really was melting from the inside out.

His head tilted slightly so their lips could press together more firmly. She clung to him, afraid he would pull back. Her hands moved from his upper arms to his shoulders, then wrapped around his neck. She couldn't get close enough. She needed more. Desperately.

"Cassie." His voice was low, thick and strangled.

She uttered two words she'd never before in her life said to a man.

"Don't stop."

He groaned, parted his lips and plunged his tongue inside her mouth.

She welcomed his assault, meeting him with one of her own. They touched and stroked, exploring each other, finding pleasure and heat and madness. She worried a little about her enthusiasm until she realized he was holding on to her just as tightly and that the hand on her waist had dropped to her rear and pulled her hard against him.

Speaking of hard…he was. She could feel the ridge of his need pressing against her belly. She'd never felt Joel's arousal before. Of course they'd never stood this close or kissed with such passion.

He broke the kiss, but only to press his lips against her cheeks, her jaw, then down her throat. Her breathing came in gasps. She didn't know how much longer she was going to be able to remain standing.

"Ryan," she whispered.

"I know," he answered. "I feel it, too."

So this was passion, she thought through a fog of desire as he reclaimed her mouth. This was the sensation that sparked the books and songs and poems. It all made sense now. For the past several years she'd thought everyone was lying to her and that this sort of thing didn't really exist. But it did.

Unfortunately, she didn't have any right to be experiencing it with this particular man.

She broke the kiss, turned on her heel and ran from the room.

CHAPTER NINE

RYAN LEANED AGAINST the windowsill and closed his eyes. He could still feel the heat of Cassie's body pressed against his and taste her sweetness on his tongue. A tremor ripped through him. It didn't matter that he was fifteen different kinds of bastard, the wanting inside of him was the most powerful force he'd ever experienced.

The sound of her footsteps died away. There was a moment of silence, followed by a door closing on the second floor. She'd run from him. He hated that she'd done that, but he couldn't blame her. What the hell had he been thinking?

He crossed over to his desk and sank into the leather chair. His breathing still came in gasps and his arousal ached. He had a bad feeling he was going to spend the next several hours in a lot of pain. Still, none of that mattered. The real problem was that he hadn't been thinking. He'd been feeling and reacting.

The questions of right and wrong, of what was proper and decent hadn't occurred to him. One minute they'd been talking and the next she'd been so damn close that he couldn't help himself.

He'd lost control. He, Ryan Lawford, who always played the mating game by the rules, had lost control with a young woman who didn't understand there was a game in progress. He'd been blindsided by a virtual innocent. Joel had been the only man in her life, so she should have been the one in over her head. Instead *he'd* been the one to plunge headlong into passion.

Guilt crept through him, seeping into the cells of his body, replacing the wanting with something cold and ugly.

He'd had no right to touch her. She worked for him. He swore again and wondered what had gone wrong. He'd never once flirted with an employee, let alone dated or kissed one. He'd always been able to separate business from pleasure. To be honest, in the past he'd never been tempted to cross the line. The fact that he'd only done it once didn't make him feel any better. What he'd done was wrong. Cassie not only worked for him, she worked for him *in his house.* She was completely vulnerable and at his mercy by virtue of her living under the same roof. He owed her respect. He owed her a work environment in which she felt safe. He owed her the right to get through her day without worrying that she was going to be groped at every turn.

But that wasn't his only sin. There was also the issue of her involvement with Joel. Cassie was practically engaged to the younger man. He, Ryan, had no business trying to seduce her. If she'd been unattached it still would have been wrong, but this made it unforgivable.

What had happened? Why her? She wasn't his type. He ignored the voice inside that whispered he didn't have a type. She was too young, too inexperienced, too different from the women who regularly drifted through his world.

He leaned back in his chair. It didn't matter, he realized. Right type or not, engaged or not, working for him or not, he wanted her. Something had happened between them. Not just tonight, although the kiss had been glorious, but before. He'd noticed her. He'd seen that she was a bright, funny, pretty, charming woman and he'd wanted her. Now he didn't know how to change his feelings so that he didn't get excited every time he saw her or thought about her.

The realization confused him. Something was happening to him—he was changing. He was no longer the man he'd been when he'd first arrived in Bradley to clear up his brother's estate. Some of the changes had come about because of Sasha. He was growing to care about the little girl. But some of the changes were about Cassie's influence on him.

What was happening to him and how could he make it stop? He'd done so well for so long by ignoring his feelings. He didn't want to have to deal with them now. Unfortunately, he wasn't being given a choice.

His world had just gotten very complicated.

He reminded himself that he didn't want a commitment. Unfortunately, Cassie was the kind of woman men married, not the kind they had an affair with. There was also the issue of her engagement, not to mention her employment with him. He didn't have a choice in the matter. He was going to have to apologize and promise that it would never happen again. That wouldn't make it right, but it was the best he could do. Actually it was the best he was *willing* to do. After all, he could offer to terminate her so that she could get back to her regular life.

But the thought of Cassie leaving was physically painful, and it wasn't all about having to deal with Sasha on his own. He knew instinctively that it would be difficult for him to go through his day without seeing Cassie. He didn't even want to think about what that meant.

So instead he would apologize to Cassie in the morning and promise that she would always be safe from him. He would hide his wanting; he would stop thinking about her as much. He would attempt to go back to the man he had been before, even though he had a bad feeling it was going to be a nearly impossible task. He'd seen the light and he doubted he would willingly return to the darkness.

THE FIRST FINGERS of dawn crept around the closed drapes. Cassie pulled her knees more tightly to her chest and watched as the room slowly brightened. She'd been awake for much of the night, thinking about *the kiss*.

It was such a simple act, she thought. A type of contact millions of people had every day. Family members kissed hello or goodbye, old friends often greeted each other with a kiss. She'd kissed her sister, her parents, her aunt and, of course, Joel. But nothing had prepared her for the impact of Ryan's kiss. She was still surprised there weren't scorch marks on her hands and face from the heat of their contact. She'd relived the kiss a hundred times in the long night and each time the memory had made her shiver with longing.

Her body had come alive in his arms. She'd finally understood why lovers risked death to be together. She'd read once that when a woman truly bonds with a man that just the idea of being with a different man could physically make her sick to her stomach. Cassie had always thought that was a lot of nonsense, but now she wasn't so sure. She didn't know exactly what steps were necessary to bond a woman to a man. She suspected they first had to make love, to establish a biological as well as an emotional connection. But she understood the part about not wanting to be with anyone else. Just the thought of another man's kiss made her flinch.

The world had become a confusing place. On the one hand, Ryan's kiss had explained so much to her. She felt as if she'd finally seen through a previously closed door. She had shared a common human experience.

Cassie dropped her head to her knees and sighed. But on the other hand, what she'd done was wrong. There were no words to pretty up the truth. She had a commitment to Joel and she'd violated his trust in her. Maybe she'd been a little annoyed because he hadn't been concerned about her living in Ryan's house, but that didn't give her the right to create a situation in which he would be concerned. She owed him her loyalty.

Ryan was just a crush, she reminded herself once again. As such, she owed him nothing. He might be a flesh and blood man, but their worlds were so different, he might as well be a movie star. She had as much in common with him as she did with someone famous. Except...

She raised her head and squeezed her eyes tightly closed. Except somewhere along the way, he'd become real to her. He wasn't just the object of her affection. He was a normal person with moods and opinions. She'd talked with him and laughed with him. She'd watched him change from a distant stranger into a warm, caring man who was coming to love his niece. She'd seen that he cared about different things, that he was honorable and hardworking. She was still smitten with him, but she also liked and respected him.

Now he'd taught her about wanting. He'd held her close and kissed her until everything had changed. Her body had come alive for him. Even this morning when she should be feeling guilty and horrible and figuring out a way to set things right, memories of their kiss intruded. If she thought about it for too long, she found herself getting warm. Her breasts would begin to ache, and that secret place between her legs would tingle and dampen.

She didn't know exactly what was happening to her, but she knew she liked it.

However she wasn't a fool. Here, in Bradley, with only his two-year-old niece for company, Ryan might think that she was great fun to be around. But she wouldn't fit into his real world. She wasn't the right kind of woman. He was older and more sophisticated, while she was just a preschool teacher. Maybe if she'd always wanted to be more they might have had a chance, but she didn't. She loved living in Bradley. She'd only ever wanted to work with children. She didn't care about wearing the right clothes or driving the right kind of car. Her idea of heaven would be a family—roots of her own.

Cassie opened her eyes and stared around at the lovely guest room. The large dresser seemed to waver in the morning light. Then she realized there were tears in her eyes. At one time she'd thought she would find everything she'd ever wanted with Joel. They'd been in love once and they'd made plans for a future. But something had happened along the way. She couldn't point to an exact date or incident, but they were different people now. The kiss between Ryan and her had been wrong, but it had forced her to face something she suspected she'd been avoiding for a long time. She had to end things with Joel.

The thought should have terrified her, but it didn't. She held her breath, waiting for the rush of disappointment or sadness, but there wasn't much of anything. Maybe a little relief, which startled her. Should she have broken things off with Joel years ago? There was no way to get that answer, she realized, and no point in second-guessing herself. She would just have to go forward now and do the right thing.

She brushed her cheek with the back of her hand and

smiled. Wouldn't it be lovely if she told Ryan what she was going to do and he was so happy he swept her up in his arms and told her he'd loved her from the first moment he'd met her? It was about as likely as winning the lottery, and she rarely bought a ticket. Unfortunately, Ryan wouldn't think anything about her breaking up with Joel. Or if he did, he would most likely be worried that she would expect something from him.

Cassie's smile faded. She didn't want that. She didn't want Ryan to think she was going to pursue him. She would have to play it very cool. As if the kiss was no big deal. Maybe he would think this sort of thing happened to her every day.

That was going to be her goal, to keep it casual. Ryan must never know how very much his kiss had rocked her world.

RYAN HURRIED THROUGH his shower, then shaved and dressed quickly. His hair was still damp when he left his bedroom and headed for the stairs. He wanted to catch Cassie before she got Sasha up.

But when he stepped into the kitchen, the toddler was already sitting in her high chair with a cup of juice in front of her. She beamed when she saw him. "Unk Ryan. Me pincess."

He gave her a quick smile, taking in the fact that she was dressed in her Halloween costume. "So you are. And a very beautiful princess at that."

His gaze swept the room. Everything looked completely normal. Cassie stood at the stove preparing his niece's hot cereal. Sunlight reflected off the linoleum floor. The smell of bacon and coffee filled the room. It was as if nothing had happened. For a second he thought maybe he'd imagined the whole incident. Then Cassie turned toward him.

"I tried to convince her to wear something else, but she can be quite stubborn, as you know." Her smile was just right, her eyes bright, her expression welcoming. There might have been a hint of weariness in the shadows under her eyes, but he wasn't sure. Still it wasn't Cassie's reaction—or lack of reaction—that convinced him last night had been very real. Instead, it was his own.

Desire slammed into him with the subtlety of a truck traveling at four hundred miles an hour. He half expected to be thrown into the wall and fall to the ground in a broken heap. He wanted her instantly. He wanted to pull her close and kiss her hard. He wanted to bury himself inside of her until they both—"Ryan? Are you all right?"

"What?" He blinked and realized that Cassie was holding out his mug of coffee. He took it from her and tried to fake a smile. "Sure, I'm fine. Thanks." He raised the mug in salute, then sipped the steaming liquid.

"Have a seat. I thought you might be tired of cold cereal so I'm making pancakes."

"Great." Except he wanted her too much to eat.

He took his usual chair at the table. Sasha banged her spoon against her tray. "Me hungry."

"I'm sure you are." Cassie crouched in front of the child. "You can tell me you're hungry and that you want your breakfast, but you're not allowed to bang on the table."

Sasha's delicate brow furrowed as she struggled to understand the information. She raised her spoon to bang it again. Cassie shook her head.

"No. Don't bang."

Sasha stared, released her spoon. It clattered to the metal table. Cassie sighed. "I suppose that's as much of a victory as I'm going to get this morning," she said as she rose to her feet and returned to the stove. "Your cereal is just about ready, young lady. Give me thirty seconds."

Ryan sipped his coffee. This scene wasn't playing out the way he'd pictured it last night and again this morning when he'd awakened before dawn. Somehow he'd thought Cassie would be more upset by what had happened between them. He stared at her. There didn't seem to be anything wrong. Was she really all right or was she pretending?

She filled a small, plastic bowl with warm cereal and placed it in front of Sasha. "Do you want a piece of bacon?" she asked the girl.

Sasha nodded. "Peas."

Cassie shot him a grin. "One of these days I'm going to forget she has trouble with her *L*'s and actually hand her a bowl of peas. Imagine how shocked she'll be."

He couldn't stand it anymore. He pushed back his chair, rose to his feet and crossed to the stove. She had several strips of bacon frying in a pan. On the counter, the electric griddle heated for pancakes.

"I'll watch these," he said, reaching for the pan.

"Thanks." She stepped to the side and stirred the batter. "You usually want four pancakes. Does that sound right for this morning?"

"Sure. Whatever." As if he cared about food. He stared at the rapidly crisping meat, then at his niece, who was happily eating, getting as much food on herself as in her mouth.

"Are you all right?" he asked, his voice low enough not to carry across the room.

Cassie poured pancakes onto the griddle, then looked at him. "Of course. Why do you ask?"

"You're many things, Cassie, but you're not dumb. You know why I'm asking."

"Okay." She turned her attention back to the pan. "I'm fine and I'm not just saying that."

"Really?" He wanted to believe her. Knowing that she wasn't suffering any aftereffects would make his whole life easier.

"Of course. You want the truth?" she asked, then continued without waiting for his response. "It was a very lovely kiss. One of the best I've had in a long time. But that's all it was. We didn't rewrite history or change the course of time. We kissed. I don't really understand exactly how we got from chatting about our pasts to a passionate embrace, but this kind of thing happens. We're two adults working in close proximity."

"This is not common practice in my line of work," he said, a little surprised she was being so sensible. Somehow he'd expected her to be upset.

"Mine either." She grinned. "But then as a preschool teacher I would have many less opportunities than you."

"So you're really okay with this?"

"Sure."

She turned the pancakes, then nodded at his pan. The bacon was done. He scooped the pieces out onto a paper towel.

"I'm realistic," she told him. "Aside from Sasha, you and I have very little in common. We had a moment, now it's over. No big deal."

Her attitude annoyed him, even though he knew he should be thrilled that she was so calm about everything.

"We have more than Sasha in common," he said. "We get along extremely well. We read the same kind of books, watch similar movies. We talk easily."

"I suppose." She didn't sound convinced.

"We're intelligent." They were also great together when it came to kissing, but he didn't think he should point that out to her. While he knew he was more experienced than she, he'd never felt the kind of instant fire before.

"And funny," she agreed. "But so what?" She put the cooked pancakes onto a plate, then poured four more circles of batter onto the griddle. "Face it, Ryan, we're from different worlds. A man like you would never be interested in a woman like me."

"Don't be ridiculous. Of course I would be interested." He'd spoken without thinking. Cassie glanced at him. "I don't think so."

He cleared his throat. The conversation had gone a lot better when he'd had it alone in his shower. Somehow she wasn't getting her lines right. "What I mean is that we have enough in common that differences in our living styles aren't significant. I'm not making a play for you, I'm just pointing out that your logic is flawed."

"Thank you for sharing."

He saw the glint of humor in her eye and knew that she was laughing at him. He didn't know whether to be offended or join in the joke. In the end, it was easier to ignore either option and plunge ahead.

"My point is," he said, moving closer and lowering his voice, "that you don't have to worry that I'm going to attack you. You're my employee working in my home. You are entitled to my respect and you have it. I promise I will never compromise your position or violate your trust again."

She flipped the pancakes. "Thanks, Ryan, but it never occurred to me that it would be otherwise. The kiss was a one-time thing. Not to worry."

Her casual dismissal made him want to shake her. Or

kiss her again. Which showed him how far he'd gone over the line.

"You're safe here," he said.

"I know."

He gritted his teeth together. "Great. Just so we understand each other."

"We do. You can stop belaboring the point."

Her smile took the sting out of her words, but he couldn't help feeling that he'd lost complete control of the situation. When and how had that happened? And why wasn't he happy with everything she was saying? It was exactly what he'd wanted to hear.

But he wasn't happy. He wanted her to be...what? Afraid? He shook his head. That wasn't right. Maybe it was that she'd put the situation out of her mind so easily, when he was finding it difficult not to pull her close and do it all again.

"Everything is ready," she told him. "Go sit down."

He did as she asked. As she put his breakfast in front of him, she spoke. "I have a couple of things I need to do this afternoon. I've checked with Aunt Charity. She can come by and baby-sit Sasha. I hope that's all right."

"It's fine. Take as long as you'd like."

Sasha claimed Cassie's attention and Ryan was left feeling as if he'd missed something very important. Everything had gone his way, so why did it all feel so wrong?

CHAPTER TEN

CASSIE SAT AT a corner booth in the small fast-food restaurant at the back of the Bradley Discount Store. She resisted the urge to check her watch. After all, she'd looked at it about thirty seconds before, so she wasn't likely to be surprised by the time.

She glanced around at the plastic furniture and wished she could have met Joel somewhere other than here. From her seat she could see out into the store. There were too many people and not enough privacy, but when she'd called Joel that morning he'd said he couldn't spare more than a few minutes for her. Her choice had been to come to the store, or put off their conversation. Cassie had agreed to come to him rather than wait another day.

She took a sip of her soda and wondered what on earth she was going to say to him. She'd practiced several different approaches in the car, but each had sounded more stupid than the last. There was no easy way to do this, but it had to be done. She had to tell Joel the truth. She wanted to be as kind and gentle as possible, but she had to get the message across.

She heard footsteps and glanced up. Joel crossed the black and white floor, moving toward the booth. He wore gray slacks and a pale blue shirt, along with a cartoon-print tie. His hair was neat, his face freshly shaved. He held a clipboard in one hand. He looked like what he was—a busy, albeit harried, manager.

"Hi," he said, sliding onto the plastic bench opposite hers. "Sorry I'm late. There were some problems in housewares."

"It's fine. I've only been waiting a few minutes." She paused. Now what? "Joel, I have something to tell you."

"Okay, sure."

But as she watched, his gaze strayed to the clipboard resting on the table. Trying not to show her annoyance, she reached out and turned it over so he couldn't read it anymore. "This is important," she told him.

"Fine. I'm listening."

"I…" Her mind went blank. "It's just…well…" Then the words came in a rush. "You didn't touch me just now. Not even a kiss on the cheek."

His mouth tightened as his blue eyes narrowed. "Is that what this is about? Are we going to talk about our feelings again? I'm willing to do that, Cassie, but not now and not here. It's the middle of my workday. We're in my store. I'm not going to entertain my employees with a passionate embrace. If that bothers you, I'm sorry."

She took a sip of her diet soda and tried to smile. "You're absolutely right. This isn't the time or place to talk about feelings and I don't expect a passionate embrace at your place of work. But you didn't touch me at all. I'm not angry, I'm simply pointing out the obvious. We don't touch anymore. We haven't for a long time."

He sighed heavily, the world-weary sound of a logical male about to be exposed to the irrational thinking of a female. Cassie promised herself no matter what, she wasn't going to lose her temper.

"Don't," she told him. "Don't say anything, just listen."

He frowned, then nodded. "If you'd prefer."

"I would." She took a deep breath. All right. She had his attention. Now what was she going to do with it?

In the car on the way over she'd discarded a couple dozen ways of telling him the truth. She wasn't sure of the correct tone, or proper sequence of the words that would explain what was going on with her. Despite the practice, all she could think of was a bald statement of the facts.

"Working for Ryan has become a problem," she said. "It's not him, it's me. I have feelings for him." She couldn't bring herself to look at him, so she stared at the hard plastic table. "It's just a crush. I mean what else could it be? I barely know the man. But it's there and it doesn't seem to be going away."

"Is that it?" Joel asked.

Cassie raised her head and met his steady gaze. "What do you mean, 'is that it?' Isn't that enough? We've been together for nine years, I confess to having feelings for another man and that's all you can ask me?"

"Oh, honey, you're making too much out of this. Of course you have a crush on Ryan. What young woman in your position wouldn't? He's older, he's successful, he's sophisticated. I'm sure he can be quite charming. If you hadn't noticed him I would have worried about you. It doesn't mean anything." Joel's smile was warm and friendly. "Is that what all this is about? Have you been worrying yourself over nothing? That's so like you, Cass."

She couldn't speak. She could only stare. Maybe it was her hearing. Maybe some connection to her brain had malfunctioned and words were getting messed up or turned around.

"You don't care," she managed between stiff lips.

"Of course I care. You mean the world to me. But I'm not worried about your crush on Ryan. As soon as he's out of your life, you'll forget all about him."

He was taking this way too calmly, she thought.

Maybe he was the one with the broken brain. "There's more," she told him.

"I'm listening."

"We kissed." She waited, but there was no reaction. "It was just once. I mean it was just one event, but during those few minutes we kissed several times."

Still no reaction. Joel nodded as if to show he was listening, but there wasn't any obvious anger or displeasure on his part. For all she knew he was thinking about his problems with the housewares department.

She set her forearms on the table and leaned toward him. "It wasn't like when you and I kiss, Joel. There was no holding back. I felt...I felt things I've never felt before. I wanted him...passionately."

She paused, then realized she was done. What else was there to say? Except maybe the obvious. "I'm sorry," she added in a low voice. "I didn't mean to hurt you."

"Ah, Cass."

He glanced at his watch. She blinked. His watch? Like he was late for something more important? "Joel, I'm telling you that I kissed another man and that it turned me on. I wanted to *be* with him. Do you want to say something about this?"

"I'm not surprised," he told her calmly. "The situation was bound to occur. Frankly, I expected it sooner, but I'm glad it's finally here. We can deal with it and put it behind us."

One of them was crazy. "What are you talking about?"

"When we started dating, you were only sixteen," he said.

"I'm well aware of that."

"I was seventeen."

She felt as if she'd been dropped into a conversation

already in progress. "What does that have to do with anything?"

"I've dated other women, but you never dated other guys."

He was comparing his few dates in high school to her kiss with Ryan? "Joel, you don't understand what I'm trying to tell you."

"Of course I understand." His smile was kindly. "I've been there. When I dated before, I kissed those girls and...well..." He flushed. "We did some things together. My point is I've experienced life. I know what's out there in the world. You haven't done that. I'm pleased that you had the opportunity to sow your wild oats and get all this out of your system."

Okay, so they weren't talking about the same thing at all and Joel didn't get it. Now what? "This is more than wild oats," she said. "A lot more."

"I know you believe it is, but don't worry. It's done and now we can get on with our lives." He reached out and placed his hand over hers. "I love you, Cass. You're the one that I want to be with. I still trust you. Isn't that what matters?"

It should, she thought sadly. It should matter a whole bunch, but it didn't.

She studied his familiar face, the shape of his jaw, the curve of his lower lip. Light brown eyes crinkled slightly at the corners. He was so honorable, she thought. So willing to believe the best of her.

"It's not that simple," she said. "I don't want to go back to what we had. It's not enough." She pulled free of his touch, and stared at her fingers. The promise ring glinted in the overhead lights. "I can't keep this anymore," she told him and slipped the slender band from her finger.

"What are you doing?" Joel asked, the first hint of concern filling his voice.

"What it looks like. I'm sorry."

"I see." Joel picked up the ring. "I hope you're not making the mistake of thinking he's going to want you."

She told herself he hadn't meant the statement as cruelly as it came out, but she wasn't sure. "I don't pretend to know what Ryan wants in life, but I'm reasonably confident it isn't me. Our kiss was just something that happened. It didn't mean anything." At least not to him. Unfortunately for her, it had not only been a wake-up call about her relationship with Joel, it had also embedded itself in her mind. She couldn't stop thinking about those few moments in his arms.

"I'm not breaking up with you because of Ryan," she continued. "I'm doing it because of me. I've experienced passion. I know what it's like to want someone so much it hurts." She drew in a deep breath. "Maybe I'm setting myself up for heartbreak. Maybe I'm reaching for the stars. I don't know. But what I *am* sure of is that I want to find this again. I want that kind of passion in my life on a permanent basis."

"It's that important to you?" Joel asked.

"Yes."

He picked up the ring and stared at the tiny diamond. "We could do that," he said without looking at her. "If you wanted to."

If she hadn't been so close to tears, his lack of enthusiasm would have made her smile. "I appreciate the offer, but no thanks. It's been nine years and we've never even tried heavy petting. It was too easy not to become lovers."

She swallowed. "I'm sorry, Joel. You are a wonderful man and I adore you. In some ways I love you. I'll always have feelings for you, but they're not the kind of feelings that a woman should have for her husband. I can't see you anymore."

He closed his fingers over the ring. "Just like that? It's been nine years."

"I know. It's what I want. If you look deep inside, I think you'll find it's what you want, too."

"All right." He slipped the ring into his shirt pocket. "If you need time, I'll give you time. We'll put the relationship on hold for a few weeks. I'm sure once you've had a chance to think about it, you'll come to your senses."

She didn't know whether to scream or cry. Anger, sadness, frustration and pain from the thought of never seeing Joel again all welled up inside of her.

"I don't want time," she said. "I want it to be over. I want you to walk away from me without any regrets. I want you to find someone else and experience a little passion of your own. It will change your life forever."

She slid out of the booth and tried to smile. She had a feeling she failed pretty badly. "Goodbye, Joel. Good luck."

Then she turned and walked away.

A KNOCK AT his office door interrupted Ryan. He called "Come in," without turning away from his computer screen, then remembered that Cassie had left for the afternoon an hour or so before. He glanced up in time to see an attractive fiftysomething woman step inside.

She was about Cassie's height, with sleek dark hair pulled back into a fancy bun. Tailored clothes emphasized her trim body.

"You must be Cassie's aunt Charity," he said, rising to her feet.

"Yes. I just thought I'd poke my head in and say hello."

She crossed to his desk and handed him a cup of coffee. As she held another mug in her hand, he figured she was expecting an invitation to join him for a few minutes.

"Have a seat," he said, motioning to the empty chair next to her. Like Cassie's sister, her aunt wanted to check out the man Cassie worked for. He appreciated that her family was so concerned about her well-being.

"Thank you."

Charity sat down and set her coffee on the desk. He did the same.

"Is Sasha asleep?"

"Yes. She was a little hyper from playing," Charity said as she crossed her legs and picked up her mug. "I supposed a game of tag in the backyard wasn't a clever idea right before her nap, but I wasn't thinking." Her easy smile returned. "It comes from not having had children of my own. By the time I moved in with Cassie and Chloe, they were far too old to play games or need naps."

"You're their aunt on their father's side?"

"That's right. So I don't have any connection with the town of Bradley." She took a sip of coffee. "Has Cassie told you that one of her relatives actually founded the town?"

"She mentioned something about it."

"It's quite extraordinary for me to imagine having roots that go down that deep. I've always been something of a wanderer." Her well-shaped eyebrows drew together. "Come to think of it, I've lived in Bradley longer than anywhere else in my adult life. I came here when the girls were nearly eighteen." She paused, then gave a small gasp of surprise. "That was more than eight years ago. Time does get away from us all, doesn't it? Eight years. Who would have thought?"

"There is something pleasant about Bradley," he said.

"I'd planned to be here a month or six weeks at most, but now I find myself considering a longer stay."

"Really?" Dark brown eyes regarded him thoughtfully. "There's a lot to like here."

He wondered if she was still talking about the town or something else. Had Cassie told her aunt about what had happened the previous night? He studied the older woman sitting across from him, but he couldn't be sure.

Charity set her mug on the desk. "I moved in with the girls as soon as I found out about my brother's death. Unfortunately, I'd been in remote sections of the Far East, so it took the family lawyer three years to find me. I couldn't imagine staying in a small town where the neighbors knew one another. Living with two teenage girls was also a shock. I couldn't wait to leave." Her expression softened. "But slowly, the town and the girls worked their magic. Cassie and Chloe have both urged me to resume my travels, but I find I miss them less and less with each passing year."

She smiled. "I stayed at first to make sure the girls got through college. Then there was always some excuse to keep me around. Now I want to stay to see Chloe's baby born. I'm beginning to suspect I've lost the travel bug. Still, I saw a great deal of the world." She paused, and leaned forward slightly. "Is Bradley anything like where you grew up?"

"Not really. My mother, my brother and I lived in different parts of Los Angeles."

"What about your father?"

"John, my older brother, had a different father. His dad left when John was three or four. My father ran out on my mother when he learned she was pregnant." Not much of a legacy, he thought grimly. How could any man turn his back on his child?

"That must have been difficult for all of you," Charity said. "Your mother sounds like a very strong woman."

"She was. She worked hard. Maybe too hard. There wasn't a whole lot of fun in our house."

"I've met people like that," Charity told him. "I can't remember the exact old saying but it's something about hard work curing every ill." She flashed him another smile. "And here I'd always thought only chocolate could do that."

"I don't know about chocolate, but there were things I missed when I was growing up. She never approved of me going away with my friends and their families on camping trips. When I was in high school, she didn't want me spending money on school dances."

Ryan had nearly forgotten about all of that. He remembered finally getting the courage to ask a girl out, only to have his mother tell him it was a waste of his hard-earned wages. In the end, he'd gone on the date, but hadn't bothered asking the girl out again.

"It was a relief to get away to college."

"You went on scholarship?" she asked.

He nodded. "I worked, too, for spending money." It was as if he'd opened a long-closed door. The past flooded over him. How he'd enjoyed being on his own and how guilty he'd been for those feelings. He remembered phone calls from his mother where she'd reminded him to keep up his grades and warned him not to be frivolous by joining a fraternity or getting involved in extracurricular activities. He'd done a few things, but the guilt had always kept him from enjoying them too much.

"A doctor and a successful businessman. Your mother must be very proud."

"No," he said quietly. "She's gone now, but it wasn't

like that." He shrugged. "She never said anything except to keep working hard."

"And then she died."

Charity said the words as if she'd actually known his mother. Ryan stared at her. He realized how much he'd revealed in the past few minutes. "How did you do that?" he asked.

She didn't pretend to misunderstand. "It's a gift," she admitted. "People often find me easy to talk with. Plus, with you, I had an advantage. I knew your brother."

"I didn't," he said without thinking, and realized it was true. "He was ten years older and had left for college when I started third grade. He would come home and visit but it wasn't the same as growing up together."

"He was a good man. You would have liked him." She tilted her head and stared at him. "More important to you, I suspect, he would have always liked you. Cassie says you're doing very well with Sasha."

"I can't take any of the credit there. Cassie has been a huge help and Sasha is a sweetheart. We have a great time together."

"You're making an effort," Charity said. "Many people wouldn't bother."

He remembered his first few days with his niece. How he'd wanted to avoid her and how desperate he'd been for someone to take away the responsibility. "Cassie had to shame me into doing my part."

"I suspect it wasn't all that difficult. You're not the sort of man who walks away from what's important. Cassie thinks too much of you for it to be otherwise."

The implied approval made him uncomfortable. He doubted Charity would be as friendly if she knew about the kiss. "Cassie is very accepting. I admire that in her. And she's a natural when it comes to kids." He thought about the laughter that always filled the house. "I've never known anyone like her. She seems to understand exactly what Sasha is thinking all the time."

"She has a college degree in child development and works in a preschool. If she didn't understand children, I would be worried. Yes, some people are better with children than others, but don't discount the training or years of experience. You wouldn't expect a new employee fresh out of school to be an expert in your line of work. Why is it different with Sasha?"

"That's what your niece told me. I guess I should believe her."

"Of course. We can't both be wrong."

"Agreed." He picked up a pen, then set it back on the desk. "The problem is I don't have Cassie's experience or her training. I worry that I'm not going to do the right thing where Sasha is concerned. With her parents gone, I'm all she has."

"Worry is half the battle," Charity told him. "It means you care. Too many people don't. You'll do your best. Sometimes you'll get it right, the rest of the time you'll fake it." She looked at him with compassion. "Believe me, I understand. I came into a household with two nearly grown young women. I wanted to share my life experiences with them, but I had to balance that with their need to find things out for themselves. Sometimes it was hard to bite my tongue, sometimes I wondered how much I was going to get wrong. But I knew I loved those girls and the loving makes all the difference."

Ryan knew that six weeks ago he would have discounted those feelings, but now he knew better. Sasha feeling that she mattered to him was half the battle. "I want to do what's right," he said. "I owe it to Sasha, and to my brother."

Knowing eyes darkened. "Maybe you owe it to yourself as well."

Once again he was surprised by how easily he shared his innermost thoughts with this woman. He'd always held that part of him back, but there was something about Charity that made him think that not only could he trust her but that she would also understand what he was trying to say. "You do have a way of making people talk, don't you?"

"As I said, it's a gift. But you're not to worry. I'm very good at keeping secrets. Speaking of which, Cassie will be turning twenty-five soon. There's going to be a party for her and I would like to put you on the guest list."

"Thank you."

Charity leaned back in her chair. "Has Cassie told you the significance of her twenty-fifth birthday?"

"Yes. She mentioned the legend of the nightgown. I know that she believes it's true. Do you?"

"Of course. I've traveled all over the world and I've seen dozens of things modern science can't explain. By comparison a magic nightgown is rather tame. Besides, Chloe dreamed about her husband when she wore the nightgown. They'd never met before, yet when they ran into each other the next day, she knew things about him that would have been impossible for her to know, unless the dream was real. It was nearly love at first sight for both of them. That's difficult evidence to dispute."

It was a tough story to swallow, he thought, trying not to play the cynic. "Do you think Cassie will dream about Joel?"

"Do you think Joel is Cassie's fantasy, or even her destiny?"

The thought made his skin crawl. "It's really not my

place to say. Besides, they've been together for nine years. Who else would Cassie be interested in?"

Charity stared at him for a long time without speaking, then she rose to her feet and walked to the door. "I'm sure you're very busy. I've kept you long enough."

She gave him one last piercing glance, then she was gone. Ryan was left with the uncomfortable feeling that she knew about the kiss…and a few other things he hadn't figured out yet himself.

CHAPTER ELEVEN

RYAN SPENT THE rest of the afternoon pretending to work without actually getting anything done. Part of the reason was he couldn't believe all the personal information he'd shared with Cassie's aunt. Spilling his guts to total strangers wasn't his style. Actually he rarely spilled his guts to anyone. How had she done that?

He hadn't been able to come up with a reason and after a while it had ceased to matter because of the second reason he couldn't work—Cassie. Where was she? She'd left in the early afternoon and it was near—he glanced at his watch—four-thirty. She never took much time off to begin with and certainly not in the middle of the day. Had something happened to her?

Even as he contemplated calling the police and local hospitals, he heard the front door open and the sound of low voices. He exhaled in relief. She'd made it home. Now he could concentrate.

But even though he turned to his computer and stared at the screen, he wasn't thinking about the spreadsheet in front of him. He wanted to know where Cassie had been and what she'd been doing. He knew it wasn't any of his business, but he couldn't help thinking it had something to do with what had happened between them last night. Even though it was probably both paranoid and incredibly egotistical, he wondered how much that kiss had changed everything.

She'd seemed all right that morning, he reminded himself. Had she been acting? Maybe he should just accept things at face value. Maybe he should believe her when she said she was fine. It was just a kiss, after all. Nothing earth-shattering. Except that the passion had nearly overwhelmed him. He'd never experienced anything like it before. But that didn't mean she hadn't.

Ryan frowned. He didn't like to think that she and Joel created the same kind of heat. They couldn't have and not bothered to get married. If he had dated a young woman who had made him feel the way Cassie did, he might have changed his ideas about getting involved in a serious relationship.

Not now, of course, he told himself. He was a mature man who understood that there was more to life than great sex. He didn't want a commitment with anyone. Sasha was going to change his life enough without throwing a wife into the mix. And if he did decide to get married, it wouldn't be just for the sex. There were other, equally important issues such as temperament, compatibility, trustworthiness. He would want someone intelligent and caring. Obviously a woman who could love Sasha as if she were her own. But he wasn't looking, nor had he found anyone.

That decided, he told himself to lose the lingering guilt, and get back to work. Before he could, there was a light tap on his door, then Cassie stuck her head into the room.

"I'm back," she said, giving him a warm smile.

He studied her face. Except for the shadows under her eyes indicating she hadn't slept well the night before, she looked fine. "Everything all right?" he asked.

"Perfect. I'd like to invite Aunt Charity to stay for dinner. Is that okay with you?"

"Yes," he said automatically, when he really wanted to refuse her request. It wasn't that he hadn't enjoyed talking with Charity, it was just that he and Cassie had things they needed to discuss. Although at the moment he couldn't quite figure out what they were.

"Great. I'll call you when dinner's ready."

She disappeared and he was left staring at the closed door.

She had seemed like her normal self, he thought. If she had let last night go so easily, he should do the same. She'd accepted his apology and his promise that it wouldn't happen again, and moved on. He told himself he was grateful. He told himself that the lingering memories of the feel of her in his arms would pass in time. He told himself he had to work when in fact he listened intently to the sounds of female voices coming from the front of the house. He told himself he preferred it this way and that he wasn't lonely, even though he longed to be a part of the laughter. And he pretended to work until Cassie reappeared to invite him into the warmth of her company.

"YOU ARE a precious angel, aren't you?" Charity said as she stroked Sasha's cheek. "This little one and I had a terrific time together. Feel free to call on me to baby-sit anytime."

Sasha beamed with the additional attention and placed her hands on her high chair tray.

"She's a charmer," Ryan said, from across the table. "She's too cute and she knows it, don't you?"

Sasha held out her arms. "Unk Ryan."

"Yeah, yeah," he grumbled as he pushed back his chair and circled around to crouch by her high chair. Her short arms wrapped around his neck. She squeezed tight while he gently hugged her back. He didn't fool himself about who had the power in this relationship, he thought with a smile. "You've got me pegged, kid. I'm a sucker for your hugs."

Sasha pursed her lips and he obliged her with a quick kiss. Her need for affection satiated, the toddler picked up her spoon and banged it against her metal tray. "Me hungry."

"We know," Ryan said as he took the spoon from her and set it on the large table just out of reach. "Sit there nicely until Cassie brings you dinner. It won't be very long."

She stared mutinously at him. Her lower lip quivered. Uh-oh, the storm wasn't far behind. Time to entertain the troops. He slapped his hand on the tray table and splayed his fingers. "Pick one," he said.

Sasha hesitated.

He faked a hurt look. "Don't you want to play?"

She pulled on his index finger. In response, he bounced the digit several times. Sasha giggled, then pulled on his middle finger. This time he raised his hand until it hovered a couple of inches above the table, all the while humming scary alien music. After a couple of seconds, he let his hand flop back to the table.

Sasha squealed with delight. "More," she demanded and tugged on his thumb.

He flopped his entire hand back and forth, moving very quickly and finishing with a lunge for her side so he could tickle her. Sasha laughed and wiggled, pushing him away, then grabbing him and drawing him close.

"You can't have it both ways, kid," he told her.

"Dinner's ready," Cassie said.

He looked up and saw her standing in the entrance to the dining room. She held Sasha's plastic plate and gazed at him with a bemused expression.

Ryan stepped back hastily. He'd forgotten that he and Sasha weren't alone. A quick glance told him that Charity had been equally amused by his game with his niece.

"She was going to cry," Ryan said defensively. "I wanted to stop that."

"You did a great job," Cassie told him. "I'm impressed." She set the plate in front of Sasha, handed the child her spoon, then patted Ryan's arm. "Everything is ready. Why don't you have a seat?"

He felt oddly embarrassed, as if he'd been caught doing something foolish. But he didn't keep defending himself. Instead he opened the red wine Cassie had set out and filled the three glasses.

"Ryan and I were talking earlier today," Charity said as her niece served tenderloins of beef and steamed asparagus. "Did you know he'd been to college on a scholarship?"

"I hadn't heard." Cassie disappeared into the kitchen, then returned carrying a bowl of mashed potatoes and a tray with French bread.

Belatedly, Ryan rose to his feet and took the serving pieces from her. "Sorry," he said, placing them on the table. "I should have offered to help sooner."

"You took care of Sasha. That was a big help."

He nodded, then held out her chair for her. What was wrong with him? He wasn't usually so socially inept. It was all the distractions, he decided. His concerns from the previous night, dealing with both his niece and Cassie's aunt, not to mention the fact that he rarely entertained at home. He'd been too busy lately, and when he did get together with friends it was usually at a restaurant.

Cassie had placed him at the head of the table with her aunt on his right. As the serving plates and bowls were passed around, Charity picked up the conversation.

"He worked part-time while he was at school, as well. Impressive determination in one so young."

Cassie took a spoonful of potatoes and flashed him a smile. "Ryan has many good qualities."

"He's doing very well with Sasha," Charity said. "He's had no training, virtually no warning, yet they've bonded."

Ryan glanced from one to the other. "I *am* in the room. You can direct some of these comments to me directly, if you'd like."

"Are you feeling left out?" Cassie asked with a grin. She lowered her voice conspiratorially and leaned toward her aunt. "Men are so sensitive."

Charity sighed. "It's a problem with the whole gender. Such delicate creatures. But what choice is there? They're all we have." She patted the back of Ryan's hand. "What would you like to talk about, dear?"

"I'm not a domineering male," he said, enjoying the banter and the feeling of being part of a family. "You can't lay that at my door."

"Of course we can," Cassie said and took a sip of wine. "There are two of us and only one of you. We can say or do anything we like."

"I see. And if I remind you that you work for me and therefore are expected to treat me with, if not reverence, then at least respect?"

"I'll point out that's an extremely domineering remark. Then I would probably take you to task for saying reverence, even in a kidding way. Reverence, Ryan? Do you secretly want to be worshiped?"

"Don't all men?"

Her brown eyes sparkled with laughter. "We'll have to set up a little shrine in one of the spare bedrooms.

Maybe put up your picture. I can come in every morning and light candles."

"Works for me, but I would prefer a large shrine, not a little one." He glanced at Charity and gave her a wink.

"You're a tricky one," the older woman said. "Be careful with him, Cassie. He's charming and they're the most dangerous kind."

"I'm not worried about Ryan," her niece said. "He's a great boss. I like working for him." Then she asked her aunt about a recent play she'd been to, and the conversation became more general.

Still, the feeling of well-being lingered for Ryan. He didn't join Cassie and Sasha for dinner as often as he should. He enjoyed the company. He kept to himself too much, he realized. Maybe it was time to change that.

When Sasha spilled her milk, he motioned for Cassie to keep eating while he took care of the mess. As he returned to his seat, Cassie put her hand on his arm.

"Thanks," she said.

"My pleasure."

His gaze dropped down to her mouth, which instantly made him think of kissing her again. Down boy, he ordered himself, then looked away. At the same time Cassie withdrew her hand. He caught the movement out of the corner of his eye.

A small alarm went off in his head. Something was wrong.

He looked at her face, trying to read her thoughts. Again she looked completely normal. Her clothes were fine, she had on her watch and her— A cold knife cut through his midsection. He blinked slowly, but the reality didn't change. Dear God, why had it taken him so long to notice? Her promise ring—Joel's promise ring—was gone and in its place was a band of pale skin.

CHARITY DIDN'T LEAVE until nearly ten that night. It had been the longest evening in Ryan's life. At first he'd tried to think of a way to get Cassie alone and ask her what had happened. Unfortunately he had a bad feeling he knew what had happened. He didn't want to know, but he *had* to know.

She'd told Joel about the kiss. They'd had an ugly fight. They'd broken up. It was the only explanation. Ryan paced back and forth in the hallway, waiting for Cassie to finish her goodbyes. She'd seemed so calm all evening, yet she had to be dying inside. This was all his fault.

No it wasn't, he told himself. All he'd done was kiss her. It had just happened. It wasn't anyone's fault. Or maybe it was both their faults and they should… Except he didn't know what they should do. He didn't know anything.

The front door closed. Ryan moved to intercept Cassie in the foyer. "We have to talk."

She drew in a deep breath and shook her head. "Not tonight, Ryan. I'm tired and I'm getting a headache. I don't usually suffer from them, so I'm sure it will be gone by morning."

He didn't think she was torturing him on purpose, but that was how it felt. "Please, just for a few minutes. I don't want to make your headache worse, but we do need to talk."

Cassie hesitated, then led the way into the living room. Ryan followed on her heels. When she took a seat on the sofa, he thought about settling next to her, but he couldn't imagine being able to stay still a minute longer. Sitting through dinner was nearly the most difficult thing he'd ever done. He glanced down at her, opened his mouth, closed it and began to pace.

Several floor lamps added light to the room. The

furniture was large but comfortable, done in blues and greens, accented by oak tables. Ryan forced himself to take a couple of deep breaths. He walked from the window to the fireplace and back, stopping in front of her.

"You're not wearing your promise ring," he blurted out at last.

A faint smile touched the corner of her mouth. "I know."

"This isn't the least bit humorous to me." His tone was sharp and her smile faded. "What happened to it?"

"I didn't lose it if that's what you're asking," she said. "I gave it back to Joel."

He'd already figured out the truth, even as he'd tried to deny it to himself. He didn't want to hear this. He didn't want to know. The guilt returned and swamped him. She'd given back her ring because of him? He refused to accept that. He paced again, then swore under his breath. They did *not* have a relationship. What the hell was she thinking?

Questions filled his mind. Questions and answers and fears and guilt. "This isn't my fault," he said quickly. "It was just a kiss. I apologized this morning. That's not a reason to break off your engagement. You shouldn't have done that. You weren't thinking."

If he was trying to make it all her fault, he was doing a poor job. Worse, he was practically squirming to get away and that wasn't his style. Ryan forced himself to stand in front of her.

"Don't panic, Ryan. Joel isn't going to come after you with a shotgun. I don't know what you're thinking, but I suspect you're making this more complicated and more personal than it has to be."

She sounded so calm. Her gaze was steady, her body language relaxed. She wore a dark green dress and matching pumps. Her hair curled away from her face, exposing her big eyes and perfect cheekbones. Not to mention her tempting mouth.

He jerked his attention away from her lips. "Then why don't you explain it to me."

"All right. I didn't give Joel back the ring because you and I kissed. I gave him back the ring because of how the kiss made me feel." She held up her hand when he would have interrupted her. "They're not the same thing at all. Let me finish. Joel and I have been together for years. In all that time, through all the kissing and hugging and hand-holding, I never once experienced anything close to the passion I felt last night."

He started to tell her that kisses were always like that, but he found he couldn't lie. *He'd* never experienced that kind of wanting before, either.

"So you told him." It wasn't a question.

"I had to. First I told him about the kiss, but he was surprisingly unconcerned."

That startled Ryan into sitting down on the opposite end of the sofa. "What do you mean?"

She recounted her conversation with Joel, sharing her ex-boyfriend's theory about the need to sow wild oats.

"He's crazy," Ryan muttered more to himself than her. If he'd been involved with Cassie and had found out she'd kissed another man, he would have gone wild with rage and jealousy. "So because he wasn't worried or upset, you broke up with him?" He shook his head. "That makes about as much sense to me as the fact that you told him the truth in the first place. You didn't have to do that. It was a one-time thing, never to be repeated."

Cassie stared at him as if he were a particularly slow child. "You're missing the point entirely," she said. "I didn't break up with him because of the kiss, or because he didn't get upset. I broke up with him because I've had a lot of questions for a long time. I couldn't figure out what was wrong with our relationship or why we didn't seem to feel any physical desire for each other." She took a deep breath and continued. "Because I had no frame of reference, I didn't know if there was something wrong between Joel and me or if all those songwriters and poets had been lying. Last night I learned there was a whole world waiting for me. A world of incredibly physical sensation." A dreamy expression crossed her face. "I want that. Not just sex for the sake of having sex, but a relationship that involves an emotional as well as a physical connection. I broke up with Joel because I'm not willing to settle anymore. This time I want it all."

Cassie had been afraid that Ryan might take her comments too much to heart. He stood up and actually backed away from her. His expression was trapped and his hands came up in a protective gesture. If she hadn't been so tired and vulnerable, she might have found the situation amusing.

But tonight she wasn't feeling especially strong. If only things had been different, she thought. If only Ryan wanted her as much as she wanted him. If only... How many hearts had broken apart on those rocky words?

"Don't panic," she said, deliberately keeping her words light. "I'm not going to beg you to come to bed or ask you to father my child. While you were technically involved in my awakening, passion-wise, this isn't really about you."

"That's not how it looks from here."

At least her headache had faded, she thought with gratitude, so it wasn't difficult to think. "We went over this when we talked this morning, Ryan. We're very different people. I'll agree that there are some similarities as far as our personalities go, but none of this is about having a relationship with you." Even though she knew she wanted one.

As long as she kept the truth from him, he would never feel obligated to try to spare her feelings. That was one thing she didn't think she could bear...Ryan's polite dismissal.

"Then what is it about?" he asked.

She motioned to the sofa and waited until he'd settled down again. "I know that you and I will never have more than a working relationship, and I'm fine with that. The kiss was a fluke. A very nice fluke, but not significant in the scheme of things."

"It was significant enough to cause you to break up with Joel."

Okay, so the man had a point. "Not exactly," she hedged. "It showed me a truth I'd long suspected. I realized I had to make a choice. For years Chloe has been telling me I was just settling for Joel. She told me there was a lot more out there and I owed it to myself to explore the world. I never thought she was right. I thought she had an irrational dislike of Joel."

She wasn't sure but his shoulders seemed to be relaxing a little. "And now?"

"Now I've had my eyes opened. I don't think I was settling for Joel. He's a wonderful man and I'll always be happy that he was in my life. But I want more than he and I can have together. I want to try to have the best of both worlds. Companionship and passion."

"And that's it?"

She nodded. "I'm being honest, Ryan. After nine years of dating Joel, what we shared is gone. When I drove home I kept waiting for the anguish. I thought it would be like losing an arm or something." She pressed her lips together and looked away. She didn't want him to see the tears filling her eyes.

"Are you crying?" he asked sharply.

She sniffed. "Yes, but not for the reasons you're thinking. All I feel is relief. Not sadness or regret or pain. I thought I would feel more."

"You might later."

"I'm sure you're right. But my heart isn't broken and I'm not sorry about what happened. Any of it," she added. "Obviously the kiss has made you terribly uncomfortable with me, and I do feel badly about that. For me it was a call to action. I hope you don't worry that it's anything else."

"I'm not uncomfortable," he said. "Kissing you did *not* make me uncomfortable."

Cassie had to suppress a smile. She hadn't meant to offend him, but the male ego was a fragile, albeit complicated, thing. "What I meant," she said carefully, "is that you have some genuine reasons for concern. I really appreciate that. I don't want you to think any of this is your fault." She drew in a deep breath.

Now came the hard part. This morning it had been surprisingly easy to "fake" being okay with everything that had happened...mostly because she found that she *was* all right. She might lust after Ryan and his body, she might think he was brilliant and wonderful and that they would be perfect together. But he didn't think that, and she wasn't foolish enough to try to convince herself otherwise. She would enjoy their conversations and contact while she could, then when it was over, she would do her best to put him behind her.

"I don't want you to worry that I'm going to make a

play for you," she said. For the first time, she felt a heat on her cheeks and it took all her strength not to turn away from his intense gaze. "Just as you were worried about me feeling in danger and took the time to reassure me, I want to do the same. I'm not going to spend my day making calf eyes at you."

His expression didn't relax at all. There was something odd in his eyes, a strange emotion she couldn't read. "What *are* calf eyes?" he asked.

She smiled. "I'm not sure either, so if I don't know, I can't make them, or do them, or whatever." She turned serious. "I'm not going to be a problem."

"I never thought you would be." He leaned toward her. "I want you to feel free to date. You still have time off in the evening and if you're giving up Joel, there's no reason to wait to 'discover the world' as you put it."

She didn't mind him not sharing her fantasy, but she deeply resented that he was so quick to throw her into the path of other men. "Gee, thanks," she said. "I think I'll wait at least a couple of days to get used to being single again. It's been a long time." She rose to her feet. "It's getting late. I'm going up to bed."

She crossed to the door, then paused and looked back at him. "Thanks for everything, Ryan. For reasons that probably don't make sense to you, I'm very grateful for what you did."

He stood, too. He was tall and broad and she found herself wishing she was standing a little closer to him.

"You make it sound like a big favor," he said. "Kissing you was my pleasure." He flashed her a quick smile. "I mean that."

She told herself to turn away, but she couldn't. If only he would walk over and kiss her again, she thought. Maybe even do more than kiss. But he wasn't going to.

She thanked him again and left. At least she would have the memory of their kiss…not to mention all the fantasies about what it would be like if they were to start that fire between them again.

CHAPTER TWELVE

THE NEXT WEEK was uneventful, for which Cassie was grateful. There had been enough trauma and change in her life for any month. Not that she would have objected to Ryan showing up unexpectedly in her bedroom, swearing undying devotion and then making passionate love to her for hours. But if she couldn't have that, peace and quiet were a very nice substitute.

Their routine continued, with Sasha in preschool Monday through Thursday morning. Ryan joined them for meals and spent his early evenings with his niece as well. Cassie wanted to believe that her witty company was what drew him, but she knew better. When it was time for Sasha to go to bed, he either took over the duties or let her handle them and disappeared into his office. Either way, once Sasha was down for the night, Ryan left Cassie alone.

"We can't have everything," she said aloud, as she slipped her jacket off its hanger and put it on. They were going shoe shopping for Sasha. In the space of a few days, the toddler's favorite shoes had gotten too tight. Visiting the mall would be a nice change, and for reasons Cassie didn't quite understand, Ryan had agreed to go with them.

She crossed to her dresser and ran a brush through her short hair. She used her left hand to push a wayward strand in place, and as she did so, she glanced at the place where her promise ring used to be. Joel was well and truly out of her life.

She'd thought he might call her. After all, his idea had been that with a little time she would come to her senses. But he hadn't tried to contact her at all. Cassie carefully probed her heart, searching for any signs of hurt or remorse. The only negative emotion there was sadness that something that had lasted so long could be forgotten so easily. She still wasn't sorry that she'd ended things between them. Her only feeling was one of relief and a nagging sense that she should have done this a long time ago.

If there was any regret, it was that this might be causing him pain. She hoped not. Their relationship had been comfortable for both of them, but she doubted Joel had given his heart any more than she had. A smile tugged at the corner of her mouth. All he needed was a hot date with a gorgeous blonde and he would forget all about her, she thought. If only she knew one who was interested in him.

"Cassie, are you about ready?" Ryan called from downstairs.

At the sound of his voice, her heart rate increased. "I'm on my way," she yelled as she hurried from her bedroom and headed for the stairs.

If Ryan could make her heart race with just the sound of his voice, imagine what would happen if they ever did the naked thing, she thought humorously. Not that they ever would, but a girl could dream. And dream she did. Nothing like having a handsome, single, charming man living under the same roof to give her a little inspiration.

She grabbed her purse and stepped outside. Ryan and Sasha stood by his late model BMW 540i. "I installed the car seat," he said as she approached.

Cassie leaned around the open rear door and stared in

to the back seat. The new toddler-size car seat had been strapped into the center. She turned to Sasha. "It's very nice and grown-up. Are you excited?"

Sasha nodded. "Unk Ryan buy for me."

"I know. He cares about you very much and he wants to keep you safe. Isn't that nice?"

Sasha grinned. "Go now."

"We've received our instructions," she told her boss. "Guess we should listen."

"Absolutely." He circled around to the other side of the car. "As this is the first time we're using this particular car seat, I'm guessing it's going to take both of us to get it right." He patted his back pocket. "I have the instruction diagram right here."

She motioned for Sasha to climb into the car. "Wow. A guy willing to read the instructions. I'm impressed."

Ryan didn't return her smile. "This is about keeping Sasha safe. I wouldn't play around with that."

Why did he keep doing that? she wondered. Saying and doing exactly the right thing. He made it very difficult for her to remember her place and keep her perspective. If only he would go back to being the silent man who didn't want anything to do with his niece. Then she would have a chance of getting over her thing for her boss.

Cassie sighed. Even though it meant the potential for more heartbreak for her, she couldn't in all sincerity really wish that Ryan changed back into the man he'd been when he first arrived. She wanted what was best for Sasha, and this new and improved uncle was definitely what the toddler needed.

Sasha crawled into the car seat and got comfortable. Cassie leaned from her side, while Ryan did the same from his. They reached for buckles and straps, occasionally bumping. At one point their hands got tangled together. Sasha thought it was all a great joke and laughed at them. Cassie smiled with her and tried to ignore the tingling that shot up her arm. She was careful to keep her expression pleasantly neutral. Despite her growing feelings for Ryan, she hadn't forgotten the trapped look in his eyes when she'd told him she'd broken up with Joel in order to find what she really wanted. The last thing the poor man needed to know was that his worst fears had come true—that his unsophisticated, much-younger nanny had the hots for him.

Cassie gave the car seat straps one last tug. "Looks great," she said and closed the passenger-side rear door. Before she slid into the front seat, she took a couple of deep breaths. If nothing else, she'd been blessed with the ability to see the truth in any situation. Ryan wasn't interested in her. Therefore she didn't want to make him uncomfortable by swooning or anything else that obvious. That gave her the determination she needed to be calm and pretend disinterest. She was able to slide into her seat and not even flinch when his arm brushed against hers.

Her resolve was strengthened by the humorous image of herself in a dead faint in Ryan's arms, while he ran around the mall begging people to help him make her not be in love with him. No, he wasn't for her, she thought, even though in her heart of hearts, she wanted him to be. But there *was* a man out there. Someone warm and caring, someone who would make her heart beat just as fast. Someone who would appreciate her good qualities. Someone who would love her back. As soon as she finished working for Ryan, she was going to go out and find her mystery man.

"What are you thinking?" Ryan asked.

"Nothing important."

"You were smiling."

"I'm a happy person."

She glanced at him and found him studying her. "Yes, you are," he agreed, his green eyes bright with affection.

She wanted to believe it was more than just friendship…wanted to, but couldn't. If only she weren't such a dreamer.

"So what kind of shoes are we going to buy?" he asked.

"You sound as if you think we get a vote."

He looked startled. "We don't?"

"They're Sasha's shoes."

"She's only two."

Cassie grinned. "You've never shopped with a stubborn toddler before, have you?"

Ryan groaned. "I don't want to hear about it."

"You don't have to. You're going to live it."

Forty minutes later Sasha sat in the shoe store and shook her head. "Pink," she said when Ryan tried to slip a yellow shoe on her foot.

He looked helplessly at Cassie. "The yellow ones are better made. They'll last longer. The only thing she likes about the pink ones is the little kitten on the side."

Cassie resisted the urge to say "I told you so." She leaned back in her chair. "I think you should explain that to her."

"Yeah, right." But he crouched in front of his niece. "Sasha, the yellow ones are very nice. They're pretty, don't you think?"

Dark curls flew back and forth as she shook her head. "Me want pink shoes. With kitty. Like book. Me like pink. Me like kitty." She kicked off the yellow shoe the salesman and Ryan had wrestled onto her right foot. "No!"

Ryan looked so shocked, Cassie had to bite her lip to

keep from laughing. Most of the time he and Sasha got along fine. There hadn't been many tantrums in his presence. Looked like that was about to change.

"What do I do?" he asked.

"It's your choice," she told him. "Pick your battle. Do you want to fight it out with a two-year-old over these shoes? You have to weigh the costs and benefits. Yes, you're the adult, you're buying the shoes, you have the final say. If you think the yellow shoes are better for her feet then you should insist." She met his gaze. "If it's just that you like the brand name better, then it's less simple. What if she refuses to wear the yellow shoes once you buy them? Do you want to have this fight every morning? Or to be more accurate, do you want *me* to have this fight every morning?"

"She'd really hate them that much?"

"I don't know. She might be fine. She might always remember the pink ones." Cassie leaned forward. "Welcome to parenting, Ryan. There aren't any easy solutions. You do have to decide what's worth taking a stand on because one of the worst things you can do is waffle once you've drawn a line in the sand. So think long and hard before making any pronouncements."

He picked up a pink shoe, then grabbed the yellow one she'd kicked away. "They're just shoes." The brightly colored footwear looked tiny resting on his hand. He turned his attention to his niece. "You're too young to be causing this much trouble."

Sasha held out her arms. "Hug," she demanded.

He obliged, all the while grumbling. "You're not going to win me over with a little affection," he said.

"Why not?" Cassie asked. "Women have been using their feminine wiles to get what they want for centuries."

"I don't think of Sasha as having feminine wiles."

Cassie didn't say anything, but she knew the exact moment Ryan made his decision and she wasn't surprised when he turned to the hovering clerk and said, "We'll take the pink ones."

As he helped Sasha back into her old shoes and socks, he glanced at her. "What are you thinking?"

That he was too cute for words, but she couldn't tell him that. "Nothing much."

"Which ones would you have bought?"

"The pink ones. It's an easy win for her. They're both well-made, she'll outgrow both of them quickly."

"So I did okay?"

His earnest, hopeful expression made her heart melt. "You did great."

"Thanks. Your opinion means a lot to me."

He flashed her a smile that, if she hadn't already been sitting down, would have made her knees collapse.

While Ryan settled Sasha on his hip and walked over to pay for the shoes, Cassie slowly collected their jackets. She needed a minute to calm down. It was difficult to pretend he didn't matter to her when her body was on constant alert. But as long as Ryan didn't figure it out, she could live with the symptoms. At least that was what she told herself.

Feeling and strength returned to her legs and she rose to her feet. As she met Ryan by the door, a young woman with two children in a stroller smiled at them. "Your daughter is very pretty."

Ryan hesitated, then thanked the woman.

When they were in the mall, he turned to her. "I didn't know if I should explain the situation or not," he said. "It seemed easier to accept the compliment. I hope you don't mind."

"Not at all. It was bound to happen."

"Thanks for understanding."

"No problem."

"So what are we going to do about lunch?" he asked.

Cassie listened while he and Sasha discussed the possibilities. She reminded herself that she had Ryan's respect and his affection. That was enough. But when the woman had assumed they were a family, something inside of her had flared to life. In that moment she realized that walking away from Ryan was going to be much harder than letting go of Joel. She hoped that there weren't any other parallels—that when she gave her heart to a man other than Ryan, she wouldn't be settling for second best again.

THE SOUND OF laughter pierced Ryan's concentration and he turned toward the window. At first it had been easy to block out the sounds of Cassie and Sasha in the house, but that was becoming more and more difficult. He supposed part of the reason was that he enjoyed spending time with them. Given the choice between them and work, there wasn't a choice at all.

He leaned back in his chair and wondered if any of his employees would believe that if he told them. After all, he was known for his long hours, a nearly superhuman ability to focus on the problem at hand, and the need to put work above all else in his life.

That had changed, too, he thought as he saved his work in progress and left the office. The truth was if he was going to stay in Bradley for much longer, he was going to have to look into getting an office. Every week he stayed in the house, he was getting less and less done, while spending more time with Cassie and Sasha.

He stepped out the back door and stood unobserved on the rear porch. The November afternoon was bright,

436   DREAM GROOM

but cool. Sasha sat on the small swing her father had
given her for her birthday. Her hair was still tousled
from her nap, while the nip in the air added color to her
plump cheeks. She was dressed in pink corduroy jeans
that matched her favorite new pink shoes, and a jacket.
Cassie stood behind her, gently pushing her on the swing.

"More," Sasha called, ever the thrill-seeker.

"This is about all you can handle, sweetie," Cassie
told her.

Her life was so simple, Ryan thought, studying his
niece. Playtime and nap time, plenty of love and affection. If she was fed and warm and cuddled, her world
was right. Adults could learn from that, he thought. His
gaze strayed to Cassie. Some already had.

Cassie was one of the most open women he'd ever met.
In a world of people being politically correct, she said
whatever she thought. She didn't play games, she didn't
pretend to care about something, even if the world said
she should. She was so pretty, he thought as he stared at
her smooth skin and laughing brown eyes. Just watching her made him feel that everything could work out.

He was still in the shadows and hadn't been spotted.
Cassie slowed the swing and wrapped her arms around
Sasha. "You are the most precious little girl," she said.
"I love you very much."

Sasha hugged her back. The child whispered something and they giggled together.

Ryan felt as if he was eavesdropping on something
very private, yet he couldn't turn away. At least he didn't
have to worry about the person taking care of his niece.
Every time he'd come into a room unexpectedly, all he'd
found was warm affection and plenty of attention. Cassie
treated Sasha with the same loving concern she would
give her own child.

Now, as the two females talked, he wished there was some way to find out what Cassie was thinking. For the past two weeks, she'd acted as if everything was fine with her. As far as he could tell, she hadn't heard from Joel. Did that bother her? Was she really all right, or was she hiding the truth from him? No matter how bright her smile, he couldn't shake the feeling of guilt inside of him. He'd been the one to kiss her, and that had, directly or indirectly, caused her to break it off with Joel. Therefore it was his fault. Therefore he had to fix the problem.

The question was how?

Maybe he could—"Unk Ryan!" Sasha spotted him and came running toward the porch. "Come pay me."

He chuckled. "I'm translating that as 'come play with me' rather than 'you owe me money.'"

"Have you borrowed any money from her recently?" Cassie asked, her voice teasing.

"No, I think our debts are cleared." He picked up Sasha and swung her around. "What do you say, little one? Do I owe you vast sums of money?"

"More!" Sasha cried out as she moved through the air. "More!"

He tossed her in the air and caught her. Sasha squealed with delight, while he marveled at her ability to trust. Finally he set her on the ground. "I need a break," he said.

"Cassie," Sasha said, pointing at her nanny.

Cassie shook her head. "Thank you, no. I don't want to be thrown into the air and I doubt your uncle wants to be the one to catch me. I would hurt his back."

Sasha frowned.

Cassie crouched in front of her. "I'm too big, sweetie. He can lift you, but he can't lift me."

"Then cull," she said with a sly little grin and rushed toward Cassie.

"What is she talking about?" Ryan asked as Cassie backed away from his niece.

She laughed, then ducked around the swing pole and moved to her left. "You're not going to get me," she cried over her shoulder, walking just fast enough to keep Sasha an arm's length away. "Tickling. She's trying to get me so she can tickle me."

Cassie made a tempting target. Worn jeans hugged her thighs and rounded hips. She wore a red sweatshirt that concealed her generous breasts, but he knew they were there. An intriguing thought occurred to him.

"Sasha, you want help?" he asked.

Sasha stopped and stared at him. Then she grinned and nodded. "Get Cassie."

She ran as fast as her short legs would carry her. He circled around from the opposite side. Cassie laughed.

"This isn't fair. Two against one." She eyed Ryan as he got closer. "Wait. Maybe we should gang up on Sasha. Wouldn't that be fun?"

"Sure, but not as much fun as this," he said as he lunged for her.

She screamed and ducked, then had to leap back to keep from tripping over Sasha. Down she went onto the soft grass. Sasha jumped on top of her and began tickling. Ryan joined the fray.

He knelt on the ground and pulled his niece toward him. As he did so, he tickled her sides. Sasha giggled and laughed, trying to squirm away.

"Thank you," Cassie said as she rose into a sitting position. Her hair was mussed, her eyes dancing with amusement. "I thought I was—"

He leaned Sasha against his thigh and kept tickling her with one hand, while with his free hand, he reached out for Cassie. She broke off in midsentence and tried to scramble away. But she was laughing too much and couldn't get to her feet. She pushed at his hand.

"Ryan, stop. You can't do this. It's not part of my job description."

Then, without warning, Sasha turned on him. Her tiny hands found that one sensitive place on his ribs. Instantly he released both her and Cassie. "No, you don't," he said, physically holding her out of harm's way.

But it was too late. Cassie had seen his moment of vulnerability. She lunged toward him and attacked. Then the three of them were laughing and tickling and rolling in a heap.

He pushed hands away, tried to pin them both down, but while Cassie and Sasha weren't that strong, they were definitely squirmy. He was also afraid of hurting them, so he couldn't use his strength against them.

"Truce," he called after a couple of minutes. "Enough."

"'Nuff," Sasha agreed and collapsed against him.

"Agreed." Cassie took a deep breath and relaxed. Her head was on his shoulder, her body pressed against his.

In that moment, he wanted her more than he'd ever wanted any woman in his life. But that wasn't what scared him. What made him break out into a cold sweat was the realization that this was exactly what he needed. Days like this. With sunshine and laughter, Sasha and Cassie. He needed them to be a family.

Fear came on the heels of desire. Fear and the sense that he was in over his head. As much as he might want to be like everyone else, he knew he didn't have the skills. He could work hard, he could build a company from nothing with only a dream and determination. He could learn that which could be taught, but he didn't know how to be a husband or a father. He'd never seen it done. He allowed himself to get close to Sasha because he had Cassie there to keep him from making any big mistakes. But who would protect her from him if they got involved?

Besides, Cassie wouldn't want a man like him. She would want someone more like herself—open and loving. Someone who believed in family and happily-ever-after. He believed in keeping an emotional distance and working eighty-hour weeks. He had nothing to offer her.

There was only one solution. He had to fix her problem. Somehow, some way, he was going to get her and Joel back together.

"HERE'S JOHN when he left for college," Ryan said, pointing to a photograph of a serious young man who looked like a shorter and broader version of his brother. "I guess I was about eight or nine. I didn't want him to go. He promised that we'd still do things together, but I knew it was going to be different."

"Was it?" Cassie asked.

He nodded. "He came home for holidays, the first couple of years, then he was too busy."

The evening was chilly, but Ryan had lit a fire in the fireplace. The welcoming scent of wood smoke filled the living room. Cassie picked up her wine and took a sip. Despite the quiet of the dark house around them and the late hour, not to mention the flickering flames, she refused to acknowledge this was the least bit romantic. Ryan had asked for her help in sorting through old pictures. He'd wanted to put a few up for Sasha to see. That was all. She was a hardworking employee helping her boss. The fire, the wine, the night…well, they were just set decorations. As real and as meaningful as a movie backdrop.

At least that was what she kept telling herself, even as her body quivered and her mouth went dry.

They were sitting next to each other on the sofa. Several photo albums were stacked around them. Ryan reached for a pale fabric-covered one and set it on the coffee table. "This is their wedding album," he said.

Helen had been a slight woman, with mahogany-colored hair and big, dark eyes. The first picture showed her and John standing together, their arms wrapped around each other. They were obviously in love. Cassie fought against the envy that swelled inside of her. She wanted that for herself—true love and someone to share it with.

"They look so happy," Ryan said. He leaned forward and rested his elbows on his knees while he studied the photo. "I still can't believe I thought my brother was crazy to cut back his hours. As I look through these pictures, I know he did exactly the right thing. I just wish I'd been able to tell him at the time."

"He knew," Cassie said. She turned several pages. In every one the couple gazed at each other, their love a tangible part of their beings. "It shows everywhere."

There was a picture of a very pregnant Helen at a summer barbecue. John stood behind her, his hands splayed across her belly.

"He loved her," Ryan said. "She meant everything to him, and him to her. I see it all so clearly now. I admire him for being able to turn his back on how he was raised. It's not easy to give up old habits and fears. My mother always told us that if we stopped working, we would lose it all. Yet, he did it anyway."

"His love was stronger than his fear," Cassie said. "But you're right, it is tough to give up old beliefs."

She held her glass of wine in both hands. She understood because she was wrestling with her own demons. She'd nearly forgotten about them in the past few years, but since her breakup with Joel, they'd started visiting her again.

They came in the night and whispered that if she wanted too much, if she tried to get what she really wanted, she would just lose it. Better to take a little less. Then she wouldn't be at risk. She'd come to realize that those fears had been the basis of her relationship with Joel. Chloe had been right—she *had* settled. Wanting Joel wasn't the same as wanting it all. Losing him wouldn't break her heart. So he'd been safe to love. Now she was thinking about going after her heart's desire, the price of which could destroy her.

What if she really fell in love? What if she gave all of herself, then lost it? She'd already been abandoned twice, first by her birth parents, then when her adopted parents had died. She didn't want to risk that happening again.

"What are you thinking?" Ryan asked.

She glanced at him and saw that he was watching her. "That no matter how scary it is, we still have to go after our dreams."

"What are you scared of?"

She shrugged. "Mostly of not belonging. That's what Joel was for me. An easy way to fit in. Now I'm feeling strong enough to go out and find a way to fit in on my own. Bradley will always be my hometown, but I'm not sure that staying here is such a good idea. I'm not going to magically finds roots. I have to go out and grow them. That might mean trying a different way of life. I need to figure out what's really important to me and then go after it."

The words sounded brave. She hoped she had the strength of character to do it, despite the demons that whispered she would only fail.

"I admire you," he said. "You're the most honest person I know."

She thought about her secret passion for Ryan. "Please don't make me out to be incredibly virtuous. I'm not at all." She wanted to say more, but he was sitting too close. She could feel his leg lightly pressing against hers. Maybe it was the wine or the fire, but she was suddenly warm.

"I'm glad you're here," he said.

She made the mistake of looking at him and found herself getting lost in his green eyes. A man shouldn't be so beautiful, she thought to herself as all the air rushed out of her lungs. It wasn't fair. How was she supposed to keep her head about her when he looked so incredibly perfect? And why didn't he just take her in his arms and kiss her? Couldn't he feel the tension between them? Didn't he know that she wanted to be with him? The image of them together, touching and tasting, holding and doing all those things she knew about in theory, if not in practice, haunted her.

Their gazes locked. The temperature in the room cranked up yet another notch until she found it difficult to breathe. The night closed in around them, making her feel isolated, but deliciously safe with Ryan. Only Ryan.

He leaned forward. He was going to kiss her. She knew it...believed it...anticipated it. He reached his hand toward her, long fingers that would stroke her skin and leave her....

"It's late. You need to be in bed. Good night, Cassie."

His words combined with his brisk tone to make her feel as if she'd been doused by ice water. She blinked twice, certain she hadn't heard him correctly. He was sending her to bed? Alone?

"Um, sure," she said. She set her wine on the coffee table and awkwardly rose to her feet. She felt like a child being sent away so the grown-ups could enjoy their evening.

"Good night," she murmured as she made her way to the stairs.

Despite her wishes to the contrary, Ryan didn't know she was alive. At least not as a woman. He knew she existed as Sasha's nanny, and no matter how she tried to convince herself otherwise, that wasn't enough for her. She wanted more. Unfortunately, she didn't have a clue as to how to get more.

When she reached her bedroom, she closed the door behind her, then leaned against the cool wood. Letting go of Joel had been incredibly easy. Despite the fact that she'd known Ryan less than two months she had a bad feeling that letting go of him was going to take at least a lifetime.

CHAPTER THIRTEEN

RYAN LOOKED OUT the front window for the third time in as many minutes. He couldn't remember the last time he'd been this nervous. Telling himself he was doing the right thing for the right reason wasn't helping. If only he'd had more time to talk to Joel. But their conversation had been rushed and he'd only had a chance to issue the invitation.

Actually, "issue" wasn't a strong enough word. Joel had practically required a summons to agree to show up for dinner tonight. No doubt the young man was still suffering, Ryan reminded himself. It wasn't every day that a man had to get over someone as terrific as Cassie. And if Ryan had his way, by the end of the evening, Cassie and Joel would once again be back together.

He dropped the curtain in place and checked his watch. Joel wasn't due for about ten more minutes. This was going to be great, he told himself. Sure, Cassie acted as if everything was fine, but what choice did she have? She couldn't really admit that she'd made a huge mistake. Still, Ryan didn't doubt that she had. She and Joel had been together for years. They obviously belonged together. Even if Cassie insisted otherwise. If he hadn't lost control of himself and kissed her, then none of this would have happened. She wouldn't have gotten it into her head that Joel was the wrong man for her. It was his fault they'd broken up and he was going to see they got back together.

But the thought of her with another man, even Joel, annoyed him. Images of them together ripped through his brain, making him want to do some ripping of his own. Like maybe taking Joel apart, limb by limb. He drew in a deep breath and reminded himself of his higher purpose in all this. While he might want Cassie, he couldn't have her. He was emotionally incapable of providing her with all that she needed and deserved. However, Joel could give her that. So they belonged together.

He walked into the kitchen to check on Cassie. Before he got there, he reminded himself he had to act casual about the whole thing. While she knew that he'd invited Joel to dinner, she didn't know that he planned to disappear right after the meal, leaving the two lovebirds to work things out.

Cassie looked up from the pot she was stirring. "I hope you like spaghetti," she said. "Charity dropped off some sauce when she was here a couple of weeks ago, and I defrosted it for tonight's meal. It's the famous Wright family recipe."

"I'm looking forward to it."

He studied Cassie's face, but as usual, she looked calm and incredibly attractive. Her soft pink sweater hugged her torso, outlining her breasts and making his skin twitch. He wanted to touch her. He wanted to hold her and be with her and…

Stop it! he ordered himself. This wasn't about him. He had to remember what was important.

"It was very nice of you to invite Joel for dinner," Cassie said. "I'd been worried that he wasn't getting out much since we broke up. Joel isn't the most social guy on the planet. Work was always his whole life."

"He seemed a little subdued," Ryan said. "I could tell he hadn't been sleeping much."

At least that part of it was true. Joel had looked exhausted, although he'd been plenty cheerful.

"You never did say what you were doing over at Bradley Discount," Cassie said, setting down her spoon and facing him. "Had you been there before?"

"I was checking out toys for Sasha. Christmas is less than two months away." It was a pitiful excuse, but the best he could come up with under the circumstances. No way was he going to tell her he'd gone to the store expressly to see Joel and had spent nearly an hour tracking the man down. Nor was he going to mention Joel's reluctance to join them for dinner.

Ryan grimaced as he remembered how he'd even taken the time to assure the younger man that there was nothing between Cassie and himself. Despite the fact that he wanted her to the exclusion of all other women.

"You were Christmas shopping? By yourself? In November?" Cassie asked the questions in a tone of disbelief usually reserved for questioning murder suspects.

"I can if I want to," he said, then practically sighed in relief when the doorbell rang. "I'll get that."

He made it halfway down the hall, paused, and returned to the kitchen. "Maybe you should get it."

Cassie stared at him. "What on earth is wrong with you?"

"Nothing."

The doorbell rang again.

"One of us had better get it," she muttered and headed out of the kitchen.

Ryan trailed after her. He didn't want to intrude on their greeting, but he also wanted to witness the event. If things looked like they were heating up instantly, he would hide out in his office and quietly drink himself into oblivion.

Cassie pulled open the door. "Hi, Joel."

"Cassie!" He swept her into a big bear hug.

Ryan had to resist the urge to jerk her out of the other man's embrace, all the while reminding himself that this had been *his* idea. Still, he hadn't thought it would hurt so much to watch her in Joel's arms. He turned away.

"Wow, you're so different," Cassie said. "What happened?"

Joel laughed. "Do you like it?"

Ryan glanced back and saw Cassie staring at Joel as if she'd never seen him before. "You're in contacts," she said and touched his face. "Your hair is styled and you're wearing new clothes."

"It's the new me."

A new look? Great, Ryan thought, trying to muster a little enthusiasm. Obviously Joel was trying to make a good impression. It seemed like everything was going to work out fine. He was thrilled. Really.

He cleared his throat and stepped forward. "Joel, thanks for joining us for dinner. Come on in."

There was the usual flurry and confusion of getting settled and taking drink orders. Cassie excused herself to check on Sasha, who had been put in bed a half hour before.

While she was gone, Ryan searched for something to say to Joel. "How's business?"

"Great. I've been talking to some people and they think I've got a real chance at making it to president of Bradley Discount." He leaned forward and lowered his voice to a confidential whisper. "I've been thinking about making a switch. There are a lot more opportunities with the big chains. I might give that a try. It would mean moving, of course, but that's not a problem anymore. Cassie never wanted to leave Bradley, but I think I would like to see the world. Maybe even move to the Bay area."

Ryan stared at the younger man. He *did* look different. The new hairstyle swept back from his face, giving him a "young executive" look. His clothes were expensive, as was his obviously new watch. Something had happened to Joel in the couple of weeks he'd been single. Something Ryan didn't like at all.

He was torn between defending Cassie's desire to stay close to home and pointing out that a move to the Bay area was hardly seeing the world. Before he could decide, Cassie returned and took her seat on the sofa.

Unfortunately, when they first came into the living room, Joel had taken one of the wing chairs, leaving Ryan and Cassie the sofa. Still, Joel was across from her and eye contact was very powerful. At least it was when Cassie looked at him.

She took a sip of her white wine. "I can't get over the changes. You look terrific, Joel."

"Thanks." He half raised his hand, then put it back in his lap. "I've worn glasses for so long that it's difficult to get used to being without them, but I like the contacts." He cleared his throat. "So how are you doing?"

"I'm fine."

She gave him one of her best smiles, the one that always made Ryan want to rush her into his bed. Joel didn't seem affected. The ungrateful twit.

"I've been keeping busy with Sasha. She's a handful, but such a sweet girl."

Cassie continued talking about her job, and then filled Joel in on news about her family. The other man pretended to listen, but Ryan could tell his attention was elsewhere. Then it hit him. Joel had asked about Cassie's life to be polite, but he wasn't interested in the answer. What he wanted instead was to talk about *his* life.

Ryan took a hefty swallow of beer and wished he'd chosen something stronger, like Scotch. He had a bad feeling about what was about to happen. He opened his mouth, but couldn't think of anything to say. It was like watching two trains on the same track. They were going to collide and all he could do was helplessly stand by.

"So what's new with you?" she finally asked, then smiled. "Aside from the great new look."

He scooted forward in his chair. "A lot. I have to tell you, Cass, when you first broke up with me, I thought you were crazy. All your talk about wanting more, about passion. I figured it was some female thing and you'd get over it in a couple of days."

He shrugged. "The thing was, I couldn't stop thinking about everything you'd told me. It started to make sense, sort of, and then I got this feeling you weren't going to change your mind. I began to realize you'd meant what you said."

"I did," she said. "I'm glad you see that. I think we're both happier this way."

Ryan had to grind his teeth to keep from speaking out. This was *not* how he'd planned their conversation. They were supposed to be talking about how much they missed each other. Maybe he was the problem. If he left the room, at least they would have privacy. But he couldn't think of a smooth way to make that happen, so he hunched down in the corner of the sofa and pretended not to be there.

"I am happier," Joel said, sounding sheepish and proud at the same time. "I got real confused about everything, so I asked Alice to dinner. She's the assistant manager of the Bradley Discount pet department. Redhead, about so tall." He held up his hand, indicating a tiny woman.

A knot formed in Ryan's stomach. The trains were only a few feet apart now. The impact was going to be felt for miles.

"I told her everything you'd said and then asked for her opinion. I figured with her being female and all, she'd have a better idea than I did as to what was going on."

"What happened?" Cassie asked.

Ryan closed his eyes. He didn't want to know.

"Well, it was the strangest thing. Partway through the meal, she told me that I should forget all about you. It seems that she's had a thing for me for about two years. She told me she was in love with me. You can imagine how shocked I was."

Not nearly as shocked as me, Ryan thought grimly. He wanted to groan out loud. He wanted to rant and rave and throw things and beat the hell out of Joel for giving up on Cassie in the first place.

He risked a glance at Cassie. She was nodding intently, as if the story was interesting but didn't have anything to do with her personally. "What did you say?"

"Nothing. I listened. Then she invited me back to her place."

Ryan thought about throwing Joel out, but it was too late. What had gone wrong? Why weren't they getting back together? He knew what the other man was going to say next. The trains impacted and the room shook. He seemed to be the only one who noticed.

"I spent the night. Actually, I spent two days there." Joel grinned like a kid who'd hit his first home run. "I even called in sick, which, as you know, I've never done before."

"That's true. You always prided yourself on your perfect attendance." Cassie's voice was calm. Ryan wanted to crawl under a rock.

"It's just like you said," Joel told her. "With Alice, I feel the passion. It's amazing. We talk about everything. There's so much to say and never enough time. We can't seem to get out of bed." He looked at her and grinned. "Cass, I owe you for this. I've never been happier. Alice is exactly who I belong with. You were right. I should have known. You always were the smart one in the relationship."

"Joel, I'm happy for you."

Ryan thought he was going to be sick.

"Is it serious?" she asked.

"Yeah. We're, uh, sort of living together."

"Already?" Ryan asked before he could stop himself. "Do you think that's wise?"

"Sure. We're getting married. I bought her a beautiful engagement ring. Nearly two carats in diamonds. It's—" Joel paused and, for the first time, seemed uncomfortable. "Sorry, Cassie. That wasn't nice, was it? I didn't mean to imply—"

She cut him off with a wave of her hand. "It's fine. You gave me the promise ring when we were both kids. Now you're a man. Of course you would do things differently."

Ryan had forgotten about the diamond-lint ring. The little piece of animal refuse had cheated Cassie out of a decent engagement ring, too.

"Anyway," Joel plunged on as if determined to tell his story, regardless of whom he hurt, "we're heading over to Las Vegas at the end of the month. This close to the holidays we had a hard time getting four days off together, but I pulled a few strings. We'll be married then. We know we want to be together forever, and don't see the point of waiting."

He made the last statement with a note of defiance in his voice, as if he expected someone to tell him that he was acting impetuously. Ryan was more than ready to do it, but he was too stunned by everything that had happened. The evening wasn't supposed to play out this way. Joel was supposed to have taken one look at Cassie and begged her to come back. They would have talked, she would have agreed, end of problem.

"I'm very happy for both of you," Cassie said. She rose to her feet, walked around the coffee table, then bent over and kissed Joel's cheek. "I mean that completely."

"Are you sure?" Joel asked, his weasel eyes searching her face. "I wouldn't have told you if I thought you still cared."

Yeah, right, Ryan thought bitterly. He couldn't wait to gloat. No doubt he figured Cassie would be destroyed by the information, kicking herself for letting him get away. Well, that wasn't going to happen. Somehow he, Ryan, would figure out a way to make it right. Although his track record at fixing things was currently pretty crummy.

"I'm completely sure," Cassie told him. "Joel, we had nine lovely years together. I'll always remember them fondly. I hope you will, too. But at the end we both knew it was time to move on. I'm so pleased that you've found your heart's desire."

"Thanks, Cassie." Weasel-boy squeezed her hand.

Cassie flashed him a smile. "I need to check on dinner. I'll be right back."

Ryan gave her a thirty-second lead, excused himself and raced after her into the kitchen.

"Cassie, I'm so sorry," he said as he burst into the room. "If I'd known that little ingrate had gone and done this, I never would have invited him over. Are you doing okay? Do you want me to send him home? I could beat him up for you."

Cassie glanced up from the tray of garlic bread she was about to place in the oven. She laughed. "What a generous offer. No one has offered to beat up another person for me before. You're being very sweet and I appreciate your concern, but I meant what I told Joel. I'm fine."

She left the garlic bread and crossed to stand by him. "I'm the one who ended the relationship. It was my idea."

"You could be having second thoughts."

"I could, but I'm not."

Ryan wanted to believe her. He stared deeply into her dark eyes, but he couldn't tell what she was thinking. Obviously the pain was too great for her to even conceive of it yet. "I'll go beat him up."

As he turned, Cassie grabbed his arm. "Don't. Joel hasn't done anything wrong. I really am happy about the new lady in his life. I swear." She made an X on her chest. "Just let it be and enjoy the evening. I'm going to."

"Sure," he muttered and stalked out of the kitchen. Enjoy the evening. No problem.

IT WAS THE longest two hours of Ryan's life. All through dinner, and afterward, while he sipped coffee and apparently had no plans to leave anytime soon, all Joel talked about was Alice. Alice was brilliant, Alice was witty, Alice was charming and insightful and well-read and probably three days away from curing several lethal diseases.

Ryan sipped his brandy and admitted the last thought hadn't been completely accurate. But, dammit, Joel was getting on his nerves. He wanted Weasel-boy out of his house.

"We're going to put off having children for a few

years," Joel was saying. "Alice and I want to spend time with each other first."

"Very wise," Cassie said. "Once the little ones start coming, everything changes."

As she'd been all evening, Cassie was the picture of poise. A lovely and gracious hostess. Ryan ached for her and wished there was something to do to help her feel better. In his arrogance, he'd tried to fix her life. Instead he'd made it worse. She must feel as if she was trapped in hell.

Finally, a little after ten, Joel pushed back his chair and stood up. "I should head home."

About time, Ryan thought. *Don't let the door hit you in the ass on your way out.* But he didn't say that. Instead he offered the other man a tight smile and led the way to the foyer.

They said their goodbyes quickly. When he was gone, Ryan closed the door behind him and leaned against the frame. "I'm sorry," he said.

"You've already apologized. I told you then there was no need. There still isn't."

She walked back into the dining room and started clearing the table. Ryan trailed after her. "I don't believe you. You have to be in pain. This is awful and it's all my fault. I was an arrogant fool who thought he could fix everything. All I've done instead is make the situation worse. I'm sorry."

Cassie sank down into a chair and wondered how offended Ryan would be if she started laughing. He obviously believed her heart was breaking and that she was within a hairbreadth of losing it completely.

"I appreciate the concern," she said as she stared at him. "You are a very kind man to worry about me. But as I said before, I'm fine."

"Cassie, a month ago you were going to marry Joel.

Now he's living with someone else who he plans to marry at the end of this month. You can't tell me that doesn't matter."

"You have a point," she said. "I feel strange hearing about the changes in Joel's life. As a friend, I'm a little worried that he's moved so quickly. But deep down inside, I don't feel anything. I'm not sorry I ended our relationship. I don't wish he were marrying me instead." She allowed herself a small smile. "I'm a little bitter about the engagement ring—it sounds beautiful. However, I would like to point out that if my biggest worry is that he spent twenty times more on her ring than mine, then I'm obviously not going to be destroyed by all that's happened. I don't have any regrets."

He studied her face. "I wish I could believe you."

"You can. I'm telling the truth." She clasped her hands together. "You're forgetting that I was questioning my relationship with Joel for a long time before I ended it. I didn't make that decision lightly. I know you feel responsible because of what happened between us, but I wish you could let that go. I have."

Okay, so that was a lie, but in the scheme of things, it wasn't a very big one. She hadn't let the kiss go. If anything, she thought about it more than ever, but only because her feelings for Ryan had changed.

The entire time Joel had been talking about Alice, she'd been thinking about Ryan. She'd realized she didn't have a crush on her boss anymore. She'd fallen in love with him.

Everything Joel had said about what it was like to spend time with Alice had made her wish it was that way for her and Ryan, too. She'd wanted to experience those things with him, she'd wanted him to return her feelings.

She wanted them both to fall madly in love, to be swept away by fire and passion, and live happily-ever-after.

She drew in a deep breath. Unfortunately, that wasn't in the cards for her. Ryan liked her and respected her, but it wasn't love. The truth didn't have to be pleasant, but she did have to accept it. There was no point in planning on something she was never going to have. So, despite the ache in her heart, she would be sensible.

She would go out and find a place in which to belong. She would find someone she could love and who wanted to love her back. She would make sure that this time there was passion as well as friendship. And eventually, she would forget Ryan and all that he'd meant to her.

But not just yet. For the next few weeks she would stay here in Bradley, in Ryan's house, and collect as many memories as possible.

"You're not even listening," he complained.

Cassie blinked. "You're right. I'm sorry. What were you saying?"

He crossed to the chair and grabbed her hand. After pulling her to her feet, he cupped her face.

"I'm more sorry than I can tell you. You've been so great and all I've done is mess up your life. I didn't mean to upset everything by kissing you. Now, by inviting Joel over, I've only made things worse. I thought that if the two of you spent some time together, everything would work out."

She loved the feel of his palms against her skin, but instead of savoring the moment, she grabbed his wrists and pulled him away. "You have an incredible ability not to hear what I'm saying. It's a gift, isn't it?" She took a deep breath. "I'll speak slowly so that you can understand. I don't want Joel. I don't miss him. I don't want to be with him anymore."

His green eyes darkened. "Really?"

Was she actually getting through to him? "Yes, really. I would rather be alone than be with someone I don't love. I don't love him."

"Cassie, I—"

She held up her hand. "If you apologize one more time I'm going to ask you to beat up yourself."

He grinned. "Okay, I won't. I'm just concerned."

"And I'm just fine. I mean that."

"All right. I'll let it go, but only after I tell you that Joel is a stupid man. He had a real prize in you."

His words warmed her. Without thinking, she leaned forward and kissed his mouth. "Thank you. That's so nice. You really—"

But she couldn't finish her sentence. Not when she saw the heat flaring in his eyes. Heat that ignited a matching fire in her body. "Ryan?"

He swore under his breath. "I promised I wouldn't do this again, Cassie, and I meant it. But you do things to me." His jaw tightened. "Just walk away. Go to bed. Leave the house if it scares you too much." He swore again. "I didn't mean for you to ever find out. I'm a real bastard. I'm sorry."

She stared at him. "You want me," she said, not quite able to believe the words even as she spoke them. Wonder filled her. Wonder and longing.

"Of course. Who wouldn't?"

She could probably come up with dozens of names, but right now that didn't seem important. He didn't love her, but he wanted her. It shouldn't be enough, but it was. She would rather have a little bit of magic with Ryan than have a lifetime of almost with someone else.

"I'm not afraid," she told him. "You're not a bastard.

I'm not leaving the house. In fact, I don't think I'm going to bed for a long time."

"One of us has to be strong."

It took all her courage, but she took a step toward him and placed her hands on his shoulders. He tensed. She leaned a little closer and felt his arousal pressing into her belly.

"I'm not feeling especially strong," she told him. "Guess it's up to you."

They stared at each other. She thought he might back off, or push her away. Instead he sucked in a breath, wrapped his arms around her and kissed her.

CHAPTER FOURTEEN

THIS KISS WAS better than the one she remembered. Cassie let herself lean into him, absorbing the heat that flared instantly. His mouth was hot and firm against hers, his body hot and hard. Passion swept through her, like a rush of light, filling every pore, every cell. She couldn't think, couldn't breathe, couldn't imagine ever wanting to stop. All she could do was kiss him back.

Ryan brushed her lower lip with his tongue. She shivered as she parted to admit him. He moved inside, stroking her, circling around, exploring and teasing. He tasted of wine and himself, a potent combination that left her light-headed.

His hands were everywhere. On her back, slipping down to her waist, then cupping her hips. He squeezed her derriere and pulled her against him so that she could feel all of his arousal, then brought his hands up her arms and began the journey again. In turn, she allowed herself to rest her fingertips on his broad shoulders. He was so strong. Every muscle tightened as she traced a pattern down his back. She could feel his rippling tension.

What was that old line? "If this is madness, then let me live with the insane." Or something like that. It didn't matter. The concept captured her feelings perfectly. She wanted to be crazy, if it meant sharing this incredible moment with Ryan. Her breasts ached and swelled until she wanted to beg him to touch her there. Her legs trembled.

Between her thighs, that most private part of her dampened. She could feel a heaviness low in her stomach and it took all her strength not to rock her hips against him.

Ryan cupped her face. He trailed kisses across her cheeks and nose, along her jaw to her ear. There he nibbled on her earlobe. Her breath caught as the impact of his teasing made her softly cry out. It was too delicious, too incredible, too unlike anything she'd ever experienced.

"Ryan," she breathed, wanting to say his name again and again so that she could know this was really happening.

He pulled back and stared at her. The fire she'd seen before had exploded into a raging storm. If she hadn't known better, she would have sworn that his hands trembled as he held her face. She noticed that his mouth was damp…from *her* kisses! *She* had done that to him. Somehow, despite her inexperience, she'd managed to arouse him and his passions.

"I want you," he said, his voice low and husky. "I want you, Cassie. In my bed. I want you naked, underneath me. I want to touch you and taste you everywhere, then I want to bury myself inside you and make you mine."

His words created an image that took her breath away. She couldn't do anything but stare at him. She'd never been naked in front of a man before, nor had a man touched her intimately. She waited for a feeling of nervousness or a voice to whisper that what they were doing was wrong, but there was only the silence of expectation.

"I want you, too," she murmured, then ducked her head as she blushed. Had she really said that?

He touched her chin and forced her to look at him. "No regrets?" he asked. "I can stop now, if you want me to." He gave her a crooked smile. "I'll want to die, but I can stop. I need you to be sure."

She knew what he was trying to say. That he wanted to make love with her, but nothing else about their relationship was going to change. He hadn't suddenly fallen in love with her. He wasn't promising her anything more than a night in his bed.

Cassie stared at his face, at the handsome lines and the need tightening his mouth, at the light in his eyes. For her it was a question of regret. Which would she regret more? Turning him away or being with him, knowing that it would never be more than a physical relationship.

She waited for the debate to begin, but there was only silence in her head. She loved Ryan. She knew him to be a good man. Despite his attempts to keep their relationship completely professional, he had stolen her heart and there was no way for her to get it back.

She'd already felt the passion of their kisses. Now she wanted to know the rest of it. She wanted to be with him in the way women had been with men since the beginning of time. As he didn't want a romantic relationship, she had to remember that this wasn't going to mean the same to him as it did to her. Eventually, she would have to get over him and find someone else. He wasn't going to be the last one…was she willing to let him be the first?

"No regrets," she said.

He brought her hand to his mouth and kissed her knuckles, then he led her to the stairs and up to his bedroom.

The room they entered was large and dark. "Stay here," he said.

He moved through the shadows. A lamp clicked on by the king-size bed, casting dim light in all directions. Cassie stared at the bed, then at Ryan. They were really going to make love. She and Ryan. She wasn't sure she believed this was happening.

"Why do you want me?" she blurted out. "I'm nothing like the women in your life."

He returned to her side. "What do you know about the women in my world?"

"Just that they're nothing like me. They're in business, or computers. They travel, wear sophisticated clothes, go to the theater and understand about wine. That's not me."

He took her hand again and pressed his mouth to her palm. "Maybe that's what I like about you," he told her. "That you're not in competition with me, that you care more about making Sasha happy than being seen in the right kind of restaurant. Maybe I like that you're honest and good, and that you don't even know there's a game, let alone understand the rules."

Game? "What game?" she asked.

He licked her palm. A shiver rippled through her and she thought she might have to sit down.

"My point exactly. I'm not claiming to understand you completely, but all the surprises have been positive ones. You're a good person. I enjoy your company, and you're sexy as hell."

She grinned. "Really?"

"I swear."

Sexy, huh? She'd never thought of herself that way. She was just plain Cassie Wright. Nothing special. Except now, with Ryan nibbling on the inside of her wrist and her whole body threatening to go up in flames, she felt very sexy and alive.

He dropped her hand and hauled her hard against him. Before she could catch her breath, his mouth was on hers, his tongue plunging inside. She met him and gave back all that he offered. When his hands slipped under the bottom of her sweater and started moving up, she didn't think about being shy or afraid. All she could do was hold herself away a little so that he could slide up to her breasts.

She'd waited for this for so long, she thought as his fingers stroked her skin. She felt him trace her ribs, then the band of her bra. At last his right hand moved up and cupped her breast.

The contact was different from what she'd expected. Firm, yet gentle, and certainly better in every way. He squeezed, then took her tight nipple between his thumb and forefinger. He rolled the beaded tip and sent jolts of pleasure through her. Her knees threatened to buckle, her thighs were on fire. She had to hold on to him to stay upright.

"Ryan," she whispered against his mouth. "Oh, Ryan."

"Tell me about it." His voice was thick. "I can't believe what you're doing to me. I want you so much, I'm about to explode."

He stepped back and with one quick, practiced movement pulled her sweater up over her head. The night air was cool on her bare skin. Cassie didn't even think about covering herself, despite the fact that Ryan was obviously staring.

"You're so beautiful," he said and stroked the valley between her breasts. "I thought you'd be perfect and I was right."

He'd thought about her? Naked? She felt a shiver in her tummy.

He took her hand and drew her to the bed. Once she was seated, he crouched down and removed her shoes and socks. He quickly did the same to himself, then settled next to her. As he kissed her, he lowered her to the mattress.

Her left arm was trapped between them, so she reached around with her right one. She explored his cheek and his ear, then ran her fingers through his hair. All the while they kissed as if they couldn't get enough of each other.

Cassie felt his hand on her belly. His splayed fingers moved in a lazy circle. He moved up and stroked her breasts with long, slow movements that had her arching like a cat. The need grew inside of her. She wanted…only she wasn't sure what. Every time he brushed against her tight nipples, she gasped. Between her legs a steady ache pounded in time with her heartbeat. She wanted him to touch her *there* but she was also a little scared, so she didn't say anything.

He continued to brush her skin, from her shoulder to her waist, pausing at her breasts with each trip. On one of the journeys, he unfastened the hook at the front of her bra. The lace fabric fell open.

He trailed kisses down her chin to her throat, then lower, toward her breasts. Her breath caught. Was he really going to kiss her nipples? Apparently he was, she thought as he nudged aside her bra and licked the hollow. The damp trail moved up the curve, then he took the peak in his mouth.

The pleasure was so intense, she made a soft whimpering sound and gripped his upper arm. It was too wonderful; she would never survive. But she didn't want him to stop. She wanted the moment to go on forever.

"Oh, Ryan, please," she begged, not sure what she asked for.

He raised his head and blew on the damp skin. The quick chill made her shiver, but before she could register discomfort, he took her in his mouth again and sucked.

A ribbon of need wove its way between her breasts and her feminine place. When his hand slid down her belly toward that spot, she didn't protest. She trusted him. Equally important, she wanted him. All that he had to offer.

His fingers pressed against the seam of her jeans. He rubbed back and forth. She shifted slightly, enjoying the pressure. It was nicer than she would have thought, even though— A jolt ripped through her. She half sat up. "What was that?"

"The promised land," he said and grinned a very satisfied male smile.

Before she could ask any questions, he began tugging off her jeans. He peeled away her panties, too, and she was naked.

Any nervousness quickly disappeared as he returned his attentions to her breasts. He kissed her curves, loving her until she nearly forgot to breathe. His hand was once again on her stomach, but this time she could feel the faint roughness of his skin, along with his warmth. His fingers followed the same trail they had before, but it felt very different on bare flesh. She quivered and jumped, but didn't protest as he made his way down to the dark curls. He slipped through them slowly, almost tickling her. Almost. There was too much anticipation for her to laugh. She wanted…so much.

He raised his head. "Cassie, look at me."

She opened her eyes, not actually remembering closing them, and stared into his face.

"I want to see you," he said. "I want to know I'm getting it right."

She couldn't imagine him doing anything wrong, but for some reason she couldn't speak right now. Not with his fingers actually sliding down from the curls into her waiting woman's place.

He stroked her lightly. "You're so wet and ready," he

said with a groan. "I want you so much. But first I want you to want me."

She started to tell him that she did. But it was hard to think of anything except the feel of him as he discovered her. He slipped inside. She felt herself clamp tightly around him.

"Oh, I..." She trailed off, not sure what she apologized for, but sure she'd done something wrong.

"No!" he said as he stared at her intensely. "I love that you want me. Don't hold back. I want to hear you."

Cassie nodded, even though she didn't have any great plans to be chatty during the event. It was going to be difficult enough pretending this *wasn't* her first time. She was hoping that Ryan wouldn't figure that out. He'd felt so responsible just for kissing her, she could only imagine what he would put himself through if he found out she was a virgin.

His finger moved in and out of her, creating an irresistible rhythm and tension. She found her attention focusing on what he was doing and all other thoughts faded. Her hips moved of their own accord, pulsing slightly to meet his every thrust. When he withdrew, she wanted to protest, but he brought his fingers a little higher, probing gently until he found a spot that made her want to cry out.

Instead she tensed and made a grab for his wrist as her eyes fluttered closed.

"There?" he asked.

She wasn't sure of the question, but she knew he had to keep touching her. If he didn't, she was going to die. "I don't know," she gasped.

He chuckled in her ear. "I do. How do you like it?"

He circled her slowly, occasionally brushing over the sensitive spot. Then he pressed a little more, went a little faster. She found herself caught in a process she didn't understand. "Like…that," she managed.

"Relax," he murmured. "We've got all night. I want to make this good for you."

His words made her uncomfortable. He was talking about that whole pleasure thing. She'd read about it, of course. For most guys it was a sure thing, but for women it could be complicated. Worry distracted her from the intense enjoyment. How was she supposed to know if it was happening to her? What would it feel like if it did? How long would it take? She didn't even know enough to fake it.

Cassie pressed her lips together. For now, what he was doing to her was amazing. She felt as if she were being carried toward the sun. Heat flooded her body, as her muscles tensed. She dug her heels into the bed and raised her hips toward him, urging him to continue.

She would let him do this for a few more minutes, she decided. Until he was probably bored, then she would plead exhaustion or nerves or something and get him to stop so they could get on with it. Yes, that was it. She would tell him to stop. Just not yet.

He continued to touch her. Occasionally he slipped his finger inside of her. Her breathing became rapid and she tossed her head back and forth. It was perfect, just like this. The rubbing, the closeness, the tension that spiraled higher and higher.

"You're getting ready," he told her. "Go for it."

She was about to tell him she didn't know what the "it" was, but she couldn't speak. A fine thread seemed to be unraveling inside of her. Heat radiated from that place in the very center of being. Heat and an odd pressure.

"Please," she breathed, hoping he would understand that she needed him not to stop.

Apparently he did because he moved faster and lighter, now directly over that one tiny point of sensation. She could feel herself gathering, reaching, straining. She clutched at the bedspread and splayed her knees wider.

"Cassie, look at me."

She opened her eyes and found herself drowning in his gaze. She clung to the edge of sanity. She was almost there…even though she wasn't sure of her destination.

He stopped moving. Her breath caught in her throat. One heartbeat, two. Then he resumed, circling and circling, faster and faster until her body peaked.

She remembered crying out his name as the ripples of release rode through her. She remembered his lips on hers and the feel of his tongue in her mouth and how he'd kissed her at the exact moment when she'd wanted to be kissed. She remembered how he'd held her afterward, hugging her close and murmuring about how beautiful she was.

Finally, when her heartbeat was nearly normal, she looked up at him. "Wow."

"Yeah? I'm glad." His pleased smile faded. "I want you."

In his arms, having just experienced the ultimate pleasure for the very first time, she found herself feeling a little bold. "I want you to have me," she said perkily.

He kissed her with a passion that made her toes curl. While he fumbled with his belt and slacks, she worked on his shirt. It was tough to undress a man, all the while still kissing him, but she liked it. It made her feel sexy and worldly.

When he was finally naked, he rolled away, opened his nightstand drawer, dug out something and closed the drawer. Then he turned back and propped himself up on one elbow.

She let her gaze drift down his broad shoulders and bare chest. While they were incredibly lovely and later she would want to look her fill, right now she was far more interested in seeing a naked, aroused man. Except for some brief, shadowy glimpses in the movies, she'd never actually seen *it*.

And *it* made her gasp. "It's so big," she blurted out.

Ryan grinned. "Why, thank you, my dear. I'm glad you approve."

Approve wasn't the word she would have chosen, Cassie thought. Suddenly fear threatened. Maybe this was a bad idea. Maybe she should tell Ryan she'd changed her mind. Maybe…

She glanced up at his face, at the wanting in his eyes, at the tender-hungry expression that made her love him more. Of course she wanted this. She wanted to finally know, and she wanted to learn it all with Ryan. She trusted him and she loved him.

He slipped on the protection, then kissed her. As his tongue plunged in deeper, his hands stroked her breasts. She hadn't thought she could want him again, but she did. Her body tensed. Between her legs, she felt the heat and swelling. Could she experience that wonderful release again? At least this time she knew what to expect.

He slipped one hand down and rubbed against her until she was breathing hard. She rocked her hips in rhythm with his movements and felt herself reaching for that perfect pinnacle. Then something hard probed at her. He pressed in slowly.

Cassie told herself not to stiffen. She took deep breaths and tried to go with what was happening. He filled her, inch by inch, stretching her. It wasn't exactly painful, but there was a little discomfort. She concentrated on the unfamiliar weight of him on top of her and how safe that made her feel. She inhaled his scent and promised herself she would remember this forever.

Ryan raised his head slightly. "You feel incredible."

His face was all harsh lines and need. His eyes opened briefly, then sank closed as he slid in deeper. He paused, flexed his hips, then looked at her again. "There's something wrong," he told her.

She'd been afraid of that. There was physical proof of her virginal state. He couldn't stop now. She was close to having all she'd ever wanted. "Everything is fine," she said and placed her hand on his hip. "Be inside of me. All the way." When he still hesitated, she pulled him close. "I want this," she whispered, then kissed him.

She felt his questions and his concern, even as she nibbled on his lower lip and plunged her tongue inside of his mouth.

"How the hell am I supposed to resist you?" he asked with a groan.

"You're not." She looked at him. "Unless you want to."

"The only thing I want is to make love with you."

She smiled. "We seemed to have undressed for the occasion and assumed the position."

"That we have."

He thrust inside with a force that made her gasp. The sharp pain faded as quickly as it had appeared. Ryan froze.

"Don't stop," she said. Then she raised her hips, offering herself to him.

For a second, he didn't move. Cassie was terrified he was going to stop. She wouldn't be able to stand that. She wanted to know. She wanted to make love with him. She wanted him to experience the same release she had.

Acting on instinct, she clenched her muscles tightly around him, then relaxed. After she repeated the action twice more, he groaned low in his throat and began moving. He withdrew only to fill her again. Her body stretched and welcomed him, the last of the discomfort faded.

"I want you," he growled. "I want to be in you, even though I shouldn't."

She touched his face, his arms, then boldly reached down and cupped his rear. "It feels too right to be wrong. Make love to me, Ryan. Show me what all the fuss is about."

"A challenge?" A faint smile tugged at his lips.

"Absolutely."

Then the smile faded and he was kissing her—the same deep, soul-touching kiss that first changed her life. He slipped his hands under her back and hauled her closer, all the while moving in and out of her. She felt herself reaching for release again, in that strange way that had happened before, except this time it was different. This time....

He tensed in her arms. "Cassie!"

The way he said her name made her shiver with incredible delight. Her body began to convulse around his. She felt the pleasure, the rightness, then he was shuddering and kissing her and the moment was as perfect as she'd known it was meant to be.

RYAN HELD CASSIE close and prayed for inspiration. Nothing in his life had prepared him for this moment. What the hell had he done? It wasn't only that he'd destroyed her life by causing her to break up with her boyfriend of nine years and then put her in a position where she'd had to hear about *his* new fiancée, but he'd just stolen her virginity. The fact that their lovemaking was the best he'd ever experienced in his life was no excuse.

"Someone should shoot me," he said, releasing her and rolling onto his back. "That's about what I deserve."

"Is this about the lovemaking not being very good or something else?" she asked.

Her voice was low and soft, laced with concern. Ryan looked at her. Cassie was as beautiful naked as he'd imagined. Now, with her hair mussed and her mouth swollen from his kisses, he couldn't imagine ever wanting to be with anyone else. Despite the fact that he'd just finished, his body stirred at the thought of being with her again. Which meant he was lower than slime. He was a single-celled creature that aspired to *be* slime.

He touched her face. "The lovemaking was wonderful. I swear." He tightened his jaw.

"But I should have told you that I was a virgin."

He'd known, of course. He'd felt the barrier, then broken through it, but still, hearing the word spoken aloud made him wince. "Yeah, you should have told me."

She flashed him a quick smile. "There wasn't much time for meaningful conversation. Besides, I didn't want you to stop."

He couldn't deal with this. Nothing made sense. "You were together with Joel for nine years. In all that time you never...."

"Obviously not. Actually, we never did anything. Not even heavy petting. I told you, there was no passion. That's one of the reasons I ended the relationship."

She rolled on her side and faced him. "Don't worry, Ryan. I'm not some innocent teenager."

"No, you're an innocent twenty-four-year-old nanny. What the hell was I thinking?"

"I'm almost twenty-five."

As if that made any difference, he thought grimly.

She touched his cheek. "Don't worry. I understand exactly what's happened here. We made love. I don't have much experience, but I can tell you it was amazing for me. It probably wasn't really smart, but it's done. I'm not going to take advantage of the situation. I'm not going to demand a relationship with you. I still work for you and I think with a little bit of effort on both our parts, we can get back to just being friendly coworkers." Her smile returned. "Just not this friendly."

He stared at her. "That's it?"

"Sure."

She was saying everything he might have said, if he'd been thinking. Why did it sound so wrong coming from her?

"Cassie," he started.

She leaned over and kissed his mouth. "No, I won't talk about this anymore." Then she stood up and gathered her clothes together. After slipping into his robe, she turned to him. "I'll return this in the morning. Good night."

With that, she was gone.

Ryan stared after her. Cassie had said everything just right. He *should* believe her. The only problem was he suddenly didn't want to.

CHAPTER FIFTEEN

As CASSIE GAVE Sasha her breakfast, she listened for the sound of footsteps on the stairs. No doubt Ryan would want to have yet another heart-to-heart talk when he came down this morning, so she had to be prepared.

She'd spent most of the night going over what she would say to him. He would be worried that she was all right, and probably worried that she would expect a real relationship. She would have to reassure him on both accounts. The first would be easy, because she was all right. In fact, she felt terrific. Ryan had made her first time wonderful. She knew she would remember everything about their being together for the rest of her life. Thinking about it now sent a shiver through her tummy. She wanted to be with him again, be held close and feel him inside her. She had a feeling that there was a lot of potential there.

Convincing him of the second issue would be a lot more difficult. Not only *did* she really want a relationship with him, but she was in love with him. She didn't know how much she was going to be able to fake about all that. At least she had a little practice at not showing her feelings, even though she wasn't sure it was going to be enough.

She wanted to be with Ryan, but only because *he* wanted it, too. She would rather be alone than have him with her out of guilt or mercy. So she was going to have to convince him that she felt only a passing interest and that she could easily walk away without a backward glance. She sighed. It sounded simple in theory—but was she going to be able to pull it off?

She stiffened as she heard his footsteps, then smiled at Sasha. "Can you eat that by yourself? I have to go tell Uncle Ryan something, then I'll be right back."

Sasha nodded and continued to eat her breakfast. She mumbled something that sounded like the two-year-old version of "big girl." Cassie kissed the top of her head.

"Yes, you are a big girl, and very special. I'll just be a minute."

She headed out the door and intercepted Ryan in the hall. From here she could keep an eye on the toddler, but not be overheard.

"Good morning," he said when he saw her.

She took in the stern set of his face, the signs of sleep-lessness, the lack of a smile and knew that she'd been right. They were going to have a serious talk. She drew in a deep breath. "While I don't mind having these talks with you, Ryan, it would be nice if all of them didn't have to happen before I've had my second cup of coffee."

He shoved his hands into his slacks pockets. "Sorry about that, but this one can't wait."

"Oh, I know." She could see him gathering himself for whatever speech he'd prepared. She didn't think she could bear to listen to his carefully worded dismissal, so she decided on a preemptive strike. "I know what you're going to say."

He raised his eyebrows in surprise. "Do you?"

"I can't be sure, but I have a fair idea. You're con-cerned that I'm upset about last night and that I blame you. You're worried that I'm going to quit or at least sulk. You're also a little worried about my assumptions that we now have an emotional relationship. You want to know my expectations. Does that about sum it up?"

She'd said everything without her voice trembling or a single slipup. There was something to be said for practice.

He stared at her for a long time, then nodded slowly. "That about sums it up."

"Good. Then let me address your concerns. First, I'm an adult. Last night I was a consenting adult. I wanted to make love with you. I'm not sorry we did it. Yes, I was a virgin and maybe I should have told you, but I didn't. I still don't have any regrets. Except for your reaction, there's nothing I would have changed about what we did."

He shifted. "It's not that I didn't enjoy it, it's just..."

"You feel guilty," she told him. "I understand that. If I were in your position, I would probably feel the same way. But it's not necessary. I wanted to be there. You gave me many opportunities to back out or to ask you to stop. I didn't. I take responsibility for that. I'm glad we made love."

She paused to catch her breath. "I think that covers your first few concerns."

"You're being very logical."

"It's a gift." She smiled. "Now, for the rest of your worries. I'm not expecting a proposal of marriage. I'm not even expecting a relationship. But I will admit things have changed."

Ryan's expression had cleared some, but now his eyebrows drew together again. "I don't dispute that, but I would like you to clarify what you mean."

"There have been a lot of changes in my life in the past couple of months. I've come to work for you, I've broken up with Joel, I've done the wild thing." She cast a quick glance over her shoulder to check on Sasha. The little girl was happily eating her cereal.

"I've made some decisions about what I want," she continued. "The only decision that affects you directly is that I can only work for you another month."

She felt her throat closing. This was harder to tell him than she'd first thought. She wanted to promise to stay as long as he would have her around, but she couldn't. She owed it to herself to be stronger than that. She deserved to love someone who loved her back. That person wasn't Ryan. She could allow herself to stay for a short period of time and be with him, but then she would have to move on. She needed to get the broken-heart part over with so she could begin healing, then get going with her life.

"You're leaving me?" He sounded stunned.

"I have to. A month gives you plenty of time to make other arrangements. If you're going to stay in Bradley, I'll help you find reliable day care. If you're going back to San Jose, then you need to start contacting places there."

She drew in a deep breath. Now for the really scary part. "I have no expectations for the time we have left. My preference is that we continue to be friends. I enjoy your company and I think you feel the same way about me."

"Of course I do. You know that."

"Good. As to our physical relationship—" She had to clear her throat before continuing. "I wouldn't object to us being lovers for the next month. We would have to be discreet. I wouldn't want to confuse Sasha or start any rumors in town." She didn't know what else to say. "It's up to you."

He looked a little stunned. "You've thought of everything."

"I tried to."

She forced herself to maintain her calm, but it was difficult. She wanted to throw herself at him and beg him to love her back. She wanted him to declare undying devotion, or at least a general fondness. She wanted him to beg her to stay forever, telling her that he couldn't possibly live without her.

"What do you get out of all this?" he asked.

"Working for you or being in your bed?"

"Being my lover."

She shivered. It was one thing for her to say the "L" word out loud, but quite another for it to come from him. "I want to be there," she answered honestly.

He sucked in his breath. "You lay it all on the line, don't you? I admire that about you, even though it terrifies me."

"I don't understand."

"I know. That's part of your appeal." He took a step toward her and tucked her hair behind her ear. "Work for me as long as you would like. I won't ask you to stay past your deadline, even though I want to. You've been more than kind in accommodating me and I don't have the right to mess with your life more than I have. As for having you in my bed, it would be my honor and privilege. But I want you to think about it a little longer. I want you to be sure this is what you want. When you leave, I want all the memories of your time here to be good ones."

"All right, I'll think about it," she told him, because that was what he wanted to hear. She didn't have to think. She already knew. But it would probably look better if she waited a couple of days before she walked into his room, ripped off her clothes and begged him to take her.

Then, when her month was up, she would walk away. Because if she couldn't have Ryan, she would have the next best thing—a life of her own.

RYAN POURED A drink for himself, then for Arizona. Chloe was out in the kitchen with her sister, and Sasha was down for the night. This was the second time he and Cassie had had someone from her family over for dinner, with Cassie's Aunt Charity being the first. He found he liked being the host and had looked forward to the evening. Unfortunately now that it was here, he couldn't concentrate on what Arizona was saying.

"I've gotten boring in my old age," Arizona said as he sat on the couch and sipped his Scotch.

"Not at all." Ryan took the wing chair opposite the sofa. "I apologize for not paying attention. I have a lot on my mind these days. I'm still putting my late brother's affairs in order. Then there's Sasha. She's a handful. I also have to decide if I'm going to stay here in Bradley or go back to San Jose."

Time was ticking away. Already a week of Cassie's month was gone. If he stayed here, he would have to relocate his business. If he left… He shook his head. He couldn't think about leaving. Not yet. Bradley was the only place he'd ever felt he belonged. Besides, if he left he would never see Cassie again. He had to see her. She was— He swore silently. He didn't know what she was to him, but he couldn't imagine living without her.

"That's not all," Arizona told him. "There's also the issue of Cassie."

Ryan thought about denying it, but figured there was no point. "There is that," he admitted.

He didn't understand what was going on. For one thing, she was handling their relationship a lot better than he was. For the past four nights, she'd stayed in his room. They'd made love until dawn, then she'd quietly crept away. He told himself he had it all—great day care for his niece and an incredible lover in his bed. What man was lucky enough to find a woman as special as Cassie, who would be with him, then at the end of a month, walk away without a second thought?

At first he'd thought she was kidding about her offer, but she was keeping to it with no apparent problem. Not once had she hinted about taking their relationship to the next level. She seemed very content to take care of Sasha during the day and him at night. She'd never once mentioned emotional entanglement.

Ryan took a swallow of his drink. He was a first-class jerk. He didn't deserve Cassie, and if he had any kind of moral character, he would break things off with her instantly. Except he couldn't imagine a world without her. Not that he was falling for her. He didn't know how to love anyone, nor did he want to learn. Love meant being vulnerable. He didn't trust emotion. Now hard work he could depend on.

"You've got it bad," Arizona said. "I recognize that fierce look."

Ryan glanced up. He'd completely forgotten the other man was in the room. "I don't have anything," he said quickly. "Cassie and I work together."

"Sure you do. And Chloe was just some reporter doing an interview." He leaned back in the sofa and rested one ankle on the opposite knee. "I'd spent my whole life going from place to place, never spending more than a few weeks under any one roof. I couldn't imagine settling down, having children. Roots didn't matter to me. Then I met Chloe and everything changed. I couldn't see it at first. All I knew was that I felt different around her. Suddenly it wasn't so easy to imagine my life the way it had been before we'd met. I told myself I didn't believe in love, and that happily-ever-after only happened in books and movies."

Arizona looked up. Ryan heard the light footsteps, too.

Chloe came in with a tray of dip and crackers. "This is to keep your strength up until dinner is ready."

She placed the food on the coffee table, flashed her husband a quick smile and left.

Ryan stared after her. At nearly seven months pregnant, she glowed. "You make her very happy," he told the other man.

"She does the same for me. I never had anyone I could depend on in my life. It took me a while to realize that's what I'd been searching for all along. Sometimes it's hard to recognize the truth."

"I'm not in love with Cassie," Ryan said flatly. "If that's what you and Chloe want, I'm sorry. It's not going to happen."

Arizona grinned. "Famous last words."

Ryan didn't know how to answer. Cassie wasn't part of his plan. He wanted— He paused and realized he didn't know what he wanted anymore. Too much was different.

"I need time to figure this out," Ryan said.

"So take it. Cassie's not going anywhere."

But Arizona was wrong. In three weeks Cassie would be leaving. Ryan didn't doubt her intention to keep to her plan. She was strong and bound by her word. Unless he found some way to keep her, she was going to walk out of his life. He told himself he would be fine, but in his heart, he was starting not to believe it.

Chloe closed the door to the kitchen. "I took them food. That will keep them quiet long enough for you to tell me what exactly is going on."

Cassie checked on the roast and the scalloped potatoes, then leaned against the counter. "I've told you I broke up with Joel," she said.

"I thought you two had a fight. I didn't know he was

already engaged to some woman from his store." Chloe looked furious. She crossed her arms above her swelling belly. "They're going everywhere together, which is surprising considering they can't keep their hands off each other. They should just stay home and not subject others to their displays of affection."

"I distinctly remember you and Arizona going through a stage like that, not too long ago. In fact, it sort of explains your pregnancy."

"That was different. Joel was involved with you for nine years. Now he's rubbing your nose in the fact that he's marrying someone else. I want him to stop."

Cassie walked over to stand next to her sister. She touched her shoulder. "I appreciate the show of support. Really, it's very sweet. But it's not necessary. I don't care about Joel in that way. I wish you would believe me. I'm not hurt by anything he's doing. He's not rubbing my nose in anything—he can't. I broke up with *him*."

"I'm worried about you," Chloe admitted. "How can this not bother you?"

"It just doesn't." Cassie got down two glasses. She poured her sister some juice, and wine for herself, then led the way to the table.

"I'll admit to feeling a little strange," she said when they were both settled. "Joel and I were involved for years. Sometimes I think I should miss him more, but I don't. I'm genuinely happy for him. I wish him and Alice the best of everything."

She stared at her sister's familiar face. "I should have listened to you when you told me I was settling. I see that now. I wanted so much to belong to someone that I stayed in a relationship that didn't have a future. I was afraid to ask for it all. I thought if I kept my hopes and dreams small enough that they would have a chance of coming true, but that if I wanted too much, I would lose everything."

Chloe leaned forward. Her long red curls tumbled over her shoulder and brushed against her forearms. "You *do* belong. You're a very special member of our family. Just because you're adopted doesn't mean you don't belong."

"It's not the same, Chloe. I have you and I have Aunt Charity. I know you both love me very much. But I wanted something of my own. I wanted to start building a history. I wanted to be married and have a family. I still want that. The difference is I've finally learned I have to take a chance on my heart's desire. I'm not going to settle again."

Chloe searched her face. "That all sounds good. So why do you look so sad?"

Cassie drew in a deep breath. She hadn't decided if she was going to tell her sister everything that was going on, but now she realized she needed the advice.

"I'm in love with Ryan."

Chloe smiled. "No big surprise there. Your crush evolved as you got to know him. He seems great. He's smart, a hard worker, Aunt Charity says he's devoted to Sasha, which means he'll be a good father. There's a slight age difference, but that shouldn't matter. What's the problem?"

"He doesn't love me back." She told Chloe about the kiss and Ryan's reaction when she broke up with Joel. "He panicked. He thought I was going to lay claim on him. It got worse when he invited Joel over for a reconciliation dinner and Joel sprang the news about his engagement to Alice." She took a sip of wine. "Ryan's never been in love. I think the emotion scares him to death."

"So there's nothing between you?"

"Not exactly." She felt herself flushing. "We're lovers." She explained how that had come to be and that she'd given herself one month with Ryan. "Then I'm leaving. I have to. If I don't go while I can, I could waste my life here. I refuse to do that again. While having Ryan love me back would be wonderful, working for him and sleeping with him without any kind of commitment is just settling."

"Do you think he'll let you go?"

The question surprised Cassie. "Of course he will. Why wouldn't he?"

"The man shows all the symptoms of someone who has it bad."

"You're mistaken," Cassie told her sister. "He likes me well enough, and I'm convenient, but I don't fool myself into thinking he wants more."

"I think you're selling yourself short. I don't think Ryan is going to give you up as easily as you think. You're everything he could possibly want in a woman. You're intelligent, you're funny, you're great with kids, and I'm going to assume the sex is amazing."

Cassie ducked her head and nodded. "*I* like it."

"Then he would be a fool to lose you and Ryan isn't a fool."

Cassie looked at Chloe. "I don't think he wants to love me—or anyone."

"People don't always get a choice in the matter. Sometimes love just happens. Don't be so quick to write him off. I agree that if nothing changes, you have to stick to your plan." Chloe gave her sister a quick hug. "I admire your ability to stand up for what you believe. I'll support you in any way I can. But don't be surprised if things start to happen. Ryan is confused right now, but I'm betting he's going to get it figured out in time."

"I can barely stand to think about that," Cassie said.

"I want to hope, but I'm so afraid he's going to let me go. I know I'll survive without him, but I would rather not."

"Have faith. You're due for some good fortune."

Cassie smiled. "You're right. And if nothing else, there's always the nightgown. It's practically my twenty-fifth birthday. Maybe I'll dream about someone wonderful."

She rose to her feet and went to check on dinner. Chloe changed the subject, but Cassie was still thinking about Ryan. It *was* nearly her birthday and she *would* wear the nightgown, hoping the family legend would work for her. But in her heart of hearts the only man she wanted to dream about, the only man she wanted to be with, was Ryan.

CHAPTER SIXTEEN

THEY CALLED OUT their last goodbyes and closed the door behind their guests. Cassie gave Ryan a big smile. "That was a lot of fun. Thanks for suggesting we invite my sister and Arizona for dinner."

Without thinking, he put his arm around her and pulled her close. "You're welcome. I had a good time, too."

Cassie slipped easily into his embrace. She was warm and willing as she leaned against him. Already he could feel the passion igniting inside of him. He didn't have to be around her very long before he found himself wanting her. He kissed the top of her head, then led them both up the stairs.

"I'm really enjoying Chloe's pregnancy," Cassie was saying. "It's a first time for both of us. I like hearing about all the details without actually experiencing it."

"Preparation for when it's your turn?"

"Something like that."

He tensed slightly. It was the perfect opening for her. Now she could casually mention something about the future, or ask if he wanted a child of his own. But she didn't. Instead she walked down the hall and checked on Sasha.

Ryan trailed after her. If Cassie were a different kind of woman, he might think that she was playing a game with him. Except that wasn't her style. She was simply being herself. She could talk about Chloe's pregnancy, or her future life, or any number of potentially awkward topics and not give it a moment's thought. She'd told him what she wanted from him and she wasn't pushing for anything more.

As she disappeared into the darkness of his niece's room, Ryan stopped in the center of the hall. Maybe the reason Cassie wasn't pushing for more with him was because she didn't want more. Maybe she wasn't interested in him for more than something temporary.

He was glad he was standing there alone because he was sure he had a stunned look on his face. All this time he'd been worried about her coming on to him when in fact she might not find him the least bit desirable. Oh, sure, she was willing to sleep with him, but was he the kind of man a woman like her would want to marry? He had no history of making relationships work. At first he hadn't wanted anything to do with his niece. While he and Cassie got along, and he was reasonably confident that she liked him, liking wasn't the same as respecting…or loving.

Cassie stepped back into the hall. "She's fine. Sleeping like the angel she is." She walked up and wrapped her arms around his waist. "What about you, Ryan? Are you tired or would you like some company?"

He stared at her, then touched her face. Less than ten days ago she'd been a virgin. Now she was asking if he wanted her in his bed. It wasn't that Cassie was arrogant or pushy, she simply had a strong sense of self. He admired that about her. He admired so many things.

"You have an odd look on your face," she said. "Did I say something I shouldn't have?"

"Not at all." He kissed her. "I was just thinking how perfect you are."

She wrinkled her nose. "That's not true, but thanks for

the compliment." She took his hand and led him toward his bedroom. "I was reading an article in this women's magazine and they mentioned something I thought we could try."

"Like what?"

She gave him a coy smile over her shoulder. "You'll just have to wait and see."

Two hours later, Cassie lay sleeping in his arms. His body was sated and pleasantly tired, but his mind wouldn't let him rest. He couldn't stop thinking about Cassie…and about what she wanted. Realizing that it might not be him had changed everything.

He stroked her short, dark hair and wondered how he was supposed to figure out what was right for either of them. He knew that in three weeks she was going to leave him and that he didn't want her to go. That much had become clear. But did he have the right to keep her? He wanted what was best for her. Could he be that? Was he capable? Or would it be kinder to simply walk away and get over her. Except he didn't think he could.

No other woman had changed him the way she had. No one else understood him or made him happy. But it wasn't all about him, either. He'd never thought about someone the way he thought about her. He wanted to make *her* happy. He wanted to help her achieve whatever she wanted in love. He wanted…

He wanted to love her.

Ryan stared into the darkness and knew he'd found a truth. He wanted to love Cassie the way she loved everyone in her world. He wanted to feel those emotions and be able to express them. But he didn't know *how* to love or to tell her that he loved her. He didn't know how to be a good husband or father. He was better with machines than people. Didn't Cassie deserve more than him?

He ran the thoughts over and over in his mind until near dawn, then he finally slept. His dreams taunted him with visions of a future he wasn't sure he could ever have.

"CATCH ME! Catch me!" Sasha cried as she ran around the backyard.

Ryan walked after her, careful to stay close enough to keep her safe, but not so close that he could reach her.

They'd been playing tag for nearly an hour and the toddler showed little sign of getting tired. Ryan couldn't say the same for himself. He hadn't gotten much sleep in the past couple of nights. He'd been too busy trying to figure out how he was going to tell Cassie all he'd been thinking about. He wanted her in his life. Of that much he was sure. The question was how did he say it? How did he make the offer so desirable that she couldn't turn him down? So far he hadn't come up with the perfect combination of words, but he was working on it.

Sasha dashed around the swing set. Ryan went after her. She made a darting move to her right, surprising him. He turned, tripped on a ball and tumbled to the ground.

"Smooth," he muttered as he lay staring up at the cloudy afternoon sky. "Very smooth."

"Unk Ryan!" Sasha rushed to his side and threw herself on top of him. "'Kay?" she asked. "Me kiss boo-boo."

"I'm okay," he told her and shifted her so she sat astride his waist. Her short legs stuck out. "Thanks for worrying. I tripped but I'm not hurt."

Sasha nodded, then leaned forward and rested on his chest. "Me tired."

Ah, so the running around had finally caught up with her. "Are you going to take a nap on me? Right now?"

She giggled and tried to fake sleep. But she kept peeking up at him to see if he was watching. Every time she showed her face, he growled at her. She giggled and retreated, only to try it again.

Suddenly, she wrapped her little arms around his neck and squeezed tight. "Me love Unk Ryan."

His throat tightened with unexpected emotion. "I love you, too, Sasha," he managed, although his voice was a little thick. "I love you very much and I'll always be here for you."

Wise toddler eyes stared at him. "Me know," she told him solemnly, and at the moment he believed she *did* know that she could trust him.

Was that all it took? he wondered. A heartfelt declaration? Could he just tell Cassie that he loved her and wanted to marry her? Would that be enough? It would have to be, he thought. He didn't have anything else to try.

Tonight, he decided. Tonight, when they were in bed together, he would tell Cassie the truth. He would explain that he didn't know how to do any of this right, but that he would always try to do what she wanted. That making her happy was the most important part of his life. Then he would confess his feelings and propose.

Before he could figure out if it might work, a voice cut through the afternoon. "Ryan? Are you out here?"

He grabbed Sasha around her waist and set her on the ground, then stood up himself. Cassie's aunt Charity came into the backyard. She smiled when she saw him. "Cassie said you two were playing." She walked over and gave Sasha a hug. "How's my best princess?"

Sasha giggled.

"I'll take that as a good report," Charity said, then straightened. "I'm just here for a second to say hi. I had a few last-minute details to work out with Cassie for her birthday party and I needed to drop off the nightgown."

Cassie's twenty-fifth birthday was at the end of the week. "She's really looking forward to the party."

"I'm sure it will be fun," Charity said. "I've even hired a high school girl to look after Sasha so you and Cassie can relax. Seven o'clock on Thursday."

"I'll get her there."

With that, Charity was gone. Ryan stared after her. Should he buy an engagement ring first, or wait until he talked to Cassie? She might want to pick it out herself, especially after nine years of wearing diamond lint.

Sasha tugged at his hand. "Drink, peas."

"Sure thing, kid." He picked her up and carried her inside.

Cassie sat at the kitchen table, reading a cookbook. She glanced up when they came in. "I saw you two out there. You were having a good time."

Her face was practically free of makeup, her clothes were sensible rather than glamorous, her hair slightly tousled. Yet Ryan thought she was the most lovely, incredibly attractive woman he'd ever seen. It was all he could do not to declare himself right there.

"We were," he said, and had to clear his throat. "Ah, Sasha wanted a drink."

"I'll get it," she said and stood up. As she crossed to the refrigerator, she passed a large white box. "It's the magic nightgown. Want to see?"

Ryan couldn't answer. He'd completely forgotten about the Bradley family legend and Cassie's hope that when she wore the nightgown on her twenty-fifth birthday she would dream about the man she was destined to marry. She'd waited for this night nearly all her life. He knew she thought of herself as an outsider in the family. Her adoption had left her feeling different. If the nightgown worked, then she would truly belong.

He told himself the nightgown wasn't really magic. She wasn't going to dream about anyone. But he also knew that his opinion didn't matter…it was Cassie's fantasy and he had no right to interfere. So he would wait until after her birthday. He would let her dream, perhaps even about another man. Then he would win her for his own.

BY THE MIDDLE of the week Cassie knew she wasn't imagining things. She drove back to the house determined to have it out with Ryan. Sasha was in preschool for two hours. That should give them plenty of time to deal with whatever was going on with him.

For nearly a week, he hadn't been himself. She kept turning around and finding him staring at her with a really strange look on his face. He would start conversations, then simply walk out of the room. Something had him distracted and she was determined to find out what.

She had a bad feeling she already knew the answer. He was ready to end their affair. No doubt he was concerned that she was getting too emotionally attached to him and he didn't want to be responsible for hurting her. So he would end it before she completely fell for him. Good thing he didn't know she was already in love. There would be no avoiding the pain this time.

She parked in the driveway, then walked purposefully into the house. It would be easier to avoid the situation, but that had never been her style. So she squared her shoulders, dug up all the spare courage she could find, then headed to his office and knocked on the door.

"Come in," he called.

She stepped inside. "Ryan, we need to talk," she began, then stopped when she saw he wasn't at his desk. Instead he stood by the window, staring out at the backyard. "Is everything all right?" she asked.

He turned toward her. "Sure."

But despite his neutral expression, she didn't believe him. "No. Something has been bothering you for several days and I think I know what it is."

He smiled. "I doubt that."

Okay, here went nothing. "You're worried about me. You're concerned that I'm going to get emotionally attached to you because we're lovers and women tend to bond when they make love with someone. I want you to know that I understand and I'm—"

"They do?" he asked, interrupting her.

"What?"

"Women bond when they make love?"

"Yes. Most of the time. If they have feelings for the man. It's pair bonding, like wolves or swans. But that's not the point. I don't want you to be concerned about me."

"Because you haven't bonded?"

This was the tricky part, she thought. She didn't want to lie, but she was afraid to tell him the truth. She took a step toward his desk. "I'm a mature person. I can handle my feelings."

"So you *have* bonded."

"I didn't say that." Except by avoiding the question, she sort of had.

He moved toward her, stopping less than two feet away. His green eyes were alight with an emotion she couldn't read. "It's one or the other. Either you've bonded or you haven't. But if it makes answering the question any easier, I can tell my bonding story."

"Okay." What was he talking about? Her stomach got all quivery and she felt both hot and cold. Dear Lord, please don't let it be bad.

He took one last step forward, then kissed her gently. "I've bonded with you, Cassie. Even before we made love, I found myself falling in love with you. I didn't recognize it at the time, probably because I've never felt this way before. You mean everything to me."

She couldn't speak. She wasn't sure she was even breathing. Was this really happening? Was Ryan actually saying these things to her?

He touched her cheek, traced her mouth, tucked her hair behind her ears and gave her a shaky smile. "You deserve so much more than I have to offer. I don't know how to be what you need, but I'm too selfish to let you go. I love you. I want to marry you. I want us to raise Sasha along with a couple dozen kids of our own. I want to make love with you every night, I want to hold you while you sleep and I want to watch you smile when you wake up in the morning."

He clutched her hands tightly in his. "Just tell me what *you* want. I can learn to be a better man, if you'll help me. I want to make you happy. I want to make all your dreams come true."

He was saying everything she wanted to hear and more. So much more. The odd light in his eyes was love, she realized. He loved her. "You *have* made all my dreams come true."

"Then why are you crying?"

She pulled one hand free and touched her face. It was

wet. "I'm so happy." Her head was spinning. "Is this really happening? Did you just propose to me?"

"Not exactly."

Her heart plunged to her toes and then broke.

"No, don't!" he said quickly. "I want to marry you. I want to elope with you tonight. But I know how important the family legend is with you. So I'm going to ask you to marry me, but I don't want you to answer. Wear the nightgown tomorrow night, then answer me in the morning."

"I don't understand. What if I don't…" She couldn't finish the statement. But he knew what she was thinking.

"What if you don't dream about me?" he asked. "If you dream about another man, I'll win you from him because I know you're my destiny. I'll sweep you off your feet with passion and devotion until you can't imagine being with anyone else. I'll earn you, and once I have you, I'll never let you go."

"I want to marry you," she said and kissed him.

"Tell me that again in forty-eight hours."

CASSIE'S FINGERS TREMBLED as she unfolded the nightgown, then slipped it over her head. She climbed into her bed and pulled the covers up to her chin.

Ryan sat down beside her and smiled. "Don't look so scared. It's going to be fine."

"I know, it's just so strange. All my life I've wanted the nightgown to be magic, and now I don't."

"You're going to dream of me. I know it. And if you don't, hey, I have a plan. Either way, I love you and want you in my life."

"I love you, too," she whispered back.

They talked for a few more minutes, then he left her

alone. Cassie fingered the lace at her collar and cuffs, then turned on her side. The bed felt odd. She hadn't slept in it since she and Ryan had become lovers.

She closed her eyes, then opened then. After twenty-five years, it was finally her turn to wear the family nightgown, and now that the moment was finally here, she was afraid to go to sleep.

"This is dumb," she told herself aloud. "Ryan is a wonderful man. I love him. I want to marry him. I should just go accept his proposal."

Except she'd tried that several times over the past couple of days and every time he told her to wait. He wanted her to have her night of magic.

She tried to relax. In an effort to distract herself, she thought about her wonderful party. All her friends had been there. Ryan had fit in with everyone. He'd made her feel so special.

Gradually, her eyes grew heavy. She fought against sleep because she was afraid, but at last it claimed her. She drifted for a while, then found herself standing on the porch of the Bradley house, staring at the wide lawn. A man appeared in the shadows. Her heart pounded in her chest. She was having a magic dream. The nightgown was about to reveal her destiny.

Even in her sleep, she found herself calling out for Ryan. She needed it to be him. She loved him.

The man continued to walk toward her. His figure was indistinct, then suddenly he was in front of her. All five feet four inches of him. She recognized the gray hair, the craggy face and the scowling expression. Old Man Withers, their caretaker for longer than she'd been alive, glared at her.

Cassie woke up with a start. She sat up and hugged

her knees to her chest. She'd dreamed about Old Man Withers. What a joke. The nightgown wasn't going to work for her.

"It's better this way," she whispered to herself. "I love Ryan."

But the sadness inside her didn't have anything to do with loving Ryan. It was about really belonging to the Bradley family. She was adopted. There wasn't a legend for her.

Coldness swept through her and she shivered. She didn't want to be alone so she got out of bed and walked down the hall. Ryan stirred as she opened his door. He raised himself on one elbow. "Good news?"

His eyes were sleepy, his hair mussed. She knew that under the blankets and sheet, he was naked and if she crawled in beside him and touched him, he would want her. He loved her and she loved him back. He'd changed in the time she'd known him. He was a wonderful father to Sasha and he would be an equally wonderful husband.

All her life she'd wanted to belong. She suddenly realized that being a part of something wasn't about a place. It didn't matter where she'd been born or who had given birth to her. Home was a state of mind. Home was where her heart was welcome. Home was with Ryan.

She smiled. "The best news," she said and slipped in beside him.

He wrapped his arms around her. "I knew you'd dream about me. Now you *have* to marry me." His voice was sleepy. "I was gonna win you no matter what, but this is better. Let's get married soon."

"I'd like that," she said.

"Good." He kissed her cheek.

He was, as she'd suspected, completely naked. And

he was half-asleep. She really should let him get his rest. Except she found herself wanting him. Not because she'd lost her dream, but because she'd finally found where she belonged—where she'd always belonged. First with her adoptive parents and Chloe, and now with Ryan.

So even though his eyes were slowly closing, she rested her head on his shoulder, then slipped her hand down his body. He made a low sound of pleasure.

"You're not going to let me get right back to sleep, are you?" he asked lazily as her hand closed over him. He was aroused in a matter of seconds.

"Pay no attention to what I'm doing," she told him in a whisper. "I'm just trying to relax you."

"Oh, yeah, it's very relaxing."

She continued to stroke him, moving up and down in that slow steady pace he enjoyed. Then, without warning, he rolled over, taking her with him, until she was on her back, staring up at him.

"I love you," he said, his green eyes bright with a combined blaze of love and passion. "You are mine and I'm going to spend the rest of my life convincing you that you've made the right decision."

"I already know," she assured him.

"Do you? I think I should start making you sure right now."

He lowered his head and kissed her. His tongue swept against the seam of her lips before slipping inside to tease and torment her in the most perfect way. They'd learned so much about each other's bodies in the past several weeks. They'd learned about the pleasures they most enjoyed together. He knew how to touch her to make her sigh, to make her catch her breath, to make her aroused. She knew how to bring him to his point of release in a matter of seconds. There were still wondrous discoveries, but already they were finding their favorite ways to make love.

He sat up and pushed down the covers, then pulled her into a sitting position and tugged off the nightgown. With her body bare to his gaze, she relaxed back onto the bed, drawing him with her. He kissed her deeply, then broke that kiss to touch his mouth to her forehead, her eyelids, her cheeks and her nose. He left a damp trail down her neck, then loved her breasts with mouth and tongue and teeth until she was shaking beneath him.

"I want you," he breathed against her heating skin. "I want to be with you and in you. I want to make love with you so much that we really become halves of the same whole. I want to be deep inside you—and I want you to have our children. I will always love you, Cassie. No matter what. Forever. I promise."

She felt the wetness of her happy tears as they trailed down her temples and into her hair. She felt her body ready for him.

"I want you, too," she whispered. "I want your babies and your arms around me at night."

She had more to say, but he was moving lower, kissing her belly, then kneeling between her legs so that he could give her the most intimate kiss of all. He parted the soft folds of her feminine place and touched his lips to her center-most place. Pleasure shot through her. Pleasure heightened by the realization that Ryan loved her as much as she loved him, and that they'd committed to each other. No matter what, they would always be together.

Then she was unable to think at all. She could only feel the sweep of his tongue against her and the pressure of the finger he'd slipped inside her. He moved in a matching rhythm designed to take her to the edge of madness and beyond. She parted her knees more to allow him to get closer, then dug her heels into the bed. As she neared her release, she half sat up to watch as well as feel his magic. She stroked his head with her fingers, giving a quiet moan as the pleasure intensified.

Then she was lost in the perfection of the moment, caught up in a storm that rearranged the universe, then delivered her safely to her lover's arms. Ryan caught her as she fell and entered her while she was still quivering. Long, deep incredible thrusts filled her woman's place and took her back up on that wonderful journey.

They opened their eyes at the same moment and stared at each other. She could not say who held the other tightest. They were so joined that she could feel his own need as well as her own—she knew the exact moment when he would find his release.

Her body shattered with his. They loved and gasped together as if they'd been born to be lovers. Perhaps they had been, she thought drowsily.

When their bodies had calmed, Ryan kissed her gently, helped her pull on her nightgown, then settled her next to him in their wide bed.

"I love you," he murmured, already half-asleep.

"I love you, too," she told him.

She fingered the lace on the nightgown and knew that despite the legend, she'd found her home and her destiny. She and Ryan were going to do well together.

Contentment filled her, warming her from the inside out. She found herself dozing off, safe in the comfort of his arms.

The dream returned. Cassie stood on the porch of the Bradley house, staring at a man walking out of the shadows. Old Man Withers appeared in front of her and glared.

"Not me, you ninny," he growled and stepped aside. "Him!"

She hadn't seen the second man before, but there he was, moving into the sunlight. "Ryan!"

In her sleep, Cassie smiled and reached for her husband-to-be. In his sleep, he pulled her close. In the morning she would tell him the truth about the dream, and that would only make him love her more.

EPILOGUE

CASSIE HELD HER breath until Sasha made it all the way down the aisle. The little girl had managed to sprinkle rose petals *and* walk on the white runner. The fact that she'd wandered a little from side to side didn't really matter.

The organ music swelled. Chloe sniffed. "It's not enough that I'm nine months pregnant," she said. "Now I'm going to cry and my face will swell up enough to match my stomach." She gave Cassie a watery smile. "At least everyone will be looking at you instead of me, so it doesn't matter."

"You look wonderful. Radiant, in fact."

"So do you. I'm glad you're marrying him."

"Me, too. Now walk down that aisle so I can follow you and get married."

Chloe made her way toward the front of the church. Her peach dress swayed with every step. Cassie waited for the music to change to the wedding march, and then it was her turn.

She still had trouble believing this had happened to her. She and Ryan had pulled together a wedding in less than a month. Fate had been on her side. Her local church miraculously had a free Saturday and could recommend a caterer who was also available. Her wedding gown had been hanging in a display window, and had fit perfectly, without a single alteration. The weather was flawless, the pews filled with family and friends. She had the oddest feeling that someone was looking out for her and Ryan.

She looked up and saw Ryan waiting for her. He was so handsome in his tux. For reasons she still didn't understand, he loved her and wanted to be with her. She knew that she loved him with all her heart. They were going to have a wonderful life together.

She was still several feet away when she heard a familiar little voice demanding, "Unk Ryan."

He walked across the aisle and picked up Sasha. They were both waiting when Cassie reached the altar.

"She wants to be with us when we're married," Ryan said. "Do you mind?"

The toddler rested on her uncle's hip. Sasha grinned and leaned forward for a kiss. Cassie obliged her. "I don't mind," she said. "It's exactly right."

Ryan took her hand in his and the three of them faced the minister, where they were joined together as a family.

Somewhere, in a place some on earth might not quite understand, an old gypsy woman smiled down at the couple destined for a life of happiness.

The legend of the nightgown had once again come true.

* * * * *

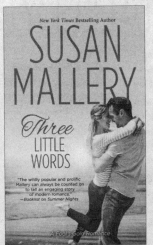

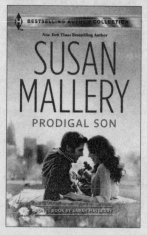

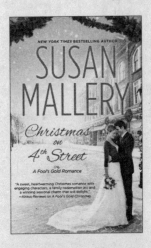

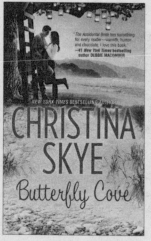

New York Times bestselling author

SUSAN MALLERY

brings readers a heartwarming tale for the holidays!

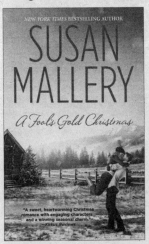

The cheer in Fool's Gold, California, is bringing out the humbug in dancer Evie Stryker. An injury has forced her to return home to her estranged family. So she won't add to the awkward scenario by falling for the charms of her brother's best friend, no matter how tempting he is. When she's recruited to stage the winter festival, she vows to do as promised, then move on, anywhere but here.

Jaded lawyer Dante Jefferson is getting used to the town he now calls home, but the pounding of little dancers' feet above his office is more than he can take. When he confronts their gorgeous teacher, he's unprepared for their searing attraction. Evie is his best friend's sister—off-limits unless he's willing to risk his heart. Dante has always believed that love is dangerous, but that was before he had to reckon with the magic of a certain small town, where miracles do seem to happen....

Available for the first time in paperback!

www.SusanMallery.com

Be sure to connect with us at:

Harlequin.com/Newsletters
Facebook.com/HarlequinBooks
Twitter.com/HarlequinBooks

REQUEST YOUR
FREE BOOKS!

2 FREE NOVELS
FROM THE ROMANCE COLLECTION
PLUS 2 FREE GIFTS!